I0779084

HENRY J. PARKS
THE ZENDER

BOOK TWO

KYLLINGMARK

This is the second book in a three part series by Jeremiah and Della Kyllingmark

CHAPTER 1

The afternoon sun was lengthening as Parks pulled out from behind Rita's apartment in Jim's truck. It rattled heavily from the damage it had sustained as he drove around the small cul-de-sac and then onto a side road. It was good distance to the abandoned warehouses, and he would need to avoid as many of the main roads as possible. Management would certainly be out looking for him.

"Barron may have checked in with the Citadel, but he couldn't do much with that crystal I put in his chest. It will keep him quiet until I get back."

Barron was only part of the problem though, and he knew it. Harry would be furious, and banging on every door in the city. It was only a matter of time before someone spilled. There was also the possibility of an insider in the ROD, as David had thought. Regardless of who or how, Parks was keenly aware things were not looking favorable.

He rounded a bend along the river when a large black SUV shot out from one of the side roads, and whipped in behind him. Parks floored Jim's rig, which responded like a wildcat, leaping forward, and ripping the road. Unfortunately, the deflated airbag from its previous accident made driving difficult, but Parks ripped it off, and threw it out the window. It bounced off the windshield of the pursuing vehicle. The two trucks were closely matched, and Parks was not able to shake them. His only chance was to outmaneuver them on the sharp corners of the winding road. Suddenly, he cut the wheel, sending Jim's truck off the road, through a shallow ditch and up the side of a small embankment before flying into a field. It bounced several times, sending a shower of mud high into the air as he raced across the field towards another road. The second vehicle tried to follow, but it was too heavy, and quickly ground to a halt.

Parks was nearly out of the field and to the safety of the side road when the blast from a Nullifier connected. It cut off the front of the truck, sending Parks sailing through the open window as the truck broke in two, and flipped over. He tucked into a ball, and rolled through the soft, muddy dirt, with the truck bouncing behind as it burst into flames.

Park slid into a shallow ditch as the burning truck stopped just a few feet from his head.

"That was close. If that guy was a better shot, I'd be toast right now."

He flattened out, and saw two men slogging through the field in his direction. The taller one was armed with the Nullifier, and his partner was carrying a military-style rifle. The field was flat and muddy with no cover, and Parks would be a sitting target if he made a break for it. Even if he could get across the road, he still had another hundred feet or so to the safety of the woods on the other side. It didn't look promising. Then he noticed a culvert running under the road about thirty yards away. Sliding down into the ditch, which was half full of water, he crawled along, careful to stay out of sight. His two assailants were still struggling across the field, and by the time they got to the burning wreckage, he had already crawled through the culvert, and was working his way towards the woods.

"I don't see him," the smaller of the two said after he scrambled up the bank to the road.

"There he goes!" the bigger one exclaimed. "He's in the ditch."

Sensing he was spotted, Parks jumped up, and began running as fast as he could. It was then he heard the distinctive hum of the Nullifier. He realized there was little chance he would make it before they got off a second shot. Planting both feet, he spun around, pulling two crystal blades from the leather belt slung around his waist. The bright flash momentarily blinded him as the energy from the weapon glanced off his blades, and cut into the tall trees behind him. Though the blades had saved his life, they weren't enough to keep him from being blasted through the air and into a massive tree. The impact nearly knocked him out, but he managed to pull several large branches over his body just seconds before the men arrived.

"Did you see where he went?" the one carrying the Nullifier said as he nearly stepped on Parks' foot.

"Not with all the dust and debris flying about," the little guy answered, rubbing his eyes. "And what caused that bright flash? I still can't see clearly."

"I've got white spots before my eyes too, but it's unlikely we'll find enough to see anyway. He had to have been blown to bits."

"That's not good enough," the small man said firmly. "We can't return without some proof. I say we circle around, and if he is still alive, we'll spot him. If he's not alive, we have to find a piece to show the boss."

Parks waited until they rounded the edge of the woods before climbing out from under the tree limbs. His choices were narrow.

If he tried to make the road, they were likely to spot him. But staying there wasn't much better. Chances were good that they had reported the events, and reinforcements were on the way. The entire area could be flooded in a matter of minutes.

It was time for the hunted to become the hunter.

With that thought, Parks slid into the woods, and moved silently along until he could just make them out through the thick branches. The one with the Nullifier was several yards ahead of his partner. He was scanning for movement, and prepared to discharge another devastating blast should he spot anything. Parks moved along until he spotted a narrow slit between two large trees. He waited until the first passed before stepping between the trees. The second one stumbled over a clump of grass, and that was all the distraction Parks needed. He leaped, hitting him square on the side of the head with his fist as he flew past.

Parks landed silently several yards beyond, and turned to see the man's body slowly sink into the tall grass. The leader hadn't heard or noticed his friend's disappearance as he continued to scan the woods. Parks slipped in behind the large man, and steadily closed the gap. He was almost ready to pounce when the man unexpectedly glanced over his shoulder. Wheeling around, the man let off a blast that just missed Parks' head as he leapt onto him, pulling him to the ground. Parks was surprised by the strength of his adversary, who easily broke free of his grip, and jumped to his feet. Parks released a devastating kick that knocked the Nullifier from his hands, and sent both it and him crashing into the woods. The large man slid into an uprooted tree, and reached for a large-caliber pistol hanging from a belt around his waist. He drew it just as Parks dove into his chest. The impact drove the man further into the woods, but he managed to hang onto his gun as he tumbled to a stop. He fired off several shots at where Parks had been, but Parks was gone.

"What is this guy, a ghost?" he asked, waving his gun around as he scrambled to his feet. "Where'd he go?"

The words were no sooner out of his mouth than another hard kick landed between his shoulder blades. Parks had darted through the woods, and moved around behind him. The impact sent the pistol spinning into the brush as the man face-planted onto the cool forest floor. Rolling over, he coughed up some dirt as Parks landed on his chest. Deflecting several of Parks's blows with his elbows, he managed to grab Parks by the forearm, and toss him into a nearby stump.

Parks was instantly up and prepared to attack again as his assailant staggered to his feet. It was then he noticed a dark red, glowing crystal hanging from a brass chain around his neck. The crystal pulsated as the man reached into his belt, and pulled out a long knife. He lunged forward, striking Parks in the face with his left hand as he tried to stab him in the ribs with his right. Parks grabbed his arm and stopped the knife, just inches from its desire. The two struggled, clenched in a death match as the red crystal glowed even brighter. The man forced Parks against a tree, pushing the blade ever closer to his heart, with his other hand fastened around Parks' throat as he choked the life out of him.

Parks held the knife at bay with one hand while he pulled a crystal blade with his free hand. With one swift upward move, Parks sliced the man's hand off at the wrist. The knife, still firmly gripped in the dismembered hand, hit the ground with a sickening thud. The man's eyes opened wide in shock as he stumbled backward before dropping to his knees.

Parks connected squarely on his chin with a left cross.

A puff of dirt and leaves shot out as he landed on his back, unconscious. Parks squatted down and rolled him over, but as he did, the red crystal dissolved into a black vapor and dissipated. Then to his amazement and horror, the man's eyes sank into his head. Parks jumped back and watched as the man's entire body collapsed, like a balloon stuck with a pin. In a matter of seconds, all that was left was a dark outline. His mind flashed back to the day in the cave with the Zender, and how it had disappeared in similar fashion.

Suddenly, he remembered the man's partner. Returning to the spot where he left him, Parks' suspicions were confirmed as he knelt to inspect the outline in the grass where he had been. Getting up, he surveyed his options.

Their backup was likely on the way, and getting close. Parks broke into a run. He would have to hustle if he wanted to make it to the warehouse.

His thoughts were confirmed as the sound of heavy vehicles broke the evening silence. From his position on the edge of the woods, he spotted three trucks filled with Cadets, rounding the bend not more than a half mile away. It would be only a matter of moments before they were combing the area, looking for him. He dropped low, his head even with the tall grass as he moved around behind the trees, looking for an escape route. He paused for a moment, and noticed a stump standing alone in the middle of an adjacent field. It seemed out of place, and it drew on his curiosity enough that he sprinted across the field, risking being spotted by the approaching troops. It was easily three hundred yards away, but the adrenaline rushing through his veins empowered each long stride as he crossed the chasm, and slid safely behind it.

"This field has been farmed for years," Parks thought as he hunkered down, "but they never removed this stump."

He examined the side he was hiding behind, and spotted what looked to be a small hairline seam, about six inches below the top. At first, he thought it was a scar from something tied to it long ago, but it was too uniform for that. He slid his hand along until he felt a small bump that felt like a button. He pushed it. The top of the stump popped open with a hiss of released air.

Parks remembered how Sterling and his brother had managed to evade capture the day he and Barron had chased them by the river. So there were more entrances to the tunnels, and they were hidden right out in the open. After all, who would expect an old stump to be an access door?

Carefully peering around the stump, he saw the troops preparing to move through the woods. They would head in his direction next, but they weren't organized yet. He seized the moment, lifted the lid, and dropped into darkness.

Parks pulled the lid shut over his head, climbed down a metal ladder, and flipped on a small flashlight he kept in his pocket. It illuminated just enough for him to see a bottom some twenty feet below. He let go of the rungs, and dropped the final six feet to a long, concrete tunnel. Rows of lights snapped on in either direction. It was a small tunnel, probably designed for surveillance, or to move troops into certain positions as needed.

A cool breeze flowing down the corridor greeted Parks as he began a steady jog in the general direction of where he thought the Island would be. However, after jogging what seemed to be several miles, the tunnel began to curve away from the city, and towards the outer region in the direction of a distant mountain range. When he came upon another exit, he climbed the metal ladder, holding his flashlight in his teeth. He slid back the latch, and slowly opened the hatch.

"Where am I?" Parks thought as he peered out into the darkened landscape.

He scanned the area for familiar landmarks, but all he saw was barren ground, and a few scrubby trees blocking most of his view. He pushed up the lid, and climbed out. The exit hatch was carefully camouflaged as the top of a large rock, and was surrounded by three strategically placed trees. The lid closed with a hiss, and Parks began surveying the area to mark the entrance in his mind in case he needed to use it again. Night was setting in, and his internal compass told him he was somewhere outside the city on the south end where the wilderness transitioned from dry scrub brush to larger trees and tall grass. It was one of the areas he had avoided as a kid, mainly because of the legends. He had heard stories of an ancient civilization that lived in a hidden village, deep in the mountains somewhere.

These could be the very people he needed to meet. They might have some of the answers he was seeking. But first, he had to return to the Island. That would likely take all night and most of the next day at a steady run, but he was up for it. He had to reconnect with Sterling and the colonel. His life, and the lives of his friends, depended on it.

CHAPTER 2

The children followed Nurse Della Larson single file into the medical facility. The smells of antiseptic and burnt flesh competed for their attention as they passed cots with people in various levels of agony. Nurses scurrying past with bandages and bed pans still managed to smile compassionately at the ragged band of kids.

"Put him down here," Nurse Larson said as they came into a private part of the infirmary.

David and Troy set Aaron's stretcher on the floor before helping him onto the bed. Isaac and Burk did the same for Joshua, who groaned as they gently laid him on a bed opposite Aaron's.

"Good job," Nurse Larson said gently as she adjusted their pillows. "One of my nurses will be right in to check on you. In the meantime, I want to talk with your friends in my office for a moment."

Just then, a tall, redheaded woman with a large smile appeared. It was Nurse Darla, and her light-hearted banter quickly relaxed the children.

"I'll see to it you two are running out of here in no time," Darla laughed. "Just relax, and let me have a look at you. Hey, I bet you could use something to eat. As soon as I'm done, I'll send over a big plate covered with potatoes and gravy and some milk to chase it with."

The rest of the kids followed Nurse Larson into her office where she had food and refreshments waiting. They grabbed handfuls of nuts, and piled their plates with fruit. Another nurse arrived with a large plate full of sandwiches that disappeared almost as fast as they arrived. After several minutes of feasting, Nurse Larson sat in the circle of chairs with them.

"There are some really good people who want to take care of you," she said as she scanned the faces of the brave kids. "If your families are found, they will help transition you back with your parents. Otherwise, they will become your new parents."

Kenzie began to cry a bit, and David hugged her shoulders.

"Look, guys," David said confidently, "we have to be strong. We don't know what's happened to anybody, but at least this will get us somewhere. The last time I saw my dad, he looked me straight in the eyes, and told me not to be afraid, no matter what happens. Well, I'm not going to let him down. You can count on me," he said, looking intently into Nurse Larson's warm brown eyes.

Kenzie wiped the tears from her eyes, and sat up straight in agreement. The rest of the children did the same, and it was settled, even though a heavy sense of unspoken loss hung in the air.

Dr. Larson's thoughts returned to the present. The eight children Parks rescued that day did make it, even though they never were able to find their real families. It was thought their fathers and mothers were either killed in battle, or disposed of somehow. No one knew for sure, but it was not an uncommon suspicion, seeing how ruthless Management could be. But Della and her team had managed to find good homes for them, and the children stayed in contact with each other as they grew up. It was as if they had become brothers and sisters. Over the years Della also stayed close, especially to Kenzie, who ended up as one of her most valued interns at the hospital. She was compassionate and smart, and the patients loved her.

Now it was time for Kenzie to know she was about to be on her own. Della couldn't risk being in the hospital much longer.

"Have a seat," Dr. Larson said warmly as Kenzie entered her office. "I need to discuss a few things with you."

Kenzie was nearly twenty two, attractive and tall, with bright blue eyes and long blonde hair. She sat across from Dr. Larson with her hands folded in her lap.

"I'm sure you've heard there have been some issues between Management and certain citizens." Dr. Larson said, leaning back in her chair. "But what you don't know is that I have now become one of those citizens. I've had a bit of a falling out, and I'm not going to be able to stay around here much longer. But you're welcome to stay as long as you wish. There's no reason for you to be concerned, and there are plenty of good nurses you can work with during my absence."

"Where are you going?" Kenzie asked intently.

"It's probably better if we don't discuss that." Dr. Larson replied. "The less you know about what I'm doing, the better."

"Well, what I do know is we are going to resist whatever is coming from Management, and will do whatever it takes to protect you," Kenzie stated flatly.

"What are you suggesting?" Dr. Larson asked as she sat upright in her chair.

"You've been the best friend we could have ever asked for," Kenzie replied. "If it hadn't been for you and Parks, we would never have made it. But we did make it, and have been busy since that day in your office when you told us things were going to be ok. We've been busy thinking of ways to bring our city back, and rescue our friends. We may have been kids then, but we're not kids anymore. Management took our families from us, but we never forgot them. The eight of us stayed together, training and preparing for this day. We'll make sure you're safe."

"Look," Dr. Larson began to protest, "I'm sure I'll be ok. You don't need to get involved. It's too risky."

Kenzie lifted a silver chain over her head, and laid it carefully on the desk. It was a diamond-encrusted pendant, and Dr. Larson could see a brightly colored blue crystal in the center.

"This is the crystal Parks gave me that day behind the facility. It's never left my possession since, and I mounted it in this setting several years ago. I thought for the longest time he gave a crystal to each of us so we would have something to hold onto. Something to remind us we weren't alone in the world. But now I realize they're much more than that. He gave them to us because he knew one day we would need their power. You see, this crystal allows me to know things. I sometimes know what's going to happen before it does."

"You can see the future?" Dr. Larson asked with a hint of skepticism in her voice.

"I know that probably sounds a little crazy," Kenzie replied. "For a long time, I just thought it was coincidence, or a déjà vu thing, but now I know it's real. I dreamed last night you would tell me about leaving for a while and needing me to step in, but that's not all. On my way over here, I saw a darkness beginning to envelope the city, and if you don't leave right away, you'll be caught in it."

"Well, I am leaving, but I can't go until I'm sure all my patients are ok," Dr. Larson replied, trying not to sound concerned.

"No, you need to go now!" Kenzie said, standing up and glancing out the window. "One of Management's vehicles just pulled up in front of the hospital."

Dr. Larson jumped out of her chair and joined Kenzie at the window. Sure enough, there was Barron, followed closely by several large men in dark suits.

"Follow me!" Dr. Larson exclaimed as she opened the secret passage into her hidden room. "We'll be safe in here."

They quickly entered the room where Jim was still convalescing with Rita close at his side.

"What's the matter?" Rita said anxiously, seeing the concern on Della's face.

"We need to keep quiet," Dr. Larson replied, "and get Jim ready to move. You should be able to travel now," She said as she quickly checked his ankle. "The swelling's down, and I don't see any signs of infection. I'll fit you with a walking cast, and get you moving." Dr. Larson continued, opening one of the cabinets and pulling out a white walking cast.

"They just came into your office," Kenzie said quietly. "We don't have much time."

"Who's in Dr. Larson's office?" Jim asked anxiously.

"No time to explain," Dr. Larson said as she slid the cast over Jim's foot. "Get up, and see if you can move."

Jim hopped off the bed, with Rita holding tight to his arm.

"I'm ok," Jim said as he took a couple of steps. "Where are we going?"

"Out," Dr. Larson replied. "We'll wait until they leave, and then get going. No one can see us in here."

They watched through the one-way glass as Barron checked her office, Nullifier in hand. Della knew Barron well, and had even provided him with medical care a time or two. But he didn't seem the same somehow. She stepped close to the glass, and watched as he rifled through the things on her desk with his back to her. Then he suddenly turned towards the hidden room.

Dr. Larson gasped at the sight. His black hair had turned snow white, and his eyes glowed an eerie red as he walked towards the wall concealing their presence. He stared, with his face mere inches from Dr. Larson.

"I think it's time to go," Jim said, pulling Dr. Larson by the arm and taking Rita with the other.

They waited a few seconds for the elevator, and then got on. The door had barely closed when a blast shook the building. Dr. Larson hit the button, and the elevator bounced wildly as it made its way down. Then, a second blast tore through the door above, severing the cables, causing the elevator to drop the final ten feet or so.

"Where to now?" Jim asked as he pushed open the doors, and they burst into a narrow, dimly-lit hallway.

"This corridor leads to a secret entrance in the underground parking lot," Dr. Larson said. "If we can make it there, we'll have a good chance at escaping."

"What a minute," Kenzie exclaimed as she stopped running. "I've seen this before."

"Seen what?" Jim exclaimed. "Come on, we have to get out of here. I see flashlights."

Suddenly, a loud crash echoed down the long corridor. Barron had jumped down the shaft and through the top of the elevator, sending shards of glass and chunks of metal flying. He was momentarily trapped by some steel wedged against the door, but that wouldn't hold him for long.

"Come on!" Jim exclaimed. "Let's go! I don't think we want to know what happens if they catch us."

"No, wait!" Kenzie said, "I've been here before."

They turned a slight bend in the corridor just as a bright flash narrowly missed them and hit the wall in front, sending tons of rock and debris crashing down. Barron had reached around the sprung door and fired his Nullifier. Now the pile of rocks blocked their escape route. It would just be a matter of moments before they were caught. They could hear metal being twisted and thrown out of the way as Barron worked his way free.

"That about does it," Jim said glumly as he examined the large rocks through the choking dust. "There's no way we're going out this way. You girls get behind me. Maybe I can take one of them down while you make a break for the elevator. If I can get one of their weapons, we may have half a chance."

"No," Rita exclaimed. "You are not going to risk your life. We'll surrender, and hope for the best."

Jim looked at Rita like he was seeing her for the first time. It seemed amazing this woman had so much interest in his well-being. A smile broke over his face as he felt her arm slip under his. He suddenly felt connected to her, and knew at that moment whatever they were up against, they would face it together.

Kenzie had been strangely quiet as she examined a section of wall behind them.

"What are you looking at?" Dr. Larson asked as she moved next to Kenzie.

"I saw this last night," she said. "I was in a hall like this, and a man reached out, and pulled me through the wall. It was weird, but I know I was standing right here."

She pulled several loose tiles from the wall, and behind them appeared the faint outline of a face carved into the rock.

Dr. Larson began helping Kenzie rip tiles from the wall, and to their amazement, the figure of a man with an outstretched hand appeared.

"That's interesting," Jim said as he peeked around the corner, "but I think Barron is nearly free. We have all of sixty seconds before he's here. Maybe we should walk back, and surrender. I don't want to see you gals hurt."

Kenzie examined the wall closely, and in the dimly-lit corridor, she could make out a small indent in the center of the man's hand. She slid the silver chain with the blue crystal over her head, and popped it out of its setting. Then she pushed it into the man's hand. For a moment there was nothing, but then the man's outline began to glow. In a few seconds the figure turned translucent, and its outline bright orange, throwing off hot, glowing sparks.

"Everybody grab a hand, and don't let go!" Kenzie ordered.

She seized Dr. Larson's hand, and stepped into the figure. In a moment, all four were passing through the rock wall, and into darkness. Kenzie pushed forward, feeling the rock in front of her turn to jelly with every step. They traveled briefly before emerging into a large underground cavern.

"Breathe," Kenzie encouraged, "take deep breaths."

She turned back to the wall, watching the outline of the man with the outstretched hand. It still glowed slightly orange, but then the blue crystal popped out of his hand and into hers. She snapped it back into its setting, and put her necklace on again.

"Kenzie, that was awesome!" Jim exclaimed, echoing their amazement. "I thought only Normand could do that."

"It's a trick Parks taught us all," Kenzie replied. "And I bet Barron is scratching his head right now, wondering where we went."

"Where is this place?" Dr. Larson asked as she examined the mammoth pillars supporting gigantic slabs of stone.

"I have no idea," Jim answered. "But that eerie green glow seems to be coming from these rocks."

"Well, they must provide light for someone." Rita observed. "But who lives down here?"

"I think it's more likely who used to live down here?" Jim answered as he looked around. "There hasn't been anyone here in a very long time. We must be under the city somewhere. Funny no one ever knew of this place. It appears we've built our city on top of those giant stones held up by these columns." Jim continued, leaning against one of them, and looking up at the rock ceiling nearly 20 feet above. "Our ancestors must have assumed they were building on solid rock, and not realized this existed below."

"Well, how do we get out of this place?" Dr. Larson asked.

"There seems to be a path down this way!" Kenzie shouted as she climbed over a large rock. "It's well-lit, and appears to head away from the city."

The group stayed close as they followed Kenzie in the dim fluorescent light. The path wound around ancient stone buildings with darkened openings. After traveling what seemed like several miles, the path widened into a large room with a central round table surrounded by ancient wooden chairs. It was dark, and difficult to make out the details, but as their eyes adjusted to the dim green lighting, things began to appear.

"Wow!" Rita exclaimed as she approached a large stone fireplace set at the end of the room. "This is really awesome. Someone knew what they were doing when they built this."

"What do you think happened to the people?" Kenzie asked. "This place feels like a mausoleum without the tombs. Why would someone just up and leave?"

"Maybe there are some answers here," Dr. Larson said as she approached a rough-hewn stone pedestal.

The surface was polished smooth and covered with silver, and an image began to appear as Della wiped off a thick coating of dust. Underneath were embossed carvings, but the dim light was not enough to see them properly.

"Just a minute," Jim said, reaching into his pocket, and pulling out a small flashlight connected to his keys. He flicked it on, and the tiny LED brightly illuminated the surface.

"I've seen these markings before," Kenzie exclaimed. "Parks once showed me a book covered with drawings like this."

Evil forms and strange creatures circled the edges, but the center was the most disturbing of all. It was an image of a frightful beast. The beast's mouth was wide open, and behind the rows of sharp teeth, were people hurting each other in the most vicious of ways.

"These guys needed better subject matter," Jim said lightly. "That thing is depressing. What else is in here?"

"I think this is here as a warning." Dr. Larson replied seriously. "Something really evil happened to these people."

"Why would people do that to each other?" Rita asked. "It's horrible."

"Dr. Larson's right," Kenzie replied. "Whoever carved that did it so that others would know what happened to them."

"A warning? For what purpose?" Jim asked, examining the drawings closely.

"To show what happens to people when the Zender comes," Dr. Larson answered.

"The Zender?" Jim asked, somewhat confused. "That's just an old wives' tale told to scare little children."

"You're wrong," Kenzie replied. "It may be an old story, but that monster is real. Kirsten told me about it. She told me how Parks killed it when they were just kids."

"It's more than that," Dr. Larson said, stepping away from the pedestal. "I know Parks's story, and about the encounter in the cave, but the really scary part is the destruction that comes every thousand years. If the Zender is real, then the thousand-year destruction is too. This is proof that the city was rebuilt on top of an old one, maybe even the original. Someone wanted to keep this place hidden, out of fear most likely. If the destroyers came again, they would have a place to hide. But it was forgotten over the ages, and its existence lost until now."

"I don't believe in fairy tales," Jim said, standing up and switching off his flashlight, allowing the green glow to return. "We need to find a way out of here. I suggest we follow this path, and see where it comes out."

They nodded in agreement, and began following Kenzie. Understanding the mystery of the city under their city would have to wait. Getting to safety mattered most.

CHAPTER 3

Parks had barely enough light to avoid obstacles as he began his journey. It wasn't easy to keep a steady pace as he jogged across the barren landscape. The way to the Island was clear in his mind, even though he was coming from a different direction. A steady, cool breeze blew across the wilderness, scattering leaves, and raising dust as Parks pushed along. He was concerned about Della, but he had to stay focused and not worry about her too much. There was nothing more he could do anyway. The Island likely held the answers he needed, and Sterling seemed to be holding something back.

The hours passed slowly as Parks made his way along. Night creatures scurried about, seeking safety in the ground, or behind shrubs and bushes as he approached. Parks remembered his youthful days spent hunting and camping under starlit skies. He enjoyed the isolation, and the wilderness had never frightened him, even as a youngster. It seemed friendly, as if someone were with him, a warm, unseen presence sharing the flickering light of his campfires.

He was nearly a full day's run from the Island when the sun began to peer over the distant mountains. The day would be equally as hot as the nights were cold. Temperatures were likely to break a hundred degrees, so Parks set up a temporary shelter using branches and shrubs cut with his crystal blade. Strapping them with rope he made from some native grasses, Parks set up a crude shelter behind a rocky outcropping, and settled in.

The bag he carried contained his heavy leather coat, supplies, and a wool blanket. Laying out the blanket on the sandy ground, Parks made himself comfortable in the shade. He ate some dried fruit and beef jerky which satisfied his stomach enough that it wouldn't be growling and keeping him awake through the heat of the day. Taking several long draws from his water bag, Parks laid back, resting his head on his backpack as he gazed across the vast terrain. But sleep eluded him.

"I made it impossible for Barron to hurt Della by implanting that crystal in his chest," Parks said to himself, "but why don't I feel things are getting better? Della puts herself in danger just because she has to. People depend on her skills and leadership. Maybe I shouldn't have left."

A warm breeze blew across Parks's face as he did his best to quiet his mind. But feelings of anger and rage roared through his thoughts. Parks got up from his makeshift bed, stepped into the heat of the day, picked up a rock and threw it at passing coyote. He purposefully missed but needed to do something to blow off steam.

"What makes them act the way they do? I never did anything but help Management build a successful organization. But here I am in the middle of nowhere, searching for answers to questions I don't even know how to ask."

Parks returned to his shelter and tried again to sleep, but the most he could do was cover his eyes with his forearm, and block out the brightness of the day. He lay there for hours, drifting in and out of consciousness. Then he gasped as he shook himself back to full awareness.

The day had passed, and the evening sky was darkening. The cool breeze returned, and swept over his sweaty face as he jumped to his feet, and looked hard in the direction of the distant city. Everything inside told him to run back and find Della. He could feel the anger boiling deep inside as he thought about all those responsible for her peril and his struggles. Barron, Harry and the rest of Management's goons were all responsible for this misery.

He slid his hand along the handle of his crystal blade as he thought of those who deserved a taste of its power.

His mind was on fire as he packed up his things.

"What if they have Della?" A voice spoke into his mind. "Management will kill her, and your friends too."

"I'd never let that happen," Parks growled as he slung the pack over his shoulder. "I would die first."

"You're too selfish to sacrifice yourself," The voice continued. "Look at you, running around in the desert like a fool. Get a clue, and turn back. Together, we'll get rid of those who resist, and you'll have everything you ever desired. Don't you want to be happy?"

"Happy? Happy!" Parks exclaimed as he stared longingly across the barrenness. "I must go back, and help Della. She needs me."

He began the descent down a steep slope towards the city, but a deep, painful pressure welled up inside his chest. He tried to push through it as he ran along, but couldn't. After only a few hundred yards, he collapsed. Struggling onto a nearby rock, Parks dropped his head into his hands. He fell face first onto the warm sandy ground. He couldn't move, and his heart was pounding like a drum inside his chest.

Then everything went black.

When consciousness finally returned, the sun was gone, and a bright round moon had taken its place. Parks took an internal inventory of his condition as he rolled onto his back. His heart had slowed, and he could sit up without feeling nauseous. He spotted the book. Apparently, it had slipped out of his pocket when he toppled to the ground, and it was lying just out of easy reach. His chest ached as he stretched out, and grabbed it.

Instantly, he felt better.

Not exactly sure why, Parks untied the leather strap, and opened the book.

"That thing can't help you," the voice inside his head challenged. "You need to get to the city before it's too late. It's time to start running again."

Parks felt sick, only this time the nausea came from images flashing though his mind of Della being attacked and hurt.

"No!" Parks said defiantly, "I'll go when I'm ready. I must read first."

His hands trembled as he opened the ancient book. It had been months since he tried to read something from it. The moon's light was not enough, so he gathered some sticks, and started a fire with matches from his bag. Before long, the fire was burning brightly. Parks sat on the edge of a rock, and began to read. Usually, the book brought only confusion and more questions, but this time was different. The book seemed to open on its own as he began to read.

It was a story of a village filled with happy people living together in peace. Life was good. They had plenty of food and fun. But there was a tall wall that completely surrounded their village. It had been there longer than any could remember, and people said it was built to protect them from an evil bear. The bear legend was told over and over again, and came with a stern warning: never go outside the wall. Oh, some villagers would venture out from time to time to gather fruit and nuts from trees that grew nearby, but they did so only in groups, and stayed within sight of the large gate. Once in a while, someone would wander a little too far away, and they were never heard from again.

However, there was one young man who didn't believe they should have to live inside the walls like prisoners. He heard the tale like everyone else, and grew up being told over and over again of the dangers of leaving the safety of the village, but he hated the feeling of fear it created. So one day, he decided something had to be done.

It was early morning when he pulled the heavy gate shut, and started off. He walked as quietly as he could through the woods, keenly aware of every sound. It was more than a little scary, being alone and outside the village walls, but he bravely worked his way through woods and brush, following what seemed to be a path.

Eventually, the woods gave way to a clearing. He saw the mouth of a dark cave set into a steep hill. Bones scattered about the cave's entrance froze him in his tracks as he realized they may have once belonged to members of his village. He took a deep breath, and unstrapped the spear he carried across his shoulders. He cautiously approached the entrance, and stood there for a few moments, staring into the quiet darkness before him. This was the day he had planned for, and the thought of running away in fear never entered his mind. He gathered himself, and yelled into the cave once, and then again.

His voice echoed back twice before dissipating into the forest behind him. All was silent for a moment. Then, from somewhere deep inside, the distant sound of heavy thuds grew steadily louder, followed by fearsome grunts and growls. The young man stepped back several paces, and dropped into a sprinter's stance with the spear held high above his head. Within seconds, the raging fury of a gigantic bear emerged from the cave, and burst into the clearing.

But in the moment of transition from darkness to bright daylight, the bear was blind for just a moment.

That moment was all the young hunter needed as he sprinted towards the massive bear, and released his spear. The sharp point of the spear sank deep into the bear's shoulder just below its neck, penetrating into its heart. Diving to the ground, the young man barely escaped being killed as the giant bear sailed over him. The bear's head drove into the ground, and its body plowed into the earth, kicking up dust and leaves before coming to its final rest. The forest was strangely quiet as the young man stood to his feet, and turned to see his prize lying motionless. His spear had done its work, and the brave young hunter had fulfilled his journey.

Later that evening when he returned to his village, all eyes were upon him. But as great as it was to have freed his people from the tyranny of a wicked beast, his prize was so much more. He proved that even the darkest fears can be defeated if you face them head on. You only have to believe in yourself.

Parks closed the book and sat quietly for a few minutes, thinking about the story.

"If I turn back now, I'll never know what lies beyond," Parks reasoned as he put the book back into his pouch. "I'll be following fear instead of faith. I trust Della, and she trusts me, and together we have agreed upon our course."

Parks slung his bag across his shoulders, taking one last long look at the distant lights of the city before beginning a steady jog towards the island. At his current pace, he would likely be there by early morning. His mind was firm now, and the pain had left his chest. Still, his thoughts regarding Management were not changed, and he was more determined than ever to find the way to defeat them.

CHAPTER 4

Kenzie climbed to the top of a large pile of broken rock, and gasped. Jim, Rita, and Dr. Larson joined her quickly. Spread out before them were the skeletal remains of an ancient generation.

"These people didn't die happy," Jim said as he hobbled down with Rita's help. "Look at them. They killed each other."

The effects of death and carnage were everywhere. Skeletal hands around the outline of a throat long since decayed away. Rib cages and backs full of knives and spears. Skulls bashed in by clubs and rocks.

"Interesting!" Dr. Larson said as she examined several skeletons. "It looks like they turned on each other, but why would they do that? This place looks like it was used for meetings or as a market or something. It seems hardly the place to stage an angry mob scene."

"I don't like it," Rita said nervously. "This place gives me the creeps."

"Over here!" Kenzie shouted. "I think I found something."

Kenzie had entered a room through two very large, ornate wooden doors. Inside were more skeletal remains. The room was full of ancient wood and stone furniture, most of it broken and smashed.

"I don't see anything," Jim said as he hobbled in. "Looks like more of the same to me."

"You passed right by it," Kenzie said as she turned to face them. "Look at the door."

They all paused and stared at two sets of three long, deep gashes ripped into the wood.

"The Zender," Dr. Larson said involuntarily. "It was here."

Jim stared at it for a long time, his mind struggling to wrap itself around the concept of an ancient, mythical beast that wasn't actually mythical. They were only stories meant to scare kids around campfires, or were they? Here in front of his very eyes was evidence of an evil so dark, it once caused the people whose skeletal remains were scattered around this dark place to kill each other without mercy. A beastly energy degrading the thoughts of reasoning people to the point where they would turn on each other, just like the scenes he had seen carved in the stone tablet. The thoughts were too painful and frightening to dwell on.

"Let's find our way out of here," Jim said, turning towards a narrow path winding its way past several large columns. "We've seen enough of this."

Quietly, they left the ancient carnage behind without saying another word. Though the events were long since buried by time, they all felt a deep sense of sadness for what those poor people must have endured.

"Do you hear that?" Kenzie said after they had traveled what seemed like several miles. "It sounds like rushing water."

They made several more bends in the path before coming to a large pool of water guarded by a roaring waterfall.

"I bet we're just outside the North end of the city where the East river spills into the wilderness," Jim shouted. "No wonder no one has ever been in here. There are millions of tons of water pounding down. Now how are we going to get out?"

"We can do this," Rita said confidently, "but we're going to need to tie ourselves together with something so we don't get separated."

"You're going to swim out?" Jim said incredulously.

"We are," Rita replied. "I'm a good swimmer, but we must work as a team if we're going to make it safely through."

"Everyone take off their jackets and sweaters," Dr. Larson commanded. "We'll make a rope from them."

In a few minutes, they were ready as they tied the ends together, making sure they were tight.

"Tie them securely around your waists," Rita said. "I'll go first, with Jim behind me."

"No way," Jim protested. "Put me at the end. I don't want to slow anyone down with my bum leg. You guys lead the way, and I'll take up the rear."

Rita looked at Jim for a moment, and saw that she couldn't change his mind. She tied the makeshift rope around her waist with Dr. Larson behind her, and Kenzie after. Jim tied his last. They moved along a steep wall to a narrow ledge. Rita wanted to be as close as possible to the waterfall before diving in. Once in the water, they were to swim close to the pounding water before taking a deep breath and diving as deep as possible. There was a danger of whirlpools, and if anyone got caught by one, they had agreed to untie themselves, and try to make it out alone. That way, they wouldn't pull the rest down if they couldn't swim free. It was risky, but they had no other choice.

On the count of three, they jumped in.

Rita was a great swimmer, as she had said. She easily dove down, and swam under the power of the pounding waterfall. Her strong strokes pulled the others as they moved beneath the crushing water. Jim pushed himself as hard as he could and tried to keep up, but he wasn't a great swimmer.

"They're never going to make it." Jim thought to himself. "I'm dragging them down."

His lungs felt like bursting as he untied the rope around his waist. Kenzie was swimming hard in front of him, and he watched as she disappeared in the mist of swirling bubbles created by the foaming water.

"I just wish I had more time to get to know you," Jim thought as Rita's face flashed before his eyes while the blackness settled over him.

Meanwhile, Barron was answering some hard questions…

"What do you mean they disappeared?" General Ivy demanded. "Nobody disappears. You're going to find them, Barron, we need them. Don't think you can excuse this."

Barron grimaced. He didn't like Harry's daughter, and he definitely didn't do well with criticism.

"I followed them down a hallway under the hospital," Barron said through clenched teeth. "There was no way out, but when I got there, they were gone."

"They must have doubled back, and you missed them." Ivy interrupted. "They have to be here in the city somewhere. You need to put together a search team, and look until you find them. I don't care if you have to go door to door. Just get it done."

Barron swallowed hard as he turned to leave.

"By the way, how's your father?" He asked as he opened the door.

"Just fine," She replied with a sneering face.

"Great! I can't wait until he's back in command again!" Barron exclaimed as he slammed the door.

He knew Ivy hated her father, and couldn't resist getting in a quick dig. But as he left, he remembered the day Parks put the blue crystal in his chest. As was expected, Harry wanted answers when Barron first returned to the city, but he couldn't tell him a thing without agonizing pain from the crystal. It wasn't until Dave Castle called him to the Citadel that things began to change.

"What's this I hear you're not talking?" Dave demanded.

"I can't say anything at this time," Barron replied calmly.

"That's insubordination," Dave snapped as he slammed his fist on the desk. "I could have you shot for that."

Barron swallowed hard as Dave sat back in his seat. He looked carefully at Barron before speaking again.

"There's something more to this than meets the eye." Dave said quietly. "You've never liked Parks, and have always been an obedient player. Why change now?"

Dave walked around his desk, and faced Barron.

"Parks has something on you, doesn't he?" Dave said as he looked square into Barron's eyes. "No, he's done something to you."

Then Dave noticed the dim blue glow coming from Barron's chest.

"Oh, so that's it," Dave said softly. "Parks has infected you with his crystal. Just stay right there while I make a call."

Dave picked up his phone, and dialed. He turned his back to Barron, and spoke quietly into the receiver.

"Follow me," Dave said as he put down the phone and headed for the door.

"Where are we going?"

But Dave didn't answer as he led the way down the hall towards the boardroom. Barron had never visited this part of the Citadel before. Neither had he met any of the Board of Directors. Sitting at the end of the long table was a quaint gentleman with a friendly, smiling face.

"Have a seat," the man said as he gestured towards Dave and Barron. "Dave tells me you have a problem and can't talk about it."

Barron glumly nodded his head in agreement.

"Well," the man continued, rising from his seat, "let's see if we can do something about that."

He came around where Barron was sitting. Barron pushed his chair back, suddenly uneasy.

"Relax," the man said, positioning himself in front of Barron. "This won't hurt much."

He reached into a vest pocket inside his suit, and pulled out a long, cylindrical glass tube. It was about an inch in diameter, and nearly eighteen inches long.

"Please remove your shirt," the man continued.

Barron obliged. As soon as his shirt was off, the man grabbed the glass tube with both hands, and buried it deep into his chest. Barron's face turned white and his eyes bulged out as he stood up, and stumbled away from the table. He looked down at the tube sticking out of his chest while pain and confusion ripped across his face. Blood spurted from the end of the tube, and he slumped forward. Finally, the blue crystal rolled out the end of the tube, and bounced several times on the table before coming to a stop.

"Don't touch it," the man said as Dave reached for the crystal. "Help me get Barron on the table."

The two men lifted Barron, and laid him on his back. Barron was mouthing words, but nothing would come out. The ceiling lights blinded him, but from the corner of his eye, he could see the man pull a bright red crystal from his pocket. He dropped it through the tube, and into Barron's chest. The pain was unbearable as the man twisted the tube, and jerked it out while Dave held him down. The red crystal was burning hot, but in a matter of seconds, the pain left. Barron blinked twice before sitting up.

"What have you done to me?" Barron asked as he rubbed the glowing red spot in the center of his chest.

"You were infected," the man replied as he returned to his seat. "Now maybe you can tell us what's going on."

Barron tensed as he swung around to face the man. Anger gripped him as he looked at the smug man sitting only a few feet away.

"You could have killed me!" Barron growled.

Dave stepped forward, but the man nodded him off.

"Sit down!" he commanded, lifting his hand towards Barron.

There was a razor-sharp pain in his chest, and Barron lost all the strength in his legs. He stumbled backwards, and fell into a chair.

"That's better," the man continued. "I suppose it was Parks who put the crystal in you. It's a good thing we were able to get it out when we did, or you would have been of no further value to us. The crystals Parks has are powerful, and must be destroyed. We must find out where he's hiding them, and maybe you can help us with that."

The man took a glass vial from his pocket, and removed the cap. Then, with the help of a piece of paper, he shoved the blue crystal off the table and into the vial, careful not to touch it. He snapped the cap back on, and returned the vial to his pocket.

"You can talk freely now," he encouraged. "Tell us everything you know."

Barron looked at Dave and then back at the man in the dark gray suit. His mind was racing, but he needed to gain control. Whatever was going on here was beyond his understanding, and he needed to be careful.

"I don't know much," Barron began. "I fought Parks, but he was able to escape after he put that thing in my chest."

"Why did he put that crystal in you?" the man pressed.

"He was afraid I would tell his secret,"

"Secret? What secret?" The man asked earnestly, growing impatient.

"Hey, what do I get out of this deal?" Barron asked looking over at Dave. "Parks rips my chest open, and then you do the same. I need some compensation for my suffering."

Dave glanced at the man in the suit, who nodded.

"What kind of compensation are you looking for?" Dave asked.

"I want General Olliver's old job." Barron answered with a smile. "You haven't found anyone to replace him, unless you're counting on Harry's worthless daughter. I can do a hundred times better than her."

"We may be able to do that, but just not quite yet." Dave replied. "Ivy's running the show for now, but I'm sure we can come to an amicable solution for you if you give us a little time."

Barron rubbed his chest, feeling the heat radiating from the crystal. He couldn't tell if he was being played or not, but he was not about to lose his advantage.

"Ok, it's Dr. Larson. She and Parks have a thing going on. He will do anything to protect her, and if you have her, you have him."

The man in the gray suit leaned back in his chair, and laughed.

"Always about love, isn't it?" The man replied, still chuckling as he stood. "Will these creatures never learn? We'll let you know our next move soon, but for right now, why don't you get some R&R. You look like you could use it."

Dave ushered Barron, to the door and shut it solidly behind him. As Barron walked down the hall towards the exit, he stopped and leaned against the wall, pondering for a moment what had just happened. "Did things just get better or worse for me?" Barron asked himself as he felt the spot on his chest where the red crystal was inserted. "Hmm, maybe I won't need as much help from Dave as I thought." Then Barron laughed and started off again with a noticeable spring in his step.

"What were you thinking?" Rita shouted as Jim coughed up half a lungful of water. "You didn't need to untie yourself. I would have pulled you through."

He lay on a shallow bank just along the water's edge with Rita.

"You're just lucky I found you when I did. Another few seconds under the water, and you would have been gone," Rita said more frightened than angry. Her voice softened as she helped him sit up. "You're not leaving me now or ever, so get used to it."

"I can't thank you enough," Jim answered warmly at her affectionate words. "But I'm ok, and I think we'd better keep moving, don't you?"

The roar of the waterfall faded in the distance as they followed the river towards the country. Rita had grown up fishing the banks of this river, and soon began to recognize familiar spots. With her leading the way, they came upon her family's old abandoned farm. After checking carefully and confirming the place was empty, Jim broke a window with his elbow, and entered through the back door. Soon a warm fire was going in the firebox, and Kenzie was busy rummaging for food.

Rita remembered the fruit cellar below the porch. It was filled with canning from many years before, and most of it was still edible. Before long, they were gorging themselves on pears and peaches. There was even some dried canned venison. It was a welcome port in a storm, but they knew they couldn't stay there long.

CHAPTER 5

"Hey, Normand," Isaac said as he jumped on the van's sideboards. "What are you doing way out here?"

"Your mom ordered something," Normand replied as he slid open the door to his van. "I don't just pick up laundry, you know."

Normand hopped out with an armload of new towels. The warm summer breeze played in the bright yellow flowers as he walked to the door with Isaac at his side. Isaac was a sturdy young man with sun-bleached shoulder-length blonde hair parted down the middle.

"Have you heard about the meeting tonight?" Isaac asked as he bounded the stairs ahead of Normand to open the front door.

"We're meeting tonight?" Normand replied as he set the towels on the entry bench. "But I thought we were lying low for a while."

"Nope," Isaac answered. "It sounds like Kirsten wants to get us all together. Lots has been happening. I saw Troy downtown at the arcade, and he told me about it. I don't know where though. Troy said Kirsten is worried we might be followed, so she's going to announce the meeting location at the last minute, just in case."

"How's she going to do that?" Normand replied with a puzzled look on his face.

Isaac pulled the bright blue crystal he kept on a chain around his neck.

"Oh, right, duh." Normand said. "What time is she thinking?"

"Don't know," Isaac replied as he picked up a football lying next to the fence that ran along their driveway. "She doesn't want any information out until the last second."

Normand snatched the football out of Isaac's hands and dropped back, pumping the ball like a quarterback.

"Go long," Normand said, and Isaac took off in a sprint. The football followed a tight spiral as it spun through the air, right before Isaac leaped up and ripped it down. He returned the ball with an equal amount of zip.

"I can't play right now," Normand said as he tossed the ball back a second time before climbing into his van. "How about I come by later tonight after dinner? We can ride together to meet up with the gang."

"Sounds great," Isaac answered as he came running back. "I've got some yard work to do for mom anyway before she gets home from work."

Normand finished his rounds, and returned to the warehouse with a full load of dirty laundry. The facility was huge, servicing the hospital, local restaurants, hotels, and some well-to-do citizens. Normand backed into one of the service docks, and began off-loading the bags of laundry into one of the stainless steel chutes took them to the sort and wash area.

He was nearly finished when he noticed a black SUV parked just outside the security fence. He pretended not to notice, but became increasingly aware he was under surveillance. Slipping into the back of the van, he cracked the slot between the cab and the van so he could get a look without being seen. The windows were darkened, but he could make out the outline of a small man or woman with a camera equipped with a telephoto lens pressed against the glass. He finished off-loading, and headed in to turn in his paperwork for the day.

"Hi, Chuck," Normand said cheerfully as he slid his paperwork into the slot next to the time clock.

"Normand," the man behind the large counter answered. "Got any plans for the weekend?

"Nah," Normand replied as he put his time card into the rack next to the time clock. "Just hanging out and playing a little ball with some friends. What about you?"

"The missus has a long list of honey-do things, but I'm going to see if I can skate," Chuck replied with a smile. "She's always thinking up things for me to do. Hey, maybe I could give you a call, and we could meet for a beer or something. I'll be out of here by five."

Normand liked Chuck and his wife, Nancy. They were regular folks who worked hard, and raised a family. Chuck was in his middle forties, but still acted like he was twenty-something.

"I wish I could," Normand answered as he opened the door to leave, "but I promised my friends. Maybe next week."

Normand pulled the rear door shut, and was greeted by the warm summer air. His sharp red convertible two-seater sports car was parked in the back of the lot behind some dumpsters. He didn't like parking it where it could get scratched or dinged in the busy lot, so he kept it stashed. But before he headed for it, he peeked around the corner of the building, and to his relief, the black SUV was gone. Normand checked up and down the fence line along the road, but didn't see it anywhere.

Maybe he was just getting paranoid, he thought as he jogged towards his car. It would certainly be understandable, considering everything that had happened lately.

He hopped in, and put the top down before heading for the exit. His curly red hair bounced in the breeze as he pulled onto the main road. He was heading for his apartment to change before going over to see Troy. Turning up the stereo, he sang along to one of his favorite groups as he whizzed along.

Twenty miles or so later, he took the off-ramp into one of the large apartment complexes on the west side of the city. His apartment was in one of the lower-rent sections. He had been working for the laundry company since coming out of high school, but they didn't pay all that much.

Still, he was taking night courses at the university, and was nearly finished with his associates degree. He wanted to get his general studies out of the way before taking his major in chemistry. His parents had offered to help, but he liked being self-sufficient. He turned down his street, pulled into his parking space, and headed to his door.

The apartment was cool as Normand threw his keys onto the small table by the door. He hit the lights, and headed for the refrigerator. He got a bowl from the cupboard, and dumped his Chinese takeout leftovers into it. In a moment, the microwave was humming, and he returned to searching the refrigerator for some refreshments. He was deep in thought as he found a half-full bottle of soda hiding behind the milk container. Suddenly, the hair on the back of his neck stood up.

"What the?" Normand said as he spun around, nearly dropping the soda.

There, standing in his kitchenette, was a small, slightly-built man with sunglasses in a dark suit.

"What are you doing in my house?" Normand demanded angrily as he quickly assessed the situation.

"I'm here to talk about you," The man said as he stepped towards Normand. "It seems you have something unusual, and I want to know where you got it," he continued, pointing towards the ring on Normand's finger.

"I don't know who you are, or why you think you can come into my house, but it's none of your business!" Normand said angrily as he slammed the fridge door. "Get out of here now!"

Normand stepped around the small dining table that divided his kitchen from the rest of his apartment, hoping to drive him towards the door, but the man just smiled. Before Normand could react, the man grabbed his hand, and effortlessly tossed him out of the kitchen. He flew into the living room, where he knocked over an end table and broke a lamp before crashing to a stop against his sofa. The little man was on him in a second, his hands gripping Normand's throat. His lungs burned for oxygen. One hand was trapped under the edge of the sofa, but the other was free, and he felt the edge of the broken lamp base.

It was heavy, made from marble, and served its purpose well as Normand smashed it into the side of his assailant's head. The impact sent the man flying into the wall of his apartment, and Normand leaped to his feet. He could still feel the man's fingers around his throat, and he gasped several times. But the man was back on his feet in an instant, with no visible effect from being smashed in the head.

"Where did you get that?" he asked again as he calmly walked around the overturned couch, and pointed towards Normand's ring.

"Like I said, what's that to you?" Normand asked as he braced himself for another assault.

"This should help you remember," The man said. He reached into his coat, and pulled out a dark red crystal about the size of a marble. "In a few moments, you'll tell me everything."

The man jumped towards Normand with the red crystal in his outstretched hand. More out of reflex than anything, Normand stuck out his hand with the crystal ring. A bright blue light instantly shone forth, filling the room. The light blinded Normand for a few moments, and when he could see again, his assailant was gone. All that remained was an acrid smell, and a wisp of gray smoke.

Normand surveyed the apartment, and looked around outside to make sure the man was really gone, and no one else was coming. He suddenly felt alone and unprotected as he put his room back together, and cleaned up the broken pieces of lamp.

He wondered if he was the only one, or if others were having similar troubles.

Kirsten was already at the meeting place when the rest of the group started to trickle in. She had chosen one of the stately homes on the upper side of the city. She knew the owners, and they had asked her to watch their house while they were gone for the weekend, so it made the perfect location. David was the last to arrive.

"Let's go into the lounge," Kirsten said as she heard them arrive. "There's plenty of room in there."

The house had every amenity, including a long bar for serving guests, and a large fireplace behind it.

"Awesome, let's turn on the game!" Troy said, pointing to the big TV over the mantle.

"Not tonight," Kirsten snapped. "We've business to attend to."

"Hey!" Burke exclaimed. "Where're Aaron and Kenzie?"

"I don't know," Kirsten replied. "All of you got my signal, right?"

Everyone nodded in agreement as Kirsten looked around at each of them.

"Strange things are going on," Normand said. He told them briefly what had happened in his apartment. "Parks always said there could be trouble, but now I think trouble is hunting us. We need to be extra careful, and on guard at all time."

"Has it occurred to anybody," Troy asked as he stood up, "that maybe they're watching us right now, or even headed our way."

Troy was a tall, well-dressed black-haired young man with dark brown eyes. Normand fought a feeling of dread. The house was located at the end of a long driveway on a dead-end street. They would be trapped if someone blocked the exit.

"Do what Normand said, and watch out for yourselves," Kirsten said as they headed for the door. "As of right now, we start operations. Remember your training, and keep in touch as much as you can. I'll try to reach Aaron and Kenzie, and let them know what's happening."

In a matter of seconds, they were piling into their respective vehicles, and ripping out. It was clear to Kirsten the years they had spent preparing to retake the city were in jeopardy. If they had been found out, she shuddered to think what would happen next. As much energy as she had put in to showing them how to use the crystals, they were still inexperienced young people. But worrying about what could happen wasn't helpful, and she knew it. She would need to pull things together, and come up with a plan.

"If we were being followed," Kirsten said to Joshua as she turned onto the main road, "they're not doing a very good job of it. There's no one around."

"It could have been a false alarm," Joshua answered as he stretched around to check the rear window. "You know Troy can get excitable sometimes. Still, it's a good idea to be extra careful, especially with what Normand said. Hey, have you heard from Parks lately?"

"I haven't seen Parks for at least two weeks," Kirsten replied as she pulled into Joshua's driveway. "But I'm sure he's ok. I'm going to be sending out some information in the next couple of days, so be listening. The time has come for us to make our presence felt."

Joshua bounded up to his front door and waved as Kirsten drove off, but she was already buried deep in thought.

Management had been tightening their grip on the city since Parks's disappearance Kirsten thought as she drove towards her parent's house. They were probably afraid, and just cracking down in general. But how could they possibly know anything of significance unless someone had talked?

Her thoughts trailed off as she looked out her side window. The moonlight glistened across the passing fields, creating long shadows that seemed to move with the tall grass.

For a moment, feelings of safety returned as her thoughts drifted to easier days of hiking trails and hunting ducks with her father and brother. Her bright headlights lit up the lines along the road as she followed a long curve before the final few miles to the family home. She slowed a bit as the road made one final sharp bend.

"What's that?" she said out loud as the lights picked up what appeared to be a herd of animals crossing the road several hundred yards in front of her.

She slowed, straining to make out what it was, when her lights reflected back a shiny red.

"Testers?!" she shouted. She slammed on her brakes, and skidded across the center line on the dew-moistened road.

A steady stream of the dark red creatures was pouring out of the ditch on one side, flowing across the road, and into the ditch on the other. Kirsten shut off her lights, suddenly realizing the shadows dancing in the moonlight across the field were thousands of Testers heading somewhere. Icy cold fingers of fear gripped her as she watched in horror. Several long minutes passed before the last of the troop disappeared into the tall grass. Kirsten waited another five minutes to make sure they were all gone before she started inching forward. She came parallel with the wide swath extending out of sight in both directions, and noted the Testers were heading in a Northeast direction, which meant they were going towards the city.

Kirsten gripped the steering wheel so tight, her knuckles turned white. Testers hadn't been seen since the city was taken. This could mean only one thing. Management was planning something terrible.

Kirsten pulled away and turned her lights back on, with a sickening knot in her stomach. The last time those awful creatures had come into the city, many people had died. She turned onto the long graveled driveway leading to her parent's new home, and the porch lights welcomed her as she parked next to her dad's truck.

She got out, and stood for a moment in the cool night air, looking up at the moon's smiling face. It all seemed surreal. The crushed rock crunched under her tennis shoes as she walked around the front of her truck towards the concrete sidewalk and up the wrought iron stairs to the porch. Light streamed from the living room window as she pushed the doorbell. In a moment, the door opened to warm hugs from her father.

"Are you ok?" her dad asked as he closed the door behind her. "You seem a bit tense."

"I'm ok," Kirsten answered, managing a weak smile. "Where's Mom?"

"Your mother had to run over to the neighbors' for a minute," Dad answered as they walked into the kitchen. "You remember Jani and her husband Darrell. Well, their daughter Angie suddenly became ill, and your mom is taking her some of that special remedy of hers. She should be right back."

"They live by the Henderson farm next to the old mill, right?" Kirsten asked solemnly.

"That's right," Mr. Parks answered. "She left about a half hour ago. You should have passed her on your way up."

Kirsten sank into the kitchen chair, suddenly too weak to stand.

"What's wrong, sweetie?" Mr. Parks asked. He sat down next to her, and took her hand.

"Nothing, I hope," Kirsten replied, her voice breaking slightly. "I wasn't going to say anything, but I passed a huge procession of Testers about a mile and a half from here, and Mom would have had to go that way."

"Testers? Out here? We haven't even heard of those awful things in nearly ten years, and you say they were just down the road. Are you sure?"

"I'm sure, Dad, and Mom would have had to pass them."

Mr. Parks jumped to his feet, and reached for the phone. In a second, he was calling his wife's cell phone. It rang and rang, but no answer. He dialed again, but still no answer. Then he called again.

"Hello, Jani," Mr. Parks said, trying not to sound anxious. "Is my wife there yet?"

Kirsten focused intently as her dad listened to the answer, watching his face for a sign of relief.

"Ok, thank you," he said. "No, no problem. I'm sure she's on her way."

Mr. Parks hung up the phone, and reached for his coat.

"I'm going with you, Dad," Kirsten said, jumping out of her chair, and following him out the front door.

Without a word, Mr. Parks grabbed the rifle he used for shooting coyotes and other varmints he kept in a closet by the front door, and threw it into the back seat of his pickup. Kirsten jumped in beside him.

"Mom's ok. I'm sure of it." she said as he sped out of the driveway. "Maybe her cell phone battery's dead. You know how she always forgets to put it on the charger."

Mr. Parks' face was tight as he sped down the country road. Within minutes, they were at the location where the Testers had crossed. Mr. Parks grabbed his rifle and a large flashlight out of the back seat. Kirsten took a second flashlight from the glove box, and together they began scanning the area. A light breeze blew the cool night air around Kirsten's neck, and she shivered slightly.

"There!" her dad shouted as he jumped into the shallow ditch.

His flashlight reflected off the rear tail light of his wife's Jeep. It was turned on its side, and wedged between two trees.

"Pearl?" Mr. Parks yelled as he climbed up the bumper and onto the side of the Jeep.

He nearly ripped the door off its hinges as he pulled it open.

"Is Mom ok?" Kirsten asked as she worked through the thick brush and broken limbs surrounding the truck to get to the front windshield.

"Pearl?" he said again in a deflated voice, scanning the empty cab with his flashlight. He stood on the truck and shouted her name with all his might into the darkened night, but no one answered.

"Mom? Mom?" Kirsten joined in as she followed him into the field.

They searched the area carefully for the next hour with no luck. Mrs. Parks was nowhere to be found.

"They must have taken her," Mr. Parks said finally as he collapsed onto one knee. "But why? Why would they take my wife? She never did anything to them."

"She's ok, Dad; I just know it," Kirsten said as she knelt down beside her father and put her arm around his neck.

Hot tears streamed down Mr. Parks' face as he leaned against his daughter.

"I sent a message to the boys," Kirsten said as she helped him to his feet. "They're on their way now. We'll have help shortly, so why don't we just take a break for a minute."

But Mr. Parks was determined to keep looking in spite of his daughter's admonition. He pushed himself, even though he was exhausted, checking and rechecking the surrounding area with Kirsten at his side. A huge weight settled into his chest as fear filled his heart, but he kept on, keeping his flashlight busy.

CHAPTER 6

The miles passed quickly as Parks moved silently through the wilderness. He crested a low, rocky ridge overlooking the entrance to the Island, and climbed down, knowing the colonel would likely see or hear him through the many sensors and cameras hidden throughout the area. He walked steadily towards the carefully disguised entrance. It was hard to locate, even if you knew it was there. The sun was hot overhead as vibrations traveled beneath his feet and up his legs while a large section of the wilderness floor rose to greet him.

"Mr. Parks," a familiar voice sounded as the entrance closed tight behind him again with a rush of cool air. "Good to see you again."

"Glad to be back!" Parks said as he shook the colonel's gloved hand.

"What brings you way out here?" the colonel asked as he led Parks down the ramp and into the expansive underground facility. "I didn't expect I'd be seeing you so soon. I trust everything's ok."

"Hardly," Parks replied as they climbed onto the tram and headed underground. "Hey, where's Sterling? He usually drives this crazy chariot of yours."

"Sterling," the colonel answered as the people mover made its way down the long series of tunnels towards the inner workings of the Island, "left several weeks ago. He said something about going home for a while."

The long electric train coasted to a stop at the main entrance. The colonel hopped off, and headed towards the elevators, which led even deeper into the lower areas and the colonel's office. Even though Parks had been there before, he still couldn't help being amazed at the enormity of the place. It was carved out of solid rock polished so perfectly the light shining from banks of overhead light fixtures reflected back at them. They entered the elevator, and the older man hit the button as the door closed behind them.

"You know, I've sent a few scouts to check on the city," the colonel said as the elevator glided to a stop. "They tell me

Management is becoming more aggressive, and there are some negative developments. Where do you think they're headed? I mean, do you think things could get bad?"

"Hi," Iris said brightly before Parks could answer as they exited the elevator.

"Hi, Iris," Parks replied with a smile as they passed the large polished granite counter.

Parks couldn't help but admire the attractive young woman. Her parents had been taken by Management when Harry lusted after their beautiful home. He had had them killed, and she was shipped out to the wilderness to die. If it hadn't been for the colonel, she would have. But this didn't seem like the right place for a young woman. She should be out with friends, discovering life, not trapped deep underground running the colonel's operations. Parks's jaw tightened as he realized how much Management had stolen from people.

"We have a lot to go over," Parks said, his mind returning to the colonel's question as they entered his office and sat down. "Things have changed in the city. I might be a hunted man, but Management suffered a severe blow too. Jim got the word out, and exposed their corruption, at least some of it. But that hasn't stopped them, at least not yet. They continue to deflect criticism, blaming it on a few "bad eggs." With all of the city's media outlets at their command, it's difficult to overcome their assertions, especially now that HOT News is out of the picture, and Jim's on the run."

"I would have expected them to move into damage control mode," the colonel interjected.

"Worse," Parks replied, scooting to the edge of his seat. "They're going after everyone they think might be part of the resistance, or anyone they suspect of supporting it. I'm worried even more people are going to get hurt."

"What do you think can be done about it?" the colonel asked, reaching across his desk for a pen and pad. "I've been evaluating our resources and options since you were here last, and I can tell you we don't have the power it would take to attack Management directly, at least not yet, but we're working on that. I've put together multiple assault teams capable of knocking out specific targets."

"You'll need to coordinate with me when the time comes," Parks said, leaning back and folding his hands under his chin, "and not move until I give the word. There are things about Management I need to understand before putting anybody at risk. What I really need is to get to Sterling. I believe he knows something that can help us."

The colonel leaned forward onto his desk, and began writing on the pad. After a few moments, he ripped off the sheet and handed it to Parks.

"Don't lose that," the colonel said as Parks looked it over closely. "That's the route Sterling took when he left. The cameras only go so far, but I followed his movements until he was out of sight. He was heading west towards the distant mountain range on the far reaches of the wilderness. No one seems to know much about that area."

"You said he was going home," Parks replied. "What do you think he meant by that? I've explored the wilderness somewhat, but have never encountered any other civilizations or seen evidence people live out there."

"I asked him about that before he left, and he wouldn't say," the colonel answered as he glanced over at the wall of video screens fed by countless hidden cameras. It was a habit formed by years of guarding the Island from intruders. "Now that I think about it, neither he or his brother ever talked about their family or where they grew up. Strange; they just showed up one day, yet it seemed they were always here."

Parks got up, and headed for the elevators with the colonel close behind.

"Excuse me," Parks said, stopping for a moment to speak to Iris on his way out, "I know what happened to you and your parents, and I'm going to make it right somehow. You deserve better."

Iris smiled, but didn't say a word. There was nothing to say. The life she should have enjoyed with her family was now but a distant memory. All this time, she had never complained or blamed anyone for her circumstance. She simply accepted the cards life had dealt her, and made the best of it. If things were going to be different, it would take a miracle, and she had never seen a miracle.

Still, something deep down inside stirred as she looked into the green eyes of the large man dressed in animal skins leaning on her desk. His face was hard, but his eyes were tender and soft. She watched as the elevator doors closed behind the colonel and Parks, and a warm sense of hope suddenly filled the dead space inside her heart. She recalled the few memories she had of fun times spent with her family so many years ago, and wiped a tear from her eye.

Maybe she had just met a miracle.

The colonel and Parks hopped onto one of the small electric cars used for moving through the vast underground labyrinth. He took Parks down a series of tunnels, stopping at a dead end. A narrow cage ladder led up into a black hole, where there was a hatch to the outside world. The area was lit dimly by a single bulb hanging from the ceiling.

"Thanks for the ride," Parks said as he hopped off, pulled his leather belt from the back, and strapped it on.

"It seems like we're always saying goodbye," the colonel said with a chuckle. "Someday I hope you can stay awhile."

"I'm sure that day will come," Parks said as he started up the ladder. "In the meantime, continue training your people. I have a feeling we'll need them sooner than you think."

The hinges on the hatch groaned as Parks pushed it open, and climbed out. It was late afternoon, and the wilderness floor was still burning from the heat of the day. The colonel tried to convince him to stay the night and start fresh in the morning, but Parks was intent on completing his journey, and nothing was going to slow him up.

The entrance had been cleverly disguised, Parks thought as he closed the lid covered with sand and native plants glued to its surface. It could be found only if someone already knew it was there.

He stood, and turned towards the path the Colonel had said Sterling took when he left. Parks had the map the Colonel drew in his pocket, but didn't really need it. He could see the way Sterling had gone by the signs he left. A partial footprint not yet absorbed by the shifting desert sands here, a broken twig there, even a small overturned rock were like neon lights to Parks. He was a skilled tracker, a skill honed from his youth.

Parks continued his quest for hours, working his way through the wilderness. He kept a steady pace, stopping only to carefully examine the area when Sterling's tracks became faint. He had traveled a good distance from the Island by the time the sun began to lower across the horizon. Darkness would soon be here.

"I've got to remember to thank the colonel," he said as he slung his bag off his shoulder, and pulled out the night vision goggles the colonel had given him. "It's like daytime all over again."

He continued through the darkness with the help of the goggles. Sterling's path led him over rugged terrain, and through dried out rivers. It was obvious no one came that way often. However, the goggles revealed a vibrant life with the heat images of various predators and prey making their nightly appearances. It was fascinating, but Parks stayed focused. He stopped only to take a drink from his water pouch a time or two. He was truly amazed at the path Sterling chose, and began to wonder where it could possibly end. There was nothing here but sand, cactus, and loneliness. Hours of steady jogging up and over countless obstacles passed before Parks finally began to tire.

Sunrise was not far off as he unwound his bag and placed its contents on a nearby rock before stretching out on the thick leather shell. The night air was cool, and a bright, starlit night greeted him as he took off the night vision goggles. The wilderness was full of sounds; familiar sounds that brought comfort to his jaded mind. In a matter of minutes, he was asleep.

"Hi, Dad," Parks said as he pulled up to the house, and hopped off his motorcycle.

Mr. Parks was sitting in an old rocker on the porch with a steaming hot cup of coffee in one hand, a paper in the other. He put down the paper as his son bounded up the steps.

"Hi, son," Mr. Parks replied with a smile. "Nice day for a ride."

He took a seat beside his father in his mom's rocker, and looked out over the field for a moment.

"It's always so peaceful out here," Parks observed, "like a little slice of heaven. Where's Mom? I need to ask her about tomorrow. She wanted me to take her grocery shopping."

Mr. Parks took a sip of coffee, and went back to reading his paper.

"Where's Mom?" Parks said again, thinking his father hadn't heard him.

Without another word, Mr. Parks got up, and went into the house. Henry sat there for a moment, confused. He got up, and followed his father inside. The house was cold, dark, and damp as the door shut behind him.

"Dad," Henry said loudly. "Dad," he said again as he walked into the kitchen and flipped on the lights.

His father was standing at the sink, staring out the window.

"Where's Mom?" he asked again.

"I've got her," Mr. Parks replied without turning.

"You've got her?" Henry asked incredulously. "What are you saying? I don't get it. What are you talking about?"

"I've got her," Mr. Parks replied, his voice becoming deeper with a sinister tone, "and you'll never see your mother again."

Henry grabbed his father by the shoulders, and spun him around.

"Barron!" he gasped, and stumbled backwards.

The man standing in front of him was no longer his father.

"Mom," Parks shouted as he sat bolt upright, sweat pouring off his face. "Something has happened to Mom."

Parks had been dreaming again.

A feeling of helplessness washed over him as he stood, and surveyed the wilderness slowly becoming lit by the rising sun. Mechanically, he put his things in order, packed them into the bag, and slung it over his shoulder. He stared for a long moment at the wilderness spreading out before him.

Doubt had sprouted tall in his mind. What was he doing way out here when his mom, Della and who knew how many others were in danger? Why was he looking for this man? What could he possibly do to change the circumstances that plagued his life? How could something as powerful as Management be stopped? Parks was only one man.

"Maybe I'm chasing a dream," Parks said with a sigh before starting off again. "But there's no hope behind me. If things are going to change, I'm going to have to keep going. I'm going to have to continue down this road, and discover what's real. If Management is meant to rule our lives, then I've lost already, and so has everybody else. But I have to find out if there is more, one way or the other."

He traveled until mid-afternoon, stopping only to take a quick drink of water. He had kept to the trail left by Sterling, but then the ground changed from the hard-packed sand and scrub brush to solid rock, and for the first time, he lost the trail. He stood for a long time surveying the area, looking for the most likely point to pick up Sterling's tracks again, but the rock bed spread out in every direction for what seemed like miles. Parks squatted down, frustrated, and wondered what to do next. Then he remembered the high-powered binoculars the colonel had given him. He pulled them out of his bag, and began to scan the distant horizon.

Suddenly, he noticed movement. He wiped the lenses, and refocused. The distant object was at the outer limits of the binoculars' range, and he couldn't tell much except that it looked like an animal of some sort.

"It's the best I've got," he said, putting the binoculars back into the bag, and taking off on a fast run in the direction of the movement. He ran at a sprinter's pace for nearly five miles before arriving at the spot where there should have been something, anything. But there wasn't.

"Aww," he groaned in frustration, "what did I see and where did it go."

It was then that he noticed the rocky surface had changed. Dropping down, brushed away some dust to discover the rocks were set together in a sort of pattern. This was not a natural occurrence. It was the result of human endeavor.

"It's a roadway!" he exclaimed, jumping to his feet. "And it looks old; really old."

The once distant mountains now loomed above as the rocky path led into a narrow valley filled with small green plants, shrubs, and trees. Parks came around a large rock, and was suddenly greeted by the roar of large, hairy animal.

It looked something like a horse or other large pack animal, with four legs and hooves. But its shoulders were massive, and its broad head sported three large, sharp horns on either side of its forehead. It snorted, and pounded the ground with its front legs. Parks froze in his tracks, and slid his hand onto the handle of the crystal blade slung around his waist. He had never seen anything like this before. His muscles tightened as he prepared for battle.

"Snuggles," a woman shouted as she came out from behind a large tree, "leave the nice man alone."

Parks relaxed a bit as a tall, dark-haired woman walked up to the large animal, and jerked the collar hung around its neck.

"You be nice," she said, and jerked it several more times.

The large animal lowered its head, and wandered away to a grassy spot, where it began grazing peacefully.

"I'm so sorry," the woman said to Parks. "She's usually friendlier than that. You must have startled her."

Just then, a sharp looking man carrying a bag over his shoulder emerged from the woods.

"Everything ok, Julie?" he asked as he approached.

"I think so," Julie answered. "Snuggles was getting a little frisky with this nice man here, but she seems ok now."

"Hello," the man said as he greeted Parks, "my name is Fred, and this is my wife Julie; nice to meet you."

"My name is Parks," Parks said as he released his grip on the crystal blade. "What is that animal? I've never seen anything like it."

"She's a Lawmule," Fred answered. "They're great pack animals, and can carry a small house on their backs. My wife and I love hiking with them. I see you're a stranger around here. How may we help you?" Fred continued, stretching out his hand.

"Well, I'm looking for someone," Parks replied, taking Fred's hand and shaking it vigorously. "I've been following him for days, but lost his trail several miles back. Then I spotted your big animal and found you. Maybe you know him; his name is Sterling."

Fred looked over at Julie with a puzzled look.

"We know most everyone who lives around these parts," Fred replied as he walked over towards Snuggles and put a leash on the large animal, "and I've never heard of anyone by that name. Maybe you should go back the way you came, and try to pick up the trail again. Obviously you missed it somewhere."

Parks felt a heavy weight of disappointment fall on his shoulders. He had come all the way out there to find answers, and returning without them seemed ridiculous.

"Just a minute," Parks said as Fred and Julie were packing their belongings onto Snuggles and preparing to leave, "you say there are people who live around here. Maybe one of them knows Sterling or where he lives."

Fred was loading the mat he and Julie had been relaxing on. Snuggles stood between him and Parks as he slung it over her back, and tied it down. Then Parks lost sight of him for a moment as Julie moved behind some trees, apparently to get the last of their stuff.

"We don't want any trouble, mister," Fred said. He stepped out from behind the Lawmule, pointing an unusual looking device directly at Parks. "I don't know who you are or how you found us, but you need to leave NOW!"

Parks stepped back for a moment, surprised by Fred's sudden change of attitude.

"I mean you no harm," Parks assured him. "Sterling is a friend of mine. He's about six feet tall with dark hair. He came in this direction, I'm sure of it."

"You heard me the first time!" Fred said more forcefully. "I don't want to hurt you, but you need to leave."

Parks squatted onto the rocky path, and glanced up the road that seemed to lead into the mysterious mountains. His best chance of finding Sterling lay up there somewhere. Turning back now would be a waste, and he knew these people were hiding something. His right hand felt the smooth, round shape of a rock about the size of a large marble next to his leg. It would take a perfect throw, but he was up for it.

"Alright," he said, standing to his feet with the rock hidden behind his back. "I'll continue my search somewhere else."

He turned as if he were going to leave, but suddenly, he spun around and let the rock fly. It hit Fred in his left arm, who winced, and dropped the strange weapon. Parks took two quick steps before Fred could recover and reach his weapon, but before he got to him, a flash of white light burst over his being. He froze, and then fell face-first, his body bouncing twice on the hard ground.

"Are you alright, honey?" Julie asked as she popped out from behind a tree with the same type of weapon Fred had.

"My arm hurts, but I don't think it's broken," Fred replied, rubbing the knot on his forearm. "That's one big guy, and he can really throw. I'm glad he wasn't aiming at my head. Nice shot, by the way. You hit him dead on."

Fred checked for a pulse as he and Julie rolled Parks over.

"Is he breathing?" Julie asked, concern rising in her voice.

"Seems to be," Fred replied quietly as he began searching Parks's pockets. "Hey, what do you make of this?!" Fred exclaimed as he pulled one of the crystal blades from his belt.

"Oh my," Julie replied, astonished. "That's incredible. What are we going to do now?"

Fred whistled for Snuggles, who had wandered off in search of more food, and was busy grazing on some bushes. She came meandering back, and lowered her massive body alongside Parks's limp frame at Fred's command. He and Julie managed to drape Parks over Snuggles's back, and strapped him down so he wouldn't fall off or escape if he woke up.

"That shot from your Whiterod should keep him down for quite a while," Fred answered as he took the Lawmule's leash. "We've little choice now but to head in, and see what the council says. In all the years we've patrolled the outer edges, we've never had anyone like him. I just hope this doesn't mean trouble."

Julie looked reassuringly into Fred's eyes as she gently took his arm. The evening sky was setting fast as they disappeared into the mountain mist.

CHAPTER 7

"I've been doing a lot of thinking lately about what really happened when Management took over," Jim said as Rita sat beside him. "I know many died in the resistance, but I'm sure there were survivors. Management did something with them, but I've just never been able to figure out what."

"I've asked myself the same question a thousand times," Rita answered, the light from the fire dancing in her dark brown eyes. "My parents disappeared without a trace, and all I can hope for anymore is a miracle."

"I've never believed in miracles," Jim said bluntly. "My life is built around science and certainty." He softened a bit as he looked into Rita's eyes. "But maybe I've been too hasty. I've seen one miracle, and if I could find you, then maybe we can find your parents–and others too. It's not over yet."

"How's your ankle feeling?" Dr. Larson asked as she walked into the parlor. "Here, let me have a look at it."

Rita moved off the couch where Jim was stretched out so Dr. Larson could examine him. She held a flashlight for the doctor as she carefully removed what was left of the cast she had fitted him with before they were chased out of the city. The swim and trek across the hard ground had pretty much destroyed it.

"Hold it a little higher." Dr. Larson instructed as she bent over his leg. "That's looking much better," she continued. "The swelling is down, and there's no sign of infection. But you're still going to need some protection if you're going to be mobile. Let me take a look around, and see what I can find to get you moving again."

"It feels a lot better," Jim said, rising up on his elbows. "With a little help, I'll be jogging out of here in a few moments."

Rita laughed as she slid a pillow under Jim's leg. In a few moments, Dr. Larson returned with some bubble wrap and duct tape she had found in a cupboard in the hall. She sat down and covered his ankle with the wrap, and began to wind duct tape around it with Rita's help.

"Hey, doc," Jim said, grinning. "Are you planning on mailing me out of here?"

"I don't think we could fit you in the mailbox," Rita smiled.

"Let's see how that feels," Dr. Larson said, patting him gently on the leg. "See if you can stand on it."

"It feels solid," Jim said as Rita helped him to his feet, "but I don't have a shoe. I can't walk around on my bare foot."

"I have just the thing," Kenzie said, coming in with an old pair of barn boots she had found. "They're a little big, but should do the trick."

Jim sat down, and Dr. Larson worked the boot onto his foot. The fit was tight, but that was just what he needed.

"How's that?" Kenzie asked.

Jim stood up on his own,, and walked carefully around the room. "It works," he said. "Now we can focus on our next destination without worrying about my slowing us down. But where are we going?"

"That's exactly what we need to discuss," Kenzie said. "I don't know this area, and I'm sure Management is looking for us."

"I agree," Jim said. "I know a place they would never suspect. I have family far out in the county where we'll be safe–if we can get there. I can't make it without help though."

"Don't worry," Kenzie said as they left the old farmhouse. "While they've been putting you back together, I've been doing a bit of checking"

Kenzie led the way across what used to be a lawn towards an old storage shed set next to the river that ran along the edge of the property. She slipped through the partially open sliding door, and pushed it the rest of the way. The afternoon sun glistened off the shiny surface of two four-wheelers.

"I forgot all about these!" Rita exclaimed, following Kenzie inside. "I thought Dad got rid of them."

"These will work," Jim said. "Plenty big enough, if there's some gas around."

"I know where there's gas," Rita said, leading the way around the shed. "Dad always kept a fifty gallon drum in the back."

A warm afternoon breeze blew through a grove of apple trees, rustling the leaves as Jim hobbled along behind Rita. A large red drum stood behind the shed, set several feet off the ground on four steel legs. A long rubber hose with a dispenser hung on the side of the tank.

Jim tapped the side of the drum. He lifted the nozzle off the hook, and pulled the lever.

A stream of gas flowed onto the ground.

"Smells ok," Jim said, returning the nozzle. "Let's get those rigs fueled up, and get out of here."

Rita, Kenzie, and Dr. Larson pushed two four-wheelers out of the shed while Jim filled two five-gallon cans he had found. They would serve as backup for the long drive. Rita and Dr. Larson strapped them on the back while he filled the tanks. Once they were gassed up, Kenzie hopped on one, and hit the starter. The motor turned over several times, but didn't fire. She waited a few more seconds and tried again but still nothing.

"The gas is shut off," Jim said, flipping a lever under the tank. "Give it a try now."

The motor sputtered several times before roaring to life. Kenzie revved it several times and then drove around a nearby tree to make sure it was in good order. Jim was on the second one and it fired off with similar ease.

"Do you think we'll be able to make it to your uncle's place?" Dr. Larson asked.

"It's a long ride, but with the extra gas we should make it," Jim said, helping Rita onto the back of his four wheeler.

"Lead on," Kenzie said as Dr. Larson climbed on behind her.

The two four-wheelers roared across the field. The ground passed quickly under their wheels, and Jim was careful to navigate around rocks and other obstructions. He didn't want to risk damaging the vehicles. They had traveled for several hours when Jim pulled up under a large oak tree, and shut the machine down.

"We need a break," he said as he hopped off. "I'm getting thirsty."

Rita pulled some refreshments out of one of the large saddle bags built into the side of the machines, and handed them around.

"How much farther is it?" Dr. Larson asked, glancing across the vast countryside.

"What is that?" Kenzie said before Jim could answer.

They saw she was looking back along the way they had just come. They gathered around Kenzie, and strained to see what she was talking about. Far in the distance was a small dark cloud moving across the horizon.

Jim bolted the rest of his sandwich, and hobbled as quickly as he could to his four-wheeler. The machine roared to life. "Let's go!" he shouted over the noise of the engine. I've seen that cloud before. We need to get out of here fast."

"What do you mean?" Dr. Larson asked as they headed back towards the machines. "It's just a cloud."

"A cloud full of Testers," Jim said. "They must be onto us somehow. We need to put some distance between us and them fast."

Jim roared off with Kenzie tight behind. He checked over his shoulder as they sped along. They were going as fast as they dared, but the cloud was gaining. He pushed his four wheeler hard. Suddenly, they came upon a narrow ditch that had been hidden by a shallow ridge. There was no time to avoid it. He pulled up on the front handlebars, trying to jump it, but the heavy vehicle caught the far edge and flipped over, sending both passengers tumbling into the sandy bank. It landed on its side several yards away.

"Are you ok?" Kenzie asked, crossing the ditch at an angle, and pulling up next to them to help.

"I'm ok," Rita answered, scrambling to her feet, and rushing to Jim's side.

"Yeah, yeah," Jim said as Rita helped him up. "I'm ok. But what are we going to do now? That cloud will be here any second."

"Get out of sight," Kenzie ordered, quickly assessing the situation.

"Get down here," Jim said, hobbling towards the empty ditch. "It's not much, but it's all we've got."

Fortunately, there was a lot of tall reed grass growing along the edge, and it provided some cover as they flattened themselves along the bottom of the dry ditch. Rita huddled tight to Jim who flinched unconsciously. Together, they watched the dark cloud moving steadily in their direction. In just a couple moments, it crossed overhead, and hovered over the four-wheelers. A red beam of light emanated from the cloud, and began scanning the area. Then the light narrowed into a solid beam, and two Testers appeared next to the overturned rig.

Jim felt Rita stiffen beside him as the short, muscular beings dressed in red armor began to inspect the crash site. One carried a large ax in one hand and a knife in the other, and the second one held a long, spear-like weapon with razor-sharp curved blades on each end. Testers had poor eyesight, but seemed to be able to sense movement.

Jim's mind raced as he tried to think of his next move. At the moment, his only real choice was to stay as motionless as possible, and hope they were not discovered. But he couldn't help wondering how they had managed to find them so quickly. No one could have followed their escape from the city, yet here they were.

The Testers moved in and around the two vehicles, and Jim began to hope they might leave, when one of them pulled a small device from a pocket inside his armor. He strained to see what it was. The Tester turned directly towards the spot where he was hiding with Rita, and both Testers walked steadily towards them. The one with the ax and knife slashed the air menacingly, and the other lowered his sharp spear.

"You stay here," Jim whispered into Rita's ear. "I'll lead them away. The rest of you break for the four wheeler, and get out of here fast."

"No!" Rita whispered, grabbing Jim's arm tightly. "Don't do anything foolish."

Jim squeezed Rita's hand, then jumped up, and started hobbling down the dry ditch, away from where the others were hiding. The Testers immediately began to pursue him, but they weren't particularly fast so for a moment, it looked like he had a chance to outrun them. Testers never tire though, and in a few seconds, they would catch up, and slice him into small pieces. Jim pushed through the pain in his bum ankle, trying to get them as far away from Rita and his friends as possible.

He didn't get far enough. Before long, he tripped over a clump of grass, and landed face down in the dusty ditch. He rolled over just in time to see the sun glistening off the edge of a battle ax raised high. He raised his arm in a reflex motion that meant nothing to the hardened steel about to send Jim the Weatherman to an early grave.

Suddenly, the Tester flew backwards over Jim's outstretched arm. Jim sat up just in time to watch the second Tester drop to his knees, and then fall limply on the ground in a small cloud of dust. Behind him stood Kenzie with a round, smooth rock in her hand. Amazingly, the Tester's helmet was not up to the task of protecting it from the blow of this one hundred and ten pound slightly built young woman.

Kenzie leapt across the field, and kicked the other Tester, which had been getting up, axe in hand. Her blow caught it flush under its chin. It staggered back, dropping the sharp knife from one hand, while trying clumsily to swing the ax with the other. Kenzie dodged him easily, picked up the knife, and in one smooth motion she deposited it squarely between the creature's eyes. It stiffened, and fell backwards into the ditch.

"Wow!" Jim exclaimed. "Where did you learn to fight like that?"

"Been practicing," Kenzie replied, checking each Tester to make sure they were not coming back for more. They weren't.

"Look at that," Dr. Larson said pointing towards the sky.

The small black cloud that had delivered the Testers to their location was dissipating. In a few seconds it was completely gone, and the bright blue sky shone clear once again.

"This is freaky," Jim replied as Rita ran up and hugged him tight. "It's like a nightmare come true. I don't get it."

"They found us somehow," Kenzie observed. "That one over there was looking at something before they went for you."

Dr. Larson reached down, and pulled a shiny silver disk out of the Tester's hand. It looked a bit like a compass. On its face was a dial with a small arrow pointed directly at Jim. She walked around him towards Kenzie but the arrow never moved off Jim.

"I don't know why this thing is so attracted to you," Dr. Larson observed, "but there's something about you it really likes."

"Why is that?" Kenzie asked.

"I have no idea," Jim quipped. "I know I have a magnetic personality, but that can't be it."

"Well, it's coming from something," Kenzie said, taking the object from Dr. Larson. "We need to figure this out before more of them show up. Do you have anything in your pockets?"

"Not much of anything," Jim said turning his pants pockets inside out.

"What about your jacket?" Dr. Larson pressed.

"Only this cigar case," Jim said, pulling out a thin silver box, "but I've had this for years, and I am the only one who ever used it. It never leaves my presence."

"Let me see," Kenzie said, taking the box. "Let's eliminate the obvious." She walked away from him. "What's happening now?" she asked Dr. Larson, who was still holding the silver disk.

"Believe it or not, now it's following you," Dr. Larson said.

"Impossible," Jim asserted, hobbling over to Kenzie, and retrieving his cigar case. "It's not been out of my possession, period."

"What about what's in it?" Kenzie asked.

"One cigar," Jim answered, flipping it open, and pulling out the cigar. "I got this from Frank when I saw him last at HOT News. We had a deal to smoke this together when this is over."

"Ok," Kenzie said, "I'll take the case, and you keep the cigar. What do we see now, Dr. Larson?" Kenzie continued, stepping away from Jim with the case in her hand.

"It's staying right on Jim," Dr. Larson answered.

"What?!" Jim protested. "That's ridiculous. How can it seek a cigar?"

"Let me see," Rita said, taking the cigar from Jim. "I know a little something about things like this."

She carefully slid the cigar ring off, and handed the cigar back to Jim. Gently unwrapping the ring, she spread it out in her palm, and slid her fingernail along the edge of the cigar ring, separating the paper as she went. She grabbed the paper between her fingers, and pulled it apart.

"I think we have it," Rita said, holding it up. "It's very sophisticated and tiny."

"I can't believe it," Jim said incredulously, looking at the device. "I, I picked that cigar up in Frank's office out of his very own personal cigar box," Jim stammered. "This means I've been carrying a tracking device from the beginning. Management knows where I've been all the time. But how can this be? Frank and I have been friends for years. He and I fought side by side, and helped slow Management's takeover. It doesn't make any sense."

"It's troubling," Dr. Larson commented. "But we need to get going, and put some distance between ourselves and this situation."

"How exactly are we going to do that?" Jim asked, suddenly feeling discouraged. "We have one four wheeler and four people. The one I flipped is toast. The front wheel snapped off."

"Not to worry," Kenzie answered. "You three mount up, and I'll follow along."

"You're going to run the rest of the way?" Jim replied in amazement. "Are you serious? We're at least thirty miles out."

"More than serious," Kenzie answered. "Let's get going, and try to make it before dark."

Jim thought he saw a blue flash from Kenzie's chest, but there was no time to ask her about it, as Kenzie had already taken off.

He mounted the remaining four-wheeler with Rita and Dr. Larson squeezed tight behind, and fired it up. He took off slowly, with Kenzie breaking into a steady jog alongside. The lifeless bodies of two Testers, a broken four-wheeler, and the remains of a gift from a once close friend faded behind them as they made their way across the open fields, and into a large wooded area. Jim drove at a slow, steady pace, his mind full of questions. Everything he had done to change the future and save people from Management's evil grip seemed futile. Even worse was the question of who had put a tracer in the cigar wrapper.

CHAPTER 8

"You rest here for a bit," Kirsten said as she led her father into the house. "The guys are there by now, and I'm going back to join them. I'll call the minute I know something. Don't worry, Dad," Kirsten said, trying to look confident.

Mr. Parks sank into one of the padded kitchen chairs. His shoulders were slumped as he took the coffee from his daughter's hand.

"What are Testers doing out here?" Mr. Parks asked in a daze as he looked down into the cup. "No one has even seen one for years, and now they're running my wife off the road. It's worse than bizarre; it's insane."

"I don't know, but try not to think about it, Dad," Kirsten said as she picked up the phone and started dialing. "Hey, Troy," Kirsten said. "Have you found anything yet?" She continued, lowering her voice, and turning away from where her father was sitting.

"Not yet," Troy said, "but we're working on it."

"I'll be right there," Kirsten replied softly. "I just want to make sure Dad is ok before I leave."

She tried again to reach Aaron and Kenzie, but they didn't respond.

"Has anybody found any clues yet?" Her father asked as he got up from the counter.

"Not yet, Dad," Kirsten answered.

"Well let's get back out there," Mr. Parks asserted. "I can't sit around here. I'll rest when your mom's safe at home."

"Are you sure Dad?" Kirsten asked. "We can handle the search."

"I'm coming, and that's it," Her father replied as he headed out the door for her truck.

"David," Kirsten said as she parked in the field, and stepped out of the truck. "It's good to see you."

"Hello, Mr. Parks," David said as he gave Kirsten a comforting hug. "I spotted lights coming up the road in this direction, so I'm sure the rest will be here shortly. What do you know?"

"Only that there was a movement of Testers, and Mom somehow got caught up in it." Kirsten replied.

"A movement of Testers," David exclaimed. "What does that mean? Should we be prepared for more than a search?"

By then the field was filling up with even more questions as the rest arrived. Kirsten quickly explained the situation, and suggested they head for where Mrs. Parks's car was found. It would be getting light in a few hours, which would make tracking easier, but until then, the search party was well-equipped with flashlights and brush cutting equipment.

"What if we run into Testers?" Joshua asked bluntly.

The group froze for a second under the dim, moonlit sky.

"Hey, I'm not saying we can't handle it," Joshua continued, his thin voice betraying his nervousness. "I just think we should talk about it. You know, have a plan."

Kirsten's first response was to rebuke Joshua for his lack of confidence, but then she realized none of them had ever fought a Tester. In fact, no one had even seen one for over a decade. Not since Management had arrived.

"Joshua has a point," David said, stepping forward. "We were just kids when those strange red creatures invaded our city. All I remember is the sound their armor made as they marched along, sort of a metallic scraping noise."

"I remember more than that," Troy interjected as he pulled a long crystal blade out of a sheath concealed beneath his heavy coat. It flashed in the light of the moon. "I also remember those little bastards killing my mother and father. Maybe I'll get a chance to even the score tonight," he said grimly, his eyes wide with anger.

"Just a second," Kirsten said firmly, putting her hand on Troy's shoulder. "We're here to look for my mom," she continued, glancing over at her father." Let's keep our focus on that, and we'll deal with Testers if we have to. Remember, we haven't been training for nothing. We'll handle whatever comes our way."

"Burke, see if you can pick up Mrs. Parks's trail on the right side," David commanded. "Isaac, you take the left."

Burke immediately headed in the direction of the overturned car. He was a slender young man with tremendous athletic ability, and easily jumped onto the overturned car, and scrambled inside. Isaac was built more like a bulldog, with a thick, round chest. He plowed his way through the tall brush, looking for signs. He crisscrossed through the brush, but was unable to pick up her trail.

"She went this way!" Burke shouted.

In a few moments, they had surrounded Burke.

"What do you see?" Kirsten asked anxiously.

"It looks like your mom made it out of the wreck ok," Burke answered as he pointed his flashlight on the ground, and felt a slight indentation made by her shoe. "But it also looks like she was pursued by the Testers. See how the ground is disturbed, and the branches heading in that direction are broken." Burke continued, shining his light into the woods. "They must have been following her."

Mr. Parks gasped involuntarily at the thought of his wife being chased through the woods.

"We'll find her," David said told him reassuringly. "Just follow Burke."

Mrs. Parks was more than just Henry and Kirsten's mother. She had been at every significant event in these kids' lives since they had been rescued. She had made it her personal goal to help them find some normalcy, and was as much their mother as anyone could be. They all loved and respected her.

Burke was already moving through broken branches and overturned trees with ease. He could not only see Mrs. Parks' tracks, he could feel her movements she tried in vain to avoid her pursuers. The blue crystal hanging on a golden chain around his neck glowed brightly as he glided over the rough terrain. It was obvious Mrs. Parks had been able to keep ahead of the Testers, but how she could find such energy was amazing. Then he remembered what a good athlete she was. She kept herself in shape by jogging several miles every day, and swimming in the pool her husband built for her after they sold the farm.

The woods were slowly starting to brighten as the morning sun began to rise.

"Hey!" Burke shouted suddenly. "Over here."

Kirsten's heart jumped into her throat at Burke's exclamation. She was working her way along the outside of the wooded area, tracking the flickering of his flashlight through the trees.

"What did you find?" she asked, pushing her way past David to where Burke was, kneeling next to a large tree.

"Your mom's down there," Burke replied, shining his light under a large tree root. "It looks like she may have hit her head on a low-hanging branch before she slid in."

"Mom?! Mom?! Are you ok?" Kirsten said, kneeling down and peering under the root. Mrs. Parks didn't respond.

"Pearl!" Mr. Parks shouted, running up. "Can you hear me?"

But the large tree had a massive, complex root system that was as much above ground as under, and Mrs. Parks was barely visible. Kirsten lay flat on the ground and stretched out as far as she could, but still couldn't reach her.

"What are we going to do?" Kirsten cried out in frustration, ripping at the roots with her bare hands. "We've got to get her out of there!"

"We'll get her out," David said confidently. "Just give me a moment to think."

The group scanned the area closely with their flashlights, looking for an answer. Mrs. Parks was pinned under one large central root of a giant tree. The gap was too narrow to get into, and even if someone could, she appeared to be pinned so tightly there was likely no way to pull her free.

"I can get her out," Isaac said suddenly, straddling the large root.

"That root is nearly two feet thick," Normand said incredulously. "What are you thinking of doing, pulling it up? The whole weight of the tree is on it. I'll go back for an ax or chainsaw."

"No time," Isaac said. He punched the root several times to create handholds before wrapping his arms around it. "Just get ready to pull her out."

Isaac strained against the ancient root as his muscles rippled under his coat. His feet began to sink deeper and deeper into the damp ground as he pulled with all his might. Then his body began to glow--dimly at first--and then brighter, until the woods filled with a brilliant blue glow. The tree moaned as leaves and small branches rained down upon them. David stepped forward in amazement, looking up as the tree began to lean noticeably. Then the root holding Mrs. Parks captive rose from the ground in a shower of dirt and leaves. Burke squatted, and gently pulled her to safety.

"She's breathing," David said, kneeling next to her. "But there is a large knot on her forehead where she ran into that branch, and her right arm might be broken. We need to get her to help right away."

Troy was already on it, finding several large limbs lying nearby.

"I need three more coats!" he shouted, stripping off his own, and sliding the end of one of the limbs into it.

Joshua, Normand, and Isaac quickly removed theirs, and helped Troy assemble a makeshift stretcher. Mr. Parks removed his coat too, and covered his wife to keep her warm.

"Great work!" Kirsten said. "Lower it next to her, and we'll work Mom onto it."

Troy and Isaac lowered the stretcher while David and Kirsten gently slid her on. The two young men stood up with Mrs. Parks nestled on their shoulders supported by the two long limbs. There was real concern Mrs. Parks could be suffering from shock and hypothermia, having been stuck under that root for nearly eight hours, but no one wanted to think about that.

"We can't take Mom to the hospital," Kirsten said as they emerged from the woods, and headed towards her truck. "It's too dangerous."

"We'll go to Dr. Flint's place," Mr. Parks said. "It's only a few miles up the road, and he'll know what to do."

"You two go on," David said as they reached the vehicles. "Troy and Josh can go too, and help get her into the Doctor's office. I'm going after the Testers to see if I can figure out what they're up to. The rest of the guys will come with me."

"I'm staying here!" Troy said forcefully after setting Mrs. Parks into the backseat of Kirsten's truck. "Anything that includes finding Testers includes me."

"Go ahead with them," Normand told Troy as he slid in beside Mr. Parks. "I'll help them."

David headed in the direction of the Testers as Kirsten took off for the doctor's house. The darkness was giving way to early morning light, so they shut off their flashlights. It was easy to follow the wide path created by the Testers as they tore through the countryside.

"Wait up!" David shouted to Burke, who was already nearly a hundred yards ahead.

Burke squatted behind a tree atop a ridge, and waited for his friends to catch up.

"Get down," Burke said quietly, motioning with his hand as they approached.

"Are you kidding me?" David said as he settled in next to Burke, being careful to keep his head down. "I've never seen that many Testers in one place before."

The ridge overlooked a valley which stood between the county and the eastern end of the city. It was a farming area dominated by ranchers and dairy farmers.

"What do you think they're doing? Burke whispered. "They're not even moving."

Below, the Testers were grouped tightly, and there was no movement or sound coming from them. The early morning light glistened off their red armor, giving them the appearance of a large lake of blood. It was an eerie sight to behold.

"I say we go down and disturb their little siesta." Troy said as he tugged on the handle of his crystal blade.

"Are you crazy?" Isaac whispered. "There are thousands of them down there."

"Who cares?" Troy snarled, starting to stand up, "I'm not afraid."

"It's not about being scared," David said. He put his hand on Troy's shoulder, and pulled him back down. "It's about being smart. We have little chance against so many, but maybe we can figure out why they're here. Look closely on the right flank," he said, pointing. "See that small tent there? Maybe we can find something in there that will give us some information. We'll follow the ridge down, and see if we can get inside. But we had better not be spotted, or we'll need more than our blades."

With that, David slipped over the ridge, and began to work his way down. The Testers did not move as the group quietly approached, being careful to stay low in the tall grass. David motioned with his hand for them to wait as he moved carefully towards the tent. It sat nearly fifty feet from the Tester formation. The canvas sides fluttered lightly in the cool morning breeze blowing through the valley. David moved as close as he could but there was still a good twenty feet between him and the tent. His body tightened as he prepared to sprint across the field, but suddenly Burke grabbed his arm.

"I'll do it," Burke whispered, "Just be ready if anything goes wrong."

Without waiting for a reply, Burke left the relative safety of the tall grass, and ran quickly across the open area, staying low to the ground. He was agile and fast, and in the dim morning light, looked like no more than a shadow. In an instant, he was next to the tent, and in the next, inside.

David's hands began to sweat, and his breathing quickened as the seconds turned to minutes. Anything could have happened, and Burke should have been out of there by now. He reached for the handle of his crystal blade. If Burke didn't come out soon, he was going in after him. Troy and Isaac were obviously thinking the same thing as they crawled up next to David with blades drawn, their bodies tensed in anticipation. A rush to the tent would certainly draw the Testers' attention and then it was anyone's guess what happens next. Then, to David's relief, Burke appeared at the tent's opening and sprinted back.

"Let's get out of here," Burke whispered as he ran past towards the safety of the ridge.

They followed, doing their best to keep up, but Burke was moving faster than any of them had ever seen. He didn't stop until he was all the way back at their trucks.

"What's going on?" David said, breathing heavily as he arrived.

"Yeah," Troy echoed. "What made you run away like that?"

"It's crazy scary!" Burke exclaimed as he spun around to face them. "When I opened the tent flap and slipped inside, I was inside a tent in a field, but then I wasn't. It was dark, so naturally I thought it was the tent, but then I noticed a sliver of light coming from what looked like an open door. I snuck over to it, and heard voices coming from the other side. That's when I realized I wasn't in a tent at all. I was in a dark room in some building somewhere. I stood at the door, listening to the conversation on the other side. Two men were talking about dividing up the city into quadrants and searching door to door. They said something about some "gifts" they wanted. I have no idea what they were talking about, but they had a map of the city up on the wall, and were outlining areas on it. I couldn't tell at first who the men were but then one of them turned and I recognized Harry, the head of the Citadel. Then the other glanced my way, and it was Dave Castle, the president. They were saying they would destroy the city and kill everyone in it if they didn't find these "gift" things they were looking for. Then, Dave started for the door I was hiding behind, and I made a beeline for the way I came in. I had no idea it would bring me back here, but that tent is some sort of a portal. I thought Dave spotted me, and that's why I was in such a hurry to get out of there."

"Wow!" David exclaimed, leaning against his truck. "That's incredible. We're going to need to find out more. I have an idea about the gifts, because I think I had one and gave it to Parks, but I don't know about any others."

"We need to get a copy of the map," Isaac said. "Then we will know their plan, but how?"

"I think I might know a way," Troy replied. "Aaron works at the Citadel, and I heard he's been promoted. Maybe he could get it for us."

"We haven't seen him for quite some time." David answered. "He hasn't been to any meetings for a long time."

"I'll drop by his place right now, and see if he's home." Burke said as he opened the door to his truck and climbed in. "I bet he could figure out a way to get that map."

"Meet me at Dr. Flint's place," David replied. "We'll regroup there, and make our next move."

Kirsten was sitting in the doctor's waiting room with her dad and Normand when David walked in. The worried look on their faces told the story as he sat down. He wanted to tell Kirsten what they had found, but this wasn't the time or place. Dr. Flint's nurse came through a nearby door, and signaled to Kirsten and Mr. Parks to follow. They made their way quickly down a long hall and into a well-lit room where Dr. Flint was holding Mrs. Parks arm and checking her pulse. He laid her hand gently down on the bed as he heard the door open, and turned to greet them.

"How's Mom?" Kirsten asked quietly.

"Have a seat over here," Dr. Flint said, pointing to a set of chairs positioned against the wall. "She's been through a lot," the doctor said as he sat across from them. "I thought at first she was just bruised from the accident you described. There's a nasty gash on her forehead. But she wasn't just bruised. It looks like her ribs were crushed by a heavy weight of some kind."

"Testers!" Kirsten gasped, glancing at her father.

Mrs. Parks groaned. They immediately got up, and rushed to her side.

"Don't exert yourself, dear," Mr. Parks said as he squeezed his wife's hand. "You're going to be all right."

"Thank you, sweetie, but I need to speak with Kirsten for a moment," Pearl said weakly. She reached over, and dropped a golden locket into her daughter's hand. Kirsten had seen her mother wear it her whole life, but now it looked different somehow.

"I, I don't understand," Kirsten said, seeing the urgency in her mother's eyes.

"It's been in our family for generations," Mrs. Parks answered, "but only a daughter born in the fourth generation will understand its purpose. You're that daughter."

"You can give it to me later," Kirsten protested, "when we get you home."

"I'm home now," Her mother replied. "You're my love, my family and my home." She looked deep into Philip's eyes, and smiled. Philip waited a few moments, then reached across, and closed her eyes.

"Mom!" Kirsten cried, bursting into tears.

Philip grabbed his daughter by the shoulders, and hugged her tight.

"I can't explain it," Dr. Flint said softly as he escorted Mr. Parks and Kirsten out of the room. "I checked her vitals when she came in, but she was already gone. I was about to tell you when she woke up. I guess she had to give you both something to hang onto, and wasn't going leave until she did."

Sunlight streamed through the truck window as Kirsten drove her father back to the farm. They were filled with sorrow and loss, but Pearl had given them something in those last few moments, something that brought a sense of peace to a very disturbing situation.

CHAPTER 9

Parks's body shuddered as his mind struggled to return to reality. A knife-like pain shot down his spine as he convulsed and fell off a narrow cot. The impact of hitting the polished granite floor returned him to the real world. Parks sat up, and shook his head several times to remove the remaining cobwebs before examining his new dwelling.

He was surrounded by four walls with a narrow window along the top on one side letting in a sliver of natural light. A fireplace with some bright embers still glowing on the hearth sat at the far end. On the opposite end stood a massive wooden door, outfitted with heavy iron hinges and a large latch with a keyhole above it.

Parks stood and then immediately sat back down, realizing the pain was coming from more than just the shot he took from the strange weapon. His mind was tangled as he desperately attempted to navigate through the conflict and emotion. His family's past and present pressed upon him.

He turned up the flame from a glowing oil lamp that was on a table next to the bed. The ancient book he had carried was set neatly on the table with the parchment folded and lying next to it. His backpack was on a small wooden chair nearby. Parks managed to get up and examine the contents, but quickly realized something was missing. The belt which held his crystal blades was not under his coat or anywhere in the room.

The last thing he remembered was meeting a couple, their odd looking creature, and a strange weapon before everything went black.

Parks gathered the book and parchment, returning them to his bag. It was likely that whoever had brought him here would be back to check before long. He examined the heavy door, looking for weaknesses, but found none. It would be practically impossible to break through it.

As he glared at it, the latch began to move, and the hinges squeaked as the door slowly opened.

The room filled with light, and the form of a very large man appeared in the doorway. Parks tensed as he prepared himself for battle.

"You're awake," came a familiar voice. "I was trying to be quiet in case you were still sleeping."

"Sterling!" Parks exclaimed in relief. "I didn't expect to see you."

"Sorry about all this," Sterling answered as he shook Parks's hand. "I guess you must have a lot of questions. If you're feeling ok, we can go outside."

"You mean after being shot?" Parks said as he grabbed his coat and bag, and followed Sterling through the door. "Couldn't you have found a larger cannon to shoot me with?" Parks added, rubbing his sore neck.

Sterling laughed. They emerged into a courtyard surrounded by mountain peaks. Below lay a valley divided in half by a large river, with green pastures and orchards dotting the landscape. It was beautiful and serene, and Parks felt a warm, gentle breeze on his face. He put his foot up on a rough-hewn fence on the edge of a steep incline, and took it all in.

"Wonderful, isn't it?" Sterling said, glancing at Parks. "My family has lived here for ages, enjoying the resources and security the valley provides. It feeds our entire village, and is a safe and sacred place for us."

"Ah, the village," Parks replied, glancing over towards Sterling. "Where did you say I was again?"

"Right," Sterling answered. "Fair enough question. There are things you need to know, but first I want to show you around, and get you some food. Can you wait that long?"

Parks was about to answer when his stomach growled and answered for him. He had found the man he was looking for, and his questions could wait a few minutes longer. Parks followed as Sterling led him towards the mountain. Glancing up, he noticed many ledges similar to the one he was standing on.

"This place is amazing," he commented as he stepped through two ornate doors into a home carved out of solid rock. The floor was polished smooth, and reflected the light coming from several large lamps hung in the middle of the entry. "Did you make this?" he asked as he sat down at a long counter facing a wood-fired cooking stove.

"Oh no," Sterling laughed, pulling out a loaf of bread. "My family has lived here for generations. According to legend, people came here eons ago, and created this. They were the first survivors, and the village has continued to evolve with each successive generation."

"You mean the people here are the ones who didn't return to rebuild the city as the legend says?" Parks asked.

"Correct," his host continued, taking some meat and cheese from an icebox. "People stay here because they feel safe."

"Then why seek me out?" Parks asked. "What do I have to do with anything if this is a safe haven?"

"That's not an easy question to answer," Sterling replied. "The destruction of the city that happens every thousand years may be greater this time. Some fear it may even affect this valley somehow. And, as far as we can tell, all signs point to this being the end of another thousand-year cycle."

"I know the old stories," Parks interjected. "I grew up with them. But that still doesn't explain why you sought me out. What do I have to do with this place, and an ancient story?"

"I'm probably not the best one to talk to about this," Sterling replied cautiously. "The council knows you're here, and we can go meet them now if you like. Oh, and you probably want these back?" He pulled Parks's belt, complete with his crystal blades, from a cabinet, and handed it to Parks. "They're very fascinating, and some might have been tempted, but we weren't going to keep them. What are they made of?"

"They came from something I found a long time ago," Parks said as he strapped them on. "Why don't we meet the council, and talk about these some other time."

Sterling nodded, and led the way out of his home and through large rock arches that led to a narrow stairway. It wound up the mountainside and entered long tunnels. By day, they were lit with sunlight that streamed in through the ends, and oil lamps hung on the walls, and were obviously for use by night. Each step led them deeper into the mountain.

Finally, Sterling brought Parks into a large auditorium that was carved like a bowl and surrounded by seats. In the center of the vast room was a wooden podium where Parks waited, while Sterling stepped away to the corner, and grabbed a long rope ascending through a hole in the rock ceiling. He pulled twice, and the loud clanging of a bell echoed through the hall. In a few moments, the room began to fill with people flowing in from rocky tunnels. They quietly found their places and stared down at Parks, making him feel more than uncomfortable.

"My apology for our rough introduction yesterday," a voice came from the crowd. It was Fred, the man Parks had met the day before. "It was our turn to patrol the east end of the valley," he explained, "and we didn't know who you were, but Sterling recognized you when we brought you in, so we gave you into his care. If you had been unfriendly, we would have carried you through the mountain, and left you on the other side. This mountain is full of undetectable passageways unless you know the secret. It's been our most effective way of safeguarding our village from those who would hurt us."

Fred was about to continue when his wife stood up next to him, and interrupted.

"Mr. Parks," Julie said gravely as Fred sat down, "we are called the Ancients. Each member of this council has a history from the beginning, and our collective story is represented in family books, and also by the engravings you see all around us," she said as she swept her hand above her head.

Parks looked up at the skillfully carved images. Many of the reliefs showed frightful scenes of battles with horrible creatures. Parks scanned them before one image set in the middle caught his attention. His mind flashed to a dark cave as a young boy facing a vicious beast with dark red eyes, a sinister, hideous smile filled with razor sharp teeth, and six long claws that ripped his flesh.

"The Zender!"

"Yes, that's its formal name," Fred said, stepping down to join Parks at the podium, "but we know it as the omen whose coming signals the end of a thousand years. Once it appears, it creates havoc and fear and, if you follow the story over here, "Fred said as he directed Parks' attention to one particular scene, "you see what appears to be a great flood that covers the city and washes it away, only we've never quite understood why they painted the water red. Anyway, the carvings are just one part of this puzzle. The rest is held in the collection of the ancient writings Julie mentioned.

"But what has always intrigued us is the reference to the sign of the Right. It's mentioned throughout the books, and pictured here." Fred continued as he pointed to a symbol resembling a heavy door with the letter "R" carved on the front.

"The Right? I don't get it. Is there a left door too?"

"I don't believe it's talking about left or right," Fred replied, somewhat indignantly at Parks's flippant answer, "but what it really means is a mystery to us. The legend says the Right comes from the sky and changes the order of things. But we have come to believe it's more a product of hopefulness than reality."

"And you think the answer is behind a door?" Parks said, a little puzzled by their seeming intellectual simplicity. "If this destruction only happens every thousand years, why all the current concern? I would think most people would have forgotten about it, and moved on by now. It's a very long time to stay concerned, don't you think?"

"You might think so," Fred replied, "and I would have to agree, if not for this."

He reached over to the wooden podium, flipped up a heavy metal ring embedded in the center, and then lifted a cylinder that clicked into place. Inside the cylinder was a long red crystal that lit the room with an eerie glow.

"Now that's interesting," Parks said, examining it closely.

"We didn't even know it was there until a little over ten years ago." Fred replied. "Our families have used this auditorium to conduct business since forever, but then one day when I was leading a meeting, the podium began to shake. It took us a little while to figure out what was causing the vibration, and that's when we discovered this crystal. We think it may have been put here as a sort of alarm, to warn us when the destroyers returned."

"It's curious, for sure," Parks noted, "but I still don't know what this has to do with me."

"It has everything to do with you!" Sterling exclaimed, jumping out of his seat. "You've done what no one ever has. You killed the Zender!"

The crowd gasped, and looked at one another in disbelief.

"Is this true?" Fred asked, his gaze boring into Parks. "You faced the beast?"

"I was just a young boy living on my parent's farm when it first appeared," Parks replied. "I had never seen anything like it, but my sister Kirsten and I found a drawing similar to it in an old book from my Father's library. My dad heard about the attack, we told him it was a bear. He took us with him to Grace Mountain to hunt it. That's a day I will never forget. We thought we were hunting it, but in reality, it was hunting us. It set a trap for me, and cornered me in a cave. It attacked, but I stabbed it in the chest with this crystal blade.' Parks continued, pulling the blade from his belt. "It vanished in a dark mist, and I've never seen it again since."

The Ancients were astonished. After a shocked silence, everyone started talking at once.

"Quiet! QUIET!" Fred shouted, waving his hands.

The crowd calmed for a moment as he continued.

"I've heard rumors of this supposed event," Fred said. He reached out to Parks, who handed him the crystal blade. "I was skeptical, but now I must admit that it seems to be true. Still, what does it all mean?"

"That's what I'm trying to figure out," Parks replied. "The blade you hold came from a glowing object that landed on our farm shortly before the beast appeared."

"Is it possible?" Fred said excitedly. "Could this have been the sign from the sky like the ancient story says?"

"I don't know your story, or whether any of what's going on is part of it," Parks said. "Certainly, there are some similarities. All I do know is I came here seeking answers, and if you don't have them, I'll have to look somewhere else."

Sterling made his way to the front, and picked up Parks's bag. He pulled out the old book.

"We all have unanswered questions," Sterling he said, "but let me try and answer at least one for you. My brother Benjamin and I were twins, and one day we left here looking for adventure.

"Along the way, we stumbled onto the place called the Island, but found it in chaos and turmoil. People were suffering from some unknown malady, but for some reason, we were not affected. We began looking around, and that's when the colonel spotted us. He was suffering as well, and wanted to know why we weren't.

"He led us to an underground room, and showed us this book and the parchment. He told us how they had discovered them buried deep in a cave out in the wilderness. It was an interesting find for sure, but when they returned to the Island and began to examine them, that's when the suffering began. They had placed the book on a pedestal, and I picked it up out of curiosity.

"As soon as I did, the colonel's pain instantly stopped. He was intrigued, and put the book into our care. He wanted to know what power it held, and with the help of some language specialists, we attempted to decipher its meaning, but we couldn't. No one could understand the writings.

"One night, I had a dream. In the dream, I was to find a man in the city, and give it to him. When I awoke, I told Benjamin, and discovered he had had the exact same dream."

"Is that why you came looking for me?" Parks asked. "Because you had a dream?"

"Yes, but it would have been impossible to find you if it hadn't been for the colonel," Sterling continued. "He showed us the tunnels that travel to the city, and sent us with the book and parchment to look for the man from our dreams. Unfortunately, we were spotted by Management patrols, and had to hide. Then they sent two men after us, but it wasn't until we saw you while we were hiding in the woods that we realized we had found the right man. I put the book in the tree in hopes you would discover it. But your weapons were strange to us, and we misjudged our escape."

"Your brother should never have been killed," Parks said. "I placed Barron under orders to capture resisters, not kill them, but Barron likes killing. I'm so sorry for your loss."

"We knew the risks," Sterling said flatly.

He looked over towards Fred, who nodded approvingly. Sterling removed the clear glass cover, and pulled the crystal out of the wooden podium. To Parks's amazement, it was actually a red crystal blade similar to his blue ones.

"We don't know who made this or why," Sterling said as he handed it to Parks, "but it seems to have been here a very long time. When we saw the blade you had, we talked it over, and decided it should go with you. Maybe you'll understand its value and usefulness."

Parks looked it over carefully, and was about to hand it back to Sterling when he began to feel lightheaded. The dimly-lit room suddenly brightened, and the carvings on the wall seemed to come alive. Memories of events and battles erupted in his mind as if he were there. He felt the deep despair of the people, and the presence of something so dark, it shook him to his core. He watched in helpless anger as the was city torn and ripped to shreds.

Sickened by the bloodbath, he tried to look away, but a singular event captured his attention. Six men sat calmly, seemingly enjoying this horror show. At the same time, they appeared to be looking for something. As Parks looked at them in disgust, they slowly turned and looked directly into his eyes.

Their gaze was hot, and Parks's heart jumped into his throat. His mind flashed to his youth, when the nightmares came, and he couldn't sleep for fear. These six, whoever they were, were seeking him.

"We're honored to give this to you," Fred was saying as Parks's consciousness returned to the room.

"One more thing, please," Parks replied as his mind sharpened. He was shaking slightly from the vision, but said nothing about it. "Have any of you ever heard of something called the Dark Matter?"

The room fell silent as Julie came forward.

"You could call it evil," Julie answered, "but that would be too simple. Our writings say only this: when the Dark Matter comes, it takes the light, and leaves only blackness behind. It's described as fear that comes at night, shakes you awake, drenches you in sweat, and leaves you trembling without an explanation. It's unseen and yet real, and we fear it more than death. Why do you ask?"

"I don't know exactly," Parks replied, "but what you describe is accurate. I have experienced it."

Parks exited the mountain with Sterling, Fred, and Julie. He was relieved to see the sun again.

"I'm so sorry I shot you," Julie said sincerely. She hugged him tightly. "I have something here that I hope will help make up for that. It's something I would like you to have." She pulled Parks to one side, lifting a chain over her head with an unusually shaped golden medallion hanging on the end. It was about three inches in diameter, a quarter inch thick. On one side was a third of the image of a six pointed star, and on the other was a sword.

"I can't take this," he protested. "It looks very old, and very expensive."

"My mother gave that to me when I turned eighteen," Julie replied. "She said there would come a day when it would help free us from oppression. I've kept it all this time, but for the life of me, I can't imagine how it could help anybody. Still, if there is something unique about it, you're the one to find out. Please take it. Mom also said I was a fourth generation daughter, and would know what to do with it. If that's true, then giving it to you fulfills my obligation."

Parks leaned down, and let as her put the chain around his neck. He hugged her, and said his final goodbyes.

"Follow the path around the edge of the mountain below," Sterling said. "You'll come to a spot where there's a narrow opening cut sideways into the rock. Once you step through, you'll be back in the wilderness, and I imagine you can find your way home from there."

"I can't thank you enough for all you've done," Parks replied, taking Sterling's hand, and pulling him tight to his chest. "I'm still confused about a lot of things, but I feel better having been here. When do you think I'll see you again?"

"My life is here," Sterling answered, "but I know we're connected somehow. We'll meet again I'm sure, but until then, be safe, my friend."

Parks followed the path Sterling had marked out for him, but as much as he had gained, pressing issues lay before him, and there was still that unexplained sorrow tugging at his heart. Parks set his face towards the city, and began the long journey back.

CHAPTER 10

Kenzie bounded over rocks and logs, and leaped over shallow ditches like a gazelle. She didn't seem to tire from their long trek across the vast countryside. Jim, on the other hand, was exhausted. His ankle was better, except for the occasional sharp pain when he shifted gears. He took his time over the rugged ground, being careful not to push the machine too hard.

As he drove, his mind was busy trying to understand how he could have been duped into taking a cigar with a tracking device. It all seemed quite impossible.

He had gone into Frank's office as he had a thousand times before. No doubt, Frank had been under pressure, but to hide a transmitter in a cigar wrap just didn't sound like him. It could have been put in there by someone else, but that didn't seem right either. No, the only one who knew his habit of taking a cigar and smoking it later was Frank. Not only that, Frank protected his cigars like a mother would a child.

Suddenly, a cold chill ran up his spine.

There was one other person with access to Frank's desk and his cigars, he suddenly realized, and she was riding behind him on the four-wheeler.

His uncle's farm finally came into view over the last remaining foothill, and they motored up the long gravel driveway. He set his suspicions aside for the moment, too tired and hungry to deal with them.

The last time he had seen this place it was brutally cold, and the trees looked nearly dead. Now it was alive with flowers and fruit everywhere. Uncle James sat on the porch with a large basket full of corn between his knees as they pulled up. He rose up to his full six-foot-nine height as Aunt Lori opened the screen door.

"Jimmy!" Aunt Lori exclaimed as she came down the porch steps. "I didn't recognize you on that thing."

Jim climbed off the four wheeler, and gave his aunt a big hug. Uncle James was right behind her with a smile. He grabbed Jim's hand in his big paw, and shook it warmly.

"Doesn't look much like the nice truck I saw you in last time," his uncle said coyly. "Did you trade it in because this one gets better gas mileage?"

"This is Rita, Kenzie, and Dr. Larson," Jim said, ignoring his uncle's quip. "We have a lot to talk about if you have time."

"Of course," Aunt Lori answered enthusiastically. "Come in. I have some cookies that have just come out of the oven, and your uncle can make a fresh pot of coffee. Are you ok?" Aunt Lori asked as she noticed Jim hobbling a bit on his recovering ankle.

"I sprained my ankle," Jim replied as Rita helped him onto the porch, "but it's getting better."

The group settled into padded chairs that surrounded the kitchen table, and for a while the only sounds were happy munching as they made short work of the cookies. Dusk rolled in, and a light mist hung over the field outside the kitchen window.

"So you're a doctor," James said as he filled Della's cup. "Dr. Larson? That name sounds familiar. Are you local?"

"I am, well was, the chief administrator at the city hospital," Della answered flatly.

"I knew it!" Lori exclaimed. "I met you once when our daughter was having her first child. You came into the room with a big bouquet of flowers, and congratulated us. You were so nice. What are you doing way out here?"

"I'll start the story if that's ok," Jim interjected. "My friends and I have been through a great deal, and we all have something to tell."

His uncle and aunt sat spellbound for nearly two hours as they revealed to them as much of the story as they thought they could comprehend. They left out a few things, such as the Testers and the Island, but Jim told them of the plot to dispose of helpless people, and how his uncle's paper collection had saved the day. It was full dark outside when they finished.

"We've plenty of room here," Aunt Lori said as she got up, and started clearing the table. "It'll only take me a minute to get some fresh sheets, and you can all bed down for the night."

"Let me help with that," Della and Rita said in unison as they began gathering plates.

Uncle James and Aunt Lori made it easy to feel at home as everyone settled into their respective rooms for the night. Rita, Della, and Kenzie were together in a large bedroom with a set of bunk beds and a daybed next to his aunt and uncle's room. Jim took the small bedroom off the kitchen.

The farmhouse had two bathrooms but only one with a shower, so they took turns while his aunt found towels and bathrobes for everybody. They were too weary to talk now, and quickly filed into their respective beds. In a few minutes, only Jim remained awake, staring at the ceiling, and listening to the distant howl of a coyote.

Why would Rita deceive him? He wondered over and over again. But perhaps she hadn't. She was nearly killed herself when that truck smashed into them. She had then gone on to rescue both Parks and himself, which was hardly the work of someone who wanted him captured. It still didn't make sense, though. How could she have known about the transmitter, or where to look for it?

He finally drifted off to sleep, but his reporter's instincts were now on high alert. The next day would be interesting indeed.

"Are you always up this early?" Jim asked sleepily as he stumbled into the kitchen.

His uncle and aunt were buzzing around the kitchen, making breakfast, and getting the coffee on.

"Early, what are you talking about?" his uncle said. "Only city folks sleep past six. We have to get started if we want to beat the heat of the day."

"All right, all right," Jim said, grinning ruefully as he sat down at the table. "I know the drill. I may not have been around for a few years, but I remember how this place works. Hey, where's everybody else? Still sleeping, I suppose."

"You mean us?" Rita answered.

She walked into the kitchen, her slender figure outlined against the small fire burning in the living room fireplace. Even early in the morning, she was a sight. Her silky black hair flowing across her shoulders outlined her long neck and pretty face. Jim forgot his suspicions for a moment as he smiled broadly, and greeted her with a warm "good morning!"

The kitchen quickly filled with cooking and table setting, surrounded by conversations. Everyone wanted to know something about everything.

"You are a most amazing cook," Dr. Larson commented as she took a second helping of Lori's homemade biscuits and fresh strawberry jam. "I've never tasted anything so good. "Did you make these yourself?"

"We have a little strawberry patch behind the house," Aunt Lori answered, "and if we can keep the rabbits out, we usually have a nice harvest. James put an electric fence up this spring, and it seems to be working. Just yesterday, I was able to pick nearly a full flat. I am planning on making some strawberry shortcake if you'll stay another night."

"That sounds really good," Jim said, "but I'm not sure of our plans yet. Hey, when did this come?" He picked up a small envelope from the holder on the kitchen window sill.

"Oh, that." Lori said over her shoulder from the sink. "All our neighbors have been getting those. It's some kind of notice, right James?"

"I read it," Uncle James replied as he took another sip of coffee. "Something about reporting to some newfangled office in the city. Seems they want to give us money or something, but I think it's just another scam."

It was a request for his aunt and uncle to report to the Human Services Division at the Citadel with their birth certificates and driver's licenses.

"From what I can tell, Management has initiated a program designed to help farmers," James said. "We just have to report for identification purposes, and sign some production agreements or something. They're going to be paying more than we can get at the local produce auctions, and are offering a three thousand dollar sign-up bonus to boot. Isn't that ridiculous? When has Management ever cared about us?" His uncle continued. "But they went to a lot of trouble making up this map. It looks like we're next, since we live between Valley View and Kickerville Road. Our neighbors to the West went last Thursday, and we're scheduled for tomorrow."

Jim looked the letter over carefully, and confirmed the offer his uncle described. Kenzie asked to see it, and he handed it over. Her attention was immediately drawn to the name at the bottom.

"Aaron Michaels!" she exclaimed.

"Who's Aaron Michaels?" Jim asked.

"Aaron Michaels is one of the eight children Parks saved," Dr. Larson explained, reading over Kenzie's shoulder. "I helped Aaron find a good home up on the hill with the Michaels family. They were an older, well-to-do couple, and seemed very willing to take on an orphan. Aaron went with them, and to the best of my knowledge, they put him through college."

"We haven't seen much of Aaron lately though," Kenzie interjected. "When we were younger, we hung out together, but then he started drifting away. He became more interested in his studies, and really didn't have much time for anything else. The last we heard he received a promotion, and was working at the Citadel. This must be his new job."

A knot formed in Jim's gut as he listened to them talk. His reporter instincts were definitely aroused, and none of this was adding up. Bringing the county folk into the city on a promise of money and prosperity seemed too easy. There had to be more to this than met the eye.

"Hey, Uncle James, can I borrow your truck for a bit this morning?" he asked innocently. "I would like to take Rita for a ride, and show her the local landscape."

James laughed knowingly, and winked as he pulled the keys from his pocket, and tossed them to Jim. Dr. Larson and Kenzie were quite content to hang around the house, and talk with his aunt and uncle which left Jim and Rita free to investigate.

He climbed into the old farm pickup. The floor boards had a fresh coat of dirt, and there were rags and tools on the seat. Rita hopped in the passenger side, and rolled down the window.

"Sure is a beautiful day," Rita said cheerfully. "And I really love your family. They're such nice people."

"They really are," Jim replied, trying not to reveal any discomfort in his voice.

The driveway quickly gave way to a blacktopped county road as the old truck lurched from gear to gear.

"Where are we heading?" Rita asked over the motor's din.

"I have a thought, but I don't want to say anything yet," Jim answered as he pulled into a neighbor's driveway.

He pulled up next to an old, two-story farmhouse with several outbuildings in the back.

"This is the Smits' farm," Jim said as he climbed out and headed for the porch. "I used to play with their daughter, Serena, when I was a kid."

Jim rang the doorbell several times before knocking, but there was no answer. He checked around back, but the house appeared to be deserted.

"They must not be home," Rita volunteered. "Maybe they had to go somewhere or something."

"Maybe," Jim answered as he knocked on the back door, "but I'm not so sure. Do you see the cows out in the field?"

"Yes, so what," Rita replied.

"Those are dairy cows, and from my vantage point, it doesn't look like they've been milked in quite some time. Come on, let's look in the barn."

Jim opened the door, and knew instantly something was wrong. The smell of death hung in the air as he checked the stalls. The calves hadn't been watered or fed in a long time.

Rita covered her nose, and gasped at the horrible sight.

"How could people do such things?" Rita asked as they walked outside. "It would take a very cruel person to let them die like that."

"It wasn't the Smits," Jim replied as they walked back towards the truck. "They're good people, and good farmers. They care for their livestock like most people care for their children. There's no way they would have allowed this."

"Then where are they?" Rita asked anxiously as they backed out the driveway. "Why aren't they here, taking care of their farm?"

"I've a hunch, but I need to check a few more homes first," Jim replied as they pulled back onto the road.

Jim and Rita visited several more homes and farms before returning to his uncle's place. They were all equally empty, with dead and dying animals everywhere. Rita rode along in silence, overwhelmed by what she had just seen. Jim jumped out, and headed straight for the house when they returned.

"How was your ride?" Aunt Lori asked cheerfully from the garden. "Did you get a chance to meet up with some old friends?"

"I need everybody back in the house right now!" Jim nearly shouted. "We need to talk."

His aunt ran without a word to the barn to fetch his uncle. In a matter of minutes, everyone was assembled at the kitchen table.

"What's this all about?" Uncle James said as he walked in. "Your aunt said you're upset about something."

"Sorry about that," Jim replied. "But what I have to say is critical. Your neighbors all got one of these invitations to come to the city just like this one, right?"

"So," his uncle replied, "I don't see the government playing favorites. If there's money to be had, we should all get our fair share. Wouldn't hurt to drive into town and get ours."

"That's just the point," Jim retorted. "There's no money for anybody."

"No money?" His aunt said. "I told you it was a scam," she said to James, "but I guess there's no real harm in it. People stay a night in the city, and then drive back. Be a nice little getaway for many of our farmer friends who seldom go anywhere."

"That's the whole point," Jim said seriously. "It's not about giving you anything. It is about getting you into the city where Management can deal with you."

"What?!" James exclaimed. "Deal with us? What are you talking about, my boy?"

"I'm talking about your neighbors," Jim said. "Look," he continued, spreading out the letter on the table. "See the map they provided dividing the county into sections. You're number three. The first two groups already went to the city, but they never returned. We found their farms and homes vacant. Everyone is gone."

"That's crazy!" Aunt Lori exclaimed. "I phoned over to Roy and Sharon's home just yesterday. They had a message on their answering machine that said they decided to stay on in the city for a little while longer, and had someone watching the farm for them."

"Who else have you contacted in the last two weeks?" Jim asked intently.

"Well, I've been thinking of calling Bill and Emily to come over for a game of cards this week," She replied. "Bill works in the maintenance department in the city while Emily manages the farm. They raise chickens and a few turkeys."

"They live way over by the river, right." Jim said. "They would have been among the first to be called up to the city. Why don't you give them a quick call just to be sure everything is ok."

His aunt hesitated for a moment before picking up the phone, and dialing. She put the phone on speaker so everyone in the room could hear. It rang three times before it picked up.

"Hi!" Came Emily's cheerful voice, and Lori was about to respond when it continued, "Bill and I have decided to stay on in the city for a while, and enjoy our good fortune. We've someone watching the house. See you all when we return."

"Oh, that's not good," Uncle James commented. "Bill works in the city, and he hates it. He can't wait to get home. There isn't much chance he would stay there for a week, let alone two."

"It's worse than that," Jim continued. "Do you remember their beautiful golden retriever?"

"Yes, Ginger," his uncle responded. "She's such a friendly girl."

"Well," Jim explained, taking a glace over at Rita, who looked down at the floor, "we stopped there last, and found Ginger tied to a tree. Unfortunately, being without food or water in this heat for two weeks was too much for her."

Everyone in the room gasped, and Rita started sobbing.

Uncle James slammed his huge fist down on the table and stood up, clearly disturbed.

"I'll call some people from the Farmer's Association right now," he said angrily as he grabbed the phone. "Then we'll form an action committee, and really get things moving. There's no way I'm going to allow any more people to go in until we get some answers."

"You may want to hold that thought for a moment," Jim said. "I believe there's more to this than any of us realize. If Management is pulling people in and holding them, it's only because they want something, and from what I see, it looks like they don't care whom they hurt to get it. Confronting them may not be the best thing to do yet."

"What do you think they're after?" Kenzie asked.

"I'm not sure," Jim replied, "but I overheard Parks mention something called "Gifts." I don't know what he was talking about, but it sounded important, and he said Management was looking for them."

"The things legends are made of," Uncle James said slowly. "They've been rumored to exist for as long as anyone can remember, but nobody has ever taken them seriously, and I can't imagine they would have anything to do with this."

"I've heard of them too," Lori said. "My mother told me they were the one thing that could keep us safe and secure forever. They're special things sent here in different forms, and are meant to be assembled somehow. Whoever has them, so the story goes, has the power to destroy the Dark Matter."

"Yeesh!" James exclaimed. "You've never mentioned that part of the story before."

"We've never talked about this before," she replied. "These kinds of subjects don't just come up, you know."

"Gifts or not," James continued, "I still think I should make some calls. We've lives and livelihoods to protect, and people need to know what's going on."

"Agreed," Kenzie spoke up. "But chances are if people don't come in willingly, they'll be sending someone out to find out why. That's likely not going to be a good thing."

"What do you propose?" Dr. Larson asked.

"I suggest we go into the city, but not report," Kenzie continued. "We need to team up with some people I know, and find out what's really going on."

"But there's going to be checkpoints," Jim said. "They'll be watching, and there's only one main bridge into the city."

"Here's what we do," Uncle James said, after thinking for a few minutes. "I'll let people know what's going on, and get some help over to the homes and farms of our missing friends. Maybe we can save something for them. Then I'll do a little quick modification to our motor home, and create some space to hide the four of you. Once we're in the city, I can let you out wherever you want. I need to meet up with my brother, and see what he knows."

"You mean Philip Parks, Henry's dad?" Dr. Larson asked.

"Yes, that's him," Uncle James responded. "He'll know what's going on, or at least have a good idea."

James called a meeting with the farmers, and told everyone what they had learned, and not to respond to the letters they received. He also suggested they arm themselves, and prepare for the worst. Not reporting was risky, and if people quit coming, Management would come looking.

In a few hours, Uncle James had the motor home ready. He removed everything from under the bench seats, and drilled some breathing holes. There was just enough room for Dr. Larson and Kenzie. Jim and Rita fit neatly under the overhead mattress. It wasn't going to be comfortable, but at least they were well-hidden. Then Lori showed James a strange box she had taken from her dresser.

"What is it?" James asked curiously.

"I'm not sure," Lori answered. "My mother gave it to me when I was just eighteen, and said one day I would need to find the person it belongs to. Mom said it was part of a "gift," but I never understood what that meant. I think I have a better idea now, and it needs to come with us."

She slid it under her seat.

James fired up the motor home while Lori took one long last look at their happy home. It was hard to imagine they might never see it again.

"You can take your positions once we get to the rest area this side of the city," Uncle James instructed as everyone piled in. "In the meantime, sit back, and enjoy the ride."

The motor home rolled down the driveway, and out onto the county road. It would be at least three hours before they had to hide. But even though there was no end of interesting topics, they were also depressing, and no one had the heart for conversation. Jim looked out the window, still plagued by the cigar incident, and no closer to an answer. But this wasn't the time or place for questions. Very shortly, they would be in the city facing unknown dangers.

CHAPTER 11

"Hi guys," David said as Burke, Normand, Joshua, Troy, and Isaac filed in through his apartment door. "Kirsten isn't coming tonight," he continued. "She's staying at home with her father. He's having a hard time coping with Mrs. Parks' death."

"I think we should go over there," Normand said. "They need our support. Maybe we can bring some pizza, and hang out for a while. It's not good to be alone when something this bad happens."

"I agree," Isaac said. "I was over there earlier today, and Mr. Parks is not doing well."

"We'll go over later," David said firmly. "I called Kirsten before you came, and she's expecting us around nine, but we need to talk business first."

He led the way into his small apartment living room. He took a seat on the couch next to Normand.

"We must stop Management. Kirsten has trained us well, and it's time to put our training to use."

"I'm ready," Troy said with a savage gleam in his eyes. "I'll head back to where we saw the Testers, and start with them."

"Whoa," Joshua said. "We have to be smarter than that. Testers are only part of the problem. We need more information before we go running out. We need to know what Management's plans really are."

"Right," David agreed, "and Aaron's our best bet. We must get word to him of what's going on, and see what he can do for us. Maybe he can get us a copy of the map Burke saw."

"He used to frequent a small tavern down on the West side of town," Isaac said. "We haven't hung out in a long time, but I know he liked listening to their bands, and even joined in once in a while."

"See what you can do," David told him. "In the meantime, I suggest we all begin contacting family and friends, and give them some advanced warning. We must be ready."

The evening sky was darkening as Isaac pulled into the parking lot behind the tavern. He walked down the narrow, cobbled street to a heavy wooden door with iron bars in its small window. An old florescent sign with the image of a large beer stein and a crack in one corner shone on the worn concrete sidewalk. Isaac stepped in, and found his place in the corner. This was his third night, and he had yet to run into Aaron, but he was hopeful his friend would show up that night, as a blues band was scheduled. Isaac ate as usual while the band warmed up, but there was no sign of Aaron. He sat through the first two songs, and got up to leave.

Just at the moment, the bar door opened, and Aaron came in with a couple of guys Isaac hadn't seen before. They were dressed in crisp dark suits and had an air of importance about them. He watched as the three men took a table at the front. When the band finished its first set, he seized the opportunity.

"Hi, Aaron," he said cheerfully, stepping up to the table.

"Isaac!" Aaron responded, standing up from the table, and hugging him warmly. "When did you get here?"

"Just a few minutes ago," Isaac lied. "I heard about the band tonight, and thought I would drop in and see if they were any good."

"Oh, they've been great." Aaron said. "They just broke for intermission, but if the second half is as good as the first, you've got some great listening ahead of you."

"Who's your friend?" One of the men sitting at the table asked.

"Sorry, this is Isaac," Aaron said, turning to the two men. "Isaac, I would like you to meet Mike and Harold, two of my comrades from work. This is Isaac, an old friend."

The two men rose, and shook Isaac's hand.

"Come on, sit with us," Aaron said encouragingly.

"Please, do!" Mike, the taller of the three said in a suave tone Isaac instantly disliked.

In a few moments, the band returned, and started the second half. There was plenty of small talk and laughter as the evening wore on. It was Friday night, and these guys were in relaxation and fun mode. Isaac was especially impressed how the waiters and waitresses paid such close attention to them. They made sure the beer kept coming, and there was no lack of food.

Isaac had never experienced this much service ever. The band finished their final song to resounding applause.

"It's still early," Mike said. "Let's go uptown, and see if we can get into real trouble. I hear there are some new bars up there with some really friendly ladies."

"I need to get rid of some beer before I do anything," Aaron said, getting up and heading for the restrooms.

"I better join you," Isaac said, jumping on the opportunity to talk with Aaron alone.

"Fun night, eh?" Aaron said, washing his hands. "Mike and Harold are great guys."

"Yeah, it's been fun," Isaac replied as he ripped a paper towel from the dispenser, "but I need to talk to you for just a minute. Is there somewhere we can go?"

"We can talk here," Aaron said. "What's up?"

"I don't feel comfortable talking in here," Isaac whispered just as another man came in, "but I only need a few minutes."

"Ok, how about I send Mike and Harold on ahead, and we talk on the way to our cars," Aaron suggested as he opened the restroom door. "We can catch up with them later if you want to come along."

Aaron's two buddies agreed to meet up with him in an hour at some place called the Big Cat, and the four of them left the tavern. . No one paid the bill, which he thought was a bit odd, but he didn't say anything.

"Nice night isn't it," Aaron said as they started the long climb up the cobblestone street towards the parking lot.

"Yes it is," Isaac said. "Aaron, we need your help. There are things happening that have us worried. Some really strange things, and I would like to explain if you can meet with us. We need some information you may be able to get for us."

Aaron froze for a moment in the middle of the street. and looked hard at Isaac.

"What are you talking about?" he asked. "What information do you need, and who is "we"?"

"The R.O.D.," Isaac said, suddenly feeling a little uneasy. "You, me, and the rest of our friends. We need your help."

"Oh, so that's what this is all about," Aaron replied, stepping to the curb to avoid a passing car. "You guys are still hanging out, prepping to fight windmills in the moonlight."

Aaron's voice sounded strained.

"I thought you guys outgrew that sort of stuff. Look, it's great to see you again, Isaac, but I'm not into these kinds of games any more. It's been over ten years, and there are no boogie men hiding behind doors. I have a lot of responsibility, and the Citadel is a great place to work."

"Just hear me out for a second," Isaac insisted. "Burke swears there's a map outlined to divide and destroy the city, and he's seen it hanging on a wall in the Citadel someplace. And Kirsten's mom died only a few days ago at the hands of the Testers. This is not a game, Aaron!"

"Pearl died?" Aaron exclaimed. "Man, I'm really sorry to hear that. She was a really sweet person; I'll make sure they get some flowers. But the rest of what you're telling me sounds like fantasy. Look, no offense, Isaac, but I've got some serious partying to do tonight, so if you'll excuse me, I must get going."

Isaac stood in the street and watched Aaron hop into a dark blue convertible, and roar up the street. His heart was heavy as he headed back to his apartment. He would need to report to the others what Aaron had said. Maybe together they could come up with a way to get through to him.

It was nearly eleven when he pulled into the parking garage below his three-story apartment building. An elevator serviced the upper floors, but Isaac liked jogging up the stairs to the only finished apartment on the top floor, his. The building was undergoing renovation, and he was helping with the work in return for free rent. Even better, he could play his music as loud as he wanted, and not worry about disturbing anyone.

He opened the heavy fire door, exited the stairs, and headed towards his room. Heavy plastic hung along the sides of the dimly-lit hall where walls were being torn out and replaced. He was just about to his door when something caught his eye.

"What's that?" he thought, stopping in his tracks.

The light from the streetlights sometimes made strange shadows out of the plastic sheets, but this time he was sure he saw movement. Isaac dropped to a crouch, and scanned the area.

Thieves came up from time to time, searching for tools or other things they could take, but Isaac had convinced the owners to build some heavy steel boxes to store stuff in. Since then, nothing had been taken, but that wouldn't stop people from nosing about.

The next flash of light was not from any streetlight; it was from thousands of electrons exploding in his brain. He tumbled through the plastic wall, and into a pile of metal studs. Before he could gather himself, his body was in the air, being thrown across another half-finished apartment, and breaking one of the fiberglass tub enclosures in half. The last thing he saw was the outline of a small, well-dressed man with sunglasses. Everything faded to black.

Flashes of hot pain shot through his body as he struggled back to consciousness. He could feel harsh, glaring lights through his closed eyelids, and there was a trickle of blood over his right eyebrow. He tried to wipe it off, but he couldn't move his hands or his feet. They were securely fastened to a steel chair, which was bolted to a concrete floor.

"So, our friend is waking up." A woman's voice. "I thought you were going to sleep all night."

Isaac's head was pounding. He blinked the blood out of his eye, and looked around the room. He was sitting in front of an old metal desk. Behind the desk sat a sharply-dressed woman with way too much red lipstick on, he didn't recognize. She seemed to know who he was though. On one side of the room was a heavy metal door, and on the other stood the small man in a black suit. Isaac recognized him as the one he had seen just before blacking out.

"Where am I?" Isaac groaned.

"Nowhere," The woman answered. "You are nowhere, and if you don't answer our questions, you'll be somewhere even worse."

The pain in Isaac's head intensified, and he struggled to remain conscious. His hands throbbed from the tight ropes, and he thought he was going to vomit. He nearly escaped back into the safety of darkness, but the little man didn't let him. He pulled Isaac's hair with one hand, and grabbed his throat with the other, lifting him off the chair. The ropes held him down, and chafed against the bruises on his wrists and legs, which were already raw. He couldn't breathe. Suddenly, the powerful grip was gone, and he fell into his chair with a thud. He gasped and coughed.

"That should help you concentrate," the woman said coldly. "It's time for questions, and I want answers. Let's start with an easy one. Who told you about a map?"

"Map," Isaac said, trying to sound confused by the question. "What map? I don't need a map."

"Don't try to be clever," the woman said. "Who told you about a map of the city with lines and markings on it?"

"The only map I ever saw was from a guy selling in the street," Isaac said. "I thought it was cool, but didn't want to pay ten bucks for it. If you want it so bad, I'll tell you how to find him."

"I see how you are," the woman said, pulling a small black bag from under her desk, and setting it in front of him. "Inside here are all kinds of sharp instruments. Each one is designed to take something specific off your body. I throw them one by one into that barrel over there until you start talking. Eventually you won't recognize yourself, but I see that doesn't frighten you." She opened the bag. "Maybe you're brave now, but we'll see how brave you are later."

She motioned to the little man, who stepped behind Isaac, and held him by his shoulders. She removed a long, straight metal tube from the bag, and set it on the desk. Next, she took a small object wrapped in cloth from inside her jacket. The wrappings fell away to reveal a dark red crystal.

"Here's what's going to happen," she said, picking up the tube, and coming around the desk. "I am going to pound this until it enters your heart, and insert this pretty little red crystal. Once the crystal is in, you'll tell me everything, even things I don't want to know. When the crystal has finished its work. you'll wish I had cut you into little pieces instead. Now, are you sure you wouldn't like to start talking while you still can? You're such a handsome young man, and it seems a shame to ruin you. We can use people like you if you're willing."

Isaac was helpless in the vise-like grip of the little man, who was stronger than he looked. The woman positioned the tube over his chest, and pulled a heavy wooden mallet from her bag.

"One last chance," she said coldly, raising the mallet over the tube. "Who told you about the map?"

"It was just an old map the guy was selling," Isaac replied, his eyes bugging out as he strained against his bonds. "Like a treasure map or something. Why do you care?"

She hit the tube hard, driving it through his skin. A second blow sent it through his rib cage, and into his chest. Isaac watched his own blood spurt out the end of the metal tube and onto the mallet.

Suddenly, he tensed. The room was somehow shrinking. The woman's eyes opened wide, and her mouth dropped open. Isaac's entire body began to glow brighter and brighter, and the ropes holding his arms and legs snapped. The small man tried to control him, but Isaac broke loose, grabbed him with his free hand, and threw him against the block wall. The man jumped back to his feet, only to be hit square in the face with the metal chair Isaac ripped from the floor. The woman jumped behind her desk, holding her arms up to shield her eyes from the brilliant blue light filling the room.

Isaac charged at the steel door, ramming it with his forearm. It blew open. Two heavy steel gates got the same treatment, and then he was free. He ran down a long corridor, and out into the cool night air. He kept running, making random turns. He had no idea whether he was being followed, or even where he was going.

He had run for nearly a mile when things became familiar. He realized he was nearing Normand's house, and slowed to an unsteady walk as he approached the door. He reached out to knock, but just then the familiar blackness returned.

"Is he going to be ok?" Normand asked as David checked his pulse. He tried not to stare at the hollow tube covered in blood that was sticking out of Isaac's chest.

"He's strong," David said. "How long do you think he was lying at your door?"

"I got home a little after eleven last night, and I leave at five to get to the depot and pick up my van," Normand said. "Obviously he came between those hours, but I never heard a thing."

Normand had carried Isaac inside, and put him on his couch before calling David. He covered him in blankets, but resisted the urge to pull out the odd-looking metal tube sticking out from his chest.

"We need to get him to Dr. Flint's place," David said. "It'll be too dangerous to take him to the hospital. Someone might be after him, and that's the first place they'll look."

Normand drove while David kept watch. It seemed like ages before they pulled into the paved parking lot in front of a small clinic. The doctor's home was in the back, and still dark when Normand rang the doorbell. When it wasn't answered right away, he started pounding.

"Hold on," a sleepy voice came from inside, "I'm coming."

The doctor peeked around the side glass before unlocking the door.

"We need your help right away!" Normand exclaimed. "Our friend is badly hurt, and he's in my truck out front."

"Let's go," Dr. Flint replied without hesitation.

Dressed in his slippers and pajamas, Dr. Flint climbed into the back of the truck, and quickly examined Isaac.

"We need to get him to the hospital immediately," the doctor said. "He is going to need surgery. I'll call the local aid station, and have them send a car over straight away. You boys should have taken him there in the first place."

"We can't do that," David said as the doctor backed out of the truck. "Somebody did this to him, and whoever that is will likely be checking the hospital. His life is more in danger there than it is here."

"I don't have the facilities needed to help him!" The doctor protested. "He must have surgery to remove whatever that is sticking out of his chest. It would likely kill him for me to pull it out."

David glanced anxiously at Normand. The thought of his own father's being nearly killed by some unknown assassin in that very same hospital was still fresh in his mind. Management was likely behind this, and waiting there for them right now.

"I have an idea," Dr. Flint said, sensing the fear in the young men. "One of the best surgeons around is a close friend of mine. He works out of the surgery center, which is just around the corner from the hospital. If I bring your friend in under my care, no one would suspect anything. We can even disguise his identity, and say he's in his seventies. I work with a lot of elderly people, so no one would be suspicious. You can trust Dr. Stevens, as he has no particular love for Management. Why don't we move him to my station wagon, and get over there. I just need a few minutes to get dressed, and make a quick call."

David and Normand had little choice. Isaac's breathing was shallow, and he had already lost a lot of blood. At Dr. Flint's direction, they grabbed a gurney out of his clinic, and loaded Isaac on it. The doctor's station wagon was extra-long and built specially for moving patients to and from his office. They locked Isaac in, and followed the doctor to the surgery center.

Normand had to get to work, but David promised to call as soon as he knew anything. David wanted to let everyone know what was going on, but was afraid to use the phone. He remembered what had happened with his father and how Management seemed to know things. They were likely listening to their calls, so he would just have to sit tight and hope for the best.

"Are you here for the injured young man?" asked a tired-looking middle-aged man in a white smock.

"Yes, I am." David said, jumping from the chair. "How's he doing?"

"He's going to be ok," the doctor answered in a soft voice. "I'm Doctor Stevens," he continued. "I removed the metal tube. He also had a broken arm and a head injury, possibly a concussion. I'm keeping him sedated for now, but he'll need time to recover. Your friend endured quite an unusual set of injuries. Is there anything you can tell me about how he got them?"

"No, sir," David answered, relieved that Isaac was going to be ok. "We found him that way. Why do you need to know that?"

"I must have something to put into my report to the insurance company," the doctor replied.

"Didn't Dr. Flint tell you we don't want any mention of him?" David said anxiously. "We think the people who did that to him are still looking for him. We think they might check the hospital, and maybe even here. Dr. Flint said you could log him in as an elderly who fell or something."

Dr. Stevens folded his arms, and held his clipboard tight to his chest as he eyed David for a moment.

"That's a crazy idea," he answered finally. "Do you know the trouble I could get into for falsifying records?" He thought for a moment. "His injuries were unusual, I'll give you that. He can stay here for now with a falsified record, but there can be no mention of it, and no visitors other than you. I'll arrange for the care he needs, but if this gets out, we're all going to be in big trouble."

"Thank you, doctor," David exhaled. "And we'll get you the money for his care. We can't use insurance, but we'll pay in cash."

"We'll talk about that later," the doctor said as he turned to leave. "Come back in a few hours if you like, and check with me on his progress."

David thanked the doctor, and headed for his truck. Isaac had been targeted somehow, but why? David needed answers, but they would have to wait until Isaac regained consciousness. It was midmorning as David headed for his parent house and some breakfast but this was becoming a puzzle of immense proportions.

CHAPTER 12

It had been weeks since Parks had last seen Della. The return journey across the wilderness seemed much shorter somehow, but the uncomfortable feeling in his gut refused to leave. The more he tried to ignore it, the more it gnawed at his mind. Behind his fears lurked a terrible anger.

He ran past the Island, not stopping to report to the colonel. He hoped the colonel would understand. He first considered returning the way he had left the city, through the hidden tunnel entrance, but he changed his mind.

He slowed to a stop on the crest of the hill that overlooked the back gate. It was the same one he and Jim had used the night they followed the black bus. The sun was beginning to set as he considered his options. The gate was unmanned, but it was equipped with cameras and sensors. Simply walking in would be impossible. As he searched, he noticed a spot where the wall dipped slightly as it crossed a wide drainage ditch. That would be his best entry point.

A large limb lay in the brush along the bank of the ditch. Upon further examination, he decided it was the perfect size for a makeshift pole. He waited for the cover of darkness, and rushed the wall. The limb bit solidly into the ground, bent under his weight, and lifted him high into the air. In an instant, he had cleared the barbed wire on the top of the stone wall, and was rolling into some brush on the other side.

He moved quickly to some cover, and watched the road carefully in both directions for a long while. There didn't seem to be any alarm or activity coming his way. He had successfully made it in.

He stayed close to the bushes on the outskirts of the city, through yards, and over fences. The night was still, and the city surprisingly quiet. It was Saturday, and normally there would be motorists and cyclists tearing about, heading to and from parties, or visiting family and friends. But as he moved along, a sullen feeling came over him. It was heavy and oppressive.

His first stop was Della's apartment, and his chosen path led him along the ridge above the HOT News station. To his surprise, the place seemed abandoned, and there were several broken windows.

He put the apartment on hold for the moment, and went in closer to investigate. A single street lamp lit the asphalted area, its dim glow enhancing the deserted air.

He sprinted to the safety of the building's shadows. There were no lights on inside. He checked the rear door, and found that it was unlocked, which he thought was strange. The building felt cold and damp as he slid inside.

It took a few seconds for his eyes to adjust to the darkened building. He passed several offices with doors half open, as if their former inhabitants were expected to return at any minute. He glanced into a few, and noted papers strewn across the floor, several broken windows, and overturned file cabinets.

Suddenly, he spotted movement along a corridor about fifty feet ahead. Something or someone had crossed the hall, but he couldn't quite make out what it was in the dark. Pulling one of his crystal blades from the heavy leather belt around his waist, he crouched down, and moved silently along the side of the hall. When he reached the cross corridor, he peered around the corner.

He stared intently for a few seconds, and not seeing any movement, stepped into the hall. He had no sooner moved into the open when a vicious blow sent him sprawling. His assailant had been hiding behind a cardboard box, and jumped up with a crowbar in hand just as Parks passed by. He was quickly joined by two others, one from behind an overturned desk in an adjacent room, and the other from the opposite end of the corridor.

Parks's head was throbbing. He raised his crystal blade just as the three dark figures closed in. Its brilliant blue light momentarily blinded the three men, freezing them in their tracks. He kicked the closest one in the midsection, sending him flying down the hall. He skidded to a stop against an overturned copy machine. The second he hit on the top of his head with the handle of the blade, dropping him to his knees. Reaching for the third, Parks was about to bury the shining blade in his chest, but his assailant cried out.

"Stop, please!" the man pled, dropping the crowbar. "I can see you're not one of them."

"One of whom?" Parks demanded to know.

He pinned the man against the wall with his forearm.

"You know, Management, the men in black suits." the man squeaked in reply. "They raided this place two weeks ago, and they still come by every now and then to check if anyone is here. They caught me cleaning out my desk a week ago, and knocked me around pretty good. We thought we could sneak back tonight and get the last of our stuff, but then you came in. I was sure our luck had run out until just now. I recognize you-- you're Jim's cousin. Parks, right?"

"That I am," Parks said.

He relaxed his grip, and let the man drop to the floor. "Who are you, and what happened here?"

"My name is Chris," the man replied, "I was Jim Banner's senior assistant before he disappeared. The big guy massaging his head is Danny, and it looks like Ray is going to be ok too," he continued as the third man came slowly down the hall, holding his stomach. "They were writers for "Jim the Weatherman's" program for nearly ten years. Now we're just trying to survive what's happening."

Parks slid his crystal blade back into its sheath. The room went dark for a moment, but Chris lit a small flashlight he was carrying. He pointed it at the floor to avoid being seen from outside, and it provided just enough light to illuminate the men's faces.

"To answer your question, things have changed," Chris continued. "First, Jim ran this program that exposed Management for what they really are--heartless, greedy people. Then Jim disappeared."

"Went into hiding, we hope," Danny interjected.

"Danny's probably right," Chris said, "but nobody knows for sure. We haven't seen him since he came in the day before he ran his program. He and Frank, the station manager, had a meeting, and then he left. The next thing we knew, Frank was laying people off. We stayed on for some time, mothballing the equipment, and making sure everything was in order. Until these guys in suits arrived and started tearing the place up. We haven't dared come back until tonight."

"What else can you tell me about the city?" Parks asked. "I've been away."

"It's a little creepy," Danny responded. "People aren't saying much, but I get the impression they're plenty scared. We were the only independent news organization in the city. Without us, people have to depend on the information Management puts out."

"Propaganda is more like it," Ray said.

"Yes, they do twist the news," Chris continued. "They've never even mentioned the situation Jim exposed at the Economic Diversity Divisions. There was money in it, I'm sure, but not a single Management-controlled station has reported on it. All they do is brag about how great things are going. They even had the audacity to run a piece on the Eastern Diversity Division, the focus of Jim's work, and make it sound like the most wonderful place in the world. It was sickening."

"More like brutal," Danny agreed. "We can't find work. People are afraid to hire us. I've had to move back in with my mom."

"He's right," Chris said. "If my wife didn't have a good job, I don't know how we would have made it. But I don't think we should hang around here much longer."

Parks agreed, but managed to secure some additional information before the three men left. He discovered not everybody at HOT News had suffered from Jim's broadcast. Frank had taken a very lucrative position overseeing Management stations. His mind whirled with questions as he left HOT News, and made his way to Della's apartment.

He carefully surveyed the neighborhood, but it didn't seem to be watched. When he was satisfied there were no spying eyes, he easily jumped the eight foot fence surrounding Della's backyard.

He found the key she kept hidden under the mat, and opened the sliding glass door, locking it again once he was inside. The room was cold, and smelled a little musty. He found the flashlight she kept under the kitchen sink, and made sure the drapes were closed before turning it on.

His first stop was the fridge. It had been quite a while since he had any decent food, and he helped himself to some leftover lasagna. He finished off with a large glass of water, and stretched out on the sofa, pulling a blanket off the back.

He was sure she had made it out safely, but he needed to find her to make sure. He would start with her friend, Darla.

Despite his anxious thoughts, exhaustion caught up with him, and he slipped into a troubled dream.

"You're such a fool," the little man in the black suit sneered. "You think you killed the Zender."

"I did kill the Zender," Parks protested. "I stabbed it with my crystal blade. I killed it when I was trapped in the cave."

"Ha!" the little man laughed. "You didn't kill the beast. You released it, and its power is growing in you even now."

Parks jerked upright, and shook himself awake. He was drenched in sweat, and his mind buzzed with confusion. It was morning. He threw off the blanket, and swung his feet onto the cold floor. He sat there for a moment, heart pounding, with his head buried in his hands.

What did the Zender have to do with him? And why did he have such a dark feeling inside? Something wasn't right, but he had no idea what to do about it."

He gathered his belongings, and slipped out the sliding glass door into the early morning air. Della's friend Darla lived about ten blocks away, and if he hurried, he should be able to catch her before she left for work.

His best hope was that Management wouldn't be looking for him in the city. They likely believed he had left for good. Even so, Parks stayed in the shadows, and crossed as many backyards and alleys as possible to avoid being seen. Along the way, he saw one old woman in a bathrobe picking her paper off her porch, but she didn't notice him, or if she did, she didn't pay him any heed.

Darla's husband Joel was in their driveway, getting his gravel truck started as Parks approached. Joel worked for the city maintenance division as one of their heavy equipment operators and truck drivers. He was a large man with a friendly face.

"Hi, Joel," Parks said as he came up.

"What the!" Joel exclaimed, spinning around. "Parks, are you trying to give me a heart attack? What are you doing here?"

"I'm looking for Della," Parks answered quietly. "Have you seen her?"

"You'd better come inside," Joel said, closing the hood on his truck. "Darla can tell you better than I can, and it's probably not good for us to be standing out here in the open."

Darla was in the kitchen making breakfast as they came in.

"Parks!" she shouted when she recognized him. "Where have you been?" She gave him a big hug, nearly lifting him off his feet.

Darla was a tall, stately woman with an engaging smile. She and Joel had been married for over twenty years, and even though they were middle-aged, they both still had the energy of teenagers. She waved him over toward one of the stools lining her kitchen counter.

"You look like you could use some coffee," she said brightly, but Joel was already pouring a cup for him.

"Thank you," Parks said as Joel set the cup in front of him, "but I'm looking for Della, and wonder if you've seen her."

"No, I haven't," Darla answered. She flashed a worried look at Joel. "Fact is, I haven't seen her in quite some time. Not since Management sent that ugly thug of theirs over to the hospital to look for that Jim fella."

"Who came over to the hospital?" Parks asked, getting more concerned by the second.

"That old partner of yours," Darla continued, "although he looks plenty different, kind of like someone beat him with an ugly stick or something."

"You mean Barron?" Parks answered, his blood beginning to boil.

"That's the one," Darla replied, taking a stool between them. "I don't know where she is, but I don't believe that Barron fella grabbed her. He was looking mighty unhappy when he left the hospital."

Parks was getting hotter by the second. If Barron was back in action, that meant trouble.

"I'm real sorry to hear about your mom," Joel said as he got up from the counter.

"My what," Parks asked as his attention returned to the moment.

"Your mom, of course," Darla replied reaching around Parks shoulders and giving him a hug. "We all loved Pearl. She was such a wonderful person."

"Was?!" Parks exclaimed, his voice breaking slightly. "What are you talking about?"

"I'm sorry," Joel said sheepishly, looking at Darla for some direction. "We thought you knew. We ran into David, and he told us she had passed away about a week ago. "

Parks's expression dropped to the floor, and his grief instantly turned to anger. Joel came around the counter and put his hand on Parks's shoulder, but he flinched and pulled away.

"I've got to go up near your folks' place this morning." Joel said. "There was some damage to the road just down a bit from their house. I can drop you off, and maybe you can find out what happened."

Parks thanked Darla for everything before he climbed into Joel's rig. He didn't speak as Joel made his way across the city and into the neighboring countryside. The dark feeling he was always battling rose inside, and gripped his throat. He should have been there. If he had been there, she might still be alive. Fear stabbed him as his thoughts returned to Della. Where was she? Rage burned in his chest, and he took comfort in its warmth.

CHAPTER 13

"What makes you so sure they'll have a road block?" Kenzie asked Jim as his uncle pulled into a rest area that overlooked the main bridge into the city.

"Just an educated guess," Jim replied. "They're gathering up all the county folk, and I'm sure they don't want to miss anybody, so we'll have to be extra cautious not to be seen."

James parked at the far end, away from any other travelers, and kept the motor home idling while they prepared for their next move. They all gathered around the tiny table in the small living quarters for one last conversation.

"I'm sure they won't search in here," Jim said confidently, squeezing Rita's hand. "I don't think they'll be looking for people sneaking into the city, since they're actively asking for people to come. However, they may want to know why you're bringing this big thing in."

"That's easy enough to explain," Jim's uncle replied. "I'll tell them we're planning on spending the weekend here, and we're too cheap to pay for a hotel room."

"And they would be right," Lori said coyly.

"The larger question is, where do we go once we're in?" Rita asked. "They may follow us, or lead us to that awful Citadel."

"We have to get to my friend Normand's place," Kenzie said. "He lives down on the West side off 4th avenue in an apartment complex. It won't be easy to get there unnoticed in this thing, though. We're like a giant moving billboard."

"Just leave that to me," his uncle replied.

He settled everyone into their hiding places, and slowly pulled out of the rest area, joining trucks and other vehicles heading towards the city. The wide, three-lane freeway wound down the steep incline before it reached the large bridge which crossed the river on the east side. The bridge dumped traffic from the country into the outer fringes of the city limits. On the north side of the freeway, the landscape was dotted with small ponds, wetlands, and an occasional home or two. The south side was filled with residential neighborhoods. A large roundabout sitting at the foot of the bridge absorbed both east and westbound traffic, dispersing them accordingly.

His uncle took note that traffic seemed to be only coming into the city; there were no vehicles leaving on the outbound lanes for the country, but there were no road blocks up either. As he crossed over, however, he spotted several black vehicles parked along the side of the road. One of them pulled in behind him.

"Are you speeding, James?" Lori asked nervously.

"No, I'm not," he answered a little defensively, checking the speedometer.

"Can't you drive a little less suspiciously?" she asked, looking out the rear-view mirror.

"I don't know what you're talking about, dear," James replied. "I'm driving as nonchalantly as I can."

Suddenly, the black car raced past, and disappeared up the road.

"Whew!" James said with a sigh of relief. "I guess they didn't want us after all. You guys can get out now."

Multiple hiding places began opening when James turned off the freeway, onto a seldom-used side road, and rounded a blind corner. He was shocked to see the same black car blocking the road. W There were several men with weapons, and they motioned for him to stop.

"Get back in," James shouted. "This thing's not over yet."

He pulled up, and rolled down the window as one of the men approached the driver's side. Another one went around behind the RV.

"How can I help you?" James asked innocently.

"Identification and registration please," the man demanded gruffly.

Lori opened the glove box, and handed her husband the information. The other cadet opened the side door, and stepped up inside the motor home.

"Where are you heading?" The first cadet asked, examining their papers.

"We got this invitation," James replied, grabbing the sheet off the dash, and handing it out the window. "It seems we might be getting some money, and a bonus or something. You know a guy can't turn down free money nowadays. Besides, it gives the wife a chance to do some shopping while we're in town. Probably just a wash, though, unless they're giving away a whole lot of money."

The Cadet looked past James and smiled at his partner.

"You missed the turnoff back there," he said, handing back their paperwork. "Just go up the road about a mile, and you'll find a spot large enough to turn this thing around."

"Thank you, sir," James replied. "Yeah, it's been awhile since I've been in this neck of the woods. Glad you came along when you did."

They got back in their car, and James watched while they pulled a U-turn, and headed in the other direction.

"Good job!" Jim exclaimed as he squeezed in between his aunt and uncle in the front seat. "You guys are great at this cloak and dagger stuff. Now, what did you mean by "leave that to me"?"

"I'll show you," His uncle said as he took another turn onto one of the roads heading towards the river, "but we'll need to get out of sight fast. They might come back, and I won't have any believable explanations the second time."

The large motor home lumbered down the street, and turned onto a narrow, seldom-used road. They traveled parallel to the river, passing old homes and farms, and after about forty minutes, pulled up into a wooded parking area next to the river.

"Here we are," James said as he turned off the motor.

"Where is here?" Kenzie asked.

She stepped outside, and looked around.

"I know where," Rita said. "My father and I used to fish up and down this river, and this was a great camping area. It was like a small park the last time I was here, but not anymore."

"We used to come here too," Lori said as she climbed out. But you're right; it doesn't look like people come down here much nowadays. There used to be some tables, and a covered area just up the bank a little, but the trail is so overgrown."

She pointed at a narrow path covered with blackberry bushes.

"Yeah, from what we hear, Management doesn't like people's disturbing the natural setting." James said as he walked to the rear of the motor home. "But I think that's just a lame excuse. What they really don't like is people having fun, period. All the years we came here, this place was immaculate. Now look at it. There's trash everywhere. The back of the river is overgrown. It's sad."

"Nice reminiscing, but we didn't come here to talk or fish," Jim said a little impatiently. "You mentioned you have something that will help us."

"Just hold on," his uncle replied.

He unlocked a storage compartment tucked under the rear of the RV.

Inside was a small jeep. He pulled ramps out of two slots, released the tie-downs holding it in place, and grabbed the bumper. The jeep rolled down. James stepped around, and set the parking brake.

"That's pretty sweet!" Kenzie exclaimed.

"We haven't used it in years, but it's in good shape, and ready to go." James said proudly. He snapped the windshield in place, and put up the canvas top. "It gets great gas mileage, and should work just fine for getting the four of you wherever you need to go. Lori and I will stay here, and enjoy the fishing while you're gone. I hear the salmon are running right now. Besides, if we get bored and want to go somewhere, I still have two mopeds tucked inside."

Jim, Rita, Dr. Larson, and Kenzie smothered his aunt and uncle with hugs and thanks. They didn't know if they would ever see each other again, but no one spoke of it. Rita took the driver's seat, Jim sat beside her in front, and Kenzie and Dr. Larson squeezed into the small rear seat.

"Where are we going?" Rita asked as they drove down the narrow, graveled road.

"We need to stay on the back roads," Kenzie answered. "Let's follow the river towards the city wall, and double back through the side streets. Then we can head to Normand's apartment, and start working on our next move."

"Just what is our next move?" Dr. Larson asked, looking out the side window, and catching glimpses of the river through the tall grass as they drove along. "We barely escaped the city with our lives the last time we were here, and now we're back."

"Our plan will have to be pretty aggressive," Kenzie responded. "We know they have a lot of resources. Guns, men, other weapons, organization--you name it, they have it.

"How can we fight them?" Dr. Larson said. "Are you saying the four of us are going to start some sort of revolution?"

"It's already started," Kenzie said bluntly. "The resistance has been building, and we've been training for this most of our lives."

"That's encouraging," Jim said, glancing over his shoulder at Kenzie. "However, between now and this epic battle you envision, I think we better be smart, and keep our heads on straight. There are a lot of innocent people who might get hurt. I suggest we find your friend Normand, and start there. We'll need a plan with an escape option before we get in too deep."

"I agree," Rita replied.

They were approaching the city wall now, and she turned down one of the back streets.

She made sure to take every side road she could find, and soon they were in a less affluent section of the city. She pulled up to a stop sign, and waited as a young mother with two small children crossed.

"Normand's home," Kenzie said as they rounded the corner to an apartment complex. "That's his car parked out front."

Rita pulled up alongside Normand's car, and waited as Kenzie went to the door. It was a modest building, with small trees planted along the walkways, and a narrow strip of mowed grass on each side of the sidewalk. Kenzie looked around carefully before climbing the three steps to the small porch and hitting the doorbell.

The door opened slowly. Normand peeked out, with the chain still latched.

"Kenzie, come in, but hurry," Normand said, fumbling with the chain.

She quickly waved to the others, and in a matter of seconds, they were all inside.

"It's good to see you, Kenzie," Normand said as they moved into his darkened living room. "I've been checking all over for you."

The window shades were drawn and the only light came from one small table lamp.

"Hey, Dr. Larson," Normand greeted her, "it's really good to see you too!"

"Good to see you again also," Dr. Larson replied. "This is Jim Banner and Rita."

"We know each other very well." Jim said with a smile as he shook Normand's hand. "If it wasn't for this young man here, I would still be in jail under that blasted Citadel."

"This place smells kind of musty," Kenzie observed as she sat on the edge of his couch. "Maybe you should air the place out a bit."

"I'm not staying here anymore than I have to." Normand replied quickly. "Especially since that little guy in a dark suit broke in here, and tried to take me apart."

"You were attacked?" Kenzie said at once.

"It was a weird moment, I must admit. "I had to use the ring Parks gave me to get rid of him. Anyway, I can explain it later, but I've made some coffee if anyone would like a cup."

"That sounds good," Jim said.

Normand led the way to a small kitchen. It consisted of four wobbly chairs set around a bright orange table, with a small stove crammed between the fridge and sink. A microwave covered most of what little counter there was. Normand handed out a hodgepodge assortment of coffee cups, pulled a stool out of the small broom closet adjacent to the kitchen, and sat down with the others.

"What's been going on?" he asked intently. "Is everybody ok?"

"It's a long story," Kenzie replied. "We've a lot to explain, but not much time. The short version is Management is pulling people from the country into the city with the promise of money, but they are not returning home to their farms. That's all we know."

"Have you heard anything about this?" Jim asked from across the table.

"I know a little," Normand replied. "In the past several weeks or so as I've been delivering to the Citadel, I've seen all different types of vehicles coming in. In fact, one afternoon I saw at least three car loads of families pull in. There were children, parents, and grandparents.

"I didn't think much of it at first, but then I noticed several of the Cadets climb into the cars, and drive them around behind the building. It's not like they have valet parking or anything, so I became curious. I had one more pickup along the rear, so I quickly finished what I was doing, and drove around behind.

"I got there just in time to see several workers closing the rear doors on a large black cargo van. I caught a glimpse of the rear of one of the vehicles. It was the one I had just seen. Anyway, I went about my business, but when I was finished and started towards the main gate, I fell in behind that same semi-truck.

"Out of curiosity, I followed it for a while, and then realized they were headed for the outer city gate. I stayed back, and parked on a high ridge where I watched as they went through the gate. They disappeared into the wilderness, and were gone. You can call that anything you want, but I say that's some weird crap."

"I doubt they're starting a used car lot," Jim interjected as he pushed himself away from the table. "This may just be a new version of what I reported on last winter, only now they're sending vehicles into the wilderness. But what are they doing with the people, and why?"

"There's more," Normand continued. "Have you heard what happened to Isaac?"

"Something happened to Isaac?" Kenzie asked anxiously.

"He's at the surgery center over by the hospital," Normand replied quietly.

"Oh, no!" Kenzie gasped. "Is he ok?"

"I found him on my doorstep early this morning. He'd been beaten pretty badly, so David and I took him to Dr. Flint's office, and he sent us to see a Dr. Stevens. I had to go to work, but David's been with him all day and called around noon to report he was out of surgery. I was just about to head over there when you came."

"Dr. Stevens is one of the best surgeons we have," Dr. Larson said, squeezing Kenzie's arm. "Whatever's happened, you can rest assured he's in the best of hands."

"Let's go over there now," Kenzie said, getting up from the table.

"I agree," Jim replied. "There should be room in that big truck of yours for all of us."

"That's not a good idea." Normand answered. "I know you all want to see him, but I've been warned to stay away as much as possible. According to David, people are looking for him, and he's being kept there under a false name. Someone might spot us, and then who knows what could happen."

"Why don't you and Kenzie go," Dr. Larson said gently. "We'll wait here, if that's ok. The two of you should be able to get in without drawing attention."

"Alright, I say we do it," Normand replied after thinking for a moment. "I can park up the street and hide my truck just to be safe, but if we're not back here by eleven, I strongly suggest you get the heck out. Whoever came here last time could come back again."

Normand and Kenzie climbed into his truck, and headed off towards the surgery center. The more Jim thought about it, the more certain he became that someone had to be working with Management. His mind began to darken as he thought about the tracking device in the cigar ring. He tapped his coffee cup with his fingernail as he stared at Rita sitting across the table from him.

CHAPTER 14

David went to his parent's house to spend the day. He hadn't seen them since they had left the city. He was confident they were safe, but the house was lonely and cold without them. Also, Management was probably keeping an eye on it, so he didn't come too often. He backed his truck into the garage, and stored it out of sight before going inside. He laid his head on his folded arms on the kitchen table, and was nearly asleep when suddenly the doorbell rang.

He crept down the hall to the front entry, and peered up under the curtains that covered a long window on one side of the door.

It was Mrs. Cantrell, the crazy old lady from next door.

He stayed still for a bit, watching the tiny, gray-haired woman ring the bell again and again. Finally he decided it would be best to answer the door, and get rid of her. He didn't want her making a scene, or calling security.

"Mrs. Cantrell," he said, stretching, and faking a yawn as he opened the door. "Can I help you?"

"I saw someone park in the garage," the old lady replied, looking up at David over her horn-rimmed glasses. "Is your mom at home?"

"Sorry, no," he said, trying to appear uninterested. "She's on a long vacation, you know, since Dad died."

"I really wanted to see her," The old lady said, peering around David into the darkened house. "I let her borrow some things, and I would like to get them back."

"Maybe you could make me a list, and I'll look for them for you," David said quickly, blocking the opening with his body.

"Why, that's a great idea," the old woman said warmly. "I have some paper and a pen across the street. Why don't you come over with me? I just made some fresh chocolate chip cookies," she said with a smile, "and I've got milk!"

David weighed his options for a moment, but then remembered the old woman and her husband. They were long-time neighbors, but her husband had died mysteriously years ago. He decided it would be easier to go to her home rather than let her snoop around in his parent's house. There was no telling what might be lying around.

He walked with the old lady down the walkway, and crossed the street to her house. The sun shone warmly, and Mrs. Cantrell chattered about her flowers. She spoke as if they were alive, but the flower beds were dead, and covered with weeds. Yet, she waived at them with her small boney hand as if to show off a beautiful display of color. David felt bad thinking age had done its worst.

He gently held her slender arm as she took each rotten step to the dingy wooden door with a half-moon window at the top. She gripped the handle, and the door opened with a long squeak. His eyes were still adjusting to the darkened room as he stepped onto the worn red carpeting.

There was a noticeable odor, and not one that he expected. The place felt like a mausoleum. An even layer of dust covered nearly everything, and cobwebs hung from lamps scattered about the room. The shades were drawn so tight, no natural light could come through, and the only illumination came from an old chandelier hung in the middle of the living room with all but two of the bulbs burned out. Mrs. Cantrell shut the door behind them, and flipped the deadbolt.

"Please sit," she said, gesturing towards a dark blue worn out couch as she sat in a rocker in similar condition.

"I really can't stay," David answered, suddenly feeling uncomfortable. "I just need that list, and then I need to go."

"It's so nice to have you here," she said gently as she rocked a bit. "You know, I don't think I've had a single visitor since my late husband died. But I've watched you grow up across the street, and you seem like such a nice young man."

He felt a little guilty for not being more hospitable, and brushed a spot on the couch before taking a seat on the edge.

"There's been so much going on lately, and I really miss your mom," she continued, rocking steadily. "Such a gracious lady. When do you expect her back?"

"Not for a while."

He was relieved the old woman hadn't offered any cookies. The smell in the house was beginning to make his stomach queasy.

"I really should get going," he said, getting up from the couch.

"Oh, just a few more minutes," Mrs. Cantrell pleaded. "What about you? What are you doing?"

David eased back down reluctantly. It was clear this woman wanted to talk, but the house was horrible. Maybe he could get some of his friends to come over and clean it for her. She was very old, and obviously not able to manage. It would take some doing, but they could definitely turn this place around for her.

"Just finished college," he answered brightly, "and I'm looking forward to getting my career going."

"Is that all you have going?" she asked pointedly, staring at him over the top of her glasses.

"I work out at the gym some," he replied lightly, ignoring the changing tone of her voice.

"That's not what I mean," Mrs. Cantrell said.

She stopped rocking, and opened the top drawer on a small table next to her chair. She reached in as David glanced over towards what appeared to be the kitchen. It was time for the list and he expected her to produce a pen and paper.

But, it was not a pen and paper and before he knew what was happening, she had gotten up from her seat, and moved halfway across the room towards where he was sitting. In her hand was a long knife, and she was coming in the direction of his throat.

"What the?!" he exclaimed, sliding back into the couch to gain a little space between him and the sharp instrument.

"You know more than you're telling," the old woman said, suddenly looking much less frail. "You and that bitch of a mother of yours are holding something I need. You have one of the gifts."

"What gift?"

"I didn't say gift I said GIFTS!" the old lady nearly screamed. "I'm only going to ask you one more time before I cut you into little pieces, and plant you with my husband in the backyard."

David's mind was reeling. He vaguely heard her saying things about Management, another city, her city that was destroyed violently, and how she managed to deal her way out.

Then he spotted his opportunity, and kicked her arm. The knife flew straight up into the ceiling, where it stuck fast. The woman screamed wildly, her eyes inflamed with anger. He jumped up, only to be met with a strike from the woman's right hand that sent him sailing over the back of the couch and into the dusty curtains. The power of the old lady's punch was amazing.

He looked up from behind the couch just in time to watch her leap, and grab the handle of the knife stuck in the twelve-foot ceiling. She planted both feet on the ceiling, pulled it free, and dropped to the floor like a cat.

He grabbed the couch, lifting it off the floor, and rammed her with it. She stabbed wildly in such a rapid fashion, the air was filled with couch stuffing. He pinned her into a corner, her eyes burning red. Then she braced herself against the wall, and pushed back.

To his amazement, his feet began sliding across the carpeted floor, and he couldn't find enough traction to resist her. The old lady glared at him with such hatred, it shook him to his core.

As he slid past a small table, he grabbed an old lamp, and swung the heavy base across the top of the couch, and into the side of the old woman's head. The impact sent her flying across the room and into a wall, where she crumpled into a small, bony, lifeless heap. He dropped the couch, and staggered back. He was sure he had killed her, but had no idea what to do next.

Suddenly, to his horror, she began to move. Mrs. Cantrell lifted her head and looked hard at him, the left side of her skull caved in by the force of his blow. He darted towards the front door as she rose to her feet. She picked up the knife with one hand, and shoved the couch out of her way with the other.

Panic washed over David as he fumbled with the lock. Finally it flipped open, and he hit the porch running. The woman screamed in a voice that sent shivers up his spine. Fortunately, he had the garage opener in his pocket. He slid under when the door was only halfway open, and jumped into his truck. It roared to life, and burst out of the garage, ripping the bottom section off the partially open garage door.

At the same time, Mrs. Cantrell jumped off her porch. He lurched onto the street, and swerved at the last instant to avoid hitting her, but as he passed, he felt a searing pain in his chest. She had buried the knife up to its handle in the truck door. It punched through the metal like butter, and penetrated his left side just below the rib cage. He was barely able to drive down the street, and fought to retain consciousness as he turned towards the surgery center. He pulled in just as Kenzie was arriving.

"David!" he exclaimed as she ran up not noticing the handle of the knife protruding from the side of the door as he lowered the window. "Are you alright?" she asked seeing the ashen look on his face.

"No," he said weakly. "I don't think I'm going to make it. That blade is deep in my side, and I can't open the door to pull it out."

Kenzie stepped back, realizing the gravity of the situation as a trickle of blood ran down the handle and dripped on the ground.

"Get a doctor fast," she yelled to Normand, who was walking towards them. "It's an emergency. David's hurt, and we need help NOW!"

"It's too late," David groaned. He slumped over the steering wheel.

Normand ran into the building to find a doctor. In a few moments, a team of doctors and nurses surrounded the truck. One of the young doctors suggested they pull the door open, and rush him inside, but another doctor disagreed, saying that might actually kill him. Pulling the knife would cause him to quickly bleed out. In the meantime, one nurse checked his vitals through the window, and another had climbed in from the passenger side and started an IV. Kenzie wanted to scream at them as they stood there, considering their options. She almost did start screaming, but just then, a small jeep pulled up, and Dr. Larson jumped out.

"Get me a sliding board," she ordered, quickly assessing the situation before climbing in the side door. "I'll need some surgical gloves, gown, and a full set of surgical instruments, plus a gurney."

The two doctors looked at each other, and one started to question her authority, when Kenzie stepped in.

"Get Dr. Larson what she needs right now!" she shouted.

The doctor took one look at Kenzie's face, and headed inside. In a few moments, he was back with exactly what Dr. Larson requested.

"We need to slide the board under him from inside the truck," she said, "and pull him straight over and off the blade."

She carefully cut the clothing from around the wound with a pair of scissors. "I'll pack it with gauze, and keep pressure on it while you move him," she continued. "He's bleeding internally, and it's likely to get worse once the blade is out, so we will have to move quickly, and get him prepped for surgery. Once he's on the gurney, I'll get scrubbed, and meet you in the surgery room."

Dr. Larson lifted David's leg as the second doctor slid the board under his buttocks. Two nurses worked in tandem, making sure the IV site and medications moved with David's body. It was a tight fit. Kenzie supported his upper body through the window as they slid him towards the passenger side, where the gurney was waiting. Dr. Larson squeezed tight against the dashboard as David passed, keeping constant pressure on his wound.

The entire process took only a few seconds, but it seemed like an eternity.

"Hold pressure right here," Dr. Larson instructed Normand as he came around the truck. "Go, go, GO!" she commanded the attendants. "I'll meet you inside." She took off for the surgery center on a dead run.

"I don't understand what's going on anymore," Kenzie said, fighting back the tears. "First Isaac, and now David. Why are people trying to hurt us, and how would Dr. Larson know to come here?"

"I called her when I went looking for a doctor," Normand answered, wiping David's blood off his hands with a towel. "I wasn't sure she would make it in time, but I'm glad she did. Remember how great she was when Parks rescued us from the Testers that day, and led us into the Citadel? If it hadn't been for Dr. Larson, none of us would be here."

Normand and Kenzie snuck into Isaac's room in intensive care to wait while David went into surgery. Kenzie sat by Isaac's side for a long time, stroking his hand, and watching him breathe. She purposely ignored the chest tube draining blood from his side into a collection chamber. The hours crept by as they waited for word.

Finally a weary Dr. Larson appeared in the doorway.

"Is David ok?" Normand asked anxiously.

"He's holding his own," she replied gently. "The knife penetrated his left lung, and lacerated one of his kidneys. It'll be a while before we know if I got the bleeding stopped. Does anyone know what happened?"

"We have no idea," Normand replied as he and Kenzie followed Dr. Larson into the hall. "It's freaking me out. Isaac gets beat to a pulp, and left with a hollow tube sticking out of his chest, and David gets stabbed through his truck door."

Dr. Larson sat with Kenzie in the waiting room while Normand went looking for coffee.

"They're going to be ok," she said comfortingly, squeezing Kenzie's hand. "I'm sure of it. You're all really more like family than friends aren't you? They're going to be ok. I mean it!"

"We've been through a lot together," Kenzie replied. "But none of us expected this."

Just then, Normand returned with three coffees. They sat talking quietly for a while before Dr. Larson left to check on David's progress. She returned in less than a half hour with encouraging news.

"I know it's early, but I like what I'm seeing. Hey, there's nothing you can do here. Why don't you two go home? You both need the rest, and I'll let you know as soon as there's any change."

"You'll call right away?" Kenzie asked.

"You know I will."

They reluctantly agreed, and Normand drove Kenzie back to his apartment. They were trying to stay calm in spite of everything, but it wasn't easy.

At the surgery center, Dr. Larson had just returned to the intensive care unit to check on David's progress a second time when a nurse poked her head in.

"There's someone at the front desk asking for you," she said. "I told him I would see if I could find you. I think it's important."

"Ok," Dr. Larson replied, making some notes on David's chart. "Make sure you check on him every ten minutes. I need to know the moment there's any change."

She wondered if it was Normand at the desk. It would be just like him to refuse rest while his friends were hurt.

"Dr. Della Larson," came an all-too-familiar voice as she rounded the corner.

"Barron!" she stammered, stopping cold in her tracks. "What are you doing here?"

"Your doctor friends gave me a call. It seems they were concerned to see you in action again," he answered, grabbing her by the arm. "They value their freedom, and don't mind reporting a fugitive, even if it is a fellow doctor. Come on, we need to have a little conversation, and some alone time."

Barron started down the hall, pulling Dr. Larson along through the heavy glass doors, and into the night.

CHAPTER 15

Joel's gravel truck slowly made its way into the nearby country on the city side of the river. Parks rode in silence, thinking about his mother. Finally, after an uneventful drive, familiar scenery greeted him, as they pulled onto the road leading to his parents' house. Joel apologized for not being able to take him all the way as he had to stop at the gravel pit, but he didn't mind. He thanked Joel, and shut the truck door. He needed to burn some energy, and jogging fit the bill. After several miles, he paused at the spot along the road where the Testers had crossed, and his mother died. The ground stretching in either direction was ripped up and small trees were overturned.

Squatting down, he heaved a deep sigh before returning to his jogging pace. It wasn't long before the house came into view. He sprinted the rest of the way up the long driveway before slowing to a walk, and climbing onto the porch. He opened the screen door, and was about to grab the handle of the kitchen door when it opened.

"Henry!" Kirsten exclaimed, "I saw you coming up the driveway. It's really good to see you." She gave him a solid hug. "Come in. Dad's in the living room."

The living room was warm, and well-lit from sunlight streaming through the windows. His mother loved plants and flowers, and always kept something growing in front of nearly every one. "They make the house feel alive," she always said, and Parks could almost feel the warmth of her kind embrace as he followed his sister.

"Hello, Dad," he said tenderly.

Mr. Parks sat quietly, staring out the front window. Standing seemed to take an extraordinary amount of effort as he got up, and pulled his son close.

"Welcome home, son," Mr. Parks said, holding Henry by the shoulders.

Parks helped his father settle back in his chair, and sat on the edge of the couch. The older Mr. Parks stared lovingly at his son, but did not speak.

"I'll go make some coffee," Kirsten said brightly, and she hurried off to the kitchen.

"What happened, Dad?" Parks asked, breaking the silence at last.

"I really don't know, son," Mr. Parks replied. "It's all very confusing."

"Here you go," Kirsten said, returning with the coffee.

"Thanks, Sis."

Kirsten placed a tray on the table, and sat across from her father.

"What can you tell me?"

"It's hard to understand where to start," She volunteered, seeing her father lower his head, and bite his lip. "For some unknown reason, Testers were moving en masse across the road, and Mom just happened to be driving over to a friend's house at the very moment they were crossing. She got hit, and then trapped."

Her voice cracked, and tears welled up in her eyes.

"I should have been here," Parks said, with a tinge of anger rising in his voice. "I never should have left the city."

"No!" Mr. Parks said emphatically, turning towards his son. "You're not to blame. No one could have changed what happened. It was an accident."

"This was no accident, Dad," Parks answered, becoming increasingly agitated. "There should be no Testers anywhere, anytime. What were they doing out here?

"We don't know," Kirsten said. "They were heading in the direction of the city, but that's all I know."

"Well, I know Testers don't appear accidentally," Parks growled. "They're always around when bad things happen."

"I'm working with the resistance, and we'll stop them," Kirsten said. "They'll pay for what they've done, but we just have to be patient, and not give anything away to Management until we're ready."

"I don't give a rip about Management," Parks retorted, rising from his seat. "I was out chasing rainbows while my mother was killed, and I have yet to find Della. I tell you, I haven't had a moment's peace since this book came into my life."

He pulled the small black book from inside his vest, and slammed it down on the coffee table. "I've been trying to figure this thing out, and all it does is cause me grief. Now look what it's done."

He stared down at it, his fists clenched at his side, and his body tight as steel.

"I had a chance a long time ago to stop these people, but I didn't," he continued. "I was trying hard to make things right, but I should have taken my crystal blades…"

Parks's voice trailed off when he saw the shock on Kirsten's and his father's faces. He stood frozen for a moment, and something caught his eye. In the long, beveled mirror set behind the mantle, he could see two glowing red eyes. Instantly, he jumped to one side and wheeled around, ready to fight. Nothing was there; just the hallway that led to the kitchen, and it was empty.

"Are you alright?" Kirsten said, grabbing Parks by the arm.

"Didn't you see that?" he said, jerking his arm away, and rushing into the hall.

"See what?" his father asked. He got up from his chair, and joined his son in the hallway. "I don't see anything. Maybe it was a shadow or something."

Parks ran into the kitchen, glanced around, and then back to the porch, but found nothing.

"Come back in and sit down," Mr. Parks said encouragingly. "We need to talk some more."

But Parks didn't feel like sitting. He paced the room and hallway several times, as the anger grew ever more powerful, with new and ugly feelings creeping in. Finally he managed to compose himself enough to sit back down, and listen to his father.

"I miss your mother more than anything in the world," Philip Parks said. He got up, walked over to one of the wide windows, and stood there for a long time before continuing.

"Your mom loved you two more than anything, and we loved her." He pulled a book from a tall bookcase and returned sitting on the couch between Kirsten and Henry, taking their hands. "We're not done grieving yet, but we are moving on. She would have wanted it that way, but before we do, let's honor her memory."

They sat there, holding hands. Henry and Kirsten each took a moment to share something special. Kirsten remembered the days she spent with her mother gardening in the greenhouse and Henry spoke of her never missing one of his ball games when he was growing up. They traded off many other stories and Mr. Parks waited until they were done before speaking.

"When you were kids, I told you the story of the city," he said, picking up the large, ornate old book he had pulled from the bookcase. "I read stories to you from this when you were little, and I know you were frightened at times from the scary pictures. But these stories had been told for so long, I think most of us just thought of them as fables.

"However, that day in the cave when the Zender attacked you was the day I felt it was real. And I can tell you it took years for your mother to forgive me for taking you and your sister on that fateful hunting trip to Grace Mountain. She was really scared when you were in the hospital, and thought we had lost you. Needless to say, I've been watching you both very closely ever since.

"Now it seems ridiculous to try and guide you along from a distance. It's time for me to step up, and get involved. It was nice being retired, and living out here with your mother. Well, that's obviously over, and you need to be careful from here on out," Mr. Parks said, making eye contact with Kirsten. "Management is very powerful, and they're running things in a direction that can only lead to one conclusion. They're planning to fulfill the story. They're going to destroy the city, and kill everyone in it."

"Dad!" Kirsten gasped. "I know Management is up to something, but wouldn't they have killed us all by now if the story is true?"

"Not necessarily, Kirsten. Remember, in the stories, people fought back, but we didn't, we surrendered. That's different. Not everyone in Management is bad. Some of them are our friends and neighbors."

"They're not all good either," Parks said, sensing the anger rising again, "especially the ones running the Citadel."

"Yes, that seems to be the center of things for sure," Mr. Parks replied, "but that's only the surface of the problem. The story I told you when you were little describes the coming of the Zender. The beast that attacked you, the one you believe you destroyed. But I don't think I ever told you much about the Dark Matter. It's the one part of the story none of us liked telling, the main reason being nobody really understood it. Dark Matter was a force that crept into the city in the dead of night, and stole the light from every corner, leaving only fear in its wake. Some say it's not real, but we know that it is."

Mr. Parks picked up his coffee, and took a few sips. His face was long, and his brow furrowed as he thought for a few moments. It was easy for Henry and Kirsten to see the strain on him.

"Our ancestors did their best to explain it," he continued, "but all they had for us were stories and poems without answers. Nothing that really explained the destruction of the city ages ago. The ancient story said the Dark Matter was what, in the end, destroyed everything. They didn't understand it either, but did their duty, and passed the story on, generation to generation. I guess the hope was someone would eventually figure it out, and end the cycle once and for all."

Mr. Parks opened the book to the back page, and took a piece of folded paper from inside the dust cover.

"This is a poem we were given to memorize," he said. "It's supposed to hold a secret that unlocks the truth:

> The light came down and hit the ground,
> Followed close by tooth and claw.
> When it tore at flesh and bone, its face we finally saw.
> A man we said with hopes held high relentless in his fight,
> But then the darkness pulled him down despite his great might.
> To our end we come to rest upon this darkest night.
> Where fear and fire burn our minds and lost hope leaves grave desire.
> Then I came upon him once again, standing in the dark.

There he turned, and with a smile, returned to us our
hearts.

The days, he said, of losing fast are done by one great
thing,

That man is more, you see, than measured by what he has.

Look up, he said, with hope restored to where the light
flows in,

And know the day darkness came is when it met its end.

"What does it mean, Dad?"

"I wish I knew, son, I wish I knew," Mr. Parks answered.
"We have a mystery filled with death and destruction that could
be starting all over again unless someone can solve the riddle.
Anyway, I'm going into the city to meet with Rich Lindberg. He
and I spoke of this long ago when you were injured, but we
haven't met but a few times since. He's still head of the city
fathers, and may know something."

He handed Parks the slip of paper.

"I need to meet some people too," Parks said, folding the
paper, and sliding it inside the black book. "And you're right,
Dad; there are things to do."

"I'll take you guys wherever you want to go," Kirsten
volunteered. "But are you sure you're up for this, Dad?"

"The time for worrying about me is over," Mr. Parks said
as he headed towards the kitchen. "Your mother would have
insisted I get my butt in gear, and do something. She would never
let me sit around and mope. But it's going to take some time for
me to get organized and set things up, so I won't be going
anywhere today."

"That's ok," Parks responded as he followed his father. "I
know where I need to go, but I don't know if I want you tagging
along. It would be better for you to stay here with Dad, and let
me do my thing."

"Your motorcycle's in the barn," his father said. "Why
don't you take it?"

"I thought Kirsten might have sold it by now," Parks
replied.

"Not a chance," Kirsten said. "I ride that thing every
chance I get, and there's even a full can of gas in the shed."

Parks grabbed his coat, and headed for the door.

"Hang on a second," she said, opening one of the hall closets. "You're going to need this, if for nothing else than to hide that face of yours."

"Thanks," Henry said as he took the motorcycle helmet with a black face shield. "I'll be back later."

He stopped at the shed, and grabbed the gas can before heading to the barn. The door slid open easily, and he reached in for the light switch. The barn was full of old machinery from their farming days, but there was some new stuff too, especially the large lawnmower his mom had purchased for his dad's seventieth birthday last year.

He found the motorcycle leaning against the back wall, and pushed it into the yard. It was a dark red, 500cc street-legal dirt bike. He topped the tank off, gave it a kick start, and revved it up as it roared to life. He pulled the helmet on, waved to Kirsten and his Dad watching from the porch, and popped a wheelie as he roared down the driveway and onto the road towards the city.

The warm air whistled past his heavy leather coat as he cruised along. The repairs to the damaged road were complete, and the county road crew had gathered their equipment, and left. As much as Parks enjoyed riding his old motorcycle though, he was in no mood for fun. Dark feelings rose, and penetrated his mind with violent thoughts as he headed towards his destination. The thoughts were growing stronger, and his desire to resist them was fading. They were becoming so powerful, he had even forgotten his real priority: finding Della.

CHAPTER 16

"Birgit," Harry barked into the intercom, "Get General Allison up here right now!"

"Yes sir," came the quick reply.

Harry walked over to the window, folded his hands behind his back and looked over the new cadets lining up along the training ground below. They were about to start their morning exercises. Harry's new directives were in play as the men faced off with a new sword-like weapon recently developed. The men practiced fighting each other, each outfitted with plenty of padding and protection, including a small shield. If he didn't know better, Harry would have thought he was watching an ancient gladiator event.

But he did know better. The weapons they were training with were just prototypes. The research department had taken red crystals provided by the board, and built a weapon that reminded Harry of Parks' blade. When the crystal was inserted into the handle, it became something much more.

"Is the old goat in a bad mood?" A tall, hawk-nosed young woman with dirty blonde hair asked as she stepped off the elevator.

"Seemed a little tense this morning," Birgit answered as she got up from her desk. "Would you like some coffee?"

"Better not," she replied as she walked through the doors towards his office, "I'll see what he wants first."

"Hi, Pops," the woman said lightly as she walked in without knocking.

"Don't give me that familiarity crap," Harry snapped as he wheeled around, and stormed back to his desk. "We need to talk."

Harry pulled back his chair, and sat down as the woman took the seat across from him. He picked up some papers and glanced over them for a few moments, ignoring her presence.

"Don't think I haven't been watching your screw-ups," Harry said finally.

He slammed the papers down, and looked hard at her. "Ivy, you got this position not only because you're my daughter, but because you have a way of getting things done. That is a skill we need more than ever now. However, that doesn't excuse anything. The board is asking questions, and you need to come up with some answers-now."

"Hey, the Parks deal was not just my thing," Ivy answered defensively. "We had to go out looking for you, remember, after Parks captured you, and left you in the wilderness. If we hadn't found you when we did, you would likely be dead. Since then, I've examined all our people. Someone had to be helping them from the inside. How else could they have escaped from that cell, and got out of the Citadel? And, even though I have yet to find out who was behind their escape, I've dealt with the men who were in charge that day."

"Yeah, yeah, that's old news," Harry injected. "Maybe you get a pass on Parks, but what about the kid you caught. How was he able to get out?"

"I don't know," she answered, agitated by his insistence. "I gave you my report detailing everything that happened."

"I need answers, and I need them now," Harry answered, slamming his gloved fist on the desk. "If you want to keep your job, you'd better find out what's going on here, and fast. I have a meeting later today with the President, and he's going to be hot if I don't have something for him."

"I'm working on it, ok?" Ivy responded coldly. "Hey, how's that new arm of yours working out?" she asked, a tinge of sarcasm in her voice.

"It's fine," Harry replied, working to calm himself. "Ivy, we need to find out what's going on; we're losing control here."

"No, you're losing control," Ivy thought as she stormed out of his office.

Harry's back stiffened as she slammed the door behind her. He lifted his gloved right hand, and manipulated his fingers.

"Parks," he said to himself, "and those blasted crystals of his. I'll see to it he pays if it's the last thing I do."

He had no sooner finished cursing Parks when a sharp pain shot through his neck. The doctors had outfitted Harry with a titanium robotic arm, but they'd had to drill into his collar bone rib-cage to anchor it after the amputation. Crystal sickness would have spread throughout his body, but now his arm was gone, and he had a mechanical replacement to remind him. Harry picked up a metal pen off his desk, and crushed it between his fingers before throwing it into the garbage.

He hated Parks more each time he looked at it.

"I'm going out for a while," Harry said to Birgit, poking his head into the main reception area. "Forward any calls to my cell if they're important; otherwise take a message."

He rode his private elevator to the parking garage below, mumbling to himself and fuming. He squealed the tires on his SUV as he left through the gate and onto the road headed for the heart of the city. Coincidently, Parks was just arriving from a different direction on his motorcycle. They missed each other by only a matter of seconds. Parks pulled off to the side of the road where he wouldn't be seen.

"Looks the same except for that new building in the back," Parks thought, surveying the high concrete wall covered with razor wire, and the heavy steel gates manned by guards toting Nullifiers. "I've never seen a duller, grayer, or more ugly place in my life." Parks murmured as he pulled out, and took the road that followed the perimeter of the compound. "I just don't remember it being this dark."

He hadn't gone more than half a mile when something caught his attention.

He wheeled around, and pulled into an open area between several bushes next to the wall. It looked like someone had been working in that spot. A steel bar gate covering a drainage outlet looked as if it had been recently replaced. The culvert ran under the wall, and he decided to get a closer look.

He pushed his motorcycle out of sight behind some dense bushes. The gate was hinged and secured, but the large lock gave way easily as Parks inserted one of his crystal blades, and twisted.

It was dark inside the culvert. He made sure to pull the gate tight, and hang the lock to avoid unwanted attention. The culvert was long, and traveled underground. He made his way using a small flashlight attached to his key chain, but when the culvert made a turn, he saw light coming from the other end. He switched off his light and proceeded cautiously, listening for any voices or sounds. He heard nothing as he approached, and found another steel gate bent inward, and nearly broken in half.

"Whatever came through here wanted out pretty bad," Parks thought as he examined the damage. "Apparently, maintenance hasn't gotten to this one yet, good for me."

He peered around the corner, and then suddenly realized where he was.

He was under the Citadel.

He stepped into the lighted corridor, keeping low as he checked the cells. There were no residents, which seemed strange. Management always had someone they were unhappy with down there. He made his way up a stone flight of stairs which wound towards the main cell entrance. He flattened himself against the wall as he approached, but from the shadows, he could see the gate was open and unmanned.

"That's weird." Parks said quietly as he walked cautiously though the steel gate. "I can't imagine why they wouldn't have someone stationed down here."

He followed the corridor towards the cadet locker room. He kept expecting to encounter somebody, but there was no one. He entered the empty locker room, and went to the clothing storage locker. There he found a uniform nearly his size. It was a snug fit, but the clothes were much less noticeable than the thick leather coat and pants he had on. He found a duffel bag and packed his clothes, but kept the belt with his crystal blades. Fortunately, the cadet coat was bulky enough to conceal it.

He swung the bag over his shoulder, pulled the cap down tight to cover his face, and headed for the parking garage. He had to go about two hundred feet, and would be exposed for a short time. If someone spotted him, he would have to fight his way out.

Parks cracked one of the double doors, and looked around. There was no one visible, so he started walking as nonchalantly as possible. He was just about to the safety of the underground parking garage when he heard several vehicles approaching, coming around the side of the building. Parks sprinted the final fifty feet, and dove behind one of the large concrete support pillars, but it was apparent they were not after him.

He watched as a parade of various types of vehicles motored past. Cars and trucks of every make and model followed one of Management's black SUVs until they came to a stop in front of the new building Parks had seen from the road. People of all ages began to file out. Some of them were children. Some were stretching and others yawning, but most just began gathering around a sharp-looking young man with a clipboard.

It was Aaron.

Parks watched for a few moments before entering Harry's private elevator. Fortunately when Harry had come down earlier, the elevator door hadn't properly closed. Parks was able to pry it open easily. He pushed the button for the top floor, and the elevator began its ascent. It dinged as the door opened onto a darkened hallway.

He stepped out and moved stealthily towards Harry's door, thankful he could make his way without being seen. He had gone only a few steps down the hall when a heavy steel panel dropped behind him, and a bank of bright lights flashed on. Once his eyes had adjusted from the blinding glare, he was stunned to find himself in a cleverly disguised hall. It looked just like the one leading to Harry's office, except this one was really a well-built steel cell. Parks pulled his crystal blade, and began to examine the room. A heavy steel door sat at the far end of the hall, and the walls were smooth, and disguised to look like painted sheet rock. He was about to cut his way out when he heard someone approaching. He tensed, readying himself for anything.

"Parks?!" came the surprised cry.

It was Birgit. Parks lowered his blade as she rushed in.

"What are you doing here?"

She held him by the shoulders, and looked into his eyes. "It's good to see you, but you can't be here. This isn't good."

"What is this place?" he asked as they stepped out of the steel box.

"It's part of Harry's new security measures," Birgit explained. "There's a combination of numbers you have to push on the elevator, and if you don't do it correctly, it deposits you on this floor and in here. He has an alarm in his office that alerts him if anyone's in here. I heard it, and came down to see who got caught. Up until today, the only people who spent any time in here were three electricians, a few maintenance people, several of Harry's friends who tried to surprise him, and me. I was caught twice."

"How do we get to Harry's office from here?" Parks asked as they walked down the hall.

"I'm real sorry to hear about your mom," Birgit continued, ignoring Parks's question. "She was such a nice lady. Hey, you can't go upstairs!" Birgit exclaimed, taking Parks' arm as he was about to start up. "You can't go up there. You need to get out of here."

"You mentioned my mom," Parks replied, "and I thank you for that. I don't want you to get hurt, but, I need you to do something for me."

"What?" Birgit gasped as Parks explained his plan. "You can't mean it."

"Just trust me on this," he said. "I know what I'm doing. I know you're not part of anything bad going on here; you're one of the good ones."

"Ok, but I have to reset the alarm system and erase the tape first," Birgit replied. "That camera up there in the corner is part of the system, but it runs through my computer. Once I've cleaned it up, I'll make the call, and then leave."

"Alright," Parks said.

He followed her up a narrow set of stairs that ended at a secret door in the hall by Harry's office.

Parks settled into Harry's chair, laid two crystal blades on his desk, and put up his feet. It wasn't long before he heard the elevator ding.

The knob turned, but, instead of Harry, in flooded a stream of cadets, each holding Nullifiers and pointing them at Parks.

"I wouldn't touch those if I were you," Harry said as he parted the line of Cadets. "These guys will blow you out that wall if you so much as move."

"Hey, I just came here to talk," Parks said. "You didn't need to bring an army unless you're scared."

"I'll show you how frightened I am," Harry said.

He walked up to Parks, and hit him square in the face with his gloved hand.

Parks fell backwards over the chair, and onto the floor. The power of Harry's punch had knocked him unconscious.

"That felt good," Harry said with a smile. "Take him downstairs, and put him in his new home. The cell I built should be able to handle Mr. Henry Jacob Parks."

Several cadets grabbed Parks by the arms, with two more on his legs. They took him to the lower floor, tied him up in chains, tossed him into the cell, and slammed the door.

"He'll be alright, won't he?" Birgit asked anxiously as the last of the cadets filed out.

"Don't worry about him," Harry responded. "He's a known criminal, and will get what he's got coming. You, on the other hand, deserve the rest of the day off with pay for your faithful service. Thank you for the call."

Birgit took her coat and hat out of the closet and left, wondering if she had done the right thing.

Meanwhile, Harry was thrilled to finally have Parks safely locked below. His plans were finally beginning to bear fruit. The next step would be talking with Dave, the president, and letting him know the good news. He expected a big bonus for this one.

"This is Harry Allison and I need to speak to the president right away," Harry said confidently into the receiver.

"Hold on for a moment and I'll see if he's available," the woman answered coldly.

"What do you want?" came the annoyed voice as Dave came on the line.

"I've got Parks," Harry said triumphantly. "He's locked up below right now."

"You stupid fool," Dave answered. "Who told you to capture him?"

"Well, you did," Harry answered, surprised by Dave's response. "You have a bounty out on him, remember."

"Yeah, so I do," Dave said, calming a bit. "Well, now that you have him, you probably think you deserve something for it. We'll see about that later. Right now, I want you to bring him over to my office. Do you think you can handle that?"

Harry hung up the phone, incensed by Dave's remark. He kicked his desk so hard, he nearly broke his foot.

"I caught him, and now they want him," Harry fumed as he limped out the door. "That's fine, but not until I have a little chat with him first."

Harry headed down to the cell where Parks lay helpless, his mind full of dark ideas.

CHAPTER 17

"Where are you taking me?" Dr. Larson demanded as Barron shoved her into his SUV, handcuffed her to the door, and put on a blindfold.

"Don't talk, Dr. Larson," Barron said as they pulled out of the parking lot. "We'll have plenty of time for conversation later."

Della sank in the seat, believing the worst. She had known Barron for years when he and Parks were partners, even friends of a sort. But he was very different now. It wasn't just his outward appearance, though his eyes were difficult to look at. They were dark, except for the center, which glowed an eerie red. His hair, once black, was now white as snow.

Della expected to be taken to the Citadel, but it didn't feel like they were going that way. The road became rough, and at times it sounded like they were on gravel. They finally rolled to a stop, and Barron unlocked her handcuffs from the door, and removed her blindfold. She saw a large, dilapidated house surrounded by a high metal fence, with a locked gate between them and the front porch. Inside the fence were two very large, very mean-looking dogs that barked, growled incessantly, and jumped against the fence as Barron approached.

"Here you go, boys," Barron said as he tossed several large pieces of meat he had stuffed in a bag.

The dogs dove, and spent the next few moments fighting ferociously over them. While they were distracted, Barron opened the gate, and dragged her into the house. Once inside, he took off the handcuffs, and stuck them into his coat pocket.

"I don't think I need to worry about your trying to escape," he smirked. "Those two brutes out there don't even like me, and they would tear you apart. I only keep them around to discourage curious neighbors.

He hung his coat in the entry, walked into the nearby living room, and flopped into a large, overstuffed chair.

"What do you want with me, Barron?" she demanded.

"All in good time, Doctor, Please, sit."

Della walked in slowly, and took a seat reluctantly. The room had a musty odor, and the ceiling was full of cobwebs, but it did appear that someone cared enough to wipe the woodwork and keep the furniture dusted. Barron closed his eyes for a moment, and folded his hands under his chin.

"I know what you're thinking," he said after a few minutes. "You think I've kidnapped you to get even with Parks. You may even be thinking I will do bad things to you for the same reason. You couldn't be farther from the truth."

"Then why did you bring me here?"

"I need some answers."

He opened his eyes, and looked at her directly.

"I think you know something, but first we need to get you settled in. I know you're frightened, but I assure you no harm will come to you if you do what I say. You will find food in the fridge, and there's plenty of water. You'll have no trouble finding what you need to cook with in the cupboards and drawers. There are several bedrooms upstairs. Take your pick. I don't sleep in beds, so use any one you like. There's also a bathroom upstairs, and one just down the hall to the left."

He closed his eyes without another word.

Well, that wasn't what she expected from a kidnapper. Despite her fear and confusion, she decided to look the place over. Perhaps she could find an escape route, or some way to protect herself.

The place was large, and must have belonged to a wealthy family at one time. There was a stairway sitting prominently in the center of the entry leading to the upper floor. A long hallway disappeared off to one side, which she imagined led to additional rooms, and she could just make out what appeared to be the kitchen through a serving counter built into the wall. Unfortunately, a diligent search of the kitchen failed to produce a knife, Barron was one step ahead of her.   She   climbed   the stairs to the second floor, and looked over the two bedrooms. From the one facing the front of the house, she could see the chain link fence and the two dogs lying in the shade of the porch. She could also just make out a few buildings on a hill in the distance. There were large warehouses in between which hid the house from the road. She made her way back downstairs, still trying to come up with escape options, but it seemed quite hopeless. Finally, she returned to the living room where Barron was sitting with his eyes closed, and his hands still folded under his chin. She found a chair and sat, watching him.

"Time to talk," Barron said suddenly after nearly an hour of sitting motionlessly.

Dr. Larson, who had dozed off, jumped. She was exhausted from the surgeries, and even in this horrible place, she couldn't help falling asleep.

"First, tell me why you were at the surgery center."

"I left some important things there," she fumbled, not expecting the question. "I thought I could just get in and out quickly, but that didn't work out the way I planned."

"Believable answer, but I don't think that's all there is to the story. You arrived to help a young man in a pickup truck who had been stabbed. You know him; isn't that right?"

"There had been an accident," she replied honestly. "I just happened upon the scene. I guess I was in the right place at the right time."

"So, it wouldn't bother you if I had one of my people get rid of the young man you worked on?"

She jumped to her feet.

"Of course it would bother me! It wouldn't matter whether I knew him or not. He deserves to live. What happened to you anyway, Barron? I knew you were tough, but I never thought you were just a robot killer for Management."

"Ok, ok," he said with a placating smile that didn't reach his eyes. "Please, sit back down. I was just testing. So you save people whether you know them or not, good for you. Well, if you are going to save any more people, you're going to need to tell me something. What do you know about the Gifts?"

"Gifts?"

She sat back down, confused.

"I don't know what you're talking about. You'll have to be more specific."

"Don't try to play me," he growled, slamming his fist on the table. "I want to know what you know. You and that friend of yours, Parks, are right in the middle of things."

She was still frightened, but less than before. Barron seemed unstable, but he hadn't brought her here to hurt her, and she was quickly realizing she had a small advantage.

"Before I say anything further," she said coolly, gathering her wits, "tell me what you think these Gifts can do for you. Even if I did know something, and I'm not saying I do, I'm not going to talk without more information."

Her captor leaned back, and looked her over closely. It seemed that he respected her bravery at least. After a moment, he relaxed into his seat, and leaned his head back again.

"Management has been looking for these Gifts for a long time," he said. "You could have one right now, and not even know it. I've heard the Board talking about them, but the only thing I know for sure is there are seven of them, and whoever has all seven will have unimaginable power."

"Well, I'm sorry to tell you," she said, "I don't know anything about them, so maybe you should just let me go."

"It's not that simple," Barron said.

He walked over to where she was sitting.

"I need you to take a look at this."

He unbuttoned his shirt, and pulled it open. Dr. Larson could see the faint image of a glowing red crystal in the center of his chest.

"What's that?" she asked, leaning in for a closer look.

"A present from some friends," he said, buttoning up his shirt. "I thought they were just pulling out the one that Parks shoved in my chest, but no, they put a different one in. It's killing me; I can feel it every day."

Suddenly, he let out a cry of pain. He dropped to one knee, clutching at his chest.

"Arrgh! Talk later. Get. It. Out."

"What?!"

"Cut this thing out of me," he ordered, sweat pouring down his face.

"But I have no surgical equipment or place to operate," she protested. "Let alone someone to assist, or provide anesthetic."

"Follow me."

He struggled to his feet, and staggered into the kitchen.

A long stainless steel counter with a row of low-hanging lights down the center occupied the middle of the room. It was surrounded by a sink and cupboards on one side, and some old appliances on the other. Natural light filtered into the room through a single dirty window above the sink. The main light came from banks of florescent lights lining the ceiling. Barron tossed two wooden stools from the counter into a side room.

"There you go," he said without any emotion. "Now you have an operating table. For surgical instruments, you'll find this sharper than any blade you've ever used."

He pulled a long thin knife from a sheath that hung on his waist, and handed it to her.

"To get through my rib cage, here is a spreader I made special just for the occasion."

He held up a locking pair of pliers with two wide flanges welded to the jaws.

"Just slide it in, and snap it."

"You can't be serious."

She looked in horror at the crude device.

"I need sterile conditions. There is no telling what's floating in the air right now, let alone what's on these things. At a minimum, the table would have to be scrubbed."

"Not a problem."

He opened a long cupboard door, pulled out a plastic gallon container full of disinfectant, and poured it over the counter until it ran down onto the floor. Then he ripped off his shirt, hopped up, and poured the remainder over his chest.

"This is crazy! I can't just start cutting on you. You could die."

"I'm nearly dead now," he said, reaching out and pulling her close to his face. "This thing is slowly killing me. Don't be afraid to hurt me. I don't feel pain the way normal people do."

He took the blade from her, and stabbed his forearm with it.

"See? No blood, and no pain. Now, let's get on with it."

He handed the knife back, closed his eyes, and relaxed. She froze for a moment, horrified. Then she tightened her jaw, walked around the counter to the sink, and began scrubbing the blade and her hands. She used what was left of the disinfectant, and when she ran out, she grabbed a bottle of dish soap, and continued scrubbing.

"Come on, come on," he said impatiently. "Let's go. I've waited long enough for this moment."

She grabbed a handful of paper towels, and returned to her patient. The counter was higher than she would have liked, so she kicked a wooden crate over, and hopped up on it. Barron's chest was glowing a dark red. It looked like he had swallowed a red light bulb that got stuck halfway down.

"What if it's in your heart?"

"It doesn't matter. It must come out. And if you are thinking of using that blade to cut my throat, just know I'll have enough strength to wring your pretty little neck before I die."

"As if I would," she responded indignantly. "Those kinds of thoughts come from people like you. I try to save lives, not take them."

Barron relaxed again at her words, and closed his eyes as Dr. Larson picked up the blade. She began with a long incision into his left rib cage, cutting through muscle and cartilage. To her amazement, there was no bleeding. Instead, it felt like she was cutting through hard-packed sand. She inserted the crude instrument Barron had made to spread his ribs. They opened easier than expected, but instead of flesh, his chest cavity was filled with what looked like fibrous jell.

His heart and lungs were illumined by the red crystal which actually made her work easier. Unfortunately, the crystal sat squarely on top of his heart, and she couldn't reach it through the narrow opening. She fumbled desperately through some drawers, and finally found an old plastic salad scoop. She took the knife, trimmed the scoop so it would fit inside his chest, and washed it as well as she could.

"You're doing fine." he said, startling her. Open heart surgery patients didn't usually talk during surgery. "I know you can do this."

She cut through the mesh of fiber and muscle that lay between her and the crystal. Once there, she sliced away whatever was growing around the crystal, but she couldn't get behind it where it was attached to his heart. Reaching in with the modified salad scoop, she grabbed the crystal, and began to pull.

It resisted at first, but she pulled harder, and it started coming free. She stretched it as far as she dared, and then Barron groaned.

"I can stop."

It was obvious this was painful, even for him.

"No," he gasped. "Get that thing out of there, no matter what."

She slid the knife blade between the scoop and his chest cavity. He writhed in pain as she carved the crystal free. Yet, in the middle of his agony he suddenly noticed the smell of her hair and instantly became aware of what could have been had he taken a different path but he had chosen Management instead.

Barron drifted in and out of consciousness as she cut the last connective tissue attached to the red crystal. She carefully removed it from his chest, and dropped it onto the paper towel, where it glowed dully. She removed the clamp holding his chest cavity open, and began to sew up the opening with the carpet needle and thin cable wire he had provided. He wasn't bleeding, but his lungs looked like gel. Even his heart had a rubbery appearance, though continued to beat steadily. Something unusual had happened to Barron's body from the presence of the crystal, but there was nothing she could do about that.

"There are no bandages," she said, covering the wound with paper towels.

He was fully conscious now, and he looked relaxed.

"No problem," he said, sitting up and holding the paper towel tight to his chest. "I don't bleed, and I don't care. You've done well."

"You need to rest," she insisted, helping him to his feet. "I just operated on your heart, and you're going to need time to recover!"

"No time. I have to be some place in an hour."

He put his shirt on.

"Stay here until I return. There are more things we need to discuss, but I don't have time for that now."

He grabbed the crystal, wrapped it in the paper towel, and put it in his pocket. Then he took a slab of meat from the fridge, and headed towards the front door. When he opened the door, the two large canines did everything they could to bite him. He knocked one of them back with his knee, and threw the meat into the yard. The two animals jumped off the porch, and repeated their vicious routine.

"They won't hurt you as long as you stay inside."

Barron grabbed his coat and shoulder bag.

"I'll be back later, but in the meantime, make yourself at home."

He jumped into his truck, and left.

"Are you kidding me?" Della said as she watched him drive away from a side window. "Things just couldn't get any weirder!"

She sat for a moment in a nearby chair, considering her options. The many years spent with Parks had given her an advantage. She had learned tactical thinking, and how to turn a bad situation around. She listened to the two animals growling and grunting from the other side of the door, and then an idea struck her. She took a large chair from the living room and a smaller one out of the kitchen. Positioning the larger one next to the door, she stacked the second on top.

"So, you want to be in the house, do you?" she said in a low voice as she climbed to the top of the chairs. "Let's see if I can help you with that."

She stretched as much as she could while balancing on the chairs, and was barely able to reach the lever handle with her foot. The door swung open against her makeshift ladder, exposing the entryway. She balanced on the chairs behind the door, and whistled. In an instant, the two dogs came rushing onto the porch and through the door, nearly knocking the chairs and Della over as they burst through.

But they came through so fast, they didn't see her as she climbed over the door, and dropped to the floor on the other side. They slid across the smooth, hardwood floor, trying to gain traction, but it was too late. She had already closed the door, and shut them in.

She stepped off the porch, feeling quite pleased with herself. She was halfway to the gate when the glass burst out of a side window. The dogs were furious. They landed in a heap, but were up in seconds and racing toward her, intent on cutting her off from the gate. She sprinted, and made it by mere inches. One of them bit onto a corner of her hospital smock, holding her for a panicked second. She ripped free, and slammed the gate.

"Have a nice day," she said, panting with relief as she turned and started down the gravel drive. "Hmm, it's probably not the best idea to stay on this road. Barron could return any moment and I don't really want to visit his house again."

She crossed a shallow ditch, ducked under a barbed wire fence, and headed across a dusty field, taking care to stay out of sight of the road. From what she remembered seeing from the upstairs bedroom window, the city must be this direction.

CHAPTER 18

Normand returned to the hospital alone. Kenzie had decided to stay with Rita and Jim to get some needed rest, and Normand promised he would call if there was any change. When he arrived, he found David in recovery, and Isaac still unconscious. The best he could do was pace the halls when he wasn't stationed at their bedsides.

"Excuse me," Normand said as he approached one of the young nurses coming from David's room. "How's he doing?"

"He's holding his own," the nurse replied. "We're keeping him sedated, and making sure there's no infection."

"Where's Dr. Larson?" Normand asked as he walked with the nurse towards the nurse's station.

"I haven't seen her since earlier today." the nurse responded.

"She went out with a strange-looking guy," another nurse said from behind the desk. "I wasn't sure why she did though, because the guy seemed kinda weird."

"Weird how?" Normand inquired, stopping in his tracks.

"He just looked different. He had this really white hair, and his eyes were very dark. They walked outside together, and that's the last time I saw her."

"Oh crap," Normand said anxiously. "I need to make a call."

He slipped off to the side, and quickly called Kenzie.

"Bad news," he said when she picked up. "Get the guys, and hurry down."

Normand was aware Management could be listening in on calls, so he had to be careful not to say too much.

"Things are going to get crazy here real soon," Normand said as he returned to the nurse's station. "That guy that took Dr. Larson is likely coming back with more bad people. They're looking for my two friends, and will kill them if we don't do something fast."

The nurse looked at Normand for a moment in disbelief, and called the doctor on duty. In a few moments, Dr. Stevens appeared from a room at the end of the corridor, and Normand quickly explained the situation.

"This isn't good," Dr. Stevens said. "What do you need?"

"We've got to move David and Isaac out of here." Normand said.

"Well, you had better hurry," a nurse said as she came running down the hall. "I just saw that same man drive up, and he has two other people with him."

"I'll do what I can to stall them," Dr. Stevens said calmly. "Just get them out of here. I'm sure they'll be checking every bed."

"Are you with me?" Normand asked the three nurses.

"Sharon, call the hospital, and see who's on duty this evening." one of the nurses said, immediately. "I'll be down at operating. Buzz me as soon as you can."

The nurses immediately began prepping their wards for transport. David was the most complicated, as he had just come out of surgery earlier in the day. However, the bed he was on was self-contained, and equipped with life support. Once she unplugged it from the wall, a battery pack took over. Life support would be operational during transport, but it was still going to take time before they were ready to go.

"Can I help you?" The receptionist said as she greeted the three visitors.

"Possibly," the woman said coldly. "My name is General Allison, this is Barron, and the man in the dark suit is Mr. Grey. We have a report there are criminals operating here, and you may be harboring fugitives."

"Well, that is shocking news," Dr. Stevens said as he came up to the desk having overheard the conversation as he was passing by. "However, I just came on duty a few hours ago, and haven't seen or heard anything of the like. Maybe you're mistaken. "

"I don't make mistakes," Barron snapped. "One of your fellow doctors called it in earlier today. They said a Dr. Larson is here helping some guy injured in a car accident. She's a wanted felon, and we need to know whom she was operating on."

"I'll help you all I can," Dr. Stevens lied, "but we serve over a hundred people here, and nearly all our beds are full. May

I suggest we start with the nursing records. We should be able to tell who was admitted and get to the bottom of this."

"That's a lie, doctor," General Allison growled. "You know where they are. Take us to them now!"

"Like I said, I just came on duty." Dr. Stevens insisted calmly. "I haven't had a chance to go over the nurses' reports, or see any patients yet. I suggest we start with the nursing records, and then you can look in on the patients as long as you don't disturb them."

"Fine," General Allison said, looking the doctor over hard, "but we're doing this my way. Barron, call the cadets in, and have them comb through each room. Mr. Grey, you come with the good doctor and me while we talk with the nurses."

Meanwhile, the phone in the ER station rang.

"Good news! Darla's on duty!" Sharon said as she ducked back into David's room. "How long before they're ready to move?"

"Another few minutes should do it," the nurse prepping David replied.

"We may not have a few minutes," Normand said anxiously as he ran into the room. "Vehicles are arriving outside, and I'm sure they'll be headed our way."

The nurse finished her work as quickly as she could, and they pushed the two beds out the rear door, and into the warm evening air just as Barron was organizing a room-to-room search. The hospital was across the street and downhill about a block.

Fortunately, the road was dedicated for emergency vehicles only, and there was no traffic. Normand helped one of the young nurses push Isaac while the other two moved David. Together, they got them up a slight incline and through a service door where Nurse Darla was waiting.

"I've got them now," Darla said as a second hospital nurse assessed their condition. "You guys hustle back before they miss you."

"Is there a security camera in back of the surgery center?" Normand asked one of the nurses from the surgery center.

"I'm not sure," she answered. "I never really pay much attention."

"Crap!" he exclaimed, stepping outside with the nurse, and looking across the street. "I see one up there in the eave of the building. Do you know where the security recorder is?"

"I think it's the room next to the restroom just past the nurse's station." she answered. "At least that's where our security guard disappears when he wants to take a nap."

"I'll be right back," Normand told Darla.

He ran across the street with the three nurses, and went in the back door. They quietly dispersed and returned to their duties while Normand checked the hall. The Cadets were working their way through the building, but they hadn't made it to the nurse's station yet. He turned his crystal ring on the thick wooden door, which instantly turned translucent. He reached through to unlock the door from the inside.

The main tape recorder was running under a bank of screens. There was a shelf loaded with tapes sitting next to the side of the desk, and one in the recorder. The tapes were marked by the date of the recording, and the tape library was about two months deep. That meant they could review this tape and the one from the day he brought in Isaac. Normand found the one he was looking for, pulled two other tapes from the previous month, and switched labels. Then he put the switched tape into the recorder, and put the rest of them back in order. He erased the tape to the end before hitting play again. That way, it would appear a new tape was recording, and no one would suspect a switch. But he still needed to get out, and the cameras were live. They would pick him up as soon as he exited.

He examined the room. It didn't only house the security system, but also the main electrical panels for the entire building. They were locked, so there was no way to flip the breaker. Normand had an idea, but it was risky.

Suddenly, he spotted the security guard on one of the screens, accompanied by Mr. Grey. It was obvious they had thought of the same thing, and were coming to check the tapes. He was out of time, and had to act fast.

He placed his ring against the electrical panel, and the metal door began to glow. He would need to reach into the panel blind, not knowing where the main breaker was. If he was wrong, he could grab live wires, and electrocute himself. He pushed his hand through the thin metal door as it glowed a bright green. He had only a few seconds before the metal turned solid again, severing his arm. He grabbed what seemed to be a handle, and pulled.

Instantly, the emergency lights came on. He pulled his hand free just as the metal door returned to a solid state. He stepped into the semi-lit hallway, and turned to leave the back way when he nearly ran into Kenzie.

"What's going on?" Kenzie demanded. "Management is crawling all over this place."

"In here, quick," Normand said, pulling her into the laundry room.

The door had just closed behind them when the guard and Mr. Grey rounded the corner, headed for the security room. Following close behind was one of the maintenance personnel with keys to the electrical cabinet, and a Cadet that stayed outside the door in the hall.

"I don't get it," the maintenance man said, fumbling for the key to the electrical panel in the dim light. "There must have been a surge or something."

He opened the panel door.

"Sure enough," he confirmed. "That's the only way you can trip a breaker like this."

The lights began to come on as he re-locked the cabinet.

"I hope we don't have any more of those," the maintenance man said, starting for the door.

"Just a minute," Mr. Grey interjected. "Has this ever happened before?"

"Never, but I've only been here six months, and I work the nightshift. This might have happened on other shifts. I don't know, but I can ask if you like when the morning shift comes in."

"No, that's ok," Mr. Grey replied. "But I will need to see the security tape for today." He turned to the security officer. "I will also need all the tapes for last week, leading up to today."

"We don't normally allow these out of our office," the man protested. "But, I'm sure it will be ok if you sign for them," he said hastily as Mr. Grey gave him a look that sent a shiver of fear racing down his spine.

The security guard put the tapes into a bag and handed it to Mr. Grey, who left without saying another word.

"I told you, we didn't have any new admissions," Dr. Stevens said as he came out of the last room with General Allison.

"I'm not sure you're telling me everything," the general insisted as they returned to the front of the surgery center. "You do realize lying to a Management official is a punishable offense?"

"As you can see," Dr. Stevens replied angrily, "I've been transparent. I'm going to send a protest to your boss regarding your coming in here unannounced and invading patients' rooms. We have many high-risk patients here who were visibly disturbed by your presence. Your intrusion is not healthy for their recovery."

General Allison sneered.

"You can go," she said. "I'll let you know if I need anything further." She addressed Barron. "Tell the cadets to go through this place again. I don't trust that doctor. They have to be here somewhere. What do you have for me?" she added as Mr. Grey arrived.

"These are the security tapes," he answered. "We can look at them when we get back to the office."

"Is that it?" Barron asked.

"I'm not sure," Mr. Grey said. "That power outage seemed plenty odd, but everything seemed to be in order. If you didn't find them, then we have to assume someone moved them, but I'm sure they were here, I can feel it. We must redouble our efforts. The Board is asking questions, and we need to have answers."

They left the building, and headed for their vehicles.

"What are we going to do?" Kenzie said as Normand cracked the door.

"The cadet is still out there, and it looks like more are coming," Normand answered.

"Hey, there are some doctor smocks folded up here," Kenzie said. "Maybe we can just walk on out."

They each put on a smock to cover their clothes, and Normand grabbed a clipboard lying on a counter. He checked the door again. The cadet had moved farther up the hall, so they quietly exited the laundry room, and began heading for the rear. Unfortunately, the other cadets had circled around the building, and were working their way up the hall towards them. Normand and Kenzie stopped, and pretended to look over some notes as four armed cadets walked past. They were almost to the exit when one of the cadets noticed Normand's bright yellow tennis shoes.

"Just a minute," he ordered, "I want to talk to you."

Kenzie and Normand took off for the exit, but were blocked by three more cadets coming in. Kenzie pulled two small crystal blades from a belt hidden under her coat. Normand pulled the long, heavy blade he had gotten from Parks which was strapped to his back. The cadets had the new blade weapons developed by Management, and blocked the exit.

Kenzie leapt into the air, and with a back flip landed behind them. Two cadets turned to face her while the other took a swipe at Normand. The next few seconds were filled with flashes of light as blue crystal blades met red crystal-powered blades. The ones built by Management failed their owners, and Kenzie and Normand destroyed them with ease.

More cadets came running to join the fray just as their three companions fell under the skill and power of the two resisters' years of training. Kenzie and Normand knew they were in trouble. A stream of cadets was now rushing down the hall, and they would soon be overwhelmed.

"Kenzie!" Normand shouted. "Point one of your blades at them."

Without hesitation, Kenzie did as Normand instructed, and he placed his ring against the side of her blade. The ring turned bright green, and her blade changed to a beautiful sea-blue color.

He grabbed her by the shoulders, and pulled his ring away.

"Hold on."

The power in her blade released, and sent a wave of energy down the hall, flattening everything in its path. It followed the corridors through the building, burst out the front doors, and into the parking lot, where it took out anyone standing before dissipating into the night.

"We've got to go." he said as one of the stunned cadets groaned, and tried to return to his feet.

"I'll take the back way out," Kenzie said, heading towards her car. "You stay with the guys."

Normand sprinted across the road, and up the drive to the hospital. The door they had brought David and Isaac through was ajar, and it was the only entrance that didn't have surveillance cameras. Once inside, he immediately looked for Nurse Darla. She had one of her nurses watching for him, and she spotted him at once.

"Whew," he said, as Darla came down the hall to meet him.

"We've only got a few minutes," Darla said firmly, looking over her shoulder. "Follow me."

She led the way down a side hall. This area of the hospital did not have any security cameras by design. When Dr. Larson designed the hospital, she had made sure certain sections were free from prying eyes. They rounded a corner where the corridor split in two, and took a sharp left turn. Darla jogged down the hall with Normand tight on her heels.

"In here," she said, opening a broom closet.

Normand looked at her, puzzled.

"Don't think about it, just do it," she ordered quietly. "There's a button in the back behind those shelves. Push it, and it will all make sense. Come on, I have to get back before I'm missed."

Darla shut the door, but left the light on as she hustled back to her office. Normand felt behind the shelves as instructed, and located the button. The wall slid open, revealing a hidden elevator.

Inside were David and Isaac on their gurneys. To his surprise, one of the young nurses he had met at the surgery center was there. This was the second elevator Dr. Larson had secretly installed in the hospital. The one to her special room had been destroyed by Barron, but this one was still operational.

"Come in, and let the door shut," the young nurse urged. "Darla said we should go up two floors, and stay inside here for the night. I have everything I need to keep these patients comfortable until morning. Darla will come back for us after things have settled down."

The light in the elevator stayed on, and they did as Darla had instructed. As the elevator came to a stop, the only sound was the hum from the fan that kept the elevator air fresh.

Normand breathed a sigh of relief, and leaned back against the elevator wall as his eyes adjusted to the dim light. The young nurse was calm and caring as she took care of his two friends. She was also pleasant to look at.

"My name's Normand," he said after watching her for a few minutes. "You're doing a great job. Thank you for everything."

"I'm Sharon," she answered brightly. "Your friends are going to be ok. By morning, they will be safely in the hospital, and under the best care."

Normand was impressed by how dedicated and caring she seemed. She was coping with an unusual setting very well. An attitude like hers was rare. He sat on the carpeted elevator floor and watched while she tended to them. He trusted her, but he was still unable to relax. She finished her work, and sat against the opposite wall, falling asleep quickly. Normand was unable to sleep; he kept replaying recent events in his mind. It seemed every turn they made, Management was waiting for them. There was no room for error.

Suddenly, a knock on the elevator door shook Normand awake. Sharon had already pushed the button to open the door, and a bright light spilled into the room, blinding him momentarily. He shielded his eyes with his arm, and blinked several times. A dark outline stood in the open elevator. He scrambled to his feet, and gripped the handle of his blade.

CHAPTER 19

"Wake up, sleepy head, it's time to talk."

Harry kicked Parks in the collarbone.

He stood over Parks with a Nullifier in one hand, and a heavy leather whip in the other. The whip was made from several braided lengths of leather with sharp metal barbs attached to each end. It was designed to cause maximum pain as it ripped flesh with each blow. Parks just groaned, and moved a little. His hands and arms were wrapped with steel chain behind his back and fastened securely between his feet.

"Come on," Harry said impatiently as he kicked Parks again, this time in the back. "I don't have all day."

Parks lifted his head, and rolled over to where he could see Harry. His face was swollen and bruised from Harry's punch, and blood was still oozing from his nose.

"Boss," Parks spit sarcastically. "I hoped we would get a chance to talk. It's been too long."

"Oh, we're going to talk alright," Harry said coldly, snapping the whip twice. "But I think it's you who will be doing all the speaking. Before I'm done, you will be begging to tell me things I don't even want to know."

"Really," Parks said evenly as Harry grabbed his collar, and jerked him to his knees. "And I thought you were the one with all the information."

"You always did have a sense of humor," Harry replied, snapping the whip menacingly several more times.

Parks was familiar with the whip, and had stopped Barron several times from using it to interrogate resisters. There was a switch on the end that sent electrical current to each barb, making for excruciating pain, and Parks believed it was the most barbaric instrument of torture.

"Before we get all hot and bothered," Parks said as the chains bit into his arms, "would you mind answering a couple of questions for old time's sake?"

"Why should I?" Harry snapped.

"Oh come on now," Parks continued. "What's this all about? Management has control of pretty much everything, and yet I hear you're amassing Testers. What are you planning on doing with them?"

"You know about the Testers?" Harry asked in amazement. "Well that's really none of your concern, but they are being called back into service you might say. But that isn't what's really important. The Board of Directors is on a mission, and you're going to help me with it."

"What mission this time? You mean killing innocent people wasn't enough for them?"

"You think you're so smart," Harry said, smirking, yet look at you. The famous Parks, trussed up like a ham hanging in a butcher shop. What a joke!"

Harry paced back and forth several times, snapping his whip. Parks could tell that he was enjoying his helplessness, and savoring the moment.

"First, I need you to tell me about the gifts," Harry said when he got tired of cracking the whip. "Only, don't answer too quickly. I want to enjoy this as long as possible. As you found out, this mechanical arm I got from those crystal blades of yours is way more powerful than my real one was. I won't even have to remove your leather coat. This whip will cut right through it.

"Oh, I see you would like one of those blades of yours right now," he sneered, pushing Parks's belt with his foot. "Too bad you can't reach them. Hey, I think I'll make sure they get destroyed, right after I destroy you. But don't worry; I'm not going to kill you, at least not yet. The Board wants to speak with you later today. I'm just going to soften you up a little first."

"That's the mission?" Parks asked as Harry prepared to make his first strike. "You want me to tell you about some mythical items. Wow, that is pathetic. But it does answer my question, and this worked out better than I expected. You wouldn't have told me anything if I had captured you instead."

"What are you saying?" Harry asked. "You've definitely lost your mind. Now for a little entertainment."

Harry lifted his arm to begin Parks' painful examination. But before he could strike the first blow, Parks tensed his body. As each muscle swelled to full size, the heavy chains began to snap and pop, sending pieces of chain bouncing off the hardened steel cell. Shaking off the chains, Parks sprang at Harry, catching him under the chin with his shoulder, and sending him sailing into the wall. The Nullifier flew out of Harry's hand and bounced into the far corner. Harry tried to strike, but Parks caught his hand in midair, and knocked the whip from his hand.

"I'll kill you with my own hands," Harry said, enraged.

He grabbed Parks by the throat. The robotic hand was as powerful as Harry had said. It squeezed Parks's windpipe shut. But Parks's anger was ignited, and rose unabated as a voice inside his head encouraged him.

"Kill him!" the voice commanded as Parks pulled Harry's hand away. Everything turned red as he ripped Harry's arm off his shoulder, and tossed it into the corner. Harry's screams of agony instantly ceased as Parks lifted him off the floor by his throat, and threw him against the wall. He fell in a crumpled heap mere inches from the Nullifier. He grabbed it with his remaining arm, before he could use it, Parks pinned his hand to the floor with his foot.

"Go ahead," Harry screamed bitterly as he looked into Parks's angry face. "You're no better than me; you're a killer. I can see it in your eyes. That wild look, and the evil you feel. Just do it."

Parks pulled his fist back, preparing to crush Harry's skull against the floor. He remembered his mother, and all the friends he lost at the hands of this monster. Harry cringed and closed his eyes, waiting for the final blow.

"No!" he suddenly shouted, and the blow meant for Harry hit the floor instead. The entire room shook from the blow leaving the distinct outline of his fist in the metal as he pulled away.

Out of nowhere, a dark, heavy-set beast appeared in the room, curving its mouth into a wicked smile that displayed rows of razor-sharp teeth.

"Zender," Parks exclaimed in shock, "but you're dead. I watched you die!"

"You can't kill me!" the beast snarled wickedly. "You don't have that kind of power. Your hatred has released me, and if you just let your anger go, we will rule everything."

"No!" Parks shouted.

He closed his eyes, and grabbed his head with both hands.

"You'll not control me," he said through clenched teeth.

"You're crazier than I thought," Harry said, watching Parks talk to no one he could see.

"Maybe I am," Parks replied, regaining his self-control, "but you should be grateful you're not dying today, no matter how much I might like that. Come on," he said, lifting Harry off the floor by his remaining arm. "I'm going to that meeting after all, just not with you. You need medical attention, and I know just the guy to help you out, even though he's not all that crazy about you Management types."

Parks helped Harry into the elevator, and took him to the parking garage. He grabbed some towels he found in the back seat of Harry's car, and used them to secure what was left of Harry's robotic arm to his side before helping him into the driver's seat. He needed to look like he was in one piece in order to get out of the Citadel.

"You're going to have to drive," Parks said, sliding into the passenger seat. "But just remember, I will take you and the guard out with this Nullifier. You say something wrong, it will be the last thing you ever say."

Harry stopped at the gate, and rolled down his window as the guard approached. He had changed the protocol since Parks first abducted him, so he could no longer just zoom through without being identified.

"Everything ok, sir?" the guard asked as he glanced over at Parks, who was slumped against the far window.

"No problem," Harry replied evenly, "just taking this guy over to the hospital for some repairs. We'll be back later for the board meeting."

The guard took one more look at Parks, who still showed the signs of the beating he took, smiled, and waved them through. Once they were out of sight, Parks took over the wheel. It was a long drive up to Dr. Flint's office, and neither man had anything to say. It was getting late when he arrived, and pulled Harry from the car. Harry had nearly lost consciousness from loss of blood and Parks had to carry him to the building.

"This guy is going to need some attention," Parks said as Dr. Flint opened the door.

"I see that," the doctor replied. "What happened to him?"

"Too long of a story to tell right now. The rest of his arm is in this bag, but I wouldn't put too much effort into reattaching it. Where he's going, one arm will be plenty. Can you get a heavy sedative?"

"And where would that be?" Harry asked through clenched teeth as the doctor went for a hypodermic.

"You'll be heading for some 'Island' living," Parks replied slyly.

"Who is he?" Dr. Flint whispered in Parks's ear as he noticed the Nullifier Parks was holding on Harry.

"You really don't want to know." Parks said. "Keep him sedated until tomorrow morning. Two men will come by and pick him up. Just remember, he's dangerous. Don't let him out of your sight, or near a phone."

"I have just the place," Dr. Flint said as he stuck the needle in Harry's arm. "Hey, you look like you could use some attention too."

"Thanks for asking, but I'll be fine. Let me help you get him into bed, and then I'll be going."

Meanwhile, back at the Citadel, General Allison, Mr. Grey, and Barron were just returning from the hospital.

"Dad's car is gone," General Allison said as they pulled into the parking garage. "I heard him say he had a meeting with the board tonight, so he must have left already. That'll give us some time to watch the security tapes before we have to explain why we don't have any suspects in tow."

The three went up the stairs to General Allison's office and began reviewing the tapes.

"I don't see anything," Barron said finally after several hours of fast-forwarding. "It looks like the good doctor was telling the truth when he said no one came in."

"I still don't like it," the general replied, tapping her long black fingernails on the desk. "That doctor seemed a little too smug to me. He has to be hiding something."

"I can go over and talk to him," Mr. Grey said emotionlessly. "I'm sure he would be more cooperative with a little persuasion."

"Not yet," the general replied. "He may have connections, and we don't want to tip our hand yet. Let's review what we know. Barron gets a call from someone at the surgery center who reports Dr. Larson is there treating an accident victim. Right, Barron?"

Barron nodded.

"We go over there expecting to find her, but there's no trace of either her or her patient. So the person who called in was playing a prank, or somebody knew we were coming, and made preparations. Either way, this thing stinks. The only reason to prank us would be to get us out of here," the general said as she began to consider other options. "But why would anyone want us out of here?"

"Maybe we better take a look around," Barron said, playing along. "If you're right, someone may have done something while we were gone.

"Barron, you take this floor and check the offices," the general commanded as she got up from her desk. "Mr. Grey, you go downstairs. We'll keep in contact with these," she said handing each of them a two-way radio from her desk drawer. "I'll go upstairs, and see if anything is out of place."

The three of them split up. Only Barron knew the truth. He had intercepted the call from his contact at the surgery center, and captured Dr. Larson before anyone was the wiser. The only reason he told them anything about the call was to protect himself if someone else called in. Getting them over there effectively muddied the waters, and put him in the clear. He had even called the security guard and had him erase his comings and goings, but he didn't understand why other things weren't on the tape.

"Get up here, now!" General Allison barked into the radio.

Barron met Mr. Grey flying up the stairs, and followed him to the top floor.

"I just spoke with Birgit," the general said. "Apparently, Parks came here looking for my dad, and got caught in his elevator trap. Birgit said they locked him in the cell below."

"Parks here," Barron said incredulously. "This I have to see."

They rushed to the lower floor and found the cell door open.

"He's not here now," Barron observed as he looked the cell over. "But it seems something happened. This didn't break itself," he commented as he picked up a section of chain. "Oh, and what's that?" Barron continued as he walked to the end of the cell, squatted down, and picked something off the floor. "Someone seems to be missing a finger."

Barron held up a metal appendage dangling from several thin wires.

"Dad's arm," General Allison exclaimed. "Something is really wrong. Did Harry leave the Citadel?" she asked anxiously into her phone as she called the guard shack.

"About an hour ago," the guard replied.

"Was he alone?"

"There was a large man slumped over in the passenger seat," the guard answered. "Mr. Allison indicated he was taking him to a meeting or something."

"Parks has your father." Barron interjected sharply.

"So, that's what this is all about." General Allison replied as she begin to pace with her fists clenched. "Parks got us running all over the place looking for phantoms while he comes in here and takes the head of the Citadel out right from under our noses. Hey, but this situation may have a silver lining after all," she said, narrowing her painted eyes. "The board wants to release the Testers and find the gifts, right? What better cover to the general public than to say we're searching for a kidnap victim? Who would be able to protest as the cadets ravage house after house? They could look for the gifts without the people knowing. It's perfect, and the board will be very pleased indeed."

General Allison slid into her father's chair, not about to let this opportunity pass. She pushed deep into the plush upholstery and slid her hands along the smooth cool leather before making the call to the President's secretary, and arranging a meeting with Dave in her father's stead. She didn't reveal any details. She would save that for a face-to-face with Dave. Her father may have been the head of the Citadel, but he meant little to her. She had learned early on to be as selfish and self-serving as possible. Now all she needed to do was convince the President she was the one to take over the Citadel, and then she would have everything her heart desired.

Almost everything.

Barron took his leave, and headed towards his house. He had succeeded in diverting General Allison's attention, and knowing that Parks was back made having Dr. Larson as leverage even better.

"It's about time things started turning my way," Barron thought as he pulled out of the Citadel. "Ivy's crazy if she thinks the president would put her in charge of the Citadel. She may be clever and cruel, but she doesn't have the experience I have. And with that crystal out of my chest, they can't push me around anymore. The board will have to acknowledge how powerful I really am, and put me in charge of the Citadel, and maybe even more."

He pulled onto the long driveway leading to the place he called home, feeling very pleased with himself. His good mood evaporated instantly however when he saw the broken windows.

CHAPTER 20

"I hope David's ok," Rita said as she flipped some burgers on the stove. "From what Normand said it sounded bad but I can't imagine why anyone would want to hurt him."

"Well, Dr. Larson will take care of him," Jim replied.

"You want something to drink?" Rita asked, setting the burger in front of him.

"Water, thanks," he said. "Hey, this looks really good!"

She sat across from him with her own burger. . Despite his comment, Jim only took a few bites before pushing back from the table.

"Are you feeling ok?" Rita asked.

"I'm confused," he said carefully, looking hard at Rita. "I can't get that tracer out of my mind. The only one who knew I had a habit of picking cigars out of that box was Frank. But why would he do that to me? We were working on the story together, and I thought we were friends. I guess you really don't know people as well as you think you do."

He got up and walked into the living room, flopping down onto Normand's couch, and closed his eyes.

"How's your ankle doing?" she asked tenderly.

She sat next to him, and patted his leg.

"Rita," he said, ignoring her question, "what really happened with that cigar?"

"I, I don't know what you mean," she stammered nervously.

"I've been a bit of a fool," he continued, opening his eyes, and looking deep into hers. "My reporter instincts have never let me down until now. Somehow, my trusting Frank and my feelings for you have clouded my judgment. You're the one who put those tracers in the cigar wrappers aren't you?"

Rita stumbled for something to say, and then started to cry.

"Nobody was supposed to get hurt," she said finally. "Frank told me he had made a deal with Management. You were to run your piece, but Frank was supposed to keep it in-house.

The day you started broadcasting, nothing was going to happen. Frank had unplugged the main feed from the back of the transmitter. But then your senior assistant, Chris, realized it wasn't broadcasting, and found the problem. He plugged it back in, and then it was too late. Everything began to play out the way you designed, and Frank couldn't stop it. I guess that's when he decided to have us both killed. To tell you the truth, I forgot about the tracer after the accident. It didn't come back to me until those Testers honed in on you."

Jim leaned back, and stared at Rita for a moment. He was angry and heartbroken all at the same time.

"Jim, you were not supposed to be hurt, just shut down. Sure, Frank told me about your plan, and how crazy he thought it was. Broadcasting an exposé on Management would only end in disaster. But after you pulled me out of the water and saved my life, I began to think differently. You weren't just "Jim the Weatherman" anymore, the guy chasing skirts and being a bigshot. Then the Testers came, and I knew right then there was no escaping. I knew you suspected something when I removed the tracer, but I had to do it. I couldn't have them find you again, but I've been terrified ever since, and afraid you would figure it out, and I would lose you."

Her voice trailed off, and she began to sob, putting her face in her hands. He sat there for a moment, not sure what to say. Rita had come to mean more to him than anyone ever had, and he couldn't imagine his life without her. They hadn't even been on a date or even kissed one time, but he was hooked.

"It's not your fault," he said tenderly, stretching his arm around her shoulders. "I don't blame you, but I do blame Frank. He and I go way back, and I thought we had an understanding. But now I see who's really behind this."

He kissed her gently on the cheek. Rita leaned into his chest, and threw her arms around his neck, hugging him tight. He sat there for a long time, holding her.

Across town, Frank was just coming out of a meeting with his station managers, and heading back to his office. He plopped into his chair, and put his feet on the desk with his hands behind his head. Programming was first on his agenda. He was starting a new series portraying Management in an even more favorable light. They were to be the heroes of every situation, and the bad guys were always those resisting Management's good efforts.

It had been the staple of programming on company-controlled outlets since the beginning, but it had been more subtle before. Now they were opening the flood gates of propaganda, and Frank was going to be responsible for the new programs. It was a huge new opportunity, and he was back in the driver's seat.

"There's someone here to see you," a female voice on the other end of his intercom said.

"I'm not taking any appointments right now," he answered gruffly. "Take a message."

"He said you would want to see him," the woman insisted. "His name is Jerry Jefferies."

"JJ?" he said, bolting to attention, and pulling his feet off the desk. "Is he a really old guy?"

"Yes, sir," she answered.

"I'm on my way out."

Jerry Jefferies owned nearly all the diamond mines in existence. When Management had come into power, they tried to take over his operations, but he had enough firepower to keep them at bay. Rumor had it he hadn't been out of his complex for the past ten years.

Frank opened his office door, and made the short walk to the reception area where a sharply dressed old man holding a gold walking stick with a huge diamond on the end sat patiently waiting.

"Mr. Jefferies," Frank eagerly, "I'm Frank, the general manager for Management productions. You probably don't remember me, but we met once before. How can I help you?"

"I have a business proposition for you," the old man said as he stood with the help of his cane. "Is there somewhere we can talk privately?"

"Of course," he said graciously. "Come into my office where we can be more comfortable."

He led Mr. Jefferies to a leather swivel chair across from his desk.

"Can I get you anything?" he asked. "My secretary can bring us some coffee or tea. I have some nice cigars here too if you like to smoke."

He opened the golden box sitting prominently on the side of his desk.

"No thank you," the old man replied, his voice cracking slightly. "I didn't come for frivolities. I've been told you are a man of action, capable of getting things done."

He tapped his cane on the floor.

"They tell me you were behind that broadcast recently. The one that exposed some wrong-doing at one of those "homes" they like to stick old people like me in. Is that true?"

"Yes, I guess," Frank replied a little taken aback at the question. "But I can't take all the credit for that. It was more the doing of one of my old reporters."

"Modesty, I like that. Good quality in a man," the old man said. "But you had to go against Management, correct?"

"Well, look around," he answered. "We're still rebuilding. Now, you mentioned something about a business proposition."

The old man swiveled the chair around with its back to Frank, and looked out the windows on the far side of Frank's office. It was a beautiful setting, with manicured gardens and several water fountains sprinkled about. It was truly the office of a man of power and influence.

"Right to the point, I like that too," the old man said, spinning back around. "My sources tell me Management is looking for something very valuable, but I want to find it first."

"You must have the wrong man," Frank protested. "I'm the manager of television and radio stations, not an investigator."

"You're the right man," the old man said firmly, leaning forward and looking at Frank over the top of his thin rimmed glasses. "You're going to run some advertising spots for me. I've prepared the commercials already."

He pulled a disk from an inside pocket in his suit coat, and set it on Frank's desk.

"You'll start running them tonight on prime time."

"I can't promise anything without reviewing them first," he protested. "I must be sure the context meets our standards."

"You can, and you will run them," Mr. Jefferies said, slamming his cane on the floor. "You don't know how persuasive I can be. You may be afraid of Management, but they are nothing like me."

"You can't threaten me," Frank said, pushing away from his desk. "I can have you arrested for that."

The old man narrowed his eyes, and laughed as he got up from his seat.

"Call whomever you think you can," he said as he headed for the door with a sinister smile, "but I doubt they will find your body. I've made a living keeping Management out of my affairs. They'll not save you. I expect to see the first broadcast tonight."

Frank trembled at the thought as the door closed behind Mr. Jefferies. He picked up the disk, and stared at it. His day had just gone from great to terrifying in less than half an hour. Now he had to figure out what to do. JJ was well known as a ruthless man in business and shady in other things. He was not someone to be trifled with.

Mr. Jefferies exited the building, and climbed into the long black limousine parked out front. A tall muscular man held the door for him and closed it as he got in.

"I can't thank you enough," Jim said as JJ settled into the plush leather interior.

"Not a problem," Mr. Jefferies replied. "I've never liked guys like him anyway. They play like they own the world, but they're just puppets. Besides, I liked your father. He and I grew up together, scratching out a living. I see a lot of him in you. What was on that disk I gave him anyway?"

"When I did my exposé on the East Economic Division, I had a lot of material, and one broadcast couldn't contain it all. So I made several episodes showing how on one hand, Management was promoting EEDs, and on the other, killing people who came to them. But I only got to run the first one before it was shut down. If he runs those, he'll be out on his ear by morning, or worse."

"Where can I drop you?" Mr. Jefferies asked.

"On the curb up there will be just fine, I can walk from there. Thanks again for the help."

Jim climbed out, and headed to the parking lot where Rita was waiting as JJ's limo sped off.

"How did it go?" Rita asked as he got in.

"We got his attention, but I know he's not going to run them," he said. "If I know Frank, he'll panic, and make a break for it. He'll hide out for a while until things cool down. I'm sure he has plenty of assistants to take care of things while he's away."

Rita pulled into traffic as Jim settled in beside her with a smile on his face.

The sky was darkening as Frank's little red sports car came bouncing down the graveled drive along the lake to his aunt's old cabin. He had told his boss at the Citadel he needed a vacation. He could hide out there for a month or so, and hopefully JJ would have moved on by then. It was a chance he had to take. Staying around the city would be too dangerous.

He rolled up to the cabin, and shut off the motor. The cabin was well stocked with provisions, and was a comfortable place to wait things out. The fishing on the lake was great that time of year, and he needed a break anyway.

He grabbed his bags out of the back, and headed towards the door. Setting a bag down, he found the key he kept hidden under the mat, and unlocked the door. He pushed it open, and hit the light switch.

"Hi, old buddy," Jim said as the lights came on. "Been a long time, Frank."

Frank dropped his bags.

"Jim! Wwhat are you doing here?"

"Just dropped by for a visit," his unwanted house guest said evenly from where he was sitting on the couch. "Come in, and have a seat. We have a lot of catching up to do."

"Hey, it's great to see you," Frank replied, gathering his composure. "But I heard you were long gone. What brings you back to the city?"

"If you remember," Jim replied, "we were going to meet up in the country somewhere after you ran my piece. But I never made it. Seems like someone tried to have me killed. Know anything about that?"

"Someone tried to kill you?" Frank asked in an innocent voice. "Who would do such a thing? Must have been after you ran that piece, and I never heard from you again. I warned you about that, remember? Management was not going to take that lying down. Anyway, I thought you were going to meet up with me, but you never came."

"Right," Jim said. "Now tell me about your promotion, and how you got a position with Management running all the stations in the city."

"Jim, baby," Frank responded thinking quickly as he walked across the room towards the kitchen, "that's a cool story. When you never came, I started thinking. What if I could return, and convince them I was abducted. Then I would become a victim, and get their sympathy. It worked great."

Frank sidled to a drawer on the end of the kitchen counter, and positioned himself where he could slowly open it behind his back.

"They bought the whole thing, and then gave me this new position. I've been using it ever since to undermine Management's broadcasting efforts. You should see how crappy their programming is."

"Is this what you're feeling for?" Jim asked as he pointed a large revolver at Frank. "I've stayed here before, and know you keep your gun in there. Now, why don't we cut to the chase, and start with how you betrayed your friends, starting with me."

"Friend?"

Frank slammed the drawer shut.

"Some friend! The only time I ever saw you was when you wanted something from me, just like the rest of your narcissistic buddies. All they ever wanted was more of the spotlight. I danced around you guys for years with Management breathing down my neck, all because HOT News was above compromise. Well that gig was getting plenty old, and I was tired of playing second fiddle."

"Yeah, maybe we never were friends," Jim said as he waved Frank over to the couch with the end of the gun. "A friend wouldn't have tried to kill me. And what about Rita? What did she ever do to you?"

"Rita, right," Frank answered as he looked down at the floor. "She was always a good trooper, but she knew the risks."

"You jerk," Jim said, getting up from the couch. "No, I'm not going to kill you unless you do something stupid. We're going to take a little trip into the city, and run a certain program you got today. I know you have complete control over all broadcasting, and there's no one on duty at night. This time, you're going to find out how bad Management really is. Come on, get moving."

He motioned towards the door with the revolver.

Frank reluctantly followed Jim's direction, stopping for a moment to pick up an overnight bag.

Suddenly, he swung the bag up, catching Jim by surprise. He grabbed Jim's arm, and tried to wrestle the gun free. They fell to the floor, wrestling for control. Frank was short and round, but stronger than he appeared.

Jim kneed him in the groin, but Frank still had a strong grip on the gun. Suddenly, there was the sound of a small explosion, and Frank relaxed his grip. Frank stared down at a bloody hole in his chest, and slumped on top of his former friend. The bullet lodged in the wall behind them. Jim got up, trembling.

"I'm sorry," Frank said as Jim knelt down to see if there was anything he could do. "I wish Management had never come here. We've never been the same since."

"I'll get you help," Jim said ripping off his shirt to plug the wound. "Just hang on."

"Look, I'm not the bad man you think I am," Frank said weakly.

A trickle of blood came from the corner of his mouth, and he gripped Jim's arm.

"I just played the middle once too often."

Jim stood outside the cabin as the flames rose nearly to the top of the nearby trees. He had placed Frank's body on the couch next to the fireplace before starting the fire. It seemed fitting somehow, in spite of what had taken place.

He remembered the good times. Happy days spent on cool nights, enjoying a few moments as the warm fire crackled, warming their faces. Management had stolen their friendship, and cost Frank his life. He vowed Frank would be remembered for more than his mistakes. He may have become something he should never have been, but he was once Jim's friend, and that meant something. He took one last long look as the roof caved in a shower of sparks before heading out the long drive in Frank's little red sports car.

CHAPTER 21

Della considered her options as she ran down the graveled drive. If Barron were to return at this moment, there was no cover, and she would certainly be caught. But even though she was not sure where exactly she was, she remembered seeing the tops of some buildings from the upper bedroom window. Her best bet was to go in that direction, and get off the road as quickly as possible.

A large, scraggly field surrounded by a barbed wire fence stood between her and the cover of the warehouse buildings. The evening air was beginning to cool as she stepped off the driveway into a shallow ditch, and climbed the barbed wire fence. She ran as fast as she could across the field, but it was scattered with small rocks, which made running difficult. She was still wearing the thin white tennis shoes used in the surgery center, and they were not designed for this. She was about a third of the way across the field when she noticed something moving on the ground in front of her. She slowed to a stop to get a better look.

"Oh, no," she shouted involuntarily, "Snakes!"

Then she looked down at her feet and around the field. There were holes everywhere. She was standing in the middle of thousands of snake dens. This was the place the snakes retreated from the heat of the day, but at evening, they came out in search of food. She stood there horrified as silver shiny heads of long, thick snakes began to pop up all around her.

Her immediate reaction was to run back the way she had come, but that way was already blocked, and the field behind her had become a writhing mass of serpents. She took off at a dead run, dodging from side to side as snake after snake popped out of the ground. Some hissed, others lunged for a strike, but most were just heading off to find their nightly meal. Miraculously, she made the barbed wire fence on the far side of the field, but there was a slithering horde tight on her heals.

She started to climb, but was shocked to find the place she had chosen to cross had a broken post. Her weight pulled against the four strands of barbed wire, and she sagged near the ground. She did her best to balance, and prayed for it to hold, even as sharp ends of barbwire penetrated her soft hands. But she didn't even feel the pain as wave after wave of serpents crossed under her precarious position. It seemed like ages before the last of the snakes had made their way out of the field, and disappeared into the nearby buildings.

"I've never seen anything like that in my life," she said aloud as she freed herself from the fence.

Her hands, arms, and legs were bleeding from the barbs, but there were no serious wounds. But her plan to use the warehouses as cover was blown as the snakes disappeared into countless cracks and crevices.

She stood there, looking for another escape route, and pondering how to get around the looming structures. There was a long, blackberry-covered chain-link fence guarding the perimeter of the property. From where she was, she couldn't tell if it was passable or not. The blackberry bushes had taken it over, and spread out in every direction. With their sharp thorns, they would not easily yield passage.

Then she heard what sounded like a car out on the main road, and the decision was made for her. Della ran for the blackberries and the fence. It looked hopeless at first, but then she saw an opening. It appeared the local deer population used this natural barrier as their highway. Being small in stature, Della carefully wound her way through the dark bushes. It was difficult going as the evening light began to dim, but the deer had done her a great favor by creating such a well-defined path. She snagged her clothes a couple of times before popping out on the other side of the warehouses. She hopped the metal pipe fence designed to keep unwanted vehicles out, and began running down the road, and away from her day of terror.

Barron could tell something was wrong the moment he arrived. His two guard dogs were still doing their thing, barking ferociously as he approached, only this time he was in no mood to throw them meat. He met the first one with a hard backhand, sending it tumbling into the side of the house and the other one he kicked so hard it landed on the porch. The two large beasts whimpered, and found a safe corner away from Barron's anger. He checked the house carefully, but the broken widows told the story, Dr. Larson had escaped.

"Come on, you worthless hounds," Barron barked as he came outside with a leash in each hand and a large flashlight.

He snapped the leash on their heavy leather collars studded with sharp metal points, and headed out the driveway. Sniffing along the ground, the two dogs eagerly led the way. Barron stopped when he spotted the place Della had crossed to get into the field of snakes.

"She's got guts!" he exclaimed. "I'll give her that. I wouldn't even cross that nasty place."

Barron followed the outline of the fence around the field, making sure she hadn't doubled back. It wasn't until he made the far corner behind the old warehouses that he saw the blood.

"Take a good whiff," Barron said encouragingly.

They sniffed the wire, and licked the blood as Barron released them. They took off with their noses tight to the ground, following Della's scent. Every now and then they would get in each other's way, which usually ended in a short, growling confrontation before they went back to work. Barron did his best to keep up as they ran along.

Once they dived into the blackberry bushes, he stayed on the outside listening to their progression. His flashlight caught glimpses of them as they pushed their way through. They beat him to the end of the bushes, and ran out and across the road. He yelled for them to wait, but the taste of blood was too strong. The last glimpse he had was their two tails disappearing around a bend in the road.

Della was a good long-distance runner and by now had put nearly a mile between herself and Barron. She hoped to find somebody at home along the way where she could hide and make a call. But as she ran, she quickly realized this was the one area of the city that was never rebuilt after Management took over. The Testers had destroyed most everything when they came through here, and the owners either didn't have the resources or the desire to put them back together again.

House after house was dark and empty, and more large, empty warehouses met her as she followed the overgrown road to the top of a small hill. She stopped for a moment, and surveyed the lights in the distance. It was another two miles before she would reach the border of the inhabited city. A long run, but she was up for it. Anything was better than returning to Barron.

Then she heard the grunting and growling of the two dogs gaining on her.

"That's not good!" Della exclaimed as she took off again.

The light tennis shoes were quickly wearing through as she ran as fast as she could over the rough, black-topped road. Her feet were bleeding from sharp rocks that had punctured the soles. Now with every step, she was leaving an even easier trail for the dogs. The houses littering the street were boarded up, but she would need to find shelter someplace before they caught her. She would be easy prey out here in the open, and she knew it. Even if Barron was nearby, she would likely be torn into pieces, and half-eaten before he got to her.

Time was running out, and desperation setting in as she started checking houses. She ran up onto the porch of one and did her best to pry the boards off the doors and windows, but they resisted her efforts. Now she could hear the heavy panting and growling as the dogs closed in. It would be a matter of moments before they had her.

Finally, she managed to pry a board off one of the windows. The opening wasn't big enough for her to get inside, but at least she had a weapon. It wasn't much, but the two rusty nails sticking out of the end would make them pay, and might be enough if she hit them just right.

"Come on!" she challenged, bracing herself.

The first one jumped onto the porch so hard it nearly crashed through the door. Its partner quickly joined it. They approached, filling the entire width of the porch with their massive bodies. There was no hurry now, and they seemed to be enjoying the moment, having trapped their prey. Then they stopped, and tightened every muscle as they prepared to pounce. A low growl preceded what would surely be a grizzly end as the moonlight reflected off their yellow teeth.

Her heart was pounding at breakneck speed, and her mind couldn't quite grasp what happened next. The two ferocious beasts leapt forward, their gaping mouths open wide, with long streams of drool running off the sides.

Suddenly, there was a rush of air that brushed her back into one of the porch posts, and she saw a dark blur go past, scooping up the two dogs. The side of the old house gave way with a crash as they disappeared in a cloud of dust and debris. Della stood there spellbound as several ferocious growls echoed into the night followed by yelps, and then silence. She wanted to run, but her feet wouldn't move. She gasped, and held her stick up as a large shape appeared in the opening.

"Are you ok, Della?" a familiar voice asked. "They didn't hurt you did they?"

"Parks," Della exclaimed as she dropped the board and fell to her knees on the porch. "Where did you come from? I thought I was dead, I thought you were dead!"

"It's ok," he said gently as he helped her past the debris.

He sat her down on a step, and threw his coat around her shoulders.

"Your feet look pretty beat up," he said, checking her over. "I can't have you walking, but we need to get out of here."

He picked her up easily.

"I have a ride for us on the other side of these woods."

He carried her through the trees to a graveled road where he had parked his bike.

Back at the old house, Barron had finally caught up to his dogs.

"What the!" he exclaimed as his flashlight unveiled the event. "That little woman couldn't have done this." He knelt down amid the remains of what were once two very powerful animals. Both dogs were obviously dead, but what amazed him was the way in which they had died. One was torn in half like you would rip a piece of paper in two. The other's head was twisted completely around, and lay grotesquely piled in a corner.

He examined the gaping hole through the wall, looking for an explanation. His flashlight reflected off a small object lying near the opening. He dropped down and examined it.

"Parks," Barron growled as he turned the shiny button over in his fingers. One of the buttons from Parks' leather coat had come off when he broke through the wall. "So you've returned, have you?"

Barron headed back towards his house. He knew there was no way to track Parks now, but somewhere along the way, he realized what a tremendous opportunity this could turn out to be. He had just learned something no one else knew, and he would find a way to use it to his advantage.

"I don't understand how you found me," Della said after they parked the motorcycle in the barn, and he carried her into his parent's home. No one was there as he set her in the kitchen, and got bandages and antiseptic for her feet. "I wasn't even sure where I was. How did you know?"

"I'm not sure I understand it myself I was heading back into the city, hoping to meet up with some of the resisters. I haven't seen anyone since I returned, except Kirsten. I was going to see if I could help them get organized, and offer my assistance."

He got up from the stool, and retrieved his bag from the entry.

"Then I started thinking about you." he said, putting the bag on the counter, and unzipping it.

He pulled out a silver object, and set it in front of her.

"It's beautiful," she said, picking it up.

It was a nearly-round object, held by a long, ornate chain fastened through a bail on the top. She admired the details as she examined the unusual markings covering its surface, and the small clear stone set in the center.

"It holds a secret," he said, taking it back for a moment.

An engraving of three linked circles with a fourth containing the small crystal covered the middle of the piece. One of the circles pushed in slightly from the pressure of his finger, and gripping it by the three unmarked circles, the fourth popped out. He twisted it, pushed it back in, and then it opened, revealing a dark blue stone and small magnifying glass.

"That's awesome!" Della exclaimed. "I've never seen anything like it. But what does it have to do with finding me?"

"David gave it to me a while ago. It was sent to his dad, Bruce, by Kevin Knobbs."

"That's why they killed Kevin and tried to kill Bruce. They wanted it."

"That's what I think too. Well, the first time I held it, I went into some kind of weird state, and then to a world filled with death and destruction. I didn't open it again until today. You see, I was riding my motorcycle thinking of you when my bag started vibrating something fierce. I pulled over to figure out what was going on. It seemed like something was trapped inside and wanted out, but it was this thing, and it was moving all over the place.

"I opened it out of curiosity, and as soon as I did, I went into another trance. That's when I saw you running down a road in some kind of danger. The magnifier scanned the area for me, and I recognized where you were. This thing showed me."

"Really," Della replied as she took the magnifier from Parks. "I've never heard anything like that before. What do you think it is?"

"I don't know," he said, relaxing a bit, "but people have died because of it. I've been holding onto it to keep it out of Management's hands. I believe they're looking for it, and other things like it, and now I'm beginning to see why. It reveals things that are really important to the one holding it. Think what could happen if it was in the wrong hands."

He put the magnifier back into its case, and returned it to his bag. It was late, and they were both exhausted. Parks knew his father wouldn't mind their spending the night in his old bedroom, and he was relieved the love of his life was finally back safe and sound. It was great to have her close again, and there wasn't another place in the world he wanted to be.

He lay next to her as she slept, and for a while, believed that life could be good again. Then that familiar dark feeling gripped him, He forced himself to think about the good days he once shared with Della and his family, the memories were mingled with pain from the loss of his mother. Despite the pain, however, Della's presence and the memories of his mother's kindness were only things standing between him and something very wrong. He didn't know how long the barrier would last against the inevitable. A hopeless feeling washed over him as he drifted off to sleep.

CHAPTER 22

"Come on you two," Darla barked at Normand and her nurse as she stepped into the elevator. "I have a room ready just down the hall, but we need to be quick about it. All these management people running around are making me nervous."

"Me too," Normand said.

He pushed David out of the elevator, through the closet, and onto the top floor of the hospital.

"Through here," Darla said as she pushed the door to a large room. "This was a private room registered to a family with two boys who were in an auto accident. They recovered and checked out yesterday, but I've switched the files. As far as anybody knows, your friends are those two brothers still recuperating from a bad accident."

Darla took David's bed from Normand, and pushed it next to the window while another nurse positioned Isaac's bed next to him. She checked their IVs and monitoring equipment.

"Dr. Stevens will be up to see them later this morning," Nurse Darla said as she turned to leave. "One of my trusted nurses is on duty. She'll make sure they're safe."

Normand was relieved as he settled into a chair. He sat there for several hours before feeling hungry, and was about to go down to the cafeteria when Isaac groaned, and opened his eyes.

"Normand?" Isaac said weakly as he recognized his friend. "Where am I?"

"In the hospital. You've been through a lot, big guy. How do you feel?"

"Like somebody hit me in the chest with a sledge hammer," Isaac said as he closed his eyes for a moment. "Man that woman is wicked."

"What woman?" Normand asked intently.

"I don't know her name, but with that nose of hers, she could sub out as a bird of prey. She and some little guy in a suit really took it to me," Isaac explained. "Hey, is that David?"

"Yes, it's David, and you're not going to believe what happened to him. Somebody stabbed him through his truck door."

"And I thought I had it rough," Isaac said, rising up on his elbows, and looking over his bed rails.

"Are you sure you should be doing that?" Normand cautioned. "Maybe we should wait until someone comes in to have a look at you."

"Screw that!" Isaac said, releasing the bed rail.

It snapped down as he swung his legs over the side.

"I don't need this anymore," he continued, pulling the IV from his arm, and ripping the sensors off his chest. "What I need is some clothes and food. I'm hungry."

Normand laughed, recognizing Isaac's familiar energy. He was not one to mess around, and if he wanted to do something, he did it. He knew right then Isaac was back. Normand found some clothes in the closet, but they weren't much. They consisted of a pair of drawstring light blue pants and a large orange shirt that fit like a tent. A pair of slip-on booties with elastic around the ankles finished out the ensemble.

"I look ridiculous," Isaac said, catching a glimpse of himself in the mirror. "We need to get some decent clothes, but not until after I eat."

He headed for the door.

"Hey, moving around the hospital may not be the safest thing to do," Normand warned. "People are looking for us."

"Well, I've got to eat," Isaac said as he paused at the door. "We'll have to chance it."

The ride down the elevator to the basement cafeteria was uneventful. It was still early, and the hospital had yet to really wake up. Isaac filled a plate with nearly everything they served with Normand close behind, and between the two of them, they consumed enough food for a family of six.

"What happened to you?" Normand asked between bites.

"Some things are fuzzy, but I do remember going to my apartment after meeting with Aaron, and running into this small guy, who by the way, is wickedly strong. He slapped the dog crap out of me. Then I woke up in some weird place with a crazy lady asking questions I couldn't answer. I got out of there somehow, and the next thing I know here I am with you."

"You met with Aaron? When was that?"

"The night we all got together, remember?" Isaac answered as he took a big mouthful of pancakes. "David said we should see if he could get a copy of that map Burke saw at the Citadel. I thought he might help us, and then he got all pissy when I mentioned the ROD to him. I don't know what's going on with that guy. He used to like meeting with us."

"Do you think Aaron sold us out?" Normand exclaimed as he pushed away from the table.

"Aaron would never do that," Isaac said defensively. "He might be a little chummy with those Management guys, but he's still our friend."

"I'm not so sure…" Normand said glumly. "Still, I need to do some checking, just to make sure. Anyway, if you're through eating, let's get you back to your room. We've been gone too long already, and you have to rest. I have a lot of things to figure out, and you need to keep an eye on David."

"I can do that," Isaac said as he got up.

Normand followed Isaac to his room, and then left the hospital. He decided the best course of action was to get over to Kirsten's parents' place, and see if he could catch her in. He didn't like the idea of suspecting one of their own, but Isaac's situation seemed too convenient to be a coincidence, and a lot of things were not adding up.

The sun was still low on the Eastern horizon as he pulled into their driveway. It was going to be another beautiful summer day.

He parked his truck in front of their porch, and hopped out. It was still early, but he hoped someone was awake. Normand rang the doorbell and peeked into the side window, but it was too dark to see. Disappointed, he headed back to his truck.

He opened the truck door, planning to call her when he got home.

"Hey!" a familiar voice came from the house. "What's going on?"

"Parks," Normand exclaimed as he slammed his truck door, ran back, and jumped onto the porch. "I didn't expect to find you here."

"Come in," Parks invited. "Just give me a minute to get dressed, would you?"

Normand followed Parks in, amused by what he was wearing. Parks had on a rather tight-fitting pink bathrobe, and was about to enter the bedroom when Normand heard another familiar voice.

"Who's there?" a female voice asked quietly.

"It's Normand," Parks said through the door. "We had better get dressed."

"Hello, Normand," Della said brightly, coming into the kitchen where he was waiting.

"Dr. Larson!" Normand exclaimed. "Wow! It's great to see you. I didn't know you were staying here."

Della ignored the awkward moment as she began making some coffee.

"Would you like some breakfast?" she asked.

"I just ate an hour ago," he replied. "Hey, what did you do to your hands?" Normand asked seeing the Band-Aids covering three of her fingers on one hand and two on the other hand.

"I got caught on a fence," Della said, and was about to explain further when Parks popped in.

"What brings you way out here?" Parks asked as he poured some coffee.

"I'm looking for Kirsten. Is she here?"

"No, she isn't home. I think she must have spent the night in the city, but I'm not sure. Dad wasn't home either, so I'm certain they had business in town. What do you need, Normand?"

"It's a hard thing to talk about. I don't know how much you know about recent events, but some really bad things have been happening lately, starting with Isaac being attacked and nearly killed."

"Dr. Larson told me some things," Parks said, glancing at Della. "But she didn't know too many details. She only helped out with David. What can you tell us about Isaac?"

"Some good news. Isaac's awake, and doing great. We had breakfast together this morning. But what seems strange is

Isaac had a meeting with Aaron the night he was attacked. He said Aaron was not all that excited about our plans to resist Management."

"Are you thinking Aaron had something to do with the attack on Isaac?"

"I don't know, I don't want to think like that. I guess I'm becoming paranoid, with people getting hurt, and weird things happening. I don't know what to think."

"You have good instincts," Parks said encouragingly, "but why don't you let me check things out while you keep an eye on Isaac and David? They're going to need a good friend like you around."

Normand felt like a heavy weight was lifted off his chest as he got up. Parks would be the right one to figure this thing out.

"Good seeing you again, Dr. Larson. I had better get to work. I've missed two days already, and can't afford to miss anymore. Oh, I just remembered," he said. "I was making a delivery at the Citadel before this all started happening, and saw the strangest thing. There were these large black vans behind one of the buildings. Do you think that means anything?"

"I don't know," Parks replied, "but I'll be checking up on that too. Let me know if you discover anything else."

"It's really great seeing you guys!" Normand exclaimed as he headed for the door.

Parks and Della waved from the porch as he drove away.

"I'm relieved to hear about Isaac," Della said as they returned to the kitchen. "I'm sure David will be alright too, but I would love to have another look at him. His insides looked like they were put through a blender, and I had to do a lot of repair work."

"It's too dangerous for you to go in there," Parks insisted, "but I'm very interested in those vans Normand mentioned. I don't know if Aaron has anything to do with Isaac or anything else Management might be up to, but I did see him at the Citadel. He was leading people into a large building I've never seen before. I'm going to need to have a look."

"That's even more dangerous," Della said anxiously as she grabbed Parks by the arm. "Why not stay here for a while with me instead."

Parks bent down and kissed Della tenderly, holding her tight.

"I'll be careful," he said reassuringly, "but I can't rest until this thing is over. We'll never have a life until it is, and you know it. But there are other things going on I haven't told you. Things I'm not sure you want to know."

"What is it, Parks?" she asked, looking intently into his big green eyes.

Parks sighed as he leaned into the kitchen stool. Della was right at eye level as she squeezed in tight between his knees. He knew he couldn't keep anything from her as he lowered his gaze.

"I've changed," he said reluctantly. "Something's wrong with me. Something I have trouble understanding. You know the story of the Zender and when it attacked me."

"Yes, you killed it, right?" Della replied.

"I thought I killed it. Now I'm not so sure. I hear a voice in my head, a voice that tells me to do things, violent things. Last night when I saw you about to be attacked by those dogs I responded instinctively."

"Of course you did," Della said softly. "You came for me. You saved me."

"I know I did, but that's not all I felt," Parks said, holding her tenderly. "I didn't just want to save you. I wanted to kill those beasts, no, I enjoyed killing them. I liked feeling their bones break and seeing their eyes glaze over as they died. I can still see it now," Parks continued, his face twisting into a strange smile.

"What are you talking about, Henry?" Della pressed, switching to a clinical mode.

"It's inside me," Parks answered, returning to his normal self. "The beast I thought I killed is in me, and I hear its voice in my head. It's getting harder and harder for me to fight the anger. I'm afraid I may even hurt someone I care about. I feel that I'm becoming more animal like all the time."

"No, you're not," Della said with a slight tremble in her voice. "You're not the Zender, Henry J. Parks, you're a kind and loving person."

She looked up at the man she loved, and felt a concern she never had before. He was different somehow, and there were changes. She reached up and hugged his neck, knowing no matter what happened, they were in it together.

Parks held her tight for a long time. It felt good with her in his arms, but he couldn't shake the gnawing, clawing presence ripping at the back of his mind. It was pure evil, and growing. He could feel it penetrating the deep recesses of his being.

"You'll be safe here," Parks said as he hopped on his bike. "If I see Dad or Kirsten, I'll tell them you're going to be staying with them for a while. I know they'll be excited having you around. In the meantime, I need to figure out what's going on with Aaron and the Citadel. Something just doesn't smell right."

He headed into the city, focused on the situation at hand. The internal battle still raged, but he felt if he kept his attention on problem-solving, he could control the strange urges. Little did he know the power of the Zender, and what was coming for him as he drove down the long gravel driveway, and out onto the road heading towards the city.

CHAPTER 23

General Allison headed across the compound towards Management's Central Control. It was a huge complex behind the Citadel, and overlooked much of the city. General Allison had only been inside once before, when her father had a meeting with the other division Managers. He wanted her to see what real influence looked like, and used that opportunity to introduce his daughter to the city's power brokers.

That was when she first met Dave Roberts, the President. He was tall and good looking, with black hair and piercing eyes. She thought he looked like a movie actor, and couldn't help staring at him. She even fantasized about him, and the power he held. She was excited to see him again. The fact his wife had recently died gave her the opportunity she was looking for, if she played her cards right.

"I'm here to see Mr. Roberts," Ms. Allison said as she exited the elevator and approached the reception desk. "I'm General Allison, and I have an appointment at twelve thirty."

The woman behind the large marble counter glanced up with a plastic smile, and ran her long polished nails down the appointment book, stopping when the General's name appeared.

"This is the way to his office," the woman said as she pulled a brochure from a drawer, and marked it with a pen. "Just follow the hall to the left, take a right, and then through the double doors. You'll find his office at the end of the hall."

The General's high heels clicked loudly on the polished marble floor as she hustled to see Dave. She was intent on selling herself, and convincing him she was the best one to take her father's position now that he had disappeared. But even more than that, she was interested in getting to know the president better.

"I'm General Allison, and I have an appointment to see the president," she said to the giant man guarding the entrance.

He looked at the slightly built woman, and then opened the door and disappeared inside. She stood there alone for a few moments, staring at the intricately carved wooden door, and the surrounding opulence. This was a building made for those with power, and it showed. Management insisted only the best materials be used, and the rarest of items were taken to adorn their structure when they renovated this building.

People had been forced to "donate" money, materials, and personal items of great value to its construction. Needless to say, there remained a lingering resentment among those required to fund such a lavish facility but that wasn't her concern. She wanted in on as much of the excess as possible.

"This way," the man said, holding the door open.

She followed him as he led the way down a plush red carpet towards a large desk with a man sitting in a high-backed leather chair looking over some papers.

"Ms. Allison," he said, rising from his seat as she approached. "Please, have a seat."

The president waited until she had seated herself before returning to his chair. She was wearing tight-fitting leather pants, and a sharply-cut suit coat that buttoned nearly to her chin. She crossed her legs, making sure he could see the six-inch high-heeled shoes she was wearing. He stared at her for a few moments before speaking.

"I was expecting your father," he said with a smile, "but you're a good substitute for now. Is Harry running late?"

"The situation is serious," she replied. "I wanted to tell you in person rather than over the phone, so I came straight over. Harry's been taken."

"Taken?" he asked intently. "What do you mean, taken?"

"Parks has Harry," she said bluntly. "He captured him in his office, and has taken him out of the Citadel again."

"Again!" Dave said, pounding his fist on the table. "That's the second time. Look, I'm sorry for your loss," he said, calming a little. "I'm sure you're upset about the situation."

"Thank you, Mr. President," the general replied, seizing the opportunity. "But I have to put my personal feelings aside. What's most important is the operation of the Citadel, and I'm not sure my father was the best person for the job."

"Oh, I see," Dave said, narrowing his eyes. "You don't think he was up to the task, eh? What would you have done differently?"

"Well, he did lose an arm in service to you and to Management," she continued, "he deserves credit for that. Unfortunately, the loss drove him to set a trap for Parks, a trap he caught himself in. Don't get me wrong, I love my father dearly," she said, doing her best to sound sincere, "but his approach was all wrong."

"Please continue Ms. Allison," Dave replied as the General paused for effect.

"Create an effective offence. People like Parks only understand one thing--force. I tried to convince Harry to let me go after him and explore more options, but he wanted to play it safe. He was afraid of doing too much, and maybe running afoul of you and the board. I understand the chain of command, but there are times you have to take the bull by the horn, and rip it off."

"I like your attitude."

He got up from his desk, and walked around to the front. He leaned back, and gave her a long second look.

"What are you suggesting?"

"Give me a list of those 'Gifts' you're looking for."

She leaned back into the chair, and looked up at Dave.

"Then I'll go to the members of the disbanded city council, and start pressuring them for information. They've been here since the beginning, and likely know something."

"You don't think we've thought of that?" the president replied sharply. "I can tell you, it's not that simple. There's not a list of items you can just go out and collect. These are unique things, and even if you had one, you might not know it. But I do like your attitude," he said, softening a little, "and it wouldn't hurt for you to initiate some conversation with the city fathers. Maybe you could do some good after all."

"And who better than the daughter of the abducted man," Ivy replied, pressing her advantage. "I'm quite capable of handling the situation, and other things as well if the need arises."

"Hmm, but I'll have to review this with the Board first. I'm meeting with them in a few hours, and we'll go over your ideas. Until then, go ahead and get things in order. You can take over his department for now, and I'll let you know what we decide."

"Thank you, sir," she said, slowly rising from her chair. "I won't disappoint you. Oh, by the way, I'm sorry to hear about your wife's recent passing," she said tenderly as she reached out and took his hand. "How are you doing?"

"I'm ok," he said emotionlessly. "It was unfortunate the way she fell down the stairs and broke her neck. She didn't suffer though, and that's comforting."

"Well, I'm here for you if you need someone to talk to," she said, squeezing his hand, and looking deep into his eyes. "You'll see how dedicated I am to Management's cause, and how useful I can be for anything you might require."

Dave watched as she exited his office, and the general made sure to sway her hips just a little more than usual to reward his attention.

"Blast that Parks!" Dave exclaimed to his empty office as the door shut behind the general. "How do you do it? Well, it doesn't matter. Harry wasn't working out anyway, and maybe his daughter could be of more use. She seems eager enough. But the gifts are elusive, and if we don't start finding them soon, we're all going to pay."

"Don't worry so much," a voice came from behind his chair.

Dave spun around to see one of the board members with his back to him, looking out the window.

"How did you get in here?" he stammered. "You startled me, sir."

"Things are progressing nicely," the man in a dark pinstriped suit said, without turning or responding to Dave's question, "but our time here is growing short. Capture the elusive man. We need to know what he knows, and whether he has any connection to the Gifts."

Dave glanced down at the floor for an instant as he considered his response. But when he looked back up, the man was gone. He leaned back, stared out the window, and smiled as he thought of his next move.

Destroying the gifts might not be the best thing for someone who wanted more than just a position in the new order. The board was powerful, but there would come a time when a new leader emerged, and then things would be different. He put his hands behind his head as a new plan began to form.

"Anybody home?" Philip asked,

He knocked on the door of the motor home, then walked around to one of the side windows and peered in.

"I never took you for a peeping tom," his brother James said as he came up the trail from the river with two fish in one hand and a pole in the other. His wife Lori carried the tackle box as they followed the narrow path.

"Looks like the fish are biting this morning," Philip said cheerfully as he met them at a picnic table.

"Good to see you, Phil," James said as he plopped the fish on the table. "How did you find us way out here?"

"Kenzie called the house looking for Henry, and told me you were fishing."

Philip put his foot on the picnic bench, and examined the morning's catch.

"I remember this place well, and figured this is where you would go. We spent plenty of days down here as kids, didn't we?"

"Yeah, those were better days," James replied seriously."

"Come in, Phil, and have some coffee," Lori said encouragingly. "I made it less than an hour ago, and it should still be hot."

Philip followed her up the three short steps and into the motor home, followed by his brother. He found a spot on the narrow couch as James occupied a cloth-covered swivel chair bolted to the floor.

"Thank you," Philip said as she put a cup of coffee on the small table next to him, and handed a cup to James. "Kenzie said you're planning on staying until you get some answers. She said you got a notice or something wanting you to go to the Citadel, but some of your neighbors went, and never came home. Is that true?"

"It seems really creepy to me," Lori said nervously. "Jim and Rita visited some of our friend's farms, and found some really bizarre things."

"What kind of bizarre things?" Philip pressed.

"He said their farms were abandoned, and their livestock dying or dead," James replied. "It's not like farmers to do a thing like that."

"Where did they go, and why isn't anyone checking on this kind of stuff?" Philip asked.

"I wish I knew," James said. "We only found out thanks to Jim, and came here looking for answers. Then the cops pulled us over once we crossed the bridge. They were really suspicious and aggressive. I've never seen them like that. That's when we decided to hide out here. One thing's for sure, we can't leave. I'm sure they're watching the main roads, and would spot us in a second. Fortunately, we have food and water for as long as we need it."

"I think some big things are coming," Philip said, leaning forward and folding his hands between his knees, "and we're just seeing the beginning. Pearl was a victim too. I lost her last week at the hands of the Testers."

"Oh no!" Lori gasped. "You can't mean it, Phil."

"I can't believe it myself," he said glumly. "I still think she'll be waiting for me at the door when I come home."

"I'm so sorry for your loss," James said, leaning into his chair, and bumping the wall with his shoulder. "But Testers? I haven't heard those mentioned in years. What would they want with Pearl?"

"I'm not sure. They were crossing the road a few miles from the house just as Pearl was heading over to help some friends. They smashed into her car, and then chased her through the woods. We found her trapped under a tree after the Testers had cleared out."

"Poor Pearl," Lori said with a sob.

"Are you doing ok?" James asked tenderly.

"No! I'm not ok," Philip said angrily. "I think the Testers are part of some larger plan, something really evil. Something connected to the ancient stories we heard growing up."

"Come on, Phil," James said, glancing at Lori, whose face had turned ghostly white. "What are you saying? You know those were just meant to scare us, and keep us kids in line. You can't really believe the boogie man is out there."

Philip scrunched his face a bit at James' attitude but knew he'd felt the same way himself at one time. And, the writings were different than what had happened to the city in the past ten-plus years. If the stories were true, the city would have been destroyed already, but that didn't mean things were right.

"Look," Philip answered as calmly as he could, "Henry met something in a cave on Grace Mountain that cannot be explained away. It wasn't like any animal I've ever heard of or seen before, and according to Henry's description and from the three wounds left on each of his shoulders, I believe it was a Zender."

"Zender," James replied. "That's just a fictitious creature. It's not real, is it?"

"I'm afraid it may be," Philip said. "Only our city is still here, so something's definitely different this time around. But I think we need to reach the city fathers as soon as possible. As far as I know, Rich Lindberg is still head, even if Management has banned them. What do you say we find Rich, and see if he can get the fathers together for a meeting? They may have the answers we need."

"I'm not staying here by myself," Lori said as she blew her nose. "I want to get over to your house, and see Kirsten and Henry. They're going to need some comforting."

"That's greatly appreciated," Philip replied. "Why don't you both stay with us until this mess is sorted out. I know you like fishing, but it must get lonely out here at night."

James looked at Lori before nodding his head in agreement. Philip had driven his pickup, and there was plenty of room to put as many belongings as they needed in the back. James locked up the motor home, and climbed into the front seat while Lori slipped into the back. Philip was careful to take the back roads to his house in order to avoid any contact with Management.

Once he dropped Lori off there, James and he would head into the city to make contact with Rich. The conversations were sparse as they drove along. Both James and Lori were still trying to come to grips with Pearl's death but it hit Lori especially hard. They had spent many years together, and were more like sisters than in-laws.

Philip, on the other hand, was deep in thought. It seemed the years of doing his level best to stay out of public affairs was coming back to haunt him. He felt guilty for not paying more attention or at least staying informed. But it had been far too easy to ignore what was happening around him. "Let someone else deal with it," he used to say, "I'm too busy." Now his apathy might have contributed to the death of his wife. It was a thought that weighed heavily on his mind.

James was feeling equally responsible. He saved every newspaper he ever bought, had seen the discrepancies and the slow twisting of truth as Management dug their claws into every story, but he had kept his concerns to himself. But now it was time to join his brother in the struggle to save as many as possible, even if it was too late for his sister-in-law.

CHAPTER 24

Jim drove to the central broadcasting station, thinking about how much things had changed. He and Frank had once been good friends. They had joined the resistance together before the city was taken, and helped secure HOT News as the only independent station in the city. Frank made Jim into 'Jim the Weatherman', and gave him a successful career, but that seemed like a long time ago now.

His mind was filled with troubling questions. Why had Frank turned against him? Did he get tired of the stress of fighting the system, and gave in to the temptation to shut up and join in? Jim had been tempted himself a few times, but he was not one for giving in no matter how tough it got. Frank had seemed much the same.

He pulled into the parking lot, and parked in Frank's spot next to a rear door that led directly to his office. He tried a few of Frank's keys before finding the right one. Frank's office was almost pitch black, with the only source of light coming from the illuminated dial on a clock on his desk.

Security could be in the building, so he kept the lights off. He pushed the button on Frank's computer, and waited for it to load. In a few moments, the flashing pointer on the screen was calling for a password.

"I hope Rita was right," he said under his breath. "If Frank changed his password, I could be here all night."

He typed in the password Rita had provided, 1CIGAR, and hit the button. Sure enough, the screen filled with icons. He remembered how much Frank had enjoyed controlling the broadcasting format at HOT News, and made sure he had the final say. That meant he could play or stop any program from his office computer, and he had brought that same level of micromanagement to his new office.

Jim had instant access to all Management-controlled stations. He loaded the disk, quickly checked to make sure everything worked, and set play for tomorrow evening when the majority of people would be home and likely to have their televisions on.

"Won't this be a surprise?" he said under his breath with a smile.

Jim was feeling good as he finished his work, and began to shut down the computer. He was hurrying to get the heck out when an icon flashing on the lower corner of the screen caught his eye.

"Message from 'Wolf Tracker,'" he said curiously. "Hmm, maybe I can find out a little more useful information while I'm here. No use wasting the opportunity."

He clicked the icon, and it opened to an email server he had never seen before. The screen slowly filled with row after row of email messages from users with strange animal names. He opened the one from "Wolf Tracker" first."

"Red eyes are grouping south," Wolf Tracker wrote. "Cannot wait much longer. Backspin will have things ready next week."

He began to check other e-mails. The conversations were purposely loosely worded, but the more he read the more, he began to understand these were communications between people who were tracking Management. Jim skimmed back through the many messages to the day last winter when he and Rita were nearly killed. There were at least ten e-mails that day from a host of unusual names. But what stood out most was one from "Weasel."

"Agreed, Backspin. Keep track of the Weather." Weasel wrote." If he's caged, we'll get him out. Have Foxtail watch and "tag" him. This will keep them busy while we get deeper inside. Be careful. Have heard they're becoming impatient. Could be stormy if we aren't careful."

Frank wasn't part of Management. The sudden realization hit him deep in his gut. He was part of some resistance. That was what he had meant when he said Jim was wrong about him. But why didn't he say anything? Jim's stepping up and becoming a reporter again probably scared him, and he didn't know if he could trust him.

Jim sat back in the darkened room as a sullen feeling swept over him. He had seen himself as the hero, riding in to save everyone, but he was really just a selfish guy wanting to get his gusto back. Frank was dead because of him, Rita had risked her life to save his, others were running for their lives, and he was sitting here having really done nothing.

He needed to figure out who these people were Frank was connected to. He began to comb Frank's computer for clues.

He pulled a pen and paper from the desk drawer, and began making notes. Suddenly, the screen went black. He checked under the desk to see if he had accidentally hit the power supply, but suddenly, the screen lit up again. He was confused at first, but then he saw the red light indicating the computer's webcam was on, and pointed right at him.

"Oh crap," he said as he started pulling plugs. "They've been watching me."

He kicked the chair back, and ripped the power cord from the rear of the computer. It faded to black as he heard footsteps running down the hall in his direction. Jim grabbed his disk from the computer, and booked it for the door.

He jumped into Frank's car just as lights came on in the office. He started the motor, and peeled out of the parking lot as several large men came rushing out. Jim saw in his rear view mirror one of them kneel down and position what appeared to be a weapon. He immediately recognized the glow of the business end of a Nullifier.

He swerved at the last second, and the blast that likely would have destroyed Frank's car cut through one of the mobile vans used for on-site reporting instead. It exploded in a ball of fire, and he swerved around the rear axle as it bounced across the road and into the far ditch. Frank's sports car lived up to its billing as he slid through the corner, past the gate, and onto the road.

There was little chance the large SUV pulling out behind him would keep up, but Jim kept the pedal mashed to the floor until he was safely out of range. He doubled back, taking the side roads to Normand's apartment. Frank's car was too noticeable to be left out front, so he stopped along a wooded area, and hid it behind some brush. His ankle was fully healed now, so he was able to jog the rest of the way to the apartment.

"Are you ok?" Rita asked anxiously as she met Jim at the door.

"Just barely," he said, closing the door and locking it. "But I'm more confused than ever. I need a shot of something."

Rita found a half-full bottle of rum in the cabinet above Normand's fridge. Jim took one shot and then another before calming enough to talk.

"Frank's dead," he said as he began to explain the events at the cabin. "But now I believe he was one of the good guys. I guess he was too proud to explain himself, and expected me to trust him regardless of the circumstances. It's a bitter pill to swallow."

Rita sobbed a bit as Jim went on to explain the weird events of the night until they were both emotionally exhausted. They talked for hours before finally dozing off, but their sleep felt as empty as the day's events.

"Where do you think Normand and Kenzie are?" Rita asked after making some coffee.

"The last thing I heard was Normand would be staying with Isaac and David until they recover," Jim replied as he poured a second cup of coffee. "We could go by the hospital, but chances are we'd be caught. I think it would be safer if you stayed here."

"You're not going anywhere without me," Rita said, her dark brown eyes flashing. "We're in this together to the end, good or bad."

"I had to try," Jim said with a slight smile. "I didn't really think you would stay behind. We need to get downtown and meet some people, people we have to trust."

They walked into the early morning light to where Jim had stored Frank's car the night before. He believed they would be looking for a red sports car, so their best move was to beat the traffic by leaving early. Once they got downtown, they could park it on the street somewhere, and walk the rest of the way. Jim took one of Normand's hooded sweatshirts to hide his face while Rita donned a loose-fitting pair of jeans, and put on a shabby coat she found in a closet. They looked like two homeless people, but they weren't alone. There was plenty of poverty and more people in need than ever thanks to Management.

They made it downtown without incident, and Jim ditched the car as planned. Soon, he and Rita were walking the sidewalks.

"Where are we going?" Rita asked as they moved with the shoppers and people heading to work.

"We're going to meet one of our friends from the list I made at Frank's office," Jim said from behind the dark glasses under his hood.

It was a long walk, and he was starting to sweat under the heavy sweatshirt. He began to feel self-conscious as he passed people in short sleeves, but he had no choice. He couldn't chance being recognized. Finally, they came to a large brick building sitting prominently in the center of the business district.

Jim strolled into the marbled entry, and pulled off the sweatshirt. A slender, red-headed older woman sitting behind a desk looked up as he approached.

"Hi, Shirley!" Jim said warmly. "It looks like your husband is still too cheap to hire a secretary."

"Jim," the receptionist replied, standing up with a wide smile. "I was just thinking about you. Where have you been hiding?"

"Not hiding so much," Jim replied, "more like running for my life."

"I heard something about that," she said coming around her desk, and kissing him on the cheek. "It's good to see you again, and who is this with you?"

"Sorry," he said, "this is Rita. Rita, this is Shirley."

The two women traded pleasantries, but Jim was staying on course.

"I need to see your husband. Is he in this morning?"

"He is," she said, "he just came from court and is doing some client calls, but I see his line is open. I'll check for you."

Shirley clicked the intercom, and in a few moments, an older gentleman with a neatly-trimmed beard and silver hair came out through one of the heavy carved wooden doors.

"Jim!" he said as he shook his hand. "Been a long time, and who is this lovely lady with you?"

"Hello, Mr. Kraft," Jim responded. "This is Rita. Can we talk for a minute?"

"Sure! Come in to my office," the man said, holding the door open. "My next appointment isn't for another half hour. We can talk, and catch up a bit."

The office was large, and filled with expensive furniture and high book cases. Boxes stuffed with files covered his desk. He quickly put them down on the plush, carpeted floor before taking his place behind the desk. Tim Kraft was full of energy, and seemed genuinely glad to see Jim. He was also full of questions, but Jim couldn't waste time, and got right down to business.

"I need your help," Jim said bluntly. "I'm sure you're aware of most everything that happens around the city, and know all about the demise of HOT News. But you should also know Frank is dead."

"Frank died?" Tim said with obvious surprise. "How? When? I just spoke with him yesterday."

"You spoke with Frank yesterday?!" Jim asked as questions exploded in his head. "Why would you be speaking with Frank? He wasn't one of your clients, unless you know something about the secret society he's involved with."

Tim pushed away from his desk with a frown on his face. Jim knew instantly he was on to something, and had come to the right place.

"Secret society?" the lawyer replied as he folded his arms, and leaned back with a hard glare. "What are you talking about?"

"Frank was in communication," he pressed, "with people who had secret identities. I found a bunch of emails on his computer last night when I was in his office. Let me guess," he continued. "Weasel?"

"If you could find out, they may have found out too." the lawyer exclaimed, slamming his hand on the desk. "There are a group of us who are working together to undermine Management, but up till now we've had little success. In fact, your broadcast last year was the best thing that happened. Oh, Frank was against it at first, but once it ran, it gave him opportunity to get inside Management's main studio, and become part of their team. He's been getting the goods on them, and we were preparing charges against them, but that may be over if Frank's dead, and they've discovered our identities."

"That would be a problem," Jim replied. "But maybe I've inadvertently put them off the track. They might think it was me behind everything. I say we continue on as if that's what they think. We can't quit now," he asserted. "Look, Rita and I need a safe place to hide and some resources, and I'm going to need a cover so I can move around the city without being stopped. Also, here's a list of people I would like you to hire from my old HOT News team." He wrote some names on a pad from Tim's desk. "These guys are good, and I trust them. Plus, they need the money. I also want to meet with your 'partners.' We must team up, and pool our resources. What do you say? Can you help me?"

"You're asking a lot, but maybe it'll work if Management hasn't cracked our identities," Tim replied thoughtfully. "If they have, we're all toast anyway. Shirley will take you to one of my vacant rentals where you can stay. I'll make sure you have transportation, and some communication equipment. Frank set up a two-way FM network out of some old equipment. No one uses the bands anymore, so Management has not been able to intercept our calls, and here's a portable unit," he said, opening his desk drawer, and handing Jim a large, hand-held transmitter and charger. "Not as inconspicuous as a cell phone, but it works. I'll send over some papers with Shirley, and give you both believable aliases. But you had best be careful. This could blow up on us all."

"Thanks," Jim said, shaking Tim's hand. "You're the best."

Jim and Rita got in the back seat of one of Tim's large town cars with darkened windows as Shirley drove them to a nondescript neighborhood in the middle of the city. It was the perfect hideaway, a small house with a garage and lawn surrounded by nearly identical homes. She handed Jim the keys and several bags of groceries.

"I'll come back later and check on you," Shirley said, glancing over at Rita. "Tim said you'll need transportation, so I'll drop something off later today."

"Thank you," Jim replied warmly. "You've been a big help."

The house was perfect, and he could hardly believe their good fortune. A few hours ago, he wasn't sure if they would live to see another day, and now he was in the middle of the resistance.

CHAPTER 25

"It's time to shake things up," Parks said to himself as he motored along on his bike. "I think I've been a little too easy on my old buddies at the Citadel. Just because Harry's out of my hair and 'chillin' at the Island is no reason to quit now; I'm just getting warmed up."

He took several side roads up the mountain on the East side to one of the road maintenance sites. A heavy steel cable attached to several large steel pipes sunk in concrete guarded the entrance. Parks pulled up, and removed one of his crystal blades from the leather belt around his waist. The cable split in two with one quick movement, and he roared through, headed towards the big equipment sheds, where he delivered a similar fate to the padlocks on a large sliding door. Parks returned his blade to its sheath, and hopped off his bike. The giant trucks were still outfitted with snowplows, even though they were not in use during the summer. He found them full of fuel, and the key in the key cabinet.

The one he chose instantly roared to life, billowing black smoke.

He pulled halfway down the driveway, and stopped in front of a heavy concrete structure built into the side of the hill. He jumped out, and addressed the heavy steel door with his blade, which sliced through like it was butter. He pushed the door open, revealing row after row of boxes filled with dynamite. He loaded fifty pound boxes onto the front seat of the truck, strapped his motorcycle to the rear bumper, and took off. The truck lumbered down the road, picking up speed as he went through the gears.

Meanwhile, the cadets were busy going through their morning routine under the watchful eye of General Allison. Most of them were rookies who had been promoted within the past six months from a large pool of eager applicants.

One of the first things Management had done when they took the city was redo the educational system. They required parents to bring their children to special educational camps, and leave them there for months at a time. This allowed them to program younger children to their methods without parental interference. These new recruits were evidence of their success, as they followed orders without questions or restraint. The general picked two cadets that morning for a special training exercise.

The group stood at attention as the two squared off in the open field. They didn't appear equally matched, as one was considerably smaller than the other. They were given their choice of training weapons. Blunt swords, wooden poles and clubs with hard rubber knobs on the end but no defensive weapons. The larger cadet chose a sword, while the smaller cadet selected a long wooden pole.

The fighting was fierce, with both young men striking their opponent, and drawing blood. It looked for a while that the smaller Cadet was outmatched, but one quick move provided a devastating blow to his larger opponent's forehead. The man fell in a bloody heap to the grassy ground, and didn't move.

"You've done well," she complimented as he returned to the cadet ranks. "That's what I like to see," she continued as she circled the barely conscious cadet. "Show no mercy, and give no quarter. You'll be of great value to the BOJ Order as we dispatch you to handle the daily offenses of this city. There are those out there who think they can oppose our ways, but you'll prove them wrong. There was one who once thought to set himself above us. He was proud, and not humble like you. He excluded many from the Band of Justice, saying you had to be patient, and learn from your elders. Well, his name now lives in infamy, doesn't it?"

General Allison walked up and down the line of cadets, looking deep into each one's eyes. "There may even be a day when you'll have to face this rogue loser called Parks. Show him less mercy than you have seen here today. Don't stop until he lies dead at your feet, for he would treat you no better. Then his memory will be forever erased, and justice will be confirmed."

She turned the remainder of the morning training over to the small, victorious cadet, and headed for her office. She purposely stepped over the wounded cadet without even looking down or saying a word. Her message was crystal clear. Win, and you are rewarded. Lose, and you will suffer. It was not new to these cadets, and they were well aware of the consequences of failure.   Most of them had at one point or another been in a similar place as their friend sprawled on the ground. But they knew helping him was out of the question, no matter how much they desired to give him a hand, and make sure he was ok. They would have to finish the morning exercises before any aid could be granted.

Parks stopped next to the wall surrounding the Citadel complex, and jumped out with two boxes of dynamite. He off-loaded his bike next, and hid it behind some bushes. He had chosen a spot where the Citadel's cameras couldn't spot him. Several passersby slowed, and stared at the huge machine idling on the shoulder of the road.

The sharp 'V' plow blade glistened in the sun as Parks hopped back in, and began accelerating towards the main entrance. He swerved onto the drive towards the gate, still picking up speed. The guard saw the plow barreling towards him, and at first, stepped out with his hand in the air. He quickly realized Parks was not about to stop, and dove back into his shack. Unfortunately, there was no getting out of the way. The machine sliced off the front of the guard shack, and sent the guard flying out a side wall. He landed in a lifeless heap several yards away.

The truck burst through the gate, and Parks had only one thought in mind: destroy as much as possible as quickly as possible. His main goal was the Citadel itself. It was Management's central command. If he could cripple or destroy it, they would be at a serious disadvantage.

The cadets froze and stared in amazement as the huge vehicle roared past and disappeared into the underground garage. They looked at each other, suddenly realizing something bad was happening. They begin running towards the Citadel, but then instantly changed direction, and dove for cover as vehicles came flying out.

Parks was crushing everything in his path while smashing through the buildings' support pillars at the same time. Along the way, he lit handfuls of dynamite, and threw them under the building. Just then, the boxes of explosives he had set outside the Citadel's wall blew, and sent a large mushroom cloud of dust and debris into the air, and rocks raining for miles around. Parks drove up and out of the garage just as the sticks of dynamite exploded behind him, sending a shock wave that knocked the cadets out of action.

Chaos was took hold as panic-stricken people streamed from the building, not sure which way to run. Parks made a big turn, revved the motor several times, and began a second run at the main support columns along the outside of the building.

"I can do better than that," he said to himself as he plowed into the wobbling building.

General Allison was having difficulty regaining her footing in Harry's old office as she struggled to grasp what was happening. The blasts sent furniture and paintings flying, and Harry's heavy desk sliding across the room, momentarily pinning her to the wall. She managed to push it off just as Mr. Grey came staggering in, having been hit in the head with a falling piece of ceiling tile. They made it to the office window just in time to watch Parks barrel by below.

"We've got to go right now!" General Allison shouted.

They raced for the stairs, with pieces of building falling everywhere. The emergency lights blinked on and off as they struggled along. They were the last two remaining people in the building as everyone else had managed to make it out. Then the building shook violently, knocking them both to the landing on the second floor as the heavy "V" blade took out the last of the support columns on the front side of the building.

Parks wheeled around the rear of the building, and tossed several more bundles of dynamite at the struggling building for good measure. They bounced into what was left of the parking garage, and exploded with such force it rocked the truck.

Suddenly, he saw a familiar face racing towards some cars parked along another building in the back. It was Aaron. He jumped into a car, and started backing out just as Parks cut him off.

"Get in," Parks commanded, opening the passenger door.

Aaron looked up in amazement at Parks glowering face. He quickly evaluated his options, and then climbed into the seat next to him.

"What are you doing?" Aaron asked as Parks took off. "Have you completely lost your mind?"

"Just the opposite," Parks retorted, "I finally found it."

He drove towards the new building on the ridge as Aaron worked to grasp the gravity of the situation. He slowed, and they watched as the Citadel swayed several times, and then slowly toppled over and smashed to the ground. A giant cloud of dust rose into the air as emergency alarms screamed for help.

The Citadel had become nothing more than a pile of shattered concrete and twisted steel.

"What's this place?" Parks asked calmly as he pulled to a stop at the main entrance of a sleek, low-lying metal building.

Aaron was in shock, and didn't respond at first. All he could see was the life he had worked so hard to build dissolving before his eyes, and Parks was to blame.

"What do you do here?" Parks asked again, more forcefully.

"Why? Are you going to destroy it too?" Aaron asked, shaking.

"No, I just want to know what you do here," Parks insisted.

"I process people for achievement awards and funding," Aaron answered bleakly. "Or at least I used to. Chances are I won't be doing that anymore."

"Where are the people you process?" Parks asked as he set the brake, but left the motor running.

"Inside or gone home, I suppose," Aaron replied, trying to decide if he should make a break for it or not.

"You would think with all the excitement going on, they would have come out by now." Parks said as he pushed his door open. "Let's have a look."

Aaron followed in a daze, finding it difficult to believe Parks was taking the time to examine the building. He guessed Parks believed it would take time for Management to respond, so he could go on a short tour. It seemed crazy, but Aaron followed him inside to a long foyer filled with tables covered with neat stacks of papers.

"Is that yours?" Parks asked, pointing towards a long dark wooden desk in the middle.

"Yes. I process their information after they fill out the paperwork."

"Then what happens?" Parks asked intently.

"Well, I take the papers back to my office for filing. Hey, don't you think you should be going?"

"Not yet. Then what happens, I mean to the people?" Parks continued, examining the building closely.

"Like I said," Aaron replied, becoming annoyed at his insistence, "they go home."

"What's in here?" Parks asked, standing in front of a set of double doors. "The building seems much larger than just this front part. Must be something back there?"

"I wouldn't know," Aaron replied. "I've never been in there."

Parks drew his blade, and sliced off the lock. Aaron was surprised how smooth it cut. It had been a long time since he saw a crystal blade. The door opened to a darkened room, and Parks felt around for the light switch, and flipped it on. The two men blinked a few times as their eyes adjusted to the light. It was a large, mostly empty room, except for a platform set against the back wall. On the platform were six chairs in a row facing forward.

"Nothing much to see," Aaron said, turning to leave.

Then he stopped as a cold shiver went up his spine. One lone bloody handprint was visible on the wall next to the light switch. It appeared someone had attempted to wipe it off, but couldn't get it all before it dried.

"Come over and look at this," Parks said as he walked towards the platform, and waved Aaron to the front. Parks squatted down, and pointed to thin red lines between the hardwood flooring. "That's not paint. That's blood. Something really bad has been happening in here, and housekeeping is getting careless with the cleanup."

"What do you think happened?" Aaron said, beginning to feel sick to his stomach. "Why would there be blood in here?"

"How much do you want to know?" Parks asked quietly. "Whatever is at the end of this rabbit hole is worse than a headhunting queen. Judging from the blood splatters on the ceiling," Parks continued, glancing up, "I would guess the good people you brought here to help are not with us any longer."

"You mean they were killed?" Aaron gulped as he squatted next to Parks.

"I can't say for sure, but my guess is yes," Parks replied sadly. "Either way, there's nothing we can do for them now."

The sounds of emergency vehicles arriving echoed through the auditorium as Parks and Aaron stepped into the daylight. Rescue workers were beginning to search the wreckage for survivors, and the remaining cadets out on patrol were arriving in droves. They set up a perimeter, and were assessing the situation when one of the Cadets saw Parks and started yelling to a commander.

"Wait here," Parks said, climbing into the huge machine, and aiming it towards the main entrance. "This should keep them busy a little longer."

He put it into neutral, released the brake, and it began slowly picking up speed as it headed down the hill. Parks took another bundle of dynamite, lit it, and threw it into the dump bed. He and Aaron ran for the gaping hole blown through the Citadel wall. There was momentary panic as the cadets tried to move their vehicles out of the way of the careening monster, but it was too late. The truck plowed into the group of shiny black SUVs, sending them flying. Then the dynamite exploded and knocked off the dump bed, sending it sailing into the hole Parks had busted through the gate, effectively blocking them in.

"Come on!" Parks shouted, climbing over the pile of rubble that once was the Citadel wall. "Our transportation is right over there."

Aaron climbed on the back as Parks fired up his bike. He roared down the main road in front of the Citadel's main entrance to get one more long, satisfying look at his handiwork before heading towards his parent's house.

Even though everyone was occupied with one crisis or another, Parks still took the back roads. In about an hour, he pulled into the yard, and parked his bike in front of the porch.

"What have you done?" Aaron demanded, jumping off the bike and facing Parks. "I have friends that could be dead thanks to you. If they saw me, they might even think I'm in on this insane event."

"You have a lot to learn," Parks replied, his eyes flashing in the sunlight. "Come in the house, and we'll talk about it."

Aaron reluctantly followed Parks inside. He was angry and confused, and it all seemed like a very bad dream. Parks, on the other hand, was deeply satisfied that the dark voice in his head was finally quiet. But as he entered his parents' home, he found a note from Della telling him she had gone to the hospital to check on David. His conversation with Aaron would have to wait as they got back onto his bike and headed towards town.

CHAPTER 26

Della couldn't wait any longer so she called Darla to see if she knew anything. Unfortunately, Darla was out on her rounds and nobody could find her on the floor. Della's first concern was to keep from being recognized so she hunted around in Pearl's closet until she found some clothes that fit. Pearl was a few inches taller but, other than that, they were about the same build. She tried on several outfits before settling on a pair of black pants and a light sweater. Fortunately, Pearl had some wigs she wore on rare occasions so Della chose a blonde one with long front bangs. It totally covered her black hair and most of her eyes. The finishing touches came with the addition of dark red lipstick and blue eye shadow.

"I wouldn't know it was me if I didn't know it was me," Della said with a laugh as she admired herself in the dressing mirror. "Now how am I going to get to town? All the vehicles are taken."

She searched the barn finding no transportation. Next she opened the door to one of the smaller storage sheds.

"Here we go!" She exclaimed as she lifted a ten speed bike hanging from a rafter hook. "I'm going to be quite the site riding into town," she thought to herself as she strapped some elastic bands around her pant legs so they wouldn't get caught in the chain. "Well, maybe it's better this way. Who would expect the city's most noted surgeon and wanted criminal to come coasting in on a bicycle, wearing a wig?"

Della peddled her way down the driveway and onto the county road. She hadn't biked competitively for years but it didn't take long for her body to remember the routine. She rose up and peddled hard on the inclines then leaned forward and peddled equally hard on the down slopes. It took nearly two hours to make it to the city limits but, once there, she made her way along the city streets.

"Ok!" Della said to herself as she coasted to a stop in front of the hospital's main entrance. "That wasn't so hard was it? Now let's see if I can get inside."

She parked the bike out front and straightened her outfit before entering through the heavy glass doors. Her goal was to blow past the nurse's station and find Nurse Darla before anyone noticed. After all, she couldn't just ask what room David was in. He must be held under a false name. Suddenly, her blood ran cold as she saw Barron standing at the nurse's desk thumbing through the patient files. He could be there for only one reason, to find out if anyone had been brought over from the Surgery Center and admitted within the last forty-eight hours. Her only hope was to keep her head down and not stop walking.

"Can I help you?" Said an observant nurse as Dr. Larson passed by on the opposite side of the hall.

"Crap," Della said under her breathe, quickly deciding whether to keep going or not. She decided to stop and turn towards the nurse. "Um, why yes, yes you can," she said walking over to the desk. "I was supposed to meet Nurse Darla for coffee this morning. Can you page her for me?" Della said, disguising her voice the best she could.

Barron glanced down at her and then went back to examining the files. She was trying to remain calm and act as nonchalant as possible. If Barron caught on she was done.

"I'm sorry," the nurse replied, "Darla is on her rounds and isn't available right now."

"Well, thank you very much!" Della answered with a bit of a drawl. "But, no matter. I'll give her a call later and we can catch up some other time."

"I'm available for coffee," Barron said turning to check her out.

"No, thank you," Della said, glancing at Barron from under the wig. "I'd best be going. My friend may need some hot soup."

Barron shrugged his shoulders and went back to reading while Della started towards the exit.

"My friend may need some hot soup," Della thought to herself as she resisted the urge to run. "Oh, brother, that had to sound stupid. I can't believe he bought it."

The glass doors opened and she turned to the left just out of sight. She grabbed her bike, still leaning against the wall, and started peddling as fast as possible. She went down the sidewalk and around the corner where she could see the front entrance from the safety of some bushes. She stayed there for about twenty minutes before Barron came out with a disgusted look on his face.

"He mustn't have found anything," Della said to herself as she watched him drive around the parking lot and towards the exit. She ducked as he came her way and was relieved he didn't spot her platinum blonde wig through the brush. "I've got to get to a phone," Della thought as she pushed her bike back to the main entrance. "But I'll never make it past that nurse. I need a better plan."

Several lower level administration offices sat next to the front office. One was for admissions and that was where Della set to work. She opened the door and walked straight towards an older, heavy set woman working behind a long counter. The woman didn't look up until Della had waited for a few moments.

"What can I do for you?" The woman asked seeming a little disappointed that she actually had to speak to someone.

"My father is starting to lose his memory," Della said, leaning against the counter. "He's beginning to become a danger to himself and I would like to have him admitted."

"Ma'am," the large woman answered indignantly. "This is a hospital not an extended care facility. Unless your father is injured, you need to call them."

"I'm so sorry," Della lied, "I was just trying to get him into a good environment and I thought this was the place to come. Do you have somewhere you could recommend?"

The woman softened a bit as she pulled out a reference book and pointed out several choices.

"Could I call one from here?" Della asked, seizing the opportunity. "My father is waiting in the car and I wouldn't want him to be alone too long."

"You can use the one on the end of the counter," The woman said as she pointed towards a black phone. "Just make it brief."

"I can't thank you enough, dear." Della said in her warmest tone as she slid down to the end of the counter and dialed the second floor again.

"Hello," Darla said, "second floor."

"Thank God," Della said quietly, turning her back to the woman. "Don't say much, but I am at the hospital and I need to know what room you put that patient in. I only have a few seconds."

"Room 413," Darla answered. "Hey, are you crazy? What are you doing here?"

"Thank you so much," Della said loud enough to be heard by the woman as she hung up on a confused Darla. "I'll take him over right away. Thank you for all your help." She said as she headed towards the door.

"Glad I could help," the woman replied, looking up from the papers she was sorting. "What place did you decide on?"

Della froze. She hadn't expected to be questioned and never looked at the list the woman gave her.

"The Western Economic Diversity Division," she answered hoping it was on the list.

"Good choice," the woman replied, after a long awkward pause, "I took my mom there a month ago. She must be doing great or I would have heard from her by now."

Della exited into the hall and released a long sigh of relief. A service stairwell stood between her and the nurse's station but it was her only hope of getting upstairs. She sat on a chair along one of the wider sections of the hall and thumbed through a magazine from a nearby table. Before long a janitor came out the locked door carrying a bag of garbage. Della got up and slowly walked towards the closing door as the janitor headed off. She got there just as the door was about to snap shut and slipped quietly in. Taking two steps at a time, she flew to the fourth floor without incident. Della checked the hall first and then ran for room 413. David was sleeping peacefully next to the window as she checked his pulse and the wound in his side.

"Unnhhh," David groaned as he slowly opened his eyes. "Hello, Dr. Larson. I'm sure glad to see you."

"Hi David," She replied, putting her hand on his shoulder. "Looks like you're doing ok. How do you feel?"

"Like somebody stabbed me, but I think I could get up if you would let me."

"I'll help you but move slowly. I don't want you popping your staples."

"Could you get me my pants?" David asked as he sat up in the bed and swung his legs over the side.

"Take it slow," Dr. Larson cautioned.

"It's plenty sore that's for sure," David answered, holding his side, "but I don't want to stay here much longer. There are so many things going on that I need to see Parks about right away."

Della found his pants in the closet and helped him slip them on. Then he headed for the bathroom while Della straightened his bed and had it ready when he returned. She helped him back in but David refused to remove his jeans. They felt good and he was not planning on staying another night.

"Hi, Dr. L," Isaac said quietly as he and Normand entered the room. "You come by to take care of that big lug?"

"And, how are you feeling?" Dr. Larson asked as she turned to greet the two young men. "You've had quite the experience yourself. Why don't you sit down for a minute and let me have a look at you."

Isaac reluctantly took a seat on the edge of his bed so Dr. Larson could check him. She found some basic examination tools in one of the drawers in a short counter along one wall. She pulled up the stool that accompanied it and checked his heart, reflexes, ears, eyes, and his arm that had been broken in his escape from the Citadel.

"You're healing nicely," Dr. Larson said as she pushed the wheeled stool back and looked intently at Isaac. "It's surprising, considering the severity of your injuries. But, I think you and David should spend one more night here just to be sure."

"Nah, I'm ok," Isaac said confidently. "We were just coming back to see how David was doing before heading out."

"Yeah, we didn't expect to see you here," Normand interjected as he stepped over and gave her a hug. "We heard you were hiding out somewhere. How did you manage to get in?"

"It wasn't easy but the wig helped," she said as she pointed over to a chair. "It's really good to see you boys but, look," she continued focusing on Isaac, "I know you want to go but I'm planning on spending tonight here with David and I want you here too. I just need to be sure you don't have any issues with the nasty hit you took on the head. Concussions are nothing to fool with. Besides, Normand can make the food runs and get some playing cards. I'll get Darla to bring a couple more beds in here and make sure no one disturbs us when she goes off shift."

Isaac acted put out but he really didn't mind the idea of spending a night playing cards and snacking. Dr. Larson was pleasantly surprised at how quickly these boys were healing and knew it wasn't just their youth. She knew the power that came with the crystals they were still wearing around their necks.

The next morning, Darla kissed Joel and headed for the hospital. The sun was just peaking over the distant mountain peak as she pulled into her parking space and entered the building. She went straight to her nursing staff and reviewed their assignments before hustling off to make her rounds. But as with any morning, she got caught dealing with night shift issues and was delayed nearly two hours. She was relieved when her fourth floor nurse pulled her aside and quietly described the goings on in room 413. Everyone was safe so she could relax a bit and get up there when she could. Finally, she was caught up and able to leave her office to head upstairs.

"Excuse me, dearie," Came a soft voice from a little old lady wearing a long coat with a thick fur collar, a large flowered hat that hung over most of her face, and a colorful purse draped over one shoulder. "Can you help me?" she asked as she slowly approached Darla who was just about to leave the nurse's station. "My nephew came in a few nights ago," she said with a smile as she looked up from under her hat. "I'm so worried about him and want to make sure he's doing ok." The old lady continued reaching out and squeezing Darla's hand.

"I'm sure we can help you," Darla responded gently. "I have the roster here. What's your nephew's name?"

"David Banner." She answered with a meek smile. "He's my only nephew and a really nice boy."

Darla cringed at the mention of David's name as her mind began racing. No one was supposed to know David was here, but Darla didn't know much of anything about David's family so maybe word had leaked out. Anyway, the old lady seemed harmless enough and if she turned her away, she might start asking questions and raise concerns. They had just succeeded in getting Management out of the building and now wasn't the time to make a fuss.

"You know," Darla lied, "I don't see his name on the schedule but we do have some late admits from last night. Would you like to see if one of them is your nephew? I can go in and ask the patients if they know you."

The old lady agreed and followed Darla into one of the elevators. She stopped on several floors showing her patients that obviously weren't David before embarking for the fourth floor. The old woman had a musty odor about her that made Darla a little nauseous as they rode the elevator together. Finally, they arrived at room 413. Della had just finished checking David and was busy putting the stethoscope away when the door opened. Normand and Isaac were dressed and ready to head for another cafeteria raid. Isaac's chest still hurt but he wanted to get out of the room for good as fast as possible.

"Hello," Darla said brightly as she opened the door.

"Hi Darla!" Dr. Larson exclaimed, spinning around.

"David," Darla said softly as she stood in the doorway, "I have someone here who wants to see you. Your aunt has come for a visit."

"My aunt?" David answered a little confused as he looked up from buttoning his shirt. "I don't have an aunt."

The old lady shoved Darla into the room and slammed the door behind her. Everyone froze as the gentle little old lady took off her hat and threw it. Hidden underneath was a hideous misshapen face flattened grotesquely on one side.

"You," David shouted, falling back against his bed. "That's the woman who stabbed me!"

"I'll kill you all if you try and stop me," the old woman said, pulling a long knife from her bag. "I want that box your father got from Kevin Knobbs," she said, returning her attention to David. "Tell me or I'll cut your heart out."

Instantly, David knew she was looking for the Magnifier he had given to Parks.

Isaac was closest to the old woman. He reached over and grabbed her arm. He was going to rip the knife out of her hand but, instead, found himself sprawled on the floor as she hit him in the groin with her free hand. Normand circled around behind and grabbed her, pinning her arms to her side. That lasted for a few seconds as she easily broke his grip and spun around with the knife. Normand jumped back, narrowly escaping injury. David pulled one of the bed rails loose and stood ready to defend himself. It was clear by the wicked look on the woman's face they weren't just dealing with a deranged human being. She was something far more evil.

"Where is it," she demanded as she took a threatening step in David's direction.

"Like I told you at your house," David answered, holding the bedrail, "I don't know."

The woman's eyes narrowed and turned dark red as she raised the knife high over her head. This thing was powerful and ready to kill everybody when, suddenly, Dr. Larson sprung off her chair with a shiny crystal blade and planted it in the old woman's heart. A surprised and shocked look covered Mrs. Cantrell's twisted face before she disappeared in a whiff of black mist, her clothes dropping into a pile on the floor. The group stood there for a moment stunned by what they had just witnessed as Dr. Larson slid the blade Parks had given to her back into the belt, under her sweater.

"Everybody ok in here?" Parks asked as he came storming in. "I heard the end of that encounter."

"Well, up until about two seconds ago," David answered, "I would say no. But Dr. Larson seemed to have handled this situation nicely."

The next few moments witnessed a deluge of questions as everybody spoke at once. Della grabbed Darla who looked like she was about to collapse and eased her into a chair.

"Are you ok?" Della asked as she squeezed Darla's arm.

"Probably not," Darla replied, stumbling towards the door. "I feel sick to my stomach and may just go home for the day."

"Here's the deal," Parks said after Darla left, "I have commandeered one of Management's SUVs. The driver won't be needing it anytime soon but we can sure use it. Normand," Parks commanded sharply, "you take David and Isaac back to your place. I think you guys would be safer there. Della will come with me and I'll get in touch with you as soon as I can."

Normand and Isaac helped David down the stairs and out into the morning light. They piled into Normand's truck and headed straight for his apartment. The young men were both relieved and encouraged by the power they had witnessed today.

CHAPTER 27

"What's happening here?" President Dave Castle said as he ran from Management's main office complex towards the Citadel only a few moments after Parks and Aaron had escaped on Parks' motorcycle.

The shock and awe of what Parks accomplished was more than could have been imagined.

"What happened here?" Dave yelled this time to the closest Cadet.

"I'm hearing different things," the Cadet replied. "Someone said there was a small troop with a tank. Someone else said it was several tanks. I was inside when it all started coming down and heard only explosions."

"What about you?" The president hollered to several Cadets working with the rescue team, "What do you know about this?"

"It was one man with a large snowplow and explosives, sir," one of the Cadets said as Dave stepped past the security perimeter. "He blew out the wall up there about a half mile," the Cadet said pointing up the road, "and threw several bundles of explosives under the building. It appears we've lost all our security vehicles except those that were on patrol this morning and a few that were parked out back. We've also lost nearly all communications since the central broadcasting came through the dish on the roof. Right now we're in touch by shortwave only with these handsets. It gives us about a mile range and that's it so we don't know what could be going on other places. Some are saying this is a coordinated attack and is continuing throughout the city but I can't confirm it."

"Who's in charge?" The president demanded. "I need to speak with him right now."

"I'm in charge," General Allison said as she appeared from the wreckage, covered with dust. "It was Parks again. I'm sending patrols after him right now."

"How are you going to do that?" Dave replied. "It looks like he's smashed most of your equipment."

"I'll take care of it!" Barron injected as he came from a meeting with the scene commander. "Parks is on the run. I just need two operational vehicles and I'll find him."

"Let's not rush out just yet," Dave said as he calmed a bit. "From what I hear, there could be more attacks and until we know the full scope let's get up to my office and figure this thing out.

This was the first time Barron or General Allison had seen Dave shook. He was fidgeting with his tie and couldn't stop pacing in the elevator as they went up. They exited onto the top floor and had to nearly run to keep up with Dave. He blew right past the large man guarding his office door and jumped into his chair. He grabbed a pencil and paper before addressing the General and Barron.

"Ideas," Dave asked, starting with Barron.

"If my sources are correct, and I believe they are," Barron began slowly, "Parks is operating solo. There's no coordinated attack on the city."

"How can you know that for sure?" the General challenged. "Parks has been seen with resisters and could have easily orchestrated a large scale attack."

"Parks and I were partners for a long time," Barron said defensively, "and he doesn't like involving others in his work. So, if he's going to do something this extreme, you have to know he's working alone. Besides, I think he wants the satisfaction of beating us himself. He's unbelievably selfish and doesn't like sharing his "glory" with anyone. Even more, when we worked together, he was always trying to outdo me and take credit for my actions," Barron lied. "Yes, it's only Parks. I'm sure of it."

"What do you propose doing?" The president asked as he relaxed a bit and leaned back in his chair.

"First, I find him," Barron answered, seizing the moment. "Once I've hunted him down and brought him to you, you can deal with him as you see fit. Just a suggestion, but I think a public execution would be most fitting for the likes of him."

"You've tried catching him before and that didn't work out so well," the General chided not wanting Barron to get too much power. "What makes you think you'll have any better success now?"

"I've got a new plan," Barron said, holding his temper in check as he ignored the General's sniping. "I went after him before but now I'm focusing on his family. Put pressure there and he'll come to me."

"Hmmm," Dave said thoughtfully, looking Barron over. "Ok, you can do whatever you want to get Parks but you had better not mess up. And, I want more than just Parks," He continued turning his attention to the General, "I want to send a message loud and clear to the city. No one comes against us without paying the ultimate price. You'll need to see to that."

Dave began meditating on the day's events after dismissing them. He could care less about the Citadel or Parks for that matter. His goal was to get to the Gifts. While contemplating, his door opened and in walked Mr. Grey.

"What do you want?" Dave asked somewhat annoyed at being interrupted.

"I came to talk," he said as he sat down.

"About what?"

"A unique proposition if you're interested," Mr. Grey said quietly. "I believe you and I are alike somewhat. We both want power, lots of power. You also know the Board is out to destroy the Gifts but if someone were to get ahold of them it's said they would be the most powerful of all."

"Yeah, old news, what does that have to do with me?"

"Because of my unique relationship with the board," Mr. Grey continued, "I'm not able to do certain things. You might say I am a prisoner of sorts, trapped in this form. Now, if I were to come upon the Gifts and bring them to you first, maybe you could change that."

Mr. Grey leaned his head forward and removed his dark glasses. The place on Mr. Grey's head where his two eyes were supposed to be, were instead black openings extending deep into his skull.

"I was taken from my home years ago," Mr. Grey said as he put his glasses back on, "and I want to return but they will never let me go. If you were to promise to help me, I could be a great asset to your future."

"Interesting," Dave replied feeling more powerful than ever, "but how do I know I can trust you."

"I'll do what I must," Mr. Grey said as he turned to leave. "And then we can discuss things further after we see how successful I am."

Dave leaned back into his chair as Mr. Grey left. This was unexpected but definitely a great opportunity. One he could take advantage of. It could also be a sign the Board was losing its grip.

"Mr. President," the intercom on his desk interrupted. "The Board is meeting right now and calling for you."

"Tell them I'll be right in." he said, standing up and adjusting his tie. "This should be interesting," he thought as he exited his office and started towards the board room. "I'm sure the Board is well aware of the events by now. I just need to steer them in my favor."

He arrived at the solid oak door with the small brass plaque fastened to the wall next to it. He entered the modest room outfitted with a large wooden table surrounded by seven chairs. Each seat, other than his, was already filled with six ordinary looking business men talking intently amongst themselves. They hardly noticed as he sat down.

"Ahum," Dave said interrupting their discussion, "you wanted to see me?"

The men at the table each had an identifying brass name plate in front of them. They were numbered one to six and liked to be identified only by number.

"We have seen the destruction of one of your buildings," number Three said emotionlessly. "What has happened out there?"

"Nothing I can't handle." Dave replied, equally as emotionless. "Parks, the man you thought was nothing more than an inconvenience, single handedly destroyed part of the Citadel. I have restored order and Parks will be in custody before he can do anymore damage."

"Parks again," number Five said calmly. "He has been quite the problem for you, hasn't he?"

Dave could feel himself getting angry at that response.

"We don't care if you capture him or not," number Six said, to Dave's chagrin. "We believe he may possess one of the Gifts."

"We want the Gift not the man," number Three affirmed.

"If I had him here right now," Dave asked, "could you at least give me a clue of what I would find on him? What does the Gift look like?"

"The reason you struggle to control him," number Four answered, "is because the gift is helping him. We believe he's looking into the past, the present and can see the future. If you find him, look for something that can fit into the palm of your hand. That's all we know."

Dave looked around at the six familiar faces, knowing they weren't real. What was real was the darkness they were hiding. He watched as they turned and exited through the rear door but he remained seated for a moment, thinking. Then his thoughts were drawn to his wife, Doris, and the Mystic she once visited.

"Doris had a warning for me," Dave remembered. "There was a group of men planning to destroy our lives, destroy the city," he remembered her saying as she retold her dream. "They surrounded you as a dark cloud appeared and then the darkness covered you. I searched for you but couldn't find you. When I woke up you were gone and I was alone."

"She had a dream," Dave repeated to himself over and over again as he returned to his office, "and that dream became her reality. Maybe that Mystic lady can be of value."

Dave grabbed his car keys and left with a smile.

In the meantime, the board had exited to the rear room. It was dark with only a dimly glowing object set on a table in the middle providing the illumination. There were no chairs, just seven octagon shaped, raised platforms surrounding the table. Each man stepped up and took a position on one of six and the room became a brilliant dark red as a beam shot from the globe into their foreheads.

"Can you feel it?" number One spoke.

"Yes!" number Three answered. "They are finally beginning to respond as we expected."

"But it's been so long," number Five replied. "Not like the other cities. The dark matter is rising and we grow weary of this place. We should have left already."

"Be patient. We cannot rush what must come," number Six said. "Their time is running out and soon we will feast."

"Yes," number Two agreed. "It will be a harvest unlike any before."

Suddenly, they began chanting over and over again: "Hard as stone, flesh and bone; hard as stone, flesh and bone," and then they were gone…

CHAPTER 28

"Hello, Dr. Larson," Aaron said peeking out from the rear of the SUV as Della climbed in next to Parks.

"Aaron!" Della exclaimed. "I didn't know you were here. How are you doing?"

"Not so great," Aaron replied, sticking his head between the seats and glancing up at Parks. "Has he told you anything about what he did yet?"

"No," Della answered, "we haven't had time to talk. We just came from a rather crazy situation. What did you do, Parks?"

"It's not what I've done," Parks replied angrily, "it's what Aaron's done."

"What I've done!" Aaron exclaimed. "I was doing my job when you started destroying the Citadel like a crazy person. Yeah, maybe I was working for Management but there are a lot of worse jobs out there. And, there are some really good people over there too, or at least there was. I'll be surprised if any of them are even alive after what you did."

"What is he talking about?" Della demanded as Parks pulled onto the main street and headed towards his parents' house.

"He's got it all wrong," Parks said, his face turning red. "He's up to his neck and he knows it. I've got information that points in only one direction-yours." Parks said as he looked hard at Aaron in the rearview mirror. "You have some explaining to do and don't think you can fool me."

"Ok, Parks, calm down," Della said. "I'm sure there's a perfectly good explanation for everything. We're all stressed so let's just wait until we get to the house to talk this out."

Aaron was disgusted at Parks' insinuations as he settled back into the rear seat. Della, on the other hand, was not clear at all, but knew something serious had happened. Neither Parks nor Aaron were in any mood to chat as silence filled the vehicle. The drive over was tense, to say the least. When they arrived, Parks stood by the door like a security detail as Aaron got out. He followed Aaron into the house as if he thought he would make a break for it. But, all he succeeded in doing was making Aaron even angrier.

"What's your problem?!" Aaron demanded as he took a defensive position behind the long counter.

"You're the problem," Parks quipped. "I think you know a lot more than you're letting on. I say out with it!"

"I know you've totally ripped my life apart," Aaron retorted, "For all I know there are Cadets out right now searching, not only for you, but for me, too. And what do you think they're going to do when they catch up with me? It's not going to be pretty, I can tell you that."

"What are you two talking about?" Della asked. "What has happened?"

"I took down the Citadel this morning." Parks answered evenly.

"You took down the Citadel," Della replied bewilderedly. "I don't know what that means."

Aaron looked over from the end of the counter and made a little mushroom shape in the air with his hands followed by the traditional, "Boom!"

"You blew up the Citadel!" Della exclaimed. "Are you crazy? We're supposed to be the good guys. What were you thinking?"

"Look," Parks replied, staring at Della through narrowing eyes, "I did what I had to do. Somebody had to do something drastic and the timing seemed right."

"Well, I guess discussing that with me first didn't enter your mind," Della challenged. "Our future could be jeopardized because of you. Did you ever think of that?"

"Look, maybe I should have said something but Aaron is the one that needs to talk," Parks said. "Don't you Aaron? Aaron has done things that have caused real suffering."

"What?" Aaron asked a little confused. "I've never hurt anyone. I have no idea what you're talking about."

"That's a lie," Parks asserted. "I've been talking with Normand and he said Isaac met with you the night he was assaulted and nearly killed. You were the only one who knew he wanted information on what Management was up to. He asked you to help him get it but you said you weren't interested in helping. He felt you had turned against the ROD and left the pub disappointed with your attitude. But, when he got home, there was an unwanted visitor waiting for him. You're the only one who could have alerted them."

Aaron looked down at the counter for a few moments before replying.

"He wanted me to jeopardize my position and I wasn't ready to do that," he said quietly. "Is he ok?"

"He's out of the hospital," Dr. Larson answered. "But he had a rough go. Someone tried to shove a metal tube into his chest. But both he and David heal very quickly."

"David? What happened to him?" Aaron asked, looking up in surprise.

"He was stabbed," Parks replied. "They're different circumstances but I believe they're related and you're behind them both. Tell me what you know!"

"Well," Aaron began, looking down at his hands, "I got a call on the way home the night Isaac came by the pub. It was from my boss, General Allison. She had some questions about a project I was working on. You see, they had decided to pull people living in the county in and begin a rewards program. They told me it would make for a closer community and bring more business into the city and so on. We got to talking and I happened to mention Isaac's ridiculous assertion that upper Management was engaging in some kind of evil plan. She laughed and confirmed how stupid that seemed. We talked more and then she asked for Isaac's name. She said she would bring him in and show him around some time. I thought that was really generous of her, especially if Isaac could see for himself the good we're doing."

"The problem is," Parks replied firmly, "Isaac was right. Management has a plan and it's not a good one. I'm afraid the program you were leading was not for the benefit of people living in the county but for their destruction. The blood we saw in that building could have only come from one source, the people you processed."

Aaron sunk his head in his hands as Della walked around the counter and put her hand on his shoulder.

"You had no way to know," She said softly. "They have the entire city living in the dark, believing they're looking out for their welfare. People don't want to think there's evil at work."

"When I was a child, I didn't think these things were real," Aaron said finally, "and those endless hours of training were just a waste of time but I did keep this," he continued reaching into his pocket and pulling out his wallet. He opened a hidden pouch with a snap and pulled out the crystal Parks had given him that fateful day years before. "I guess I know now why I've kept it. Somewhere deep inside I believed all those things you and Kirsten taught us," he said as he lifted it up by the long thin chain and slid it over his head.

"As wild as this may sound," Parks said, his expression brightening. "This may not be such a bad thing."

"What are you thinking?" Della asked.

"What if Aaron can return to his duties?" Parks suggested. "He could become our inside man."

"That seems a little out of the question now don't you think? I mean I don't even have a place to go back to. You wiped out the Citadel, remember. Not only that, you took me with you. I'm sure they think I was in on it too."

"Not necessarily," Parks continued with a twinkle in his eye. "No one got a good look at you and I'm sure they're still trying to figure things out. It's risky, I know, but what if you just showed up and blended into the chaos. Maybe no one would notice."

"I'm willing to try anything to help," Aaron said boldly.

Della took over the moment by making some coffee and turning the conversation to more pleasant and ordinary things for just a moment. But then it was back to the situation at hand.

"It's probably not safe here anymore," Parks said. "I think we should move to another location and I know just the place. We'll drop Aaron off as close to the Citadel as we dare and he can walk in from there. I don't want you to know where we are going," Parks said to Aaron as they got in the SUV. "The less information you have the safer you'll be if people start asking questions. However, we do need a way to stay in touch," Parks said. "Squeeze the crystal I gave you until it glows and I'll know your thoughts and you'll know mine."

Aaron didn't need to question anything. He knew exactly what to do as Parks dropped him about three blocks from the Citadel on a side street. Parks plan was to head for Dr. Flint's house and see if the doctor would put them up in one of the servant apartments. Dr. Flint lived in an old family mansion he had bought. He turned it into a small hospital. It was large enough to contain living quarters for both his family and people he hired to tend the place. Unfortunately, his wife had passed away several years ago and, since then, he had been slowly downsizing.

The only problem left for Parks was what to do with the black SUV he had grabbed from several Cadets the day before.

"What do you think we should do with this thing?" Parks asked as they drove along.

"First of all, we don't need to head to Dr. Flint's quite yet," Della responded eagerly. "Take the next turn onto River Road."

Parks followed her directions as they drove down a long graveled drive to where a large motor home was parked.

"Hello." She said as she knocked on the door. "It's Della and Parks." She said again. "That's strange," she continued as she turned back to Parks, "It's dark inside and they should be here."

"Whose motor home is this?" Parks asked as he tried to peek through the curtains.

"It belongs to Jim's Aunt and Uncle," she replied as she stepped down from the door.

"You mean my Uncle James and Aunt Lori?" Parks responded.

"Right, I forgot you two are cousins."

"Why are they parked way out here?"

"They received one of those letters Management sent inviting them to the Citadel," Della said as she walked with Parks. "Your cousin Jim checked the homes and farms of neighbors who got similar letters and found some disturbing things. It appears the people came into the city but never returned home. That's when they decided to come here and wait until we could figure out what's going on but I don't understand why they're not here."

"No worries. Maybe they needed to go to town and get supplies. Either way, you're right about this being a good spot to rid ourselves of that black machine."

Parks pulled the truck over to an overgrown blackberry bush covered boat loading dock, opened the rear door, and pulled out his motorcycle.

Parks gave the truck a push and they watched as the large SUV picked up speed tearing through the blackberries on the way into the river. The swift current took it several hundred yards downstream before it slowly slipped below the waterline.

"What now?" Della asked as they walked back towards the motor home.

"I guess we could stay here until they get back," Parks replied taking one more look around the campsite. "They always kept a spare key in the gas cover."

Parks opened the motor home and he and Della began making themselves at home while his father, uncle and aunt were looking for him elsewhere.

"Nobody's here." Philip said as he checked his house. "I guess Henry and Kirsten must be out somewhere but you're welcome to wait. I'm sure they'll be back soon."

Lori thought about it for a moment and then answered.

"I'm not feeling that safe. I would rather stay with you guys."

"That's ok with me, Honey," James replied, "I would rather have you along anyway."

"You guys need to change," Philip said, ducking into the bedroom, "We'll be heading downtown and we need to look the part. As soon as you're ready we can get out of here."

"Downtown?" James asked after they got out onto the road. "Where exactly are we going?"

"Rich has a large office overlooking the business district," Philip replied. "We'll meet him there and see what he says."

Philip slowed slightly as they passed the spot where the Testers crossed the road and killed his wife. It was difficult for him to think about the long night Pearl spent alone, trapped under the tree.

"Here we are," Philip said as he pulled his truck into a space in front of an imposing building set in the middle of the most powerful economic district in the city. "Let's go up and see if Rich is in."

The foyer was bustling with people in suits and fine clothes as they entered. Philip, James, and Lori blended right in as they took the elevator to the top floor. It deposited them into a plush office setting.

"Can I help you?" The tall well-spoken young man behind the counter asked as Philip approached.

"We're here to see Rich Lindberg."

"Rich Lindberg?" The young man replied with a quizzical look on his face, "just a moment."

He reached down and picked up the phone. Turning his back to Philip, he spoke quietly to the person on the other end.

"You may have a seat over there," the man said after hanging up. "Someone will be right out to help you."

They relaxed for a moment in black leather chairs hoping Rich was in. A small pile of magazines sat in the middle of a large heavy glass table and James picked up one and thumbed through it while Philip and Lori sat quietly. In a few minutes a tall stately woman in a dark suit came around the corner.

"Hi," she said warmly, "I'm Lucy Lane and who may I say you are?"

"My name is Philip Barker and this is my brother, Jacob, and his wife, Virginia," Philip lied as he reached out to shake her hand. He was taking extra precautions just in case. "We came up to see an old friend, Rich Lindberg. Is he in?"

"Why don't you come on into my office for a moment?" The woman said as she turned and started walking down the wide hall to the office on the end. "We can talk there."

They followed her, glancing back and forth at each other, wondering what was going on as she led the way into a large office overlooking the entire financial district. Philip remembered the last time he was in this office when they discussed the situation with Henry and the Zender. The woman took a seat behind Rich's desk and motioned for them to have a seat.

"So, you came to see Rich Lindberg?" Lucy asked politely as she folded her hands and looked intently at them.

"That's correct," Philip replied, "is he in today?"

"Unfortunately, no," The woman replied as she noted something on a piece of paper. "I haven't met him personally," Lucy continued, "as I just transferred over here but I understand he had taken ill and sold the business. I understand he's living at one of the Economic Diversity Districts. The West one, I believe. What's your business with Mr. Lindberg?"

"We're just trying to reestablish an old relationship," Lori blurted out not sure why she suddenly felt uncomfortable, "we haven't seen him in a long time and just wanted to drop by and say hi."

"Sorry I don't have better news," the woman said with a slight smug smile. "But I would like to hear more about how you met Mr. Lindberg."

"We grew up together is all," Philip replied as he started to get out of his chair. "But we should probably get going. It was very nice meeting you."

"I'll walk you to the elevator," Lucy said as she got up.

"Oh, that's not necessary," Lori said a little louder than she intended. "We've disrupted your day too much already. Thank you again."

They quickly exited and made their way to the elevator, not saying a word along the way.

"Yeesh," James exclaimed as they pulled out of the parking lot. "I don't believe I've ever met a creepier woman in my life."

"No kidding," Philip replied. "I was glad to just get out of there. Did you see how she looked at us when we asked about Rich? You would think we were trying to rob the place or something. I'm glad you spoke up," He continued glancing at Lori in the back seat, "my mind went blank there for a moment."

"We need to get over to that EDD and find Rich," Lori said boldly.

"Do you really think that's a good idea, dear?" James asked. "He's probably in pretty bad shape."

"I don't believe a word that woman said," Lori answered. "If Rich is over there, it's not by his own doing."

"I agree," Philip said. "I say we drop in on him and see for ourselves what's really going on."

"How are we going to do that?" James exclaimed. "I'm sure that Lucy person has already told someone of our visit. She's likely on the phone right now."

"I know just what to do," Lori replied. "My oversized husband here needs some specialized assistance. He's been acting a little strange of late, you know, and I'm sure they would make room for another customer, especially a paying one."

James face took on a puzzled look as his wife smiled back brightly. One thing he had learned through years of marriage, if she thought she had a good idea, watch out. It was her way or else. But he couldn't for the life of him figure out what she had in mind.

CHAPTER 29

Kirsten arrived early to the barn they used as their headquarters. It was nestled behind an old torn up and abandoned farm house, a product of a battle long since forgotten. And, the land which once produced hay and grain now lay overgrown with weeds and brush.

Kirsten put her thoughts together as she waited for the rest to arrive. She had contacted the ROD members through the crystal mainly because using cell phones was too dangerous. Someone could be listening in.

"Hi Kirsten," Normand said brightly as he opened the door, "am I the first one here?"

"You are," Kirsten replied, giving Normand a hug. "Good to see you."

"I really like what you've done with the place," Normand joked. "It has that cow-ish feeling."

Kirsten sat on a milking stool while Normand watched for the others to arrive. There was no question Normand liked Kirsten, but he was too shy to express his feelings. He liked hanging out with her and missed the days they used to train together.

Before long, the rest of the group arrived, except Aaron, who was under Parks' direction to return to the Citadel.

"Good to see you guys!" Kenzie exclaimed as they each found something to sit on around the old wooden door set on blocks of wood they used for a table. "But it seems every time we get together something bad is happening to someone somewhere."

David agreed and went about describing the recent events with both him and Isaac. The attacks they endured revealed their skills needed upgrading and more training was in order. But Troy felt they couldn't wait.

"I say we start acting more like Parks," Troy suggested. "He kicked some serious butt at the Citadel. Why not mount up and go after them."

"There's only one problem with that idea," Joshua replied, "we aren't Parks. We try something like that and we're likely to be wiped out unless we have a darn good plan."

"I get that!" Troy said. "But isn't that why we're here. Burke got inside their place and saw a map we could use. Whatever happened to that? Wasn't Aaron supposed to get us some information or something?"

"I spoke with Parks," Kirsten answered, "and he says Aaron is doing his best but we have nothing yet. We have to remain patient. As soon as he knows something he'll pass it on. In the meantime, there are some things we can be doing, and that's why I called you guys together. You're right Troy that people are feeling something but, from what I'm hearing, it's not hope. Everyone I talked to is terrified Management is going to get even, at their expense. You know I work for the road division as an engineer and the rumors running around our office are crazy. Some of my coworkers say they heard talk about some major changes coming down the pipe. They say an announcement is coming soon and it's not going to be good."

"So let's go get them!" Troy said angrily, slamming his fist on the makeshift table. "Why wait until they act. We act first and knock them out before they even get started."

"Come on, Troy," Burke responded. "Kirsten's right. We have to be patient and wait for Parks."

"I agree," Normand said, standing up to stretch. "David and Isaac got pounded because they were snooping around. Management's on to us so we need to be smart. There's no telling what they might try next."

"Hey!" Isaac said suddenly. "What if they've been watching us? Maybe they found a way to track our movements and they know about the ROD."

"Right," Kirsten replied. "That's why I didn't contact you by phone. We need to use our crystals and our heads."

"Guys," Normand exclaimed, glancing out an old cracked window. "You have got to see this. If I'm not mistaken, those are Testers coming across that field."

They were up and at the barn windows in an instant and, sure enough, a small troop of Testers, their red armor glistening in the afternoon sun, were moving steadily in the barn's direction.

"So much for more training," Kenzie exclaimed as she opened the door and ran for her truck.

In a few seconds, they were roaring away from the barn but, as they drove down the narrow gravel drive, it became apparent more Testers had already cut off their escape route. A group of ten were marching side by side with weapons drawn. Kenzie made a quick decision to run straight at them with her powerful four wheel drive truck in hopes they would jump into the ditch to get out of her way. But, instead, they fanned across the road blocking her escape. Kenzie hit them at over fifty miles an hour sending Testers flying in all directions but the impact also sent Kenzie's truck sailing across the ditch and into a nearby field. It flipped several times before coming to rest on its top.

"Oh no!" Troy shouted as he watched in horror. "We've got to help her."

He slammed on his brakes and jumped out but several Testers were already back on their feet and heading towards Kenzie's truck. Kenzie had suffered a serious blow to her head but was conscious enough to release her seat belt. She dropped to the roof of her overturned truck and managed to crawl out the broken passenger side window. A small trickle of blood flowed down her forehead as she staggered to her feet. She could hear the heavy thud of the Tester's footsteps approaching as they came running. She dropped down and attempted to pull one of the crystal blades she kept behind the front seat but it was wedged tight. She struggled to free it as the Testers rushed across the field. It would be but only a matter of seconds before they reached her. She felt one of the blades coming free just as the first of the Testers came around the end of her overturned truck with a wicked looking blade in its hand. It was curved with a razor sharp end and several shorter similar curved ends on both sides of the blade. The Tester held it high as it approached and was just about to slice Kenzie in half when a dark blue blur flashed between her and the Tester.

Troy had dove across the underside of the overturned truck with crystal blade in hand. The blade easily knifed through the Tester's heavy armor. It froze for a second with its mouth hanging open as Troy tumbled to the ground and quickly jumped back onto his feet. He turned ready for battle but instead watched as the Tester dropped to the ground into two separate pieces.

Troy's blade had cut it in half.

But they were not out of the woods yet as two more came around the rear of the truck. But Troy's training days paid off as he kicked one in the chest sending it flying into the side of the truck while he sliced an arm off the second. A few more well placed moves with his blade and they were finished.

"We've got to get out of here," he yelled as Kenzie worked to free her blade. "There's more of them coming and I can't fight them all."

Just then, Kenzie's blade broke free and she joined Troy in a sprint for his truck. Burke was running in their direction and met them half way.

"You ok?" Burke asked as they ran back together.

"I'll let you know," She replied.

A group of Testers were coming down the road from behind as Kenzie jumped into Burke's car. The rest of the ROD set up a defensive posture in hopes of stopping them but, once they saw Kenzie was safe, they piled back into their rigs and ripped down the road. Troy's truck was built for off road action and its front end outfitted with heavy steel pipes. As he punched the powerful motor sending a spray of gravel from all four tires, two of the remaining Testers came crawling out of the ditch. Troy swerved at just the right moment to send their lifeless bodies twisting through the air and into a large rock. A third Tester had taken up a position in the middle of the road with its sharp weapon raised high but, before it could strike, Troy plowed into it. The creature managed to hang onto his grill and was attempting to climb onto his hood for another strike when Troy slammed on his brakes. The Tester flew off and onto the road, stunned. Troy got out and walked around the front of his truck where the Tester was trying to get up.

"This is for my parents!" Troy exclaimed as his blade separated the Tester's head from its body. "That'll teach you to mess with me." He continued as he kicked the body into one ditch and the head into the other. But then a sharp pain shot up his arm as he climbed back into his truck. He winched and glanced at his right hand as it began turning a light shade of blue.

"Are you ok?" Burke asked Kenzie again as they sped along.

"I think so," She answered feeling the knot on her head and wiping the blood from her face with a napkin she had found in the glove box. "What I don't get is how they knew we were there."

Then it dawned on her.

"Someone must have planted a tracking device on my truck. That's why they came after me. I've seen them do that before when I was traveling with Dr. Larson, Jim and Rita. They hone in on the device and follow it relentlessly."

"Who could have done something like that?" Burke asked. "No one knows what you're doing or about us, do they?"

"That I don't know," Kenzie replied. "But I'm equally sure I can't go home until we find out what's going on."

They drove out onto the main road and then split up as was their protocol if they were attacked. They would reconnect at a predetermined safe place in two hours.

Meanwhile, Jim was planning his next step from the hideout Tim, his lawyer, had provided.

"Thanks for the car," Jim said to Shirley as she handed him the keys.

"It's full of gas and not one to draw attention," Shirley responded as she turned to leave. "Just be careful."

"Let's go!" Jim exclaimed. "It's time to rally the troops."

Jim put the large hand held walkie-talkie in the back seat and threw a blanket over it. He was heading to see Chris, his senior assistant from HOT News. It was time to take a fresh look at what they could do to get his message to the people and Jim had some wild new ideas.

"This should come in handy," Jim said as he tested the old four door bluish grey sedan. The car wasn't attractive but he found it in excellent mechanical condition and fast. "Maybe Tim used this thing to get his guilty clients out of town."

"Let's just hope we don't need a fast getaway," Rita replied seriously.

"Hey!" Jim exclaimed as he pulled to a stop at an intersection. "Isn't that Kenzie over there?"

Burke had driven to a nearby gas station to get some bandages for the cut on Kenzie's head. She was waiting outside while he went in to make sure she wasn't spotted on a security camera.

"Hi Kenzie," Jim said as he pulled next to Burke's car. "I didn't expect to see you way out here. Hey, are you bleeding?"

"A little but let's not talk about it here," Kenzie replied as Burke came out of the store. "Just follow us."

Jim pulled in behind them and soon they were weaving their way through miles of side roads until they came upon an old abandoned middle school. Management had centralized all education and only those teachers with the correct attitude were allowed to teach the children. They had eliminated any schools which were community centered in favor of bussing children to ones where they had maximum influence. Several of the group had attended this school but now they used it as their emergency meeting place.

"Hey!" David said in surprise as he recognized Jim. "I haven't seen you in quite some time. How have you been?"

"I'm good," Jim answered as the rest of the group gathered round. "But I think we better get inside," Jim said anxiously. "I can't help feeling we're being watched, if you know what I mean."

They quickly moved inside as David led the way through a covered walkway and then a set of double doors before arriving at a large basketball auditorium. The doors were chained shut but David knew the combination and let them in. They gave Jim the short version of what they had just been through and then it was his turn. They huddled around as Jim explained the recent course of events.

"We've got to work together as a team." Jim went on. "It's our only chance. If I can find a way to tell people what's happening, we may be able to create a full scale revolt."

"That's what I'm talking about." Troy injected.

"The information I'm holding could be the catalyst needed to change everything," Jim continued. "We just need to get it out there."

"That may be," Kirsten replied. "But I don't think that many people are really paying attention. Management has been doling out so much propaganda do you really think they'll buy the truth now?"

"You have a point," Jim admitted, "even worse, people seem to have amnesia or something. They've forgotten what happened when Management first took over and now appear to have become dependent on their programs. It's like they've been fattening us up and I'm not sure there's enough left to resist but I know we have to keep trying regardless."

"Then what are you suggesting?" David asked. "Every time we do something, something bad happens."

"I get that," Jim replied. "It's a dangerous world out there but we may have some advantages. First, they don't know where we are now, and anytime we can move behind the scenes we have opportunity. Second, we have each other. If we network together, we can watch each other's backs. Third, you guys have some unique weapons. I've seen those crystals Parks gave you and they're powerful. Look, there has to be more like us out there. We just have to wake them up."

"We all want that," Kenzie affirmed.

"And, I say we get started now!" Isaac exclaimed. "Let's start pulling people together and get after these guys. What're we waiting for?"

"Just be careful, that's all I ask," Jim cautioned. "Management has proven they have power. What we need is to get Parks on board with us. He's out there tearing things up on his own. It could backfire and maybe already has. You can bet Management's reaction to his attack on the Citadel will be nasty. Give me two days and then we meet back here again. By then I should have more information. In the meantime, you guys stay out of sight."

Jim had just finished speaking when Troy groaned and fell to the hardwood floor.

"What's wrong?" David asked of a nonresponsive Troy as he knelt to check him out.

"He's cold as ice," Kenzie observed, "and look at his arm. It's turning blue."

"I've heard of this before," Kirsten interjected as she knelt next to Kenzie. "Parks called it crystal sickness. He told me it comes from using our crystal blades with malice. I thought he was exaggerating but apparently he wasn't. Troy must have done something he shouldn't have."

"What're we going to do?" Kenzie asked anxiously. "We have to help him."

"Parks is the only one who can," Kirsten replied. "I'll try to contact him while you guys get him into my truck."

David and Isaac carried Troy to Kirsten's truck and laid him in the back seat. He looked even worse in the daylight as his arm's bluish tint was extending to his shoulder and his eyes were glazed over.

"I'll go with Kirsten," Kenzie said, hopping into the front seat.

"You two be careful but hurry," David said as he closed the door, "He doesn't look good. Let me know what happens as soon as you can. If all goes well, we'll meet back here in exactly forty-eight hours."

They all agreed but a heavy feeling settled over them as they drove off. It was bad enough they were in danger from Management but seeing Troy suffering was hard, especially since they were thinking it could be from using the very weapon they all carried, the weapon designed to protect and save them. If there was any hope, it now seemed to lay with Parks.

CHAPTER 30

Barron was determined to succeed at capturing or killing Parks and was not about to let anything stand in his way. He also knew Della was his Achilles' heel even though she had managed to escape his clutches. His plan to use her to draw Parks out had failed but that didn't mean he would lose this time. Barron laughed to himself as he envisioned his plan while returning to his house to pick up supplies.

"Parks, Parks," Kirsten thought as she held the crystal from around her neck tightly in the palm of her hand. "I need your help."

Parks felt the blue crystal he kept in a small pouch in his backpack begin to vibrate. He had given Kirsten the other half in case of emergencies.

"Hi Sis," he thought, "everything ok?"

"Troy's in trouble," Kirsten answered. "His arm is cold to the touch and his skin turned blue. I think he might have crystal sickness. Can you help him?"

"Where are you?" Parks asked.

"I'm heading towards dad's house," Kirsten replied. "Can you meet us?"

"Don't go there," Parks said, "meet me at Dr. Flint's instead. I'll be there in an hour."

Parks had left Della at the doctor's house earlier and was sure she could help Troy until he got there. He wasn't through with Management yet so Troy would have to wait for the moment. He expected Management would be hunting him, but they wouldn't be thinking he was hunting them. This that gave Parks a distinct advantage.

He headed towards a spot where he expected to find them watching for him and pulled onto a side road where he could hide his bike. Traffic was heavy as he dropped into a ditch and crawled through several large culverts, moving silently to a favorite stakeout spot. The spot was nothing more than grass and gravel and mostly hidden by a large advertising sign. It was perfect for catching unsuspecting motorists. Parks climbed out of the culvert and stayed low behind the tall grass as he came up behind some bushes. Sure enough, there were two large black SUVs each filled with four heavily armed cadets. He moved silently behind the first rig, keeping low to the ground. He could hear them talking as he pulled his crystal blade and slit the brake line on the first truck. But just then, one of the cadets opened the rear door and walked around behind to urinate. Parks pulled his feet in and held his breath. The Cadet walked around a bit, stretching, before returning to his friends. Parks finished his work on the second truck and then headed for his motorcycle. He pulled onto the main road and took off in the direction of their trap. He slowed as he passed just long enough for them to get a good look and then took off.

"That's him!" one of the Cadets exclaimed. "Get him!"

The powerful vehicles tore out of their hiding place and began pursuit. Parks slowed enough to make sure they didn't lose him and then made a sharp turn down a side road. The road snaked along one of the many rivers traversing this area of the city. The two SUVs were tight on his tail but, as they braked to make the turn, the cut brake lines did their work, sending them sailing through a fence into the river. Parks made a U-turn and arrived just in time to watch the men struggling against the current, their heads bobbing in the water. Two cadets managed to scramble on the top of one of the SUVs before it disappeared under the water.

"I hope you boys know how to swim," Parks shouted with a laugh before popping a wheelie as he drove away.

He knew every Management trick in the book because he had written most of them himself. His goal was to make them suffer as much as possible and fear the very mention of his name but, for now, his thoughts needed to return to Troy. Crystal sickness was nothing to be trifled with and every case so far had ended in amputation or death.

"How's Troy doing?" He asked quietly as he stepped into the small waiting room where Kenzie was sitting.

"Parks!" Kenzie exclaimed. "We've been waiting for you." She jumped up, nearly running down the hall. "He's in here," she said as she opened the door to Room Four.

"I'm glad you're here," Kirsten said, relieved. "Troy needs you."

"What do you think, doctors?" Parks asked.

"I've never seen anything like this," Dr. Flint replied as he pulled his stethoscope from his ears, "come to think of it, there's a lot lately I've never seen. His temperature is low and his right arm seems to be changing from flesh to something else."

"You've got to do something!" Kenzie pleaded as she grabbed Parks by his arm.

"Can you wake him?" Parks asked.

"He was barely conscious when they brought him in," Doctor Flint replied. "And he seemed to be in a lot of pain. I gave him some pain medication to keep him comfortable but then he basically passed out."

"I can get him awake if you need him," Dr. Larson said as she looked up from checking his pulse. "One shot of narcan should do it."

"It's the only way," Parks said as Della prepared the syringe. "If he stays asleep he may never wake up."

Dr. Larson gave him the shot and, within seconds, Troy's eyes popped opened and he groaned.

"Parks," Troy said through clenched teeth, "what's going on? What's wrong with me?"

"Calm yourself Troy, you'll be ok. I just need you to answer a few questions." Parks replied as he motioned everyone away from the bed. "What did you kill last with your blade?"

"Just those lousy Testers," Troy answered, his face flushing red with anger. "And I would do it again if I could."

"You really hate them, don't you?" Parks pressed.

"They killed my parents," Troy answered as his body tightened. "I can't get my mother's face out of my mind, it haunts me daily."

"You were little then, right?" Parks said, looking hard into Troy's eyes.

Troy nodded yes as he stared back.

"But sometimes hatred can hurt even if it's justified. Can you sit up?"

He took Troy's left arm while Dr. Larson slid a pillow behind his back and stayed next to him to keep him from falling over.

"I read something a while back," Parks said pulling the black book out of his bag. "It goes like this," he said flipping to the page, 'Vengeance belongs to the one whose heart and mind is pure but he who takes vengeance without understanding, risks his own life.'"

"Parks, are you saying killing the Testers was wrong?" Troy asked becoming increasingly agitated.

"Maybe. Why did you kill them?"

"They were attacking Kenzie and I had to protect her," Troy continued, "tell him Kenzie. Tell him how they came for you."

"It's true Parks. They would have gotten me if it wasn't for Troy."

"That's my point," Parks replied. "You shouldn't have any issue if what you say is true. Look, there has to be more to this than you're letting on. What else did you do?"

"Well," Troy said reluctantly, "I stopped on the way out and killed a Tester that was in the road but was not part of the ones that were coming for us."

"If you use your blade with the wrong motive this is what can happen," Parks explained. "But all may not be lost. I have something here that may help." Parks said as he pulled a small ornate box from his bag.

It was the Magnifier. Parks opened it up as before revealing the blue stone and small magnifying glass.

"I've had some experience with this thing. Take the magnifying glass and look into the blue stone. You have to think about that moment when you lost your parents no matter how painful that may be."

"Are you sure?" Troy said, glaring at Parks. "I can't do that." Then a sharp pain shot up his arm and into his neck. Troy nearly screamed as his shoulder cramped.

"You have to try," Kenzie pleaded as she came to the end of his bed. "I can't bear the thought of losing you."

Troy looked around the room at the caring faces then reluctantly took the magnifying glass and blue stone from Parks' hand.

"I don't see anything," Troy said impatiently, staring through the magnifying glass.

"Keep trying," Kenzie encouraged.

"Wait, there is something in there. It looks like..." Then Troy went silent as the room around him disappeared in a swirl and suddenly he was back in his Parents' house.

"They're coming down the street, Honey," Troy's mother said as she knelt by his side and hugged him tightly. "You have to run son. Dad and I will hold them as long as we can but you have to go."

"Why can't we all run, mom?" Troy asked, fighting back the tears.

"Look son," his Dad said as he knelt next to his wife with his hand on Troy's shoulder. "There's nowhere for us to hide. They've blocked the city exits and are closing in on us. But you can make it to your friend Normand's house. We'll slow them down."

Time for talk was over as the tip of a sharp ax smashed through the front door. Troy's father had wedged a baseball bat against the latch but it wouldn't hold long. He was armed with a long broom handle and his wife had a frying pan in one hand and her iron in the other."

"Run, Troy, run!" His mother shouted.

A few more hits with the ax and, in an instant, Testers were flooding the narrow hallway. Troy started to run and looked back over his shoulder just as his mother and father were engulfed by a red wave. It was a memory that was burned into his mind.

Troy watched himself as a child through the magnifier run out the back door towards Normand's house. The Testers barely missed him as they closed in, grasping at his feet as he dove through the fence. Then something surprising happened as he continued watching. The Testers didn't kill his parents like he had thought. Instead, they subdued them and then herded them out the door and into a waiting bus full of more captives. They were driven to a holding area filled with hundreds of city people. Troy couldn't believe his eyes. He held his breath as an ordinary looking man in a dark suit stood outside the barbed wire fence. He looked the crowd over and then began randomly selecting people and sending them into a large building. His parents were chosen and disappeared into the building.

"Are you alright?" Parks asked as Troy's mind returned to the room.

"I don't know," Troy said, trembling. "I'm not sure what just happened but this magnifying thing showed me something impossible. My parents might be alive. No, I know they are. I can feel it."

"That's the way it works," Parks replied. "The Magnifier doesn't show you everything but it does show enough. The rest you have to get on your own. How do you feel?"

"Confused," Troy answered. "But I don't feel angry the way I did. It's like a weight has been lifted off my mind. But where are my parents?"

"That question has to wait for now," Parks answered. "We need to deal with the crystal sickness and get you back to normal. Hold this in your right hand," Parks said as he pulled a large crystal from his bag. "Start squeezing it as tightly as you can."

Troy did as instructed and at first nothing happened. But then, after a few moments, the crystal began to glow brightly. Troy winched in pain as the bluish color drained from his neck and shoulder and down his arm into the crystal. Then the crystal flashed so brightly it blinded everyone in the room before returning to its normal state.

"That did it!" Parks said.

Troy looked up at Parks with a weak smile and then down at his arm. He clenched his fist and opened it again as he raised it in front of his eyes.

"We have a lot to learn about these crystal don't we Parks?"

"We have a lot to learn about everything. Now you need to get some rest."

Kenzie raced around Parks and gave Troy a big hug. A wave of relief spread over their faces as they realized he was going to be ok.

"Let's drive by my folks' house," Parks said after everyone left. "I would like to pick up a few things. We may be staying here longer than we think. Besides, it's a nice day and this will be the first time we're not being chased by someone."

Della agreed and soon they were cruising down the road on his motorcycle. He hadn't bothered to put his helmet on as it was a beautiful day and was enjoying the scenery rushing past. He was taking deep breaths as Della held tightly to his waist. This was the most fun he'd had in a very long time. Parks was about a mile from his Parents' home when he began to smell something burning. He came over a small ridge below their property when he saw smoke rising above the trees.

"Now what," Parks shouted as he hit the accelerator.

Ripping around the corner and up the long driveway Parks was mortified to see his Parents' house in flames.

"It's too late!" Della screamed. "Don't go in there!"

But Parks had already jumped onto the porch and through the front door. He held his breath and covered his face with his thick leather coat as he started checking rooms. But, the heat was overwhelming and quickly drove him outside.

"I don't think anyone's in there," Parks said, coughing and gasping for air. "But what started the fire? Dad's so careful with everything. We have to get the fire department up here right now. I'll go down to the neighbor's house and use their phone."

"Oh, I wouldn't bother," came a familiar voice that made the hair on the back of Parks' neck stand up. "You see, there's no need to stop the fire as you won't need the house any longer anyway."

Barron was standing in the door to the barn with his favorite weapon, the Equalizer, pointed directly at Della.

"I have a nice exploding tip on this one," Barron said coldly. "So if you're thinking about doing anything foolish, I wouldn't, or your little lovely will be splattered all over the yard."

"What do you want?" Parks growled, turning to face him.

"Can't you tell?" Barron asked in a sarcastic tone. "I've come for you. You're going to get everything I've lost, back," he said, walking towards Parks with his weapon still trained on Della. "You're going to put these chains around your feet and hands and lock yourself up tight." Barron continued, throwing several lengths of chain at Parks. "Then we are going to take a little trip into town where I'll finally get the credit I deserve for capturing the vaulted Parks."

All of a sudden, a blast from inside the house blew out a window sending shards of glass at Barron's face. Instinctively, he ducked and covered his head with his arm. That was all Parks' needed. Parks took a quick step towards Della grabbing her by the waist and then dove for the safety of a large cherry tree. Looking up, Barron pulled the trigger without thinking but his shot was off the mark. Instead of hitting where Della was mere seconds earlier, the projectile, filled with tungsten steel pellets, exploded near Parks' bike. Meanwhile Della and Parks were safely behind the tree and, in an instant, Parks was up and racing towards Barron as he frantically worked to reload. Parks caught him just as he fired the second time, only this shot went harmlessly across the field, blowing several bales of hay apart.

Parks ripped the weapon from his hands and hit Barron in the chest so hard he bounced off the barn and back into Parks' fist. Barron gasped for air as Parks lifted him over his head and slammed him to the ground. Grabbing Barron by one leg, he threw him across the yard and into the very tree Della was still hiding behind.

Just then a section of the porch collapsed from the fire and one of the large supporting timbers fell onto the lawn. Parks walked over and picked it up, his eyes dancing red in the light of the flames. He carried it like a giant flaming club as he strolled across the road towards the semiconscious Barron. Parks raised it high and was about to smash Barron's head when Della raced around from behind the tree.

"Henry," Della cried. "What are you doing?"

But Parks didn't even see or hear her as his body tensed and a dark smile broke over his face.

"You can't do this!" Della screamed as she yanked on his coat.

Parks was unresponsive. It was if it was all in slow motion and surreal as his eyes, once a warm shade of green, were now burning red.

"Kill him, kill him," came the voice in Parks' head. "Kill them all."

It was then something happened deep inside his being as Della's pleading began to penetrate his mind. He shook himself, as if out of a dream state, realizing suddenly he was feeling hatred and anger he had never experienced before.

He pushed Della aside, raised the beam at full height and then slammed it onto the grass mere inches from Barron's head before tossing it aside.

"We have to help him," Della said as she knelt next to Barron. "His head is bleeding and I'm sure there are multiple broken bones. We must get him to Flint's office or he'll die."

"Why do you care?" Parks asked. "He just tried to kill us. Leave him."

"What's going on with you?" she demanded, as she checked Barron's injuries. "You've never been like this."

"Maybe not," Parks snapped, "maybe not."

Della nearly gasped as she glanced up at Parks' face. It was all twisted and hard and his eyes still a dim red.

"I know that look Della. But you can't fix me," Parks said in a voice that nearly growled, "no one can fix me."

Parks picked Barron up by the collar and literally threw him into the back of the SUV. The drive to Dr. Flint's office was far from pleasant.

CHAPTER 31

"Lori, you can't be serious," James exclaimed. "You expect me to enter one of those blasted EDDs as a spy? Are you kidding me?"

"Relax, honey," Lori assured him. "All you need to do is pretend to be a little off. That shouldn't be too hard for you."

James looked over his shoulder at his wife who just smiled back innocently.

"You know," Philip said, "I like that idea and it just might work. You're not going to be in any real danger and we can tell them it's a test to see how you handle it. I'll stop by the bank right now and pick up enough cash to buy us through the door. I also have a friend with a wheelchair, and, with a few modifications, it'll work just fine. Once inside, you just have to look around a bit and find Rich. Then just give us a call and we'll come get you both."

"You make it sound so easy," James answered nervously. "Just cruise in, find Rich, and say, 'hey, let's just take a stroll and get on out of here.'"

Obviously, James was not excited about the prospect of staying at the Western Economic Development District but his wife could be quite persuasive. Not to mention, if they were holding Rich against his will, someone would have to get him out and he knew that. By the time Philip had withdrawn the money and they had stopped for lunch, James was willing to spend a week at the facility. Philip pulled into the WEDD parking lot and parked in one of the handicap spots.

"I'm going to wait here for you," Philip said as he turned off his truck, "just in case that Lucy person called over and warned them about us. They will be expecting three people not two and you don't look nearly as tall in that wheelchair," Philip joked as he pretended to help James into it in case anyone was watching.

Lori pushed her husband up the slight incline, through the automatic doors and into the foyer. Clean white tiles and polished woodwork gave the building a sterile feeling as she approached the main desk. A noticeably overweight man in his mid-fifties was sitting with his head down reading a book as Lori arrived at the counter.

"Can I help you?" The man asked, looking over his black rimmed glasses.

"Why yes," Lori replied politely. "My husband needs care and I was hoping I could find someone here to talk with about him."

"Do you have an appointment?" The man asked impatiently.

He obviously didn't like having his reading interrupted.

"Sorry no," she replied. "I didn't realize I would need one. You see we live out in the county and I have such a hard time getting him in and out of the truck so I seldom take him to the doctor or the city for that matter. It was quite the struggle getting him this far but I thought someone might be able to see him. We have plenty of money and would be willing to put him here on a trial basis. He's really no trouble at all."

The man reluctantly stood up and looked over the counter at James who was doing his best to appear disoriented and half asleep.

"I'll call but I can't promise anything," The man said as he picked up the phone.

In a few moments, a tall stately looking gentleman, in a trim white sport coat, came out of an adjacent office.

"Why hello," He said cheerfully as he put his hand out to Lori. "My name is Gary Reynolds. I understand you're seeking assistance for your husband, correct?"

"Yes. This is my husband James," Lori said, taking the man's hand and squeezing it gently. "I was hoping someone could help me. We're getting older and he's becoming too much for me to handle anymore."

"I understand." The man replied, "We see this all the time. Come into my office and let's see if there's something we can do to help."

Gary held the door open as Lori pushed James into his office. She took a seat while her husband continued his disabled act. Mr. Reynolds proceeded in explaining the various levels of care available and the cost associated with each. He droned on for nearly fifteen minutes showing brochures and explaining how the facility worked.

"I really like this one," Lori said finally, holding up one of the brochures.

"That's our most expensive option," Mr. Reynolds replied as he looked her over closely, "and will cover every need he could have but are you sure you can afford it?"

"Well," She said quietly as she reached into her purse and pulled out a large wad of hundred dollar bills, "we would have to pay privately. You see my husband never was one for insurance. He believed money in the bank was all the insurance a body needed. He made sure we have plenty of it. If it is ok, what I would like to do is try out your facility," Lori continued, "and see if he would be happy here. Can I give you enough for say a month? That should be long enough for me to see if he's happy or not. Once I'm satisfied he's in a good space, I'll pay for a year, in advance."

James cringed at the thought of being here a month. They told him he would only have to stay a week then he realized she had to make it worth the man's while and a week wouldn't do it.

"I think that can be arranged," The man said pulling a pile of forms out of his desk as he eyed the cash. "We just need you to fill these out and then we can get him started."

"Not a problem," Lori said with a smile as she wrote down a false last name for James. "The good news is, he isn't allergic to anything and he has quite the even temperament."

"That's just fine," The man said as she handed him the forms. "It comes to an even fifteen thousand."

Lori began counting the money out on the man's desk in fifteen neat piles of one thousand dollars each. Gary scooped them up and put them into a locked drawer at the bottom of his desk. He tucked the forms in another drawer without even looking at them while still eyeing the five thousand she put back into her purse. Gary made a quick call and, in a few moments, a young nurse appeared in his office.

"This is Nurse Jennings," Gary said as he introduced them. "She will be his personal nurse while he stays here. She will take you to his room so you can get a look at his accommodations. Visiting hours are from eight to six weekdays and nine to seven on weekends. If you want to see your husband on off hours, just let her know a day in advance and she'll arrange it for you."

Lori thanked him and then followed the nurse as she pushed James down the hall and onto a waiting elevator. They went up two stories before landing on a brightly lit hallway leading to a large nicely furnished room.

"Is there anything I need to know?" The nurse asked as she helped him out of his wheelchair and into a comfortable chair.

"He likes to watch cartoons and old westerns," Lori answered. "Just keep the TV on and he'll be fine. He doesn't speak but can take care of himself, use the bathroom and that sort of thing. He sometimes walks around a bit but he won't hurt anything. You'll just need to bring him back if he wanders too far."

"We have something just for that." The nurse said as she snapped a bracelet around his wrist. "This lets us know where all our patients are and makes it easy to keep track of them."

Lori thanked the nurse and made her way back down and into the parking lot.

"How did it go?" Philip asked as Lori climbed into his truck.

"Just like clockwork," Lori replied. "He's in but I don't know how good he'll be at finding Rich. It's not like he's inconspicuous or anything as big as he is. But I bet he'll enjoy the attention he gets. The nurses are cute and they have plenty of food. He even whispered in my ear when I kissed him goodbye that he's finally getting that vacation he always wanted. I love him but sometimes he can be such a putz."

Philip headed back to his house not knowing it was burned to the ground. That was a shock he couldn't have anticipated. Meanwhile, James settled into the routine at the EDD pretending to be mentally deficient. He was very cooperative and, before long, became the darling of the nurses and staff. They would push him to the cafeteria or take him for walks so he could get some exercise. Yet, all the while, James was scoping out the building and looking for Rich. Then, one afternoon, he noticed a locked section of the building. It seemed out of place as the rest of the halls were open with people coming and going, but not that one. He managed to wander to the entrance once and glanced through the small wired glass window in the door before his nurse caught up with him. Inside was a hall with a row of locked doors. It was obvious they were keeping certain people there and it would be up to him to figure out how to get in and see if Rich was one of them.

James had noticed every hall was outfitted with a security camera which made moving around unnoticed very difficult. However, he also noted the lights on the cameras would switch from red to green because they were timed on in sequence. They switched from hall to hall as the security guard watched. He timed the one monitoring his hall and learned it was red for nearly a minute which was plenty of time for him to make his exit while not being seen.

By the sixth night, he had wandered the halls enough to note the location of every security camera and that security after midnight consisted of one maintenance man who doubled as the security guard.

That's when he came up with his plan.

The bracelet easily unsnapped as it was designed for people who didn't have the mental wherewithal to even realize they were wearing one. It was two thirty AM as he watched the camera switch to red. James slipped out of his room, into the stairwell, which had no cameras, and then down to the second floor. He needed to keep the maintenance man busy long enough for him to get inside the locked area. James waited for the camera light to change to red and dashed for the bathroom where he shoved a roll of toilet paper into the toilet and flushed. In a few seconds, water was pouring over the tiled floor and beginning to run out the door. He went back into the stairwell and headed downstairs where he could just see the security office through the small window in the door.

Meanwhile, one of the nighttime nurses noticed water running into the hall from the bathroom. In a matter of seconds she was on the phone and James watched as the maintenance man came sluggishly out of his office and headed for the elevator.

James skillfully maneuvered the remaining hall cameras making sure he was never in sight when they were green. This would have recorded his movements. He was feeling plenty proud of himself and, with the nurse and the maintenance man busy on the second floor, he had clear access to the locked door guarding the mysterious hall. James examined the handle for a moment before putting his full three hundred plus pounds on it. The handle held for a few seconds before the mechanism inside yielded.

The lock sheared off with a metallic crunching sound as he slid inside.

In an instant, James was in and quickly unplugged the final camera mounted over the door. That was one time being six foot nine helped. The then began checking each room. The doors had one small window for viewing and a holder on the wall with a plain manila file in it. James looked in the first window but it was too dark to see who was in there so he pulled the folder with a large green dot on the front. He looked quickly but Rich's name wasn't in it. He checked each file as he went down the hall, but still no Rich. The folders either had a green or yellow sticker just under the occupant's name. He was beginning to worry, believing the maintenance man had likely fixed the toilet and was probably cleaning up the water by now. He would likely have only a few more minutes before he would be returning to his office and he might run into him. Then he reached the final room at the end of the hall. There was no name on the file just a single black dot on the file folder.

He had no other choice but to check this room for himself. The lock gave way just as the other had. He flipped on the light and in the corner was a worn cot with a frail looking man curled up under a thin sheet, lying against the wall.

"Rich?" James said quietly as he rolled the man over.

James gasped at the sunken eyes and gaunt face of a man who obviously hadn't eaten much in a long while.

"James," Rich said weakly. "What're you doing here?"

"I'm here to get you out," He said gently helping Rich sit up. "Can you walk?"

Rich tried to stand but didn't have the strength so James picked him up and carried him into the hall and shut the door. James was heartbroken at the sight of his old friend. Rich was only skin and bones as James carried him through the halls and up the stairs to his room, making sure to avoid being recorded. He laid Rich on his bed. He got him some water and fed him some saltine crackers he had stashed. Rich was in bad shape and would need medical attention but getting him out of the facility would be no easy matter. Chances are they would quickly discover Rich's escape and start an all-out search. The first order of business would be getting word to Lori and Philip. Lori had hidden a small cell phone in an inside pocket of his suitcase for just this reason.

He let the phone ring three times and then hung up. Then he called right back and let it ring twice, before hanging up again. It was their agreed upon signal. All he could do now was wait and hope they got it. It was nearly nine AM before one of the nurses discovered Rich was gone and by mid-morning several large black SUVs had arrived at the main entrance. Groups of heavily armed men began working their way through the building. James pretended to be asleep when they arrived at his room. He had tucked Rich behind him and pulled the blanket over them both. James' large body made it easy to hide his friend.

"What's this guy's story?" one of the officers asked as he started looking through the closet and bathroom.

"He's been here for a while," The nurse responded. "He has Alzheimer's and doesn't do much. He can't talk and we keep him on a tight lease. He wears a bracelet that lets us know where he's at all times. He never left his room last night. I checked this morning."

James' stomach jumped into his throat as he realized he forgot to put the bracelet back on. It was on the small table next to his bed but they hadn't spotted it yet. The nurse went over to check the bathroom as the officer rummaged through the closet. James quickly reached out from under his covers and pulled the bracelet off the table. He snapped it back on just before the officer addressed his bed.

"Can we get him up? I want to see that bracelet you mentioned."

"He usually sleeps until midafternoon," the nurse replied, "we keep him medicated most of the time but I can pull his arm out."

She pulled back the sheet enough for him to see the bracelet on James' left wrist. Satisfied, the officer turned and left the room while the nurse put everything back in order. She was just about to exit herself when she paused for a moment at the door. Looking intently at James, her thought, for a second, was that the bracelet should have been on his right wrist not his left. Then she shrugged her shoulders and followed the investigator to the next room.

"Are you ok?" James asked with a sigh of relief.

"I'm alive," Rich replied trying to sit up.

"You rest easy," James instructed, making sure they had left the floor before getting Rich more water and some cookies he had stashed in his drawer. "We'll have to wait until help arrives. In the meantime, you stay covered and out of sight. I'll meander down to the cafeteria after a little while and get you more food. They're used to me wandering around looking for food. I'll just stash some fruit and other stuff and then come right back."

The place was really hopping as James walked in his familiar daze down the halls and into the cafeteria. In the meantime, Lori and Philip had arrived amid the heightened security.

"You're going to have to bluff your way through this," Philip said as he unloaded the wheelchair. "I just hope you don't get caught."

"Don't worry about me," Lori answered, as she pushed the wheelchair towards the building. "Just be ready to go when I come out."

Lori went straight up to the counter and to the overweight man with the round rimmed glasses, who was trying his best to appear busy as the area buzzed around him.

"I've come to visit my husband," Lori said after waiting a few minutes behind two other people. "Is it ok to go up?"

"It's not a good time for a visit," the man replied, seeming much more annoyed than ever. "But, I guess it'll be alright if you don't stay long."

She pushed the empty wheelchair down the hall, passing stern looking men in dark suits, interrogating staff members. She rode alone in the elevator and then quickly entered room 304.

"Lori," James exclaimed as he hugged his wife. "I was hoping you got my message. This place is going wild."

"Good to see you, Rich," Lori said as Rich managed to sit up. "You just relax and don't worry. We'll have you out of here in no time." She continued, shooting a worried glance at James. Rich looked horrible and she could tell James was deeply concerned.

Before long, Lori was pushing James off the elevator and towards the exit. She passed through the frantic activity and was almost to the exit doors when the fat man noticed.

"Where are you going?" He nearly shouted from across the busy hall. "I don't have a release order for him yet."

"Oh, we're not leaving," Lori lied, leaving James by the door and walking over to the counter. "I'm just taking him out for some air. He loves being outside and it's such a beautiful day. I'm going to let him enjoy it for a minute."

"Let me get his nurse first," The man replied, picking up the phone. But, just then, two men in dark suits approached his desk and began asking questions. They wanted to look at his admission log for the past week.

Lori nonchalantly walked back to where James was sitting.

Suddenly, a tall man in a dark black suit with dark glasses, carrying a clip board, came walking down the hall in her direction. The man at the desk watching Lori saw the man stop and address her. He asked some general questions and then moved on. The fat man was distracted for a moment by some questions on his admission logs and when he turned back she was gone.

"Let's move," James said as he took over pushing the wheelchair. "We've got to do this fast."

Philip was waiting with the side door open as James pulled a plywood panel up. Philip had modified the wheelchair with a hidden compartment under the seat. They quickly helped Rich into the truck.

The man behind the desk looked up and scanned the foyer for Lori after the two men finished looking over his log. He walked around, checking up and down the hall, before stepping outside. His face turned white when he saw the abandoned wheelchair sitting in an empty parking space.

"It's good to see you," Philip said as he sped away.

"I didn't think I would ever see the outside of that place," Rich replied as energetically as he could. "I don't see how you guys managed this but you have my eternal gratitude."

"All due to my great acting skills," James replied with a smile.

"Yeah, and do you know how hard it was to find a suit large enough to fit you?" Lori bantered. "Gorilla sizes don't grow on trees you know."

"Hey, where are we going?" James noticed as they took a side road away from the city. "I thought we were going up to your house."

"We can talk about that later," Lori answered as she glanced at Philip's pained face. "There's been a fire at Philip's house. We're going to be staying at our motor home, honey, until further notice."

James leaned back and shook his head. One minute they're rejoicing in the rescue of a good friend and the next they're dealing with a new kind of tragedy. Would there be no end to the misery? Then Philip turned and smiled at his brother. James knew instantly the house wasn't what was important. It could be replaced, but not Rich. James smiled back and relaxed into the seat feeling very proud of what they had just accomplished.

CHAPTER 32

The drive to Dr. Flint's was filled with arguing as Della did her best to keep Barron comfortable.

"Why save him?" Parks challenged.

"It's my duty," Della replied firmly. "Besides you and Barron were friends once, right? What happened between you two?"

"We were never truly friends," Parks snapped. "I was forced to take him as my partner, that's all. He never felt the things I did."

"You're wrong," Barron said weakly. "You never saw me because of all your rules and regulations but I was there for you."

"You're lying," Parks growled. "You never cared about the Order. Getting ahead and being noticed was all that mattered to you. You hated me from the start and there was nothing I could do to change that."

"Easy Henry," Della said calmly. "He's lost a lot of blood and needs medical attention."

"That's all you care about isn't it?" Parks said pounding the steering wheel, "keeping him alive. Why is that? What is it about this inhuman creature that attracts your attention?

"Henry," Della replied incredulously. "What's wrong with you? Of course I want to keep him alive. I would help anyone in need, you know that."

"Where do you want me to leave him?" Parks asked abruptly ignoring Della's response as they drove into Dr. Flint's. "I say dump him in the parking lot and leave."

"We're not dumping him in the parking lot!" Della replied indignantly. "You're going to help me carry him in."

Parks slammed the door as he got out and stormed around to the rear. He opened the door and grabbed Barron by the ankles and jerked him onto the gravel driveway.

"Carry him in yourself," Parks growled again without even looking at Della.

"Parks, you can't leave him here like this," Della pleaded as she checked Barron's condition. "You're the one who said you cannot use the power you have with ill intent. Now you want to take matters into your own hands and mete out your own form of justice. I am afraid that's going to take us places we can't come back from."

"You might be afraid," Parks snarled, "but I'm not and if you're so concerned about them maybe you should join them."

Della was pierced to the heart at Parks statement. They had been married for over ten years and in all that time Parks had never said a sharp word to her. Oh, they had some disagreements, as any couple would, but they always ended in an apology and a hug. But this was different. Parks was serious and his voice cold. Yet before Della could say another word, Parks barreled out of the parking lot.

Della felt her heart sink as she watched her future disappear around the corner.

"I love you," Della said quietly, "and I always will. The day you come back is the day I am going to tell you you're the luckiest man alive. You're going to be a father Henry J. Parks. We're going to have a baby boy."

Dr. Flint heard the commotion and came out to help. Between the two of them, they managed to get Barron onto a gurney and inside.

Meanwhile, Parks was headed in any direction that brought suffering to Management. In his mind the best thing would be to take out the head. He had eliminated Harry and destroyed the very building he helped build. Now he needed to set his sights higher. It was time to deal with the President and the Board.

While Parks was planning his next attack, Dave had just left his office with one goal in mind, he needed to find the Mystic his wife, Doris, once used. Doris was superstitious and would go to her house located in one of the deserted streets in a distant part of the city. Dave had held back his laughter as his wife spoke of her "sessions." Yet, there was the day she told him of the dream she had that night. A dream in which she saw her husband disappear into a dark mist and not return. Her dream came true in a strange sort of way as Dave experienced the power of the Six and then returned home to kill her the following night.

Dave arrived at the address his wife had written in the back of her address book. The house was rundown and the porch full of numerous eclectic things hanging from the rafters, including a strange looking doll he brushed aside, as he walked to the door. He raised the heavy brass knocker and hit the door twice.

"The door is open," an old voice from behind the black painted door said.

Dave laughed to himself as his eyes adjusted to the décor. It was as expected, candles burning on small tables, various carvings of strange creatures, and the heavy smell of incense. The walls were decorated with paintings filled with mystical scenes topped off by the old woman sitting in a creaking rocking chair next to the fireplace. She wore a dark red dress covered with strange embroidery.

It was classic decorations to impress the simple mind.

"How may I be of service, Mr. Castle?" The old woman asked.

"How do you know my name?" Dave replied indignantly.

"I know many things," The old woman said. "Why have you come here?"

"I came to be read, what else?"

"Oh, you mean a reading," the woman corrected, "that will cost twenty five dollars and must be paid in advance."

Dave pulled three tens out of his wallet and took one more look around the room before handing her the money.

"Now what?"

The old woman opened an old carved wood box sitting on a small white marble table in front of her and pulled out five dollars in change. She started to hand it to Dave but he waived it off.

"Keep it," he said as he grabbed her hand, twisting it slightly. "But this had better be good or I'll want more than just my money back."

The woman eyed him for a moment and then returned the bill to the box before setting it on the floor.

"Please be seated," she said as she pointed to the chair across from the marble table. Several burning candles sent flickers of light across Dave's face as the woman pulled a hood over her head. Her face was barely visible as she closed her eyes and began waving her hands over the table. Dave was quickly becoming annoyed as he waited. The dark room, candles and supposed trance the woman was in seemed phony and predictable. He was really beginning to think his wife was the weak minded fool he thought she was. But then his attention became drawn to the table as its appearance changed from stone to what appeared to be liquid glass. He caught glimpses of images floating across the surface as the old woman began speaking in a strange language. Then the table changed to a brilliant red before returning to its solid state.

"You hold a dark secret," the woman said, still hunched over the table and keeping her eyes beneath the hood.

"What secret?" Dave demanded suspiciously. "What has my wife told you?"

"Your wife told me you killed her," the woman said as she looked up into Dave's eyes. "Doris was an innocent caught in a sinister web of your making. Now you come here looking for answers. What answers did you expect?"

"Knowledge like that could be dangerous," Dave replied in a dark tone. "But if you are as 'seeing' as you say I must know more. What else have you seen?"

"I know someone is searching for you." The old woman said as she leaned back and began to rock.

"Searching for me? Why?"

"You took something precious and now he's seeking justice."

"And why should I care?"

"Because you seek the 'Gifts'."

"What do you know of the Gifts?" Dave demanded as he became increasingly intrigued. "Tell me what you've seen."

"His face is hidden from me," She replied. "But I can feel him. He doesn't understand what he has but he's learning."

"How can I find him?"

"You'll not have to find him, Dave," the old woman said with a slight smile. "He'll find you."

Dave suddenly felt the urge to leave. Her words were like hot embers burning in his mind and he was becoming increasingly uncomfortable.

"You paid your fee," the old woman said as she reached inside her dress and pulled out a leather pouch. "But that's not enough for what I've given you. You still owe me."

"Owe you what?" Dave said as his eyes narrowed.

"It's in your pocket," she said as she pointed to the vest he wore under his suit.

Dave looked down and was surprised to see a red glow coming from his suit. He reached into his coat pocket and pulled out a dark red crystal. He didn't know how it got there but suspected one of the board members must have slipped it in for some unknown reason. He placed it in the woman's bag which she returned to the pocket in her dress.

"Take care, Dave," the woman said darkly. "Even you may not be powerful enough to face what lies ahead."

"I don't know what your game is," Dave replied sharply, "but I'll be back and you had best be ready with some real answers. I didn't get to where I am by being played."

With that, Dave turned and stormed out the door, which slammed shut behind him of its own accord.

"Crazy old woman," Dave muttered to himself as he drove towards his house. "If she thinks her mumbo jumbo is going to fool me she's wrong, dead wrong. And so what if someone is coming for me. When has that ever been different?"

The air was cool for a summer night as he parked along the wide sidewalk bordering the front of his beautiful house. His large assistant came out of the house in a heavy hooded coat and opened the door for him. Dave walked towards his front door, buried in thought, as he pondered his next move. His servant helped him off with his coat and he headed straight for the library to work on his plan. He decided the best course of action would be to hold a public engagement where he would be seen. That would expose whoever was after him but, in reality, he would have troops stationed where they could get the jump on the person the old woman had seen. He opened the ornately carved wooden door to his library and hit the light switch.

"What the...?" Dave exclaimed as he saw his servant tightly bound in one of his leather chairs, "who? what?" he stuttered in confusion as he turned to confront the man in the hooded coat.

"Parks," Dave nearly shouted. "The old woman was right after all."

"I have no idea what you're talking about," Parks said as he backed Dave against his desk. "I'm here for one reason. You are going to call a meeting of the board tonight."

"What makes you think I am going to do anything you ask?" Dave said as he slid around Parks and moved behind his desk. "You're a wanted criminal, terrorist even. You've destroyed property, stolen vehicles as well as injured Management personnel. I think you would be better off surrendering to me now and let me take you in before I have you killed."

Parks laughed involuntarily at Dave's assertion.

"I don't think so," Parks said as he put his fists on Dave's desk and leaned forward. "You're going to pick up the phone and call the board together. You'll make up some story about how you have some new information they need and you'll do it now!"

Dave sat down behind his desk to gain a little distance. He leaned back and looked into Parks' eyes. They glowed a dim red.

"Seems you have problems of your own," Dave said as he rocked back a bit. "Is there something you're not telling me?"

"I didn't come here to play games," Parks snarled as he lifted Dave's servant with one hand and threw him across the room. Books of all sizes and shapes cascaded down on the man's head as he returned his attention to Dave. "My next move is going to be on you. Now make the call!"

"So you're a tough guy." Dave responded without flinching. "But that isn't going to help you here. I understand you have some Gifts and I want them. Why don't you just place them on my desk and I'll let you walk out of here. Otherwise, I'll have to take them from you."

Parks eyes turned completely red as his face twisted into a hideous smile. He slammed down both fists on Dave's desk busting it in half. Then, kicking the desk aside, Parks grabbed Dave by his shirt with his left hand as he clenched his right into a fist. He started to deliver a devastating blow bent on smashing Dave's face when Dave caught his fist.

"You think you can come in here and bully me?" Dave said to a wide eyed Parks. "I've seen countless men like you in the cities we've destroyed. Men who thought they could stop us. Well, you are just as big a fool. Now get off me." Dave said as he shoved Parks so hard he flew across the room and smashed into the door and landed in a pile on the floor. "You wanted it this way and now you're going to get it!"

Parks struggled to his feet, shocked by Dave's power. He steadied himself as Dave calmly fixed his tie and then strolled through the splintered wood that once was his desk. He pulled Parks close and looked into his burning red eyes.

"Why, you're scared," Dave said sarcastically. "Isn't your mommy here to help you? Don't worry, you'll be joining her soon."

Parks hit Dave in the chest with his forearm driving him backwards as he opened the door and burst out of the house and into the cool night.

"You got away this time!" Dave shouted after Parks as he realized he couldn't catch him. "But next time things will be different"

He stood for a moment in the street as Parks disappeared into the darkness. "I should have knocked him out when I had the chance." Dave said dejectedly as he walked slowly into the house.

Parks plowed through brush, jumped over fences, ran up steep slopes, down ravines, across dry creek beds and didn't stop until he was at the edge of the wilderness. There he collapsed, exhausted, on a large flat rock.

"I've never felt fear like that before," Parks lamented. "The man practically admitted killing my mother and I ran away. All I could think of was getting away. There's something I'm not seeing. I have to figure this out."

Parks loosened the belt full of crystal weapons that was strapped to his waist. He let them fall to the hard rocky ground along with his backpack. But, as he did, the small black book fell out.

"You've been the source of so much pain." Parks said as he picked it up and held it in one hand. It was open and in the bright light of the moon he strained to make out the words.

"The beast rages and steals the bounty of the land and those who step on others are themselves in dark prisons. But the one who listens and heeds my words will discover the power to end the terror."

Parks set the book down in his lap for a moment as he pondered the statement. He leaned back but then groaned as pain shot up his arms. Parks shook off his leather coat to expose the long sleeved white linen shirt he wore underneath. He looked down at his left arm and then his right. The linen shirt was matted with blood in three distinct lines running from his shoulders to his elbows and then his hands.

The blood was flowing from the old scars left by the Zender's claws.

He looked up at the sky, raised his bloody arms, and screamed into the night.

Yet there was no answer as Parks stood there, alone, feeling the anguish of many things. But then a fresh realization began to filter into his thoughts and with it a renewed strength. He suddenly realized the energy driving him wasn't his, even though it was in him. He also saw that the enemy he must defeat first was himself but the sword for this fight wasn't found among his crystal blades. His new weapon was understanding.

CHAPTER 33

The boys pulled out of sight behind the abandoned elementary school a few minutes ahead of Kirsten and Kenzie. David led the way into the large auditorium which once doubled as a basketball court. The light coming from a bank of clear panels lining one end of the building let in plenty of afternoon sun.

"I don't get it!" Joshua said anxiously as Kirsten walked in. "We've trained our whole lives to fight but, when we do, we run the risk of dying. This just isn't right and, I don't know about anyone else, but I'm giving my blade back."

He laid it respectfully on one of the bleachers and then backed away.

"I don't blame you for being afraid," Kirsten said as she addressed the worried faces. "If you remember, one of the foundational tenants of our training was motive. If the blades are used out of anger or hatred they can work against you."

"Sure we remember," Burke responded. "And that was all fine and good when we were practicing on straw dummies or sparing with each other, but you're talking real Testers now, and Troy isn't alone in his feelings about those things. There's not a single one of us that didn't lose someone because of them, not to mention they were chasing and trying to kill us when Parks intervened. You really believe we're not going to have hard feelings if we run into one of them? Come on!"

"I never said it would be easy," Kirsten replied as she took a seat on the bleachers, "and I totally understand what you all went through."

"So what do you expect us to do?" Normand asked.

"I saw something I can't explain in the Magnifier Parks had," Troy interjected. "Somehow my parents could still be alive and yours may be too. They're connected to the Testers in some strange way."

"Connected to the Testers?" Isaac said incredulously. "Those are the very things responsible for most of our pain. How can that be true?"

"This sounds incredible," Troy answered as he looked at Kirsten, "but if we kill another Tester, we could die too. Is that a risk we should be taking?"

"I can't tell you what to do," Kirsten replied. "All I know is your motives must be right. The power of the blades cuts both ways and you're in danger if your thoughts are wrong."

"But Troy proved there's no amount of training that can stop this kind of anger." David interjected. "I nearly lost my adoptive parents and my life because of them. You have to know what we feel is deep. Who's to say how I'll react if I see them again. Chances are it won't be warm and fuzzy."

"Everyone needs to sit for a moment," Kirsten said as she stood in front of the bleachers. "You may think the crystals are just inanimate objects like metal or wood but they are much more than that. Parks and I discovered early on they not only provide strength and do unusual things but they also draw off your energy. Your heart must be innocent or they will hurt you because they don't know evil, only good. So, if you defend yourself or help a friend in need, they'll work for you. But if you attack without cause and become the aggressor, the blade cannot tell who you are and the very energy that could save you turns on you and, well, I guess you know what happens then."

Kirsten looked from face to face as they thought over what she said. Then, to everyone's amazement, Joshua stepped forward and picked his blade up off the bleacher.

"I get it," Joshua said as he slid it into the leather sheath he kept hung around his waist. "We're in this to win and these give us the best odds. Hey, if I'm going to turn to stone it'll be because I'm fighting for the right cause and alongside the people I trust the most. That's a risk worth taking."

The room filled with positive energy as each one of the ROD agreed with his assessment. The future they imagined was in their grasp and no one could take that from them if they worked together.

"Where are we going to stay?" Normand asked. "My apartment has been invaded and David's Parents' too. We're going to need another safe place."

"Kirsten can stay with me," Kenzie replied. "I have a spare bedroom she could use."

"Well, that takes care of two of us." David said.

"My house is big enough," Joshua replied, "and you know my parents have been supporting us from the start. They'll do whatever we need."

"That settles it then," Kirsten said. "I'll go with Kenzie and the rest with Joshua. I don't imagine there's any reason for me to remind you to keep a low profile. See if you can get in touch with the resistors and let them know what's happening. This is no drill. They need to be ready."

There was no doubt the danger was real and bad things could happen, but the feeling in the air was of optimism and a sense of relief. They said their goodbyes and left.

Jim pulled into the safe house and waited for the garage door to shut before getting out. Management was likely going all out to find them and anyone else that might be resisters. He was worried. He checked the house carefully just to be sure they were really alone.

'This isn't over yet," Rita said as she took a seat at the small kitchen table.

"No it's not," Jim replied. "But, I think I may have an answer. We went to Frank's office and got caught. That may have been the best thing that's happened so far."

"You're not serious," Rita said with a puzzled look.

"Just listen for a minute," Jim continued. "What if Management believes we're on the run and unable to do anything."

"That does seem to be the situation."

"Not completely. I know we talked with the kids about another broadcast but I think it has to be more than that. We have to crush their ability to broadcast, while getting our own information out."

Rita sat back and studied Jim's determined face for a moment. It was not an easy thought but she trusted him in a way she had never trusted anyone before. Seeing her worried look, Jim changed the conversation and began talking about what their future might look like if they succeeded. It didn't make Rita feel much better but, for the moment, that's the best they had.

"Good morning," Dr. Flint said as he opened the door.

"Is Della still here?" Parks asked quietly as he stepped inside.

"She's been up most of the night," Dr. Flint replied softly. "That patient of hers, Barron, looks like he is going to pull through."

Parks was not overly excited to hear Barron had survived. If he managed to make a full recovery, there was no doubt he would come after them again. Fortunately, Parks had taken the time to blindfold him before bringing him here so there was little chance he knew where they were keeping him but getting him out of here would be trickier. He couldn't risk another transfer to the Island or leave him here indefinitely. Something else would have to be done.

"Hello Della," Parks said quietly. "How are you doing?"

She was leaning against the wall staring at Barron as Parks came in.

"I'm alright," Della replied.

"I'm glad to hear that," Parks said tenderly, "can we talk for a moment?"

Della followed him into the hall.

"What's the chance we start over?" Parks said tenderly. "You know, set the clock back, say, ten years or more?"

Della smiled at the thought. She knew the years had taken their toll on them both and it would be nice to go back to better times, but then her thoughts returned to reality, as Parks continued.

"But maybe that's not so easy," Parks said seriously. "Things have changed in me, some good, some not so good. I'm not sure even my mom would recognize me, that is, if she was still alive. What I'm trying to say is I'm sorry for my behavior the last few weeks. I've been focused on something and have been blaming my troubles on it. Unfortunately, that something finally caught up to me. Really, it all goes back to the Zender, the thing I thought I had killed."

"What are you saying, Henry?" Della asked, not really hearing him.

"This may sound strange but I know the beast from the cave has followed me my whole life. Yet, I see it clearly now and

I know the only way to keep us safe is to destroy it once and for all."

Parks looked tenderly into Della's eyes and smiled.

"It's going to be alright," he said, "I promise."

Della took Parks by the hand and led him to an empty office.

"You had better sit down," she said. "We have bigger issues."

Parks was definitely confused. What could be larger than the internal battle he was fighting?

"We're going to have a baby," Della said calmly. "It's going to be a boy to be exact. Whatever you're talking about will just have to wait."

Parks sat there just staring straight ahead. He started to say something and then stopped. His brain had somehow forgotten how to communicate with his mouth.

"Henry, did you hear me? I'm pregnant with our son."

"Yes. Yes!" Parks exclaimed as he hugged Della. "I'm going to be a father. You're going to be a mother. We're going to be parents."

Parks hugged Della tightly to his chest and kissed her face softly. But inside he felt a sudden jolt of fear more real and powerful than ever. He knew Della didn't understand the energy he was fighting, but he did. He had to do whatever it took for his family and his city.

"We need to get you out of the city," He said. "You're not safe here and I can't afford to have the two of you in danger. We'll leave tonight."

"You can stay here with us as long as you need," the Doctor volunteered. "There's plenty of spare bedrooms in the main house."

"I can't thank you enough for your generosity," Parks replied. "But, nowhere in the city is safe with me around. I hit them hard and they won't quit until they find me."

"What about Barron?" Della asked intently.

"Can he be moved?" Parks asked.

"He does seem to heal quickly," Della said. "But I would have to check first. What are you thinking?"

"You prep him and I'll make sure he gets to the hospital," Parks replied. "After that, he's on his own."

Della agreed and before long Parks had him loaded in the back of his SUV. Barron was neatly deposited, blindfold and all, at the main entrance of the hospital.

Della knew Parks was telling the truth and that they would have to leave. But somehow, tomorrow seemed so much brighter. They were together again with a promise of peace and love. However, deep down, Parks could sense the claws sinking into his soul. There was a power so evil and dark he knew it would have to be stopped. Management couldn't be allowed to rule any longer if there was to be a future for anyone, especially his beloved Della and his unborn son. The time was fast approaching when he would have to deal with the Dark Matter.